THE SECRETS TO HEARTBREAK

BOOK TWO: THE HEARTBREAK SERIES

BRITTANY TAYLOR

 Created with Vellum

THE SECRETS TO

Heartbreak

BOOK TWO: THE HEARTBREAK SERIES

For Jase
My first
I love you to the ends of the earth and back
I hope you never stop climbing those monkey bars

Vada

I STILL REMEMBER HOW MY BACK PRESSED AGAINST THE cold, hard glass, the way his warm hands molded to my flesh, heating me from the inside out. They soothed the places on my body that ached for him, wrapping around me like a warm blanket on a winter day. The way Colton moved me from the bar counter to the tabletop, savoring every inch of my skin, never fully deciding if he wanted to use his hands or his mouth...

Our secret was spoken out loud, the words dangling between us in an invisible contract. He sealed our secret with unrelenting kisses and illicit touches. In truth, our secret was only supposed to be the one time.

Colton could never give me more, and I understood—or at least that's what I've told myself since that night in the restaurant dining room. He's my brother's best friend and, by his own admission, too busy to ever take our relationship further.

I was used to being in second place. I was used to playing second fiddle to everyone in my life—a lesson well taught by my father growing up.

It was supposed to be easy to keep this secret to ourselves. We chose to bury it, the memory now etched into the wood of table number eight, situated in the middle of the dining room of his restaurant.

Now, that's all that's left: memories.

Although it's been over a year since I've felt Colton's lips pressed against my skin, sparking my insides like a firecracker, I haven't been able to stop thinking about him, or our secret.

That's the thing about secrets.

They aren't meant to be kept forever.

SECRET #1

I've never been very good at letting go of the past.

CHAPTER ONE

Vada

Table number fucking eight.

Every time I look at it, my body immediately reacts. What's it called? Muscle memory? I've heard about it before when talking about people learning to walk again or when you lift weights, but could it be true for people you've slept with?

I've never had to learn how to walk again, and the thought of going to the gym specifically to pick things up and put them down couldn't sound any more awful than it already does.

But muscle memory from sleeping with someone? It's a possibility, and if it is, I'm fairly certain that's what I'm experiencing.

It's pretty fucking stupid actually.

Part of me is thankful today is my last day at my brother's restaurant, if only for the sake of not having to look at table number fucking eight every single day.

"Remember, your shift ends at six. After that, we're celebrating."

"It's six right now," I tell my best friend, Sloan, as I fill a few glasses of beer—for table fucking eight.

"Oh shit," she says, spreading her eyes wide. She quickly

grabs the beers from my hands and nods toward the computer behind me. "Clock out."

The beer foam spills over her hands, dripping onto the floor. I freeze, my body stiffening in shock at what she just did. She hasn't always been the best at bartending. She's been working here for the past three months. After Colton hired her, she started seeing my brother, and they've been together ever since. I have a feeling Sloan is here to stay since she's the only one who's managed to bring Dallas back from the dead, and he wouldn't take a chance at screwing that up.

She also happens to be my best friend.

I watch Sloan as she puts the glasses down on the counter and grabs a fistful of napkins, hastily cleaning off her fingers. It barely does anything before she tosses them in the trash and picks up the beers again.

She nods toward the computer again when she sees I haven't moved. "I'm serious, Vada. Clock out. I've got this."

"Do you?" I ask her, stifling a laugh.

She rolls her eyes, already heading toward the end of the bar to walk out to the dining room. "Yes. Now go."

"Wait—before you go, I need to close out my tab." I turn around to find Cassidy standing on the other side of the bar.

She's leaning over it with her hands wrapped around the edge. Her mouth is spread into a wide grin, displaying her perfect white teeth. They're blinding, even in the dim lights of my brother's restaurant.

"Fine," Sloan says, stopping mid-stride. The beers are still perched in her hands as she talks to us over her shoulder. "Close her tab and then clock out. You can't be wearing those clothes for your going away celebration."

I look down at my shirt, spotting a barbecue stain near my shoulder and a wet spot on the bottom hem from leaning over the counter to clean spilled drinks all night. "Yes, ma'am." I chuckle as she walks away, all the while keeping a smile on her face as well.

When I turn back to Cassidy, she's already pulling her card out of her wallet.

"Here you go." She holds it out for me. Her long blonde hair is pulled back into a high ponytail, the ends dancing across her bare back. She's wearing a thin-strapped tank top, her gold necklace resting against her chest. Her lips are painted a pale pink, the same shade as her cheeks.

Cassidy is a photographer for *The Daily News*. Our newest hire, she's only been working at the paper for the past month. Even though I've just been popping in every now and then, writing articles whenever I can find the time while working at the bar full time, Cassidy and I became quick friends. She's younger than me and fresh out of college, but I like her. She fit in easily, and I know she's here waiting to celebrate my last night at the bar with me before I go back to the paper full time. I swipe her card for the two drinks she's had since she sat down an hour ago.

By the time I give her card back and she signs the receipt, Sloan's already returning. This time her hands are now full of dirty dishes.

"Did Cassidy cash out?" Sloan asks, dumping them into the bin we keep behind the bar to save us from always having to run back into the kitchen.

"Yes." I laugh, giving Cassidy a side glance in response to how Sloan is rushing me.

"Good. Get out of here and go out back. Colton's taking you home to change while we close up. It'll be an early night for us."

"Why is Colton taking me?" My heart skips a beat. See? Pretty fucking stupid.

"Because Dallas is out grabbing the rest of the supplies for your party," she explains. What supplies he needs, I have no idea. "And I'm here covering the front," Sloan adds. "The kitchen isn't serving food anymore, so Colton's the only one who is free."

I open my mouth to object, knowing full well I can drive myself, but I don't. I can tell how excited Sloan is for this party.

I stop arguing with her and clock out, mostly because she saved me from having to walk to table eight, forcing me to remember how Colton's tongue slid between my—

"Fuck." I gasp when I suddenly slam into a firm wall of muscle. I look up, and my eyes land on familiar ones staring right back at me. Light brown irises narrow as he presses his lips together. Hot breath comes out of his nose as he stares at me, his lips separating just enough for him to blow it across my skin.

I must not have seen him push through the door connecting the bar to the kitchen.

"There you are." He lifts his hand and gently grabs my arm. His warm, strong fingers wrap around my bicep as he pushes back through the door, pulling me to the back. Maybe going to the gym wouldn't be such a bad thing. The way Colton's fingers easily press into my flesh has me reconsidering the idea, but only for a few seconds. His touch is soft...too soft.

"What are you doing?" I ask, trying to keep up with him.

He wraps his arm around me, leading me through the kitchen and down the small hallway that opens to the back porch where all the smokers are. I look up at him, catching how his light brown hair moves across his forehead as he walks, flecks of gold peeking through the strands under the warm light. He's wearing his black-rimmed glasses as usual. They're sliding down the bridge of his nose a little. He catches it and pushes them back up with his finger. The stubble lining his nearly perfect chiseled jaw has grown out, leaving a short beard. He twists his mouth, and I can't help remembering how once upon a time long ago, those same lips were pressed against me.

I'm doing it again. *Fuck.*

My mind always seems to wander back to our secret when I'm around him. It's been over a year since I've been with Colton in that way, but time doesn't seem to matter. I still think about it.

Colton is not only my brother's business partner and co-owner of Dallas' BBQ and Brew, he's also my brother's best friend. For a time, I considered how my brother would take knowing Colton and I have been closer than what he assumes we are, but deep down, I don't really care. I'm old enough to handle my own relationships; plus Colton's been clear in letting me know he's always felt the same about me.

My thoughts haven't always been one-sided. After our one night, Colton would come over to my place. We never went too far, always pushing the boundaries. We'd order dinner and watch a movie. Sometimes I'd fall asleep with my head in his lap and his hand on my hip, his fingers dancing close to the waist of my pants. As the year has gone on, those nights have become scarcer the more Colton's been involved with graduate school and running the restaurant. Still, he finds his ways to touch me, like right now as he wraps his arm around my waist, keeping my body pressed against him.

Most of the time it's been at work: brushing past me in the refrigerator in the kitchen, leaning over me to grab a few coasters from behind the bar. Every day he's found an excuse to touch me. We've simply never acted on it because we remember the deal we made.

The deal that our secret would only be the one time. Never again.

Instead, we allow ourselves to indulge in moments like this, pretending we aren't scavenging for some sort of loophole in our deal. We agreed we wouldn't sleep together again, not that we wouldn't touch each other.

Colton doesn't answer my question of where he's taking me. Puffs of smoke continue to pour out from the small chimneys of the smokers, the leftover embers still smoldering from cooking meat all day.

But it isn't the smokers that have me surprised; it's how Colton's truck is parked out back. The engine rumbles and the doors are propped open. He's parked it so the passenger door is open on the same side where I'm standing.

He lets go of my arm and stands by the door, holding it open for me. I swallow my nerves as he stands in front of me in his usual torn jeans and faded black Dallas' BBQ and Brew t-shirt. His shirt stretches around his broad muscles, his forearms swelling as he holds on to the door.

"Get in." He nods toward the open door.

I cross my arms over my chest and narrow my eyes. "Are you kidnapping me?"

"No, I'm not kidnapping you. What the—" He shakes his head, holding out his hand. "Just get in. If you don't, Sloan will kill me for not bringing you back here on time."

I step toward him, kicking up the dirt along the way. "I have my own car here. I can drive myself."

"You can…" He holds out a hand. "But where's the fun in that?"

I give him a pointed look. "Fine." I unravel my arms and step up into the truck without grabbing his hand, and he laughs then closes the door behind me. He climbs into the driver's seat, not wasting any time leaving the restaurant.

When we pull up outside my apartment, I wrap my hand around the door handle but stop when I notice he isn't going with me. He stays in the vehicle, his hand still wrapped around the steering wheel.

"Are you not coming with me?" I ask him.

"I mean…" He shrugs, flexing his fingers on the wheel. The

leather rubs against his skin as he lets out a breath, his shoulders falling. He pauses, the muscles of his jaw ticking. "How long do you think it'll take you?"

I raise my eyebrows. "Are you kidding?" I look down at my shirt, pointing to the barbecue stain I found earlier. "It might take a minute."

He swipes his thumb across his bottom lip, looking out the window to his left, away from me. He inhales a deep breath then opens his door. "I'll go in with you, but try not to take too long."

"You're ruthless, you know that?" I hop out of the truck and shut the door behind me, not waiting for him.

He follows behind me slowly. He keeps his distance, the sound of his boots hitting the pavement filling the night air. I push through the wrought iron gate and hold it open long enough for him to grab it.

I let my hand fall away, and we walk in silence until we reach my apartment. I unlock the door and keep it open for Colton to follow me again. I can sense the mood between us shifting, enough so he doesn't follow me all the way in. He moves to the couch and sits down, pulling his phone from his pocket. He immediately starts scrolling.

"I'll try to be quick."

He looks up long enough to give me a weak smile before he returns to whatever it is he was looking at.

I walk down the hall and into my bedroom, closing the door behind me. When I lift my shirt over my head, my nose immediately fills with the scent of barbecue sauce and vodka. It's enough to make me gag.

Even though Colton's out in the living room, my cheeks redden in embarrassment. I can't believe that's how I've been smelling all day, especially sitting in the cab of Colton's truck. I grab a few strands of my long, curly hair and bring it to my nose.

At least that still smells good. The lingering scent of my coconut shampoo replaces the gross concoction from my shirt.

I undress, tossing my clothes in the hamper. I don't rush getting into the shower like Colton was urging me to, but I try not to take my time either. Once I squeeze a dollop of shampoo in the palm of my hand, I'm quick to work my fingers through my hair. As I rinse it out, I start thinking of what they have planned for my last night celebration. Sloan said Dallas was out getting supplies, and honestly, the thought of what it could be terrifies me.

When I'm finished quickly shaving my legs, I rinse and step out of the shower. I wrap a towel around myself, tucking the corner in over my chest. I step out into my bedroom, gathering my hair into my hands, pulling it away from my back.

"Shit." I try to pull again, realizing my hair is somehow tangled in my necklace. I look down at the diamond resting in its rose gold setting. It's a necklace my mother gave me when I graduated college three years ago. I try to turn the chain around to get a better look at how it's tangled, but I can't. There are too many strands caught around the clasp for me to be able to pull it out or undo it. I must have been too distracted in the shower to remember to take my necklace off before stepping in under the water. Between me working all day and jumping into the shower without brushing it, it's become a tangled mess.

I stand in my bedroom, the back of my neck stinging from where my hair is pulling against the necklace. I'm about to walk over to my closet to get dressed and deal with it after when I hear Colton's voice coming from the other side of my bedroom door.

"Vada?" He knocks.

"Yeah." I sigh, wondering how in the hell I'm going to get my hair out of this thing without ripping an entire chunk out. "You can come in."

It isn't until he's stepped into my room that I realize I've invited him in when I'm completely naked. Well, at least I am under this thin towel I have wrapped around me.

"I heard you hiss and say shit, so I figured I'd see if you were okay."

I wince, giggling under my breath. "I was that loud?"

"A little." He steps closer to me, his eyes wandering over my body. The flash in his eyes is enough to make me wonder if I'm still wet from my shower, or if it's me, watching him look at me the way he is now.

"I'm okay." I wave him off then bring my hand up to the back of my neck. "I just got my hair caught in my necklace and I can't get it out. I'm afraid I'll break my necklace, or my hair."

Colton walks over, immediately moving behind me as my hair drips between my shoulder blades. "Here," he says, his voice a near whisper. "I'll take a look."

Here he is again, finding his excuse to touch me.

Loophole.

A chill immediately spreads across my skin, goose bumps breaking out the second his fingers touch me. My throat swells and I hold in a breath as he slides his fingers along my shoulder, slowly dragging my wet hair to one side. He drapes most of it over my other shoulder, careful to not pull on the hairs caught in my necklace.

"Shit, Vada."

"It's that bad?" I ask, glancing over my shoulder. I can only see his face in my peripheral vision.

He keeps his fingers on my skin and leans forward. "Don't worry," he whispers. "Nothing I can't fix." He starts to pull strands of my hair from the clasp one by one. It's a slow, tedious process, but he doesn't stop. By the time he's done, my skin is nearly dry. I still have the towel wrapped around me as I turn around. His hands fall at his sides. I hadn't noticed until now that I was standing close to the wall beside the doorway to my bathroom. Now that I've turned around to face Colton, my back is nearly pressed against it.

"Thank you," I whisper, looking up at him with hooded eyes.

This is truly the closest we've been in a long time. My heart thrashes in my chest and my skin heats in reaction to feeling him this close. He lifts his hand, using two of his fingers to move the hair back off my shoulder. Him moving it causes him to move his hand around my neck.

I slide my legs back and forth, my thighs tightening from his touch. I press my lips together then slide my tongue between, wetting them. Colton's eyes fall to my mouth.

"Sloan asked me a question earlier that got me thinking," he says, his eyes bouncing between my eyes and my mouth as if he can't decide what to focus his attention on.

"Oh yeah?"

We're incredibly close, too close for two people who aren't meant to be close. The issue with me is I want to uphold my deal with Colton because I shouldn't want to be with someone who can't give me more than he's willing to give, but it's also hard to stick to it when he's this close.

His touch is always both fire and ice. My skin burns as his skin meets mine, but then he's quick to soothe it.

Like him, I can't decide what I want to focus on.

"Yeah," he says. "She asked me if I was going to miss you working at the bar."

I giggle. "And will you?"

He smirks, the corner of his mouth tilting as he lifts his hand, swiping a drop of water still above my eyebrow. "I haven't decided yet."

I push against his chest. "You're the worst."

He laughs, wrapping his hand around mine. "Mmm, I believe there was a time when you didn't think so."

Loophole. There goes another one.

Colton's hint at our one time is different than outright speaking about it. Our deal was to never speak of it again, and that's just what we're doing. Or at least we're telling ourselves that.

The longer I stand here in nothing but a towel with his body nearly pressing against mine, the harder it is for me to decide what to do.

I search his light brown eyes, the ones that are almost the same color as his hair, and try my hardest to put my head before my heart.

Maybe I can find another loophole, one that'll guard both.

CHAPTER TWO

COLTON

Table number fucking eight.

I walk past it as I head toward the bar. I lean over the edge, reaching back for an orange slice from the garnish tray Dallas keeps by the well. I bite into it and turn back around to face the dining room. I lean back, resting one elbow on the counter as I chew on the fruit, pulling it away from the peel with my teeth.

I try to avoid looking at table number eight because Vada is all I can think about every time I do.

I watch her as she crosses the dining room, headed to the stage where Sloan is setting up the microphone. She avoids looking in my direction. She avoids looking at table number eight. She purposely moves around it, taking the long way around, keeping her eyes glued to the stage.

I stifle the grin wanting to come out. I feel the exact same way she does.

I haven't been able to look at table eight the same way since our one time together. Since then, it's been a struggle not to get close to Vada again. I had one taste and wanted more. I craved more of her.

I remember the heat of her skin under my touch, the taste

that hit my tongue the moment I slid my tongue between her wet folds, her back arching in response to me.

Dammit. I really need to stop.

She's my best friend's little sister. Not exactly off limits, according to her brother. I don't think Dallas would care if he knew about Vada and me. I have a feeling he might already know. My reservation about us is more due to the fact that the restaurant and school are my whole life. Vada deserves someone who can put her first, and I know right now, I can't exactly give that to her. Or at least I don't think I can. I just can't think of a way it can work.

I'm still watching Vada as she meets Sloan over near the stage. She starts gathering up one of the cords, and Sloan leaves her. She walks over to where I'm standing, pulling a few shot glasses from the counter. She starts filling them with tequila.

"Thanks for taking Vada home to clean up." Her voice is nearly drowned out by the music playing overhead. Although it's quieter than when we're open, it's still loud enough to muffle even the loudest of voices. Country music blares overhead as Dallas emerges from the back, standing beside Sloan.

"It was no problem." I'm lying; it was a big problem. Admittedly, I didn't rush to answer Sloan when she asked if I'd be able to take Vada home to change out of her work clothes before bringing her back here, mostly because I know when Vada and I are by ourselves, we test the waters more and more.

It's as if we've both buried our secret, pretending it doesn't exist. Instead, we push the boundaries, never taking it far enough to be considered anything. A relationship? No. A one-night stand again? Nope.

Our touches are both innocent and dangerous at the same time.

I watch Vada as she bends over, her curly hair falling off her shoulder. It covers her face like a curtain, and I'm immediately reminded of what it was like being in her apartment earlier. She stepped out of the shower, and I heard her curse. I remained on the couch for a moment, curling my hands into fists. I didn't want to go back and see her, risk seeing her in nothing but her long hair cascading down her back, her skin damp.

But like a moth to a fucking flame, I went anyway. Thankfully, she had a towel wrapped around her, at least. My cock nearly sprang to life at the sight of her, and I tried to keep it calm as I helped untangle her hair from her necklace. Afterward, I told her we needed to leave or else we truly would be late.

Ever since then I've had a difficult time forgetting the way my fingers grazed her wet skin, and my dick has been hard.

I take my attention away from Vada and watch Sloan pour the rest of the shots, placing the tequila back on the shelf. "If we hang out in here too long, people will start thinking we're still open."

"I didn't plan on staying in here," Sloan says. Dallas loads the shots onto a small drink tray.

"Where are we going?" I ask her.

She nods her head back toward the swinging door to the kitchen. "I set up chairs and string lights on the side patio. I even made a fire pit in the middle of it using some of the pecan wood from the smokers."

"This is nice of you, Sloan." Dallas leans down and gives her a kiss before heading to the back.

Sloan nods toward Vada. She's still wrapping up a few cords, carrying one of the amplifiers over to the corner of the stage. "Cassidy is meeting us out back, and I asked Vada if she didn't mind cleaning up the stage for me while I made the drinks."

"Do you need help?"

She shrugs and pouts, her eyebrows dipping in concentration. "Not over here, but you can get started on the fire out back."

"Sure." I give Sloan a smile before looking over my shoulder at Vada. I turn back to Sloan. "Dallas is right—it is nice of you to do this for Vada."

Sloan grins and shrugs. "Of course. I love her, and I thought she could use a sendoff party since she put so much time into the restaurant after Hailey died."

"She has." I nod, thinking back to the day Vada offered to help me open the restaurant after Dallas lost his wife, Hailey.

The three of us were caught up in our grief, not knowing where our lives were going. I guess when you lose someone you love, they take a piece of you with them. Then you're left to rearrange the pieces that remain, hoping it'll resemble the life you had once before.

I'm assuming that's what Dallas had to learn to do: build a life of his own with only the memory of Hailey.

I leave Vada and Sloan inside, meeting Dallas out back. We start arranging a few of the logs from the smoker, making a makeshift fire pit in the center of all the chairs Sloan has set up.

I've placed the last log onto the pile when my phone vibrates in my pocket. I pull it out and see a text from my brother, Ryan. I read it, resisting the urge to roll my eyes. Instead, I scoff and shake my head, sliding my phone back into my pocket.

"Who was it?" Dallas asks, chuckling.

I wave him off. "Oh, it was Ryan. He just told me he's on his way home after having dinner with our dad. He's asking when I'll finish school so he'll get off his back about taking over the business. I guess Ryan is still hoping I'll change my mind so he won't be going into it alone, or I'll take it for him."

"I already know you won't," Dallas says.

"Ryan knows too, but I guess he's still holding out hope that

I'll change my mind. I don't think it's what Ryan wants either. He's never said it to me, but I can tell."

"I'm sure everything will work out."

I nod and leave Dallas to head back over to one of the smokers, closer to the back of the restaurant. Sloan and Dallas set up the fire pit off to the side of the building, partially facing the side road running adjacent to the main road. There's a wooden fence dividing the smokers from the patio.

Vada and Sloan step out from the kitchen. They're each carrying a drink in their hands. Sloan passes me, joining Dallas around the corner by the fire pit, but Vada joins me when I reach the smoker.

She hands me the other beer in her hand. "I thought you might like a drink."

"Thanks." I smile and take it from her. She's chewing on a piece of licorice, her pink lips wrapping around the red candy. "Did you really bring those to your going away party?" I ask, remembering the first time I saw her chew a piece. She told me it's become a habit of hers to keep them in her car. The day I caught her chewing one, it was early in the morning of the first day I trained her to start bartending here at the restaurant.

"I have my car here, remember?" She smiles around the piece of candy. "I ran out and grabbed a piece."

"Oh." I nod, my heart skipping a beat. I bite down on the side of my cheek, resisting the urge to step forward and claim her mouth with mine.

I can't do it, at least not in front of Dallas and Sloan.

"Can I tell you something?" I ask Vada. She's standing with her back pressed against the brick wall, her face covered in shadows. Her green eyes stare up at mine. They're dark in the moonlight, and a soft orange glow peeks through the gaps in the small fence dividing us from the patio.

"Sure." She swallows the last bit of red licorice, and I step closer to her. It's wrong for me to bring myself this close to her again, but I can't help it. Like I said, I'm a fucking moth drawn to a flame. She's covered in orange and silver, the colors mixing over her tan skin. I step forward, resting my arm above her head. I'm partially caging her in. I lift my other hand and tuck her curly hair behind her ear, swallowing. She smells like coconut and strawberries. The scent alone causes my cock to pulsate.

She tips her chin up, resting her head against the wall behind her. She gives me a small smile, and it's expressions like this one that tell me she enjoys being this close to me. She's thinking about me as much as I am her.

"I wanted to tell you..." I drag a finger down her cheek, tracing an invisible line down the side of her neck. She holds her breath, her neck bobbing as she swallows. "Being back here reminds me of the day you offered to help with the grand opening."

"I remember," she whispers.

She reaches up and places her hand over mine, flattening my palm against her chest. I can feel her heart beating against my palm. She glances over to the side, checking to see if Dallas and Sloan can see or hear us. Their hushed conversation can't be heard from where we are, letting us know they can't hear us.

I tip my head lower, looking at her with hooded eyes. "I also wanted to thank you."

"I told you before—I didn't mind helping. You and Dallas needed it, and I'm glad I was available to do it."

"You were here a lot longer than you were supposed to be."

"Honestly, I think I'll miss this place more than I realize."

"Yeah?"

"Yeah. Did you decide?" she asks, tilting the corner of her mouth into a smirk.

"Decide what?"

"If you're going to miss me or not?"

"Oh." I pretend to think on it, knowing I'll miss the fuck out of Vada. Not simply because I won't see her face every day, but more because I genuinely enjoy having her around. Something about her lights a fire to my insides. I've never felt more alive than I do when I'm with Vada.

"I want to tell you something. I have to make a confession," Vada says, not waiting for me to answer her first question.

I lower my hand and relax it by my side, not wanting to push us too far. We're constantly stuck in the middle, pushing the envelope far enough but never crossing the line.

We're fools. Both of us.

"Okay," I tell her.

"Part of me is thankful to not be working here anymore."

"Really?" I can feel my eyebrows shooting up and across my forehead.

She's quick to stop me from speaking. She swipes her tongue across her lips, and I smell strawberries again. She looks up at me with green eyes, the colors flickering with the orange from the fire. "You push me to the edge. Every day."

"What?"

"It's torturous." Her eyes move back and forth between my eyes and my mouth. "I can't stand it. I know neither of us are in a place for anything more and I know we said we're not to talk about our one time, but I can't help—"

I stop her words with my mouth, slamming my lips to hers.

She immediately releases a moan, her mouth vibrating on mine. Her mouth is warm, and she tastes sweet. With a shaky hand, she wraps her palm around the back of my neck, keeping me pressed against her.

I groan, pressing my hips into her. I can't take this too far. I won't. I won't give Vada false hope. It's horrible, and the thought of having to push her away right now causes my chest to ache.

I grip her waist, pressing my fingers into her. I slide them under the bottom of her shirt, lifting it high enough to dance along her skin. She parts her lips, allowing my tongue access. When my tongue meets hers, all my nerves spark like tiny bursts of fireworks. My cock hardens, and I press my hips to hers. She gasps, catching her breath against my mouth. I squeeze my eyes shut, gathering up the courage to pull away. I do but keep my hand wrapped around the side of her face, keeping her to me.

Our breaths mingle between us, our chests rapidly rising and falling. I take a moment to catch my breath, not wanting to break my eyes away from hers.

"Vada."

"I know," she says. "I know. It's okay." She slowly drags her finger across my mouth from one side to the next. "I just wanted to remember, even if it was only this."

"Me too." I slide my hand along her jaw and press my thumb to her bottom lip, pressing it into her pink flesh. Her mouth is swollen from my kiss. "I just…" I squeeze my eyes shut and sigh. When I open them again, I look into her eyes, making sure I see straight through to her. "Four months."

Her brown eyebrows dip in confusion, but only for a second before she understands what I mean. I'll be done with school in four months.

It's not a promise, but it's a possibility.

"Four months," she repeats.

I slide my thumb across her lip once more, telling myself to remember the way she tastes: sweet strawberry.

I allow my hand to fall away from her mouth, and I step back, never once taking my eyes off her. She pushes off the wall and runs her fingers through her hair, then she slides them down her neck. She's still attempting to catch her breath.

I'm about to tell her we should head back over to the patio to join everyone else when my phone vibrates in my pocket again. I pull it out and read the name across my screen. It's my mother.

I lift my phone and wave my hand at Vada, letting her know I'm getting a call. "I'll be over there in a minute. I should answer this."

She gives me a small smile, and I can't help noticing the sadness lingering in her eyes, even after the moment we've had.

"Colton?" My mother's voice shoots through my phone, piercing my ear as she yells.

"Mom? Are you okay?"

"It's Ryan. You need to come to the hospital."

"Why?" My chest caves in, and my feet are already carrying me over to my truck where it's parked out front.

"It's Ryan," she repeats, sobbing. "There's been an accident."

CHAPTER THREE

COLTON

Gold and silver streamers line the walls, stretching from one corner of the ceiling to the next, making the bar nearly unrecognizable. Rows and rows of green garland hang from the base of the bar top, leading all the way to the back. The second I step inside the restaurant, I'm hit with a strong scent of cinnamon and pine, a stark difference from the usual smoky brisket and barbecue sauce smell coming from our kitchen. It's as if the holidays have hurled all over the dining room, covering it in various shades of reds, greens, and golds.

Although Sloan decorated the restaurant for the holidays, I know that's not the real reason for the immense number of lights and garland. Aside from the decorations, the atmosphere in the bar is different than usual. There are more people than I anticipated being here, though I shouldn't be too surprised since it's New Year's Eve.

I was incredibly happy for my best friend when he told me he'd proposed to Sloan a few weeks ago. At one time, I never thought he'd be able to climb his way out of his grief, much less come out of it enough to want to marry again.

In a way, I can relate to Dallas. I may not have lost a spouse, but losing a brother cuts just as deep. I fell down a dark hole, grieving the one person I've been able to count on. It's been four months since Ryan's sudden death, and I've only just now started to feel myself climbing out of that dark hole.

Where Dallas turned into a recluse as far as the restaurant was concerned when Hailey died, I did the opposite. After Ryan passed away, I threw myself into work. I focused only on perfecting my food, trying every different combination possible. I was spending eighteen hours a day here, but lately, I've started to pull back, finally allowing myself the time to move on. I watched Dallas turn in on himself for over a year. I didn't want the same for myself.

I make my way further into the dining room, weaving between the crowded tables. It's incredible to see this place packed considering we closed the restaurant down for the celebration. Dallas and Sloan must have made quite a few friends since they started performing on stage together. I recognize a few of them and give polite waves on my way over but mostly keep to myself.

When I reach the center of the dining room, I stop in front of an empty table. Three empty glasses are scattered on it, but no one is sitting in the chairs. I stand near one of the seats and scan the dining room, hoping to spot Dallas or Sloan, or even Vada.

I glance over my shoulder, back toward the front door, hoping to catch a glimpse of her dark, curly hair or her green eyes.

"She's already here, you know. In the back."

I turn back to find Sloan standing on the other side of the table. She's wearing a long-sleeved, deep red velvet dress, the perfect complement to Dallas' dark blue suit. She grabs two empty glasses, and a hint of light reflects off the simple diamond ring wrapped around the fourth finger on her left hand.

"I don't know what you're talking about," I say, pretending I don't already know who she's referring to. I grab the empty beer glasses in front of me, avoiding Sloan's pointed stare.

She shakes her head. "You both are ridiculous."

"How are we rid—" My question is cut off when Dallas joins us, sliding in next to Sloan.

He wraps his arm around her waist, pulling her to his side. His eyes move to the glasses in her hands, and he grabs one from her, placing it back down on the table. "What are you doing?"

Once Dallas looks at me, I give him a small smile, but I can't help feeling Sloan's comment digging into the back of my brain. I know Sloan is referring to the silence Vada and I have given each other these past four months. When Ryan died and I poured myself into my work, it also pulled me away from Vada. With her no longer working at the restaurant, I haven't seen her. She hasn't stopped by, and I haven't gone over to her place. She's given me the space I know I needed. It still doesn't erase the fact that I miss her.

Sloan knows tonight is big, and not just because of her and Dallas' engagement. She's anxious for the moment Vada and I see each other. I can tell in the way her eyes move from the swinging door that leads to the kitchen then back to me. She's anticipating the moment Vada steps out and I see her for the first time.

"I was just going to take these back to the kitchen really quick." Sloan shrugs, then turns in Dallas' arm, keeping herself against him.

"*We're* not working," he says. "We're celebrating us tonight."

"I know," she says. "Habit, I guess."

I'm watching as Dallas pulls Sloan closer to his side, placing a kiss on her temple. She closes her eyes then pulls away.

Dallas nods his head my way. "You're not supposed to be working either. I hired a catering team for tonight, remember?"

He's telling the truth. I glance around the dining room as several waiters wearing white collared shirts and black aprons mill about, small trays perched on their hands. One of them walks by, picking up the glasses Sloan and I tried to clear away.

I open my mouth to give Dallas some smartass retort but stop when my attention is pulled away to the woman emerging from the kitchen behind him.

There's a crowd of people standing between us, and she hasn't seen me yet, but I've never seen her look as beautiful as she does now. Her long, twisted brown curls frame her face in a way that accentuates the sharp curve of her jawline. The smooth plane of her nose is situated perfectly between her pale, mossy green eyes. Her lips are painted a deep purple color that matches her dress. Her dress stops just above the middle of her thighs. The fabric clings to her body, accentuating her smooth, round curves. I bite the inside of my cheek, forcing myself to keep calm as she walks around the bar, bringing her body into full view.

My hand twitches, remembering how her body once melded to my fingers. I flex them, remembering the sound she made when I slammed my hips into hers.

It's been four months since I've spoken to Vada, since I spent the night with her the night Ryan died.

There have been times I've thought about texting her, most of them just to check in, see how things are going with her job. I want to know how it's been since she left the restaurant and went back to the newspaper full time, but like I said, I've only just now begun to crawl out of my grief.

My arms and legs vibrate with electricity at the sight of her. She's fucking gorgeous, always has been. For the past two years, she's the one woman I haven't been able to stop thinking about.

Maybe it's because she's the one woman I've never allowed myself to fall completely for. She's the one woman I keep at a distance.

As it is with most men my age, I've had my fair share of relationships and one-night stands. Most of my relationships only lasted six months or less, and all my one-night stands took place either in my dorm room or against the bookshelves in the back of the library in my first few years of college, even a few times in high school.

But now, ever since I've been working on my master's and opening the restaurant, I simply haven't had the time to indulge in my old lifestyle—or that's what I've been telling myself. Deep down in my chest, I know my decision to keep Vada away had to do with Ryan's death.

My decision to keep Vada at basically a friendship level hasn't been an easy one to maintain. Honestly, I fucking loathe it. It doesn't feel right or natural. It's as if I'm trying to push together two wrong sides of a magnet.

Vada doesn't turn in our direction when she rounds the bar. Instead, she heads over to the stage and adjusts the microphone, plugging it into the amplifier set in the corner.

She's keeping herself busy. Fuck if I know I'm the reason, but hopefully I can find more answers tonight.

I'm itching to make my way across the dining room but stop when Sloan speaks up.

"How's school going? It feels like you've been working on your master's forever."

I give her a subtle laugh, hoping it sounds convincing. I can't help it. The combination of seeing Vada and thinking back on our silence these past few months has me a bit distracted. Tonight is supposed to be all about Dallas and Sloan. I know they deserve it, but my mind is elsewhere.

"It's going great," I reply, shifting my eyes back to Vada

every few seconds. "I actually only have one more class this semester and then all I'll have left is my seminar paper."

"You're getting your degree in business, right?" Sloan threads her fingers through Dallas', clutching him as if he were an extension of her body. Where she goes, he goes. It's amazing to see the love grow between them, as if they need the other one just to stay afloat.

"Yeah." I clear my throat. "I'm getting my MBA."

"Finally." Dallas groans. Then his mouth transforms into a hint of a grin. "I can't tell you how tired I am of hearing how *busy* you are. Maybe then we'll see you more often."

"Maybe." My eyes shift to my left, catching Vada joining our group.

Finally. I hold my breath and clear my throat as she joins us. I wonder if I'll see the same desire that sparked in her eyes the last night I saw her, the desire for us to be more. How deep her desire goes, I've never been sure. I don't even know if she feels the same anymore. It's been four months since I last saw it in her eyes.

I attempt to give her a smile, the electricity returning to my veins. It thrums and vibrates, waiting for the moment she swings her emerald gaze to mine...but that electricity leaves me when she keeps her focus on the two people standing opposite me.

"All set up for you two." She smiles, displaying her perfectly straight, white teeth. They remind me of the time she grazed those same teeth across my collarbone, biting down on my flesh as I gave her an orgasm on the table only ten feet from where we're standing.

Dallas nods his head and thanks Vada. He turns, kissing Sloan on the cheek before tugging on their clasped hands, pulling them to the stage.

I run my fingers through my hair and readjust my sleeves, pushing them further up my arms. Vada still hasn't bothered to bring her eyes to me. She stares at her brother and her best friend as they step up onto the stage set in the back of the restaurant. I cross my arms over my chest, wondering how long it'll take for Vada to acknowledge me standing next to her.

Ten seconds.

I've counted to ten by the time she finally turns to me.

"Hi, Colton." She gives me a devious grin as if she's able to read my mind. She knows I've been standing here in silence waiting for her.

"Hey." My voice is drowned out by the music playing overhead. The usual country playlist has been swapped out for a compilation of songs that sound like the ones Dallas plays on stage, a mixture of folk and alternative.

Her eyes widen slightly as they roam across my body. Her mouth twists in thought, and she tucks her bottom lip under her teeth. Perhaps she's surprised by my change in clothes. I hardly ever wear a collared shirt, much less tucked into a pair of black slacks. Usually, I'm wearing some sort of worn t-shirt and roughed-up jeans.

"How have you been?" I ask, moving around the table, closer to her.

One of the waiters Dallas hired passes by us with a tray. Half of it holds some sort of pink cocktail, and the other has what looks to be beer. The waiter offers me a beer and I take it, but when he offers Vada one, she gives him a silent wave, letting him know she doesn't want one.

Her fingers twirl the gold chain dangling from her neck. The white stone at the end rests between the smooth swells of her breasts. It shimmers against the light. It's the same necklace she's worn since I've known her. She was wearing it the night we spent together.

It's hard not to think about our secret when I'm around her.

"I'm good." She gives me a tight-lipped smile and a nod so

subtle I'm almost wondering if she did it at all. "Just busy, that's all." She pauses, raising her eyebrows.

There's a hint of playfulness to her gaze, but I can't help the pin prick to the chest with her remark. It's always been a contentious subject for us, the number one reason I gave her as to why we could never have a relationship, even before Ryan died.

With my back to the stage, I keep my gaze pinned on Vada. I take a sip of my beer, eyeing her over the rim of my glass. The bitter foam hits my tongue followed by the crisp, cold liquid.

I swallow and give her a smile back, hoping to keep our conversation light. "Guilty."

It's true. Some days I feel as if my own life will swallow me whole.

Growing up, my parents always instilled a fear in me, a fear that if I didn't stick to a plan and follow through with it, I would be considered a disappointment. My life has constantly been measured not by my successes, but by my failures. Although I'm almost twenty-seven years old, I still try to gain their approval in one way or another. It's fucked up, but after Ryan was struck by a drunk driver four months ago, I'm all they have left.

Vada's chest swells as she breathes in, holding the air in the space around her beating heart. She releases it, and her shoulders fall with her chest.

"I guess we're both guilty as charged then."

For a moment, I try to decipher her answer, dissecting her meaning. I'm unsure if she's still talking about us both being too busy to be involved in a relationship or something else entirely.

Were we both guilty of being too consumed with ourselves to bother looking at the prospect of a relationship? Or are we both guilty of thinking back on that night, remembering it but never speaking of it? I told her I only needed enough time to finish school. Now that I'm approaching graduation, I'm unsure where we stand. Did Ryan's death have the power to erase the words I told her that night?

"So," I start, "*The Daily News* is keeping you that busy, huh?"

She blinks several times as she swipes her tongue across her mouth. Her eyes shift between mine as she inhales a deep breath and holds it. "Yep, they are."

Her gaze quickly shifts over my shoulder to the stage behind me. I turn and look over my shoulder in time to see Dallas stepping up onto the stage. Sloan isn't far behind him.

"Attention, everyone," Dallas starts. He leans into the microphone, straightening the black tie wrapped around his neck. He slides his arm around her again, pulling her to him without hesitation. "I'd like to start off by wishing you all a happy new year and to thank all of you for being here tonight with Sloan and me. Each of you is here for a reason, whether that be because we met here at the restaurant or through our small performances either here or throughout the city. We're grateful you're with us celebrating our engagement."

I listen to Dallas as he continues talking about how in love with Sloan he is, but it doesn't take me long to get distracted by the woman standing beside me. She's standing between me and the table. Her arm is outstretched, her fingers dancing across in small circles. They bend slightly as they ghost across the smooth surface. The black polish painted on her nails is pristine. The color shines against her pale skin. It looks fresh. Her focus hasn't moved away from the stage, and the shadows cast across her face highlight the subtle hint of a smile growing across her mouth as she listens to her brother's words.

My attention shifts back to the stage when the crowd starts to applaud Dallas. Once the sound fades, Sloan's voice fills the dining room.

She breathes in deeply, tears lining her eyes. She scans the room then her eyes fall on the center, directly onto Vada. It's then I realize Vada's eyes are just as emotional as Sloan's. They shine like glass.

"I want to thank everyone for being here as well." Sloan's voice wobbles, and her chest shudders. She attempts a small smile as she stares at Vada. "When I first moved here, I never expected to be standing where I am today." She turns to Dallas and gives him a large grin and a sweet, soft laugh before turning back to Vada. "Love hasn't always come easy for me. I don't just mean the romantic kind because I know I've found that with Dallas, but I also mean the kind of love that holds on to you forever, the kind you forge in friendships."

Sloan pauses as her eyes shift between me and Vada. I glance between the two women, watching as happy, emotion-filled tears stream down their faces. Not once does Vada move. She's frozen, her expression transforming to one of surprise.

I've never seen her this emotional before. An aching pain twists in my chest at the sight of her. Despite knowing they're tears of joy from watching her brother and her best friend, it still hurts to see her cry. It's an odd feeling and one I realize I've never had until now.

With her focus still on the both of us, I give Sloan a reassuring smile back, waiting for her to continue.

"Life can be unexpected sometimes. I didn't expect to fall in love so soon after moving here, and the day I walked into Dallas' BBQ and Brew, I certainly didn't expect to find my best friends. Colton, I can't thank you enough for being so kind to me that first day we met and for giving me a job. You're incredibly intelligent, and you make the best damn brisket I've ever tasted." The crowd gives a quick laugh, and I find myself doing the same before Sloan keeps going. "And Vada, I not only gained a friend in you that day...I gained a sister. I could never come up with the right words to describe what you mean to me."

Vada presses her hand to her chest, attempting to contain her sobs.

Sloan brushes a falling tear from her cheek. "You're the best friend I've ever had, and I love you for seeing me for who I was... for who I *am*."

Vada mouths *I love you, too* back to Sloan.

Dallas gives Sloan a gentle nudge with his shoulder, and she shakes her head, all the while never allowing her smile to falter.

"Right," she says on a breath. "With all that said..." Her voice trails off as she steps back from the microphone, and Dallas leans forward, his gaze moving from Vada to me.

"Hey man, you're like a brother to me, so there's only one person I could ever ask. Would you do me the honor of being my best man?"

I fight the emotion threatening to build in my throat at Dallas' question. I've been in this position before with him, when he married Hailey, but this is different. His love for Sloan is entirely different, and I wouldn't want to be anywhere else than there to support him.

I'm ready to answer Dallas when Sloan leans into the microphone again, not giving me a chance to respond.

"And Vada, there's no one else I'd like standing next to me on our wedding day. Will you be my maid of honor?" Her grin spreads from nearly ear to ear, and she bounces on her toes with excitement.

Vada's head twists to me, and her mouth pops open as she gasps. It's subtle, and if I weren't standing so close to her, I wouldn't be able to hear it.

But I am, and I do.

Another tear streaks down her cheek. Her glance toward me is quick and guarded. I can't tell if she's surprised Dallas would ask me or if she's simply caught up in the emotion of tonight. She quickly turns her attention back to the stage.

The music in the dining room quickly seems quieter, or perhaps it's the utter silence from the crowd surrounding me and Vada. Suddenly, the attention is on the two of us, and when I look back at Dallas and Sloan, Vada's voice is the only sound to break the deafening silence.

"Of course we will."

CHAPTER FOUR

Vada

When I first decided to leave *The Daily News* four months ago, Cassidy tagged along, promising our new boss we were a package deal. Considering I'd written a few freelance articles for *The Austin Chronicle* when I was working full time at my brother's bar, I knew it wouldn't be difficult for me to find a new job here.

A few days after I returned to work, I found out my old editor-in-chief, Randy, had basically done a vanishing act into retirement, bringing all hopes of my promotion to a complete stop, and I tried to get along with his replacement.

Daniel Jensen was an absolute nightmare. Not only did he treat half the staff as if they were incompetent, he also didn't even bother to learn who we were. He, admittedly, stated he'd not once read an article from our paper in the last ten years and had only taken the job offer because he was getting paid three times what he was making in New York. Part of me wondered who he'd fucked in the corporate office to be given that sort of deal. Part of me knew he was probably just an asshole, plain and simple. Regardless, I gave him a shot and hoped he would learn to appreciate the work I put into the newspaper. I wrote several articles in the first seven days, only for him to send me a one-word email.

No.

I'd spent over a year away from working out of the office full-time, counting on the promotion Randy had promised, and I knew I wasn't going to get it under the hellish reign of Daniel fucking Jensen from New York.

So, I decided to leave, and so did Cassidy.

Now that it's a new year, I'm determined to start over.

I set the cup of coffee I picked up for Cassidy on my way into the office this morning down on her desk. Hers is quite a bit different than mine and in the furthest corner of the office level from mine. The art department is located on the eastern side of the building, primed for the best morning sunlight. Half of Cassidy's desk is covered in photographs. On the other half, she has her computer, the screen opened up to the hundreds of photos she's taken across the city.

I find Cassidy bent over her desk, examining one of the photos closely. She's standing within inches of it, and it makes me wonder how on earth she hasn't blown out her back by now. A red pencil is pinched between her fingers when she spots the coffee I've set down beside her.

"Have I ever told you how much I love it when you bring me a coffee in the morning?" She brings the cup to her mouth, inhaling a deep breath before taking a sip.

I twist my mouth, pretending to think back on a time when she's told me. I'm just glad to have made her day. It isn't even eight in the morning yet.

"Have I ever thanked you for coming to *The Chronicle* with me?" I ask her back.

She gives me a tight-lipped smile before letting it fade. "You don't have to thank me, Vada. The job was shit the second

Randy left. You and I both know that. Plus, it wouldn't have been worth it to stay if you weren't there."

"I appreciate that." I cross my arms and lean on her desk. I slide one of her photographs toward me. It's a picture of the capitol building at sunset. The deep purple of the coming night sky blends with the orange and light blues of the day. It's beautiful.

"What are you doing tonight?" Cassidy asks while she's examining one of the photos in her pile. She sets it aside and picks up another.

"Oh..." I blow out a heavy breath. "Dallas and Sloan are having a dinner tonight to go over plans for the wedding."

"Oh yeah." She nods. "They're getting married soon, right?"

"In three months."

"It'll be a beautiful time of year." She grins, looking up at me from her photos.

"It will. I haven't had much to do yet, but then again, I just found out I'm maid of honor, so I guess the real fun hasn't begun."

"Probably not." She laughs. "I always thought I'd want to be a maid of honor, but I have a feeling it's not everything it's cracked up to be."

"I guess I'm about to find out." I smile and nod, a warmth spreading across my chest. I am thrilled to not only witness my brother falling in love for the second time, but also to be in the wedding.

When Sloan asked me to be her maid of honor at the restaurant the other night, I was caught by surprise. It's not that I didn't suspect she would ask me. My emotion came from the realization that I'd never thought I'd be as close to anyone as I am with Sloan. I never thought I'd have a friend close enough to want me in their wedding, much less as their maid of honor.

Then when I think about the other night, I think about

Colton. I didn't realize how much I'd missed him until I was standing next to him. His mere presence is enough to leave me breathless. It felt like my chest was going to cave in and my heart was going to pop out of my chest. I'd nearly forgotten how gorgeous he is. He was wearing a simple button-down shirt and tie, but I couldn't stop thinking about the way it would feel to have his arms around me again. He stood beside me, swiping his tongue across his mouth, teasing me. My insides twisted and ached for him, but when my eyes met his, I could see the pain behind them. He was wearing a well-worn mask, pretending he wasn't still grieving the loss of Ryan.

"Are you taking a date?"

"What?" I blink several times, breaking my gaze away from the photo of the capitol building I've been staring at for the past few minutes. Cassidy's still sipping on her coffee.

She lifts her shoulders. "Are you taking anyone?"

"No." I shake my head. "I don't think so. I don't know. I haven't really thought about it."

Thinking about bringing a date leads me to wonder if Colton will be bringing one. It shouldn't, considering I haven't spoken to him since the night of the engagement party. It was the first time I'd seen him since Ryan died four months ago. My heart broke for him and at the same time grieved knowing Colton was doing what he thought was best. His silence has been tough, sitting like a rock in the center of my chest, unwilling to move.

But still, he's always known I've never been one to settle. My head and my heart have always been at war for him. My head knew he needed time to grieve the loss of his brother and best friend. My heart wished I could have been the one to help him through it, but a part of me knows Colton has always lived his life to others' expectations. It's become instinct for him to push away those closest to him, telling himself he can pull himself out of it. I gave Colton the space he needed. He hasn't gone out of his way to speak to me, not the way we were months ago. I figure he'll come in his own time.

Starting with tonight.

The thought of sitting with Colton through an entire dinner brings a fluttering sensation to my stomach that makes me feel slightly sick. I dig deep to let the feeling go away and take a sip of my coffee. If I spend my entire day thinking about it, I'll drive myself insane.

"Is it normal for a maid of honor to take a date to a wedding?" I ask Cassidy.

She's sitting on her stool, her large eyes staring up at me. "I don't know. I've never been to one."

"I would think I could." I shrug. "I'll ask her tonight."

"Oh." Cassidy's back straightens as she sits up. "If you decide to take a date, you could always take Levi."

She glances over her shoulder at the same time I move my eyes to the left, spotting Levi sitting at his desk. He's sitting back in his chair and his eyes are narrowed on the computer screen as he reads whatever it is he has pulled up. His long white sleeves are rolled up his arms as he rests his elbows on the arms of his chair. He twirls a pencil between his fingers.

Levi is our newest reporter. My new boss, Nate, hired him about two months ago, and for the most part, I like him. He's quiet, and his work is always turned in on time. Not that I've been paying too much attention, but he's fairly attractive as well —a fact Cassidy has pointed out to me more times than I care to count.

"What?" I ask her, scrunching my nose. It's not that I'm opposed to the idea of taking Levi; it's simply that I never considered it. "Don't you think that would be strange?"

"No." She frowns. "Why would it be? The man is gorgeous. Like, on a scale of one to ten, I'd say he's a solid nine point five. Maybe a full-on ten."

"Then you go on a date with him." I laugh, stepping away from her desk. I really have a lot of work to do, and I've clearly already spent way too long talking to Cassidy. Now she's setting me up on dates.

Her grin immediately fades, the curve of her mouth turning into a flat line. She scratches her thumbnail on the plastic edge of the lid of her coffee. She lifts one shoulder. "Meh, I don't think he's my type."

I raise my eyebrow, unconvinced. "You just said he's gorgeous and now you're saying he's not your type?"

"Whatever." She rolls her eyes and rests her elbows on the edge of her desk, lifting her coffee in front of her face. She has both hands wrapped around it as if using the cup as a shield. "I haven't had enough coffee yet to have this sort of conversation."

"That's what I'm saying." I mutter the words, directing my comment toward her suggestion of me taking Levi to Sloan and Dallas' wedding. I haven't known Cassidy long enough to start prying into her dating life or why she's now all of a sudden looking at Levi as if he were the complete opposite of a nine point five. Taking my coffee with me, I spin around to head back in the direction of my own office. "I'll see you at lunch."

I smile against my coffee as my heels click across the tile. Maybe I'll pay for Cassidy's lunch to make up for my comment.

I turn my phone over in my hand as a text from Sloan pops up on my screen.

Sloan: Don't forget—we're meeting Dallas and Colton for dinner at the Tea Garden at 7. Super excited to finally have you two together to talk about the wedding!

The familiar pit in my stomach twists at the thought of seeing Colton after all this time. I'm no longer thinking of our one-time secret. I'm thinking of the way he held me against the wall outside the restaurant the night he found out Ryan died, the way his fingers danced along the skin of my neck.

He was on the edge of diving all in with me, reminding me he only had five months left before he graduated, but I could see the hesitation in his eyes. Ryan's death only solidified his decision to keep me at a distance.

I've nearly made it to my office and I'm about to reply to Sloan when Levi stops me.

My feet slow then pull me to a full stop outside the door to my corner of the floor. Not only did I succeed in leaving that fucker Daniel behind at my old job, my new boss, Nate, promoted me from copy editor to managing editor.

"Good morning, Vada." Levi gives me a lazy grin with his greeting. My eyes move down to the small stack of papers in his hands.

He still has his sleeves rolled up his arms as if he's been working hard to crank out thousands of words on his newest article.

"Morning, Levi." I give him a small nod. "What's going on?"

"I have the last few paragraphs of that article I wrote up last week. Since I tweaked a few things, I thought I'd bring them over to get your approval."

"Oh." I straighten my back, taking them from him. "Thanks. I'll look it over and let you know by the afternoon."

"Great." His eyes roam over me for a brief moment before he chances a quick glance over his shoulder, back toward his desk. "Anyway, I'll start working on finding another story."

"Okay, thanks."

Levi starts heading back to his desk on the other side of the floor, closer to Cassidy's desk. He runs his fingers through his hair as he hurries across the large open space, passing cubicle after cubicle.

The entire time I watch him walk away, I can't understand what Cassidy sees. I feel nothing, absolutely nothing.

At least not the way I would with him.

CHAPTER FIVE

COLTON

I'M DONE. I'M FINALLY FUCKING DONE. AND FREE.

I never thought this day would come, the day where I've finally earned my degree and all that's left for me to focus on is the restaurant...and maybe pick up what's left of my personal life. As if I've even had one the past five years.

I don't quite have the official copy of my degree in my hands yet, but after graduating only two days ago, the feeling of complete freedom has finally started to pump through my veins. The thought of finishing without Ryan has been a tough pill to swallow. I missed him this year, and I couldn't bear the idea of having a ceremony to celebrate. It didn't feel right.

Not only did finishing school open more free time for myself, the extra staff Dallas and I hired has been a godsend. Between Dallas' increasing performances around the city and my finishing up my dissertation the past two months, we desperately needed the help. I've been thankful too. Although there were moments when I still felt like my life might swallow me whole, the feeling transformed to something less intense, less life-altering.

Hiring on new bartenders, servers, and cooks, however, still hasn't stopped me from checking in on the restaurant on my days off. It's a slow night tonight, but I'm thankful since I'm supposed to be meeting Dallas, Sloan, and Vada for dinner across town. Sloan insisted we needed to meet up to discuss wedding plans. As far as I understand, Sloan knows Vada and I haven't exactly been talking much the past few months. I'm even starting to believe Dallas has noticed.

I haven't intentionally been keeping my history with Vada a secret from her brother. It was in the beginning. Dallas was falling fast after losing his first wife, Hailey. We were all grieving in our own ways, but Dallas' was different. His pain was deep and visceral. The loss of Hailey made him nearly unrecognizable—until he met Sloan. She changed it all for him, but at that point, Vada and I were in too deep with our secret. It's easier to go along with the secret when you pretend your secret never existed in the first place. No sense in bringing Dallas into it when there was nothing for him to get into.

The frustration I've had with myself for keeping her at a distance is eating away at me. I know everyone's decisions are their own. I don't blame Vada for the decisions I've made, but I also know if I don't decide soon, she won't wait around for me forever—if that's even what she's doing. She could be involved with another man by now, and I wouldn't blame her, as much as it would fucking suck.

Our night together feels more like five years ago than almost two. The way her body reacted to my touch and the way it felt with her legs wrapped around my waist, keeping my dick inside her, feels like some far-off dream, a dream that was never a real-ity. It's as if the more time that passes, the more I'm convincing myself it never happened in the first place.

Even our heated kiss at her last-night celebration...it's all a fucking memory.

"I don't understand," Dallas says. "I checked the temperature on that refrigerator before I left this morning. I know it's been iffy these past few weeks, but I never expected it to go out completely."

"I don't know, man." I pinch the bridge of my nose, pushing my glasses up. I adjust them before I continue speaking. "I think we're going to need to get a new one. Thank god we invested in more than one cooler. We're all good for now, though. Calvin's heading the kitchen tonight."

Dallas groans into the phone. I have it wedged between my face and my shoulder as I walk out of the kitchen through the swinging door leading to the bar. I'm supposed to be on my way out the door to head to the restaurant to meet him for dinner, but there was an issue when one of the chefs I recently hired on told me an entire batch of brisket didn't cook correctly.

"I guess we'll have to look into the numbers on getting a replacement," he says. "This fucking sucks though."

"It does." I find myself smiling, hoping to lighten our mood before dinner. "Remind me why we wanted to open a restaurant again."

Dallas laughs into the phone, and I only feel slightly better.

I'm walking out from the back of the bar when I pull myself to a full stop.

"Anyway," Dallas says, "since you figured it out, that means you're on your way, right?"

"Of course. I'll be there in ten."

"Good, or else Sloan will kill you." He scoffs. "And if not you then me."

"I'll be there."

"Okay," he concedes.

When I hang up, I slide my phone into my back pocket and back up a few steps, my eyes shifting to one person sitting on a stool situated in the middle of the bar counter.

It's nearing the beginning of the dinner rush, so the bar has yet to start filling in. The dining room is packed, each table filled with families and friends chatting. The bar, however, only has a total of three people.

I look down the length of the bar behind the counter and catch my bartender, Felicia, chatting with the customer at the other end. Her back is turned toward nearly the entire restaurant. It's something I'll have to talk to her about later.

I step back behind the counter and walk toward the customer. He doesn't have a drink in front of him, or any food. He must have just sat down.

He's young—too young to be sitting at the bar. It's the reason I stopped altogether.

He notices me when I'm within a few feet of him. His brown eyes widen slightly, but then he immediately looks down, focusing on his hands resting on the counter. He wrings his fingers nervously as his eyes shift back up to the TV high up on the wall above us.

"Hi," I say, sliding my hands into my pockets. I lean back slightly and bend my knees, dipping down, hoping to draw his attention back toward me.

"Hi," he mutters. He still hasn't moved, refusing to take his eyes away from the screen above us.

The boy's hair is a light shade of brown, and by the looks of it, he hasn't had it cut in months. The ends are bristled and tangled. He's wearing a bright blue baseball shirt, the words *Austin Little League* printed across the front.

Yeah, he's definitely too young to be sitting at the bar. He's by himself, and I look around, hoping to find one of his parents or any sort of adult who will give me any indication he's with them, but there isn't one.

I lean forward and cross my arms on the edge of the counter, bringing myself to his level. He still keeps his eyes glued to the TV.

"I'm sorry, buddy, but kids aren't allowed to sit at the bar." I sigh. "It's illegal."

"What does illegal mean?" he asks.

"It's when you're doing something you shouldn't be doing." I sigh again. "Like you are now." I'm unsure how to handle this kid, and I can't quite figure him out. He's only half invested in our conversation.

"I didn't know it was illegal to watch TV." He lifts one shoulder, shrugging off my comment.

"It's not." I grin, despite his brushoff.

He still hasn't looked away from the TV, even through our conversation. I'm impressed considering he can't be any older than six or seven.

"Where's your mom?" I ask, hoping he might budge if I start asking more questions. "Or dad? Or whoever is supposed to be watching you..." I chance a look down the bar and notice Felicia talking to the same customer. I really will need to fucking talk to her about that.

"Outside," the boy says. When I turn my attention back to him, he's finally broken his concentration on the TV. He's staring up at me with those large round brown eyes. "My aunt's watching me today. We ate here a little bit ago and we were on our way out when she got a phone call. She's always on the phone." He points to a woman standing outside the restaurant. I can't see her face. She's on the sidewalk, facing the street, keeping her face out of view. Her hand disappears underneath her long blonde hair as she presses her phone to her ear.

"Does she know you're in here?" I ask him, shocked his aunt wouldn't notice him missing. Is she that involved in her conversation not to notice her nephew isn't standing beside her? I'm not a parent, but I'm fairly certain it's frowned upon to let a young child wander on his own, especially when they sit down at a bar, this kid being exhibit A.

"I don't know." He shrugs again. "I figured she would come back in when she's done talking."

"Oh, so you thought you'd just come back in and sit at the bar? You know, if a policeman saw you here, you'd be in big trouble."

He turns his head, looking over each of his shoulders. When he's done, he turns his attention back to me. "I don't see any in here," he reasons. His mouth pouts into a frown as he brushes off my comment. "The Rangers are playing."

His eyes move back to the TV, and I turn around. He's right. A Texas Rangers baseball game from last season is playing on the screen above us. They're in the final inning.

I turn back to the kid. "You're a Rangers fan then, I take it."

"Uh-huh." He dramatically nods his head. I can't see much below his neck with how small he is, but his whole body starts to move back and forth. He must be swinging his legs underneath him. "I like baseball, but I'm not very good at it. Are you?"

My eyes move to the little league logo on his shirt. "Not really. I was never into sports when I was growing up." I lean forward on the counter. "I was too busy reading comic books."

"I love superheroes! I've never read a comic book before, but I just learned how to read. I'll see if my aunt will buy me one." He smiles, his brown eyes sparking under the light.

I'm about to suggest walking him out of the restaurant and safely back to his aunt when she beats me to it.

He looks out the window to where she's standing on the sidewalk. She still has the phone pressed to her ear, but it's clear she's noticed her nephew missing. She snaps her head up and down the street, looking both ways before she spins around, peering into the restaurant.

"Uh-oh," the boy says, jumping down from the stool. His eyes are wide, and his cheeks flush a light shade of pink. "I should go." He takes a few steps before he pulls himself to a stop. "I'm sorry I was being illegal."

I laugh and give the kid a smile. I open my mouth to tell him it's okay, but he's gone before I have the chance. He disappears behind the group of customers walking in through the door. I start to walk out from the bar because I know if I don't head out now, Dallas and Sloan will both kill me for being late.

Through the window, I can see the kid as he steps up to his aunt. Her back is turned toward the restaurant. It's impossible to see her face, but she pulls him in for a hug then wraps her hand around his, tugging him down the sidewalk and out of view. I only get a glimpse of her profile before they disappear.

When they're gone and I hear the last bit of the Rangers game coming from the TV above me as I walk out the door, I realize I never even got the kid's name.

💔

MY STOMACH IS past the point of hunger when I finally reach the table at the restaurant.

Everyone's eyes immediately shift up toward me, and I sit down in the empty seat beside Vada.

I haven't chanced a look at her for fear of what it might feel like to see her again. Seeing Vada every day never used to bother me. In fact, it only fueled my desire to touch and feel her, to know what it might feel like to have my cock inside of her. But now, without seeing her in months, I'm unsure of what it might do.

Instead, I focus my attention on my friends sitting across from me and the basket of bread. I reach my fingers under the cloth and pull out a slice. I pick up the knife beside my plate and dig the tip of it into the cup of butter beside the basket. I slather it across the bread in one swipe.

"I hope I'm not too late," I say to the table. They've fallen silent, watching me as I shove the bread into my mouth.

I don't know why, but I can feel my shoulders tense and the emptiness in my stomach swell. The only thing I can think to do is stuff my face with the mound of carbs in front of me.

"Are you okay, man?" Dallas asks.

I slow my chewing, realizing just how my best friends are looking at me. Both Dallas and Sloan's eyebrows are arched over their foreheads. Vada hasn't made a sound since I sat down, but I can feel her shift beside me.

I swallow my bite and drop the piece of bread. "I'm fine. Just wanted to catch up with you guys."

Their small plates are scattered with breadcrumbs and their glasses are half empty.

I brush my hands off on my pants and lean forward, crossing my arms over the edge of the table. I'm not sure what has my nerves feeling as if they're tangled up inside me into one large knot. Maybe it's my interaction with the kid back at the bar and how I've never met a kid as bold as him before, bold enough to sit at the bar illegally. If a policeman had been in there, I'm not entirely sure what would have happened. The restaurant's reputation could have been tarnished, and on top of that, mine and Dallas'.

Indecision starts to pull at me. I want to tell Dallas because he deserves to know, even if nothing came out of it. Half of the bar is owned by him. His name is painted all over the four brick walls and every coaster that gets placed under a drink.

But at the same time, I don't want him to worry for nothing. This night is supposed to be all about him and Sloan and their wedding. This isn't the time to talk about business.

Then again, I've known Dallas for years. He would want to know.

"Actually," I start to explain, "something happened when I was at the bar."

"Oh," Vada says, cutting me off. "Dallas mentioned how the refrigerators cut out and spoiled everything. Were you able to salvage anything?"

I finally look to my left at the sound of her voice, and the second I take in the sight of her, I'm wishing I had done so when I sat down. Then I would have already gotten over this fucking feeling.

Seeing her for the first time in a few months brings on a new reaction every time. Not only does a chill prickle down my neck and my throat swell, but my fingers also tighten their grip around my glass of water. I'm going to need something stronger if I'm going to be sitting through a dinner talking about wedding shit with Vada sitting less than six inches from me.

As if he's read my mind, the server comes up to the table to ask for my drink order.

"Tall beer, please."

He simply nods before walking off toward the bar set in the back of the restaurant.

"So, what happened?"

I turn my attention back to Vada. She's wearing a simple black dress. It's hard for me to tell how long it is with us sitting down, but I can see part of her thigh when I chance a glance down. The smooth neckline dips down her chest, stopping above the swell of her breasts, and the fabric comes back up, wrapping around her long neck. Her shoulders are bare, and her skin has subtle hints of gold highlighting her pale complexion. Her long brown hair is pulled back into a high ponytail, allowing her full face to be on display.

I swallow back the swelling in my throat and consciously loosen my grip around my glass of boring-ass water. It takes effort, but I'm able to do it.

She's still waiting for my response, her eyebrows arching across her forehead.

"Happened with what?" I've truly forgotten what we were talking about.

"The food—were you able to save any of it?"

"Oh." I nod. "Yeah, we lost some of the produce, but nothing we can't easily replace."

"Good." She leans forward and crosses her arms over the edge of the table.

"Well," Sloan interjects. She sighs, allowing her shoulders to rise and fall dramatically. "I know we could all use a little catching up, but I want to make sure we still talk about the wedding."

"Right," Dallas says. "Honestly, Sloan and I don't want anything too big."

"Yeah," Sloan agrees, twisting her fingers around the stem of her wine glass. "I really only plan on having my brother, Liam, and his husband, Mark. Maybe a few other teachers I work with at the school."

The server comes back and places my beer in front of me.

"What about you?" Vada asks Dallas. "Who do you want to invite?"

Her expression softens. I've never known much about their family other than the few things Dallas has shared with me over the years. All I know is Dallas and Vada's mom had them when she was only a teenager and decided to leave their dad not long after she had Vada. Despite the obvious tension they have with their parents, Dallas and Vada have remained close, more so since Dallas' first wife passed away.

"I'm inviting Mom, of course," Dallas says.

"And Dad?" Vada asks. Her voice has suddenly grown quieter with her question, almost as if she's immediately regretting her decision to ask it.

"Haven't decided." Dallas blows a hot breath from his nose and looks away from Vada. Sloan reaches down, beneath the table, most likely grabbing his hand.

"Okay." Vada nods, her green eyes turning watery. "Whatever you decide is fine with me." She gives him a reassuring smile, and deep down I'm left wondering the story behind her relationship with her dad.

I ignore the pull inside me to ask for more information. This dinner is supposed to be happy, and I don't want to be the one to ruin it.

"Dallas and I still need to figure out catering and flowers, but I was hoping your co-worker Cassidy would be interested in being our photographer," Sloan says to Vada. "I know she's not specifically a wedding photographer, but we want this to be a close-knit kind of wedding, and I like Cassidy. Do you think she would do it?"

"I can definitely ask her, and I bet she would love that you thought of her." Vada grins. Her fingers play with the end of her necklace, twirling the crystal back and forth between her fingers.

"Great." Sloan sighs. "Since we want this to be a small, intimate wedding, I'm thinking there will be maybe thirty guests altogether."

"I love that," Vada says, giving Sloan another smile. It's as if she hasn't been able to stop. Her once watery eyes have now gone back to normal. "The less the better in my opinion. Large weddings are overrated." She lets out a laugh, and I feel it shoot straight through my gut.

"Of course, that all depends on if you and Colton plan on bringing a plus-one."

"Oh." Vada sits up, pulling herself away from the table. She straightens her back then slowly leans back in the booth. She plays off her sudden movement as casual, but I didn't miss the way her eyes widened slightly with Sloan's comment.

"What about you?" Dallas asks. "Do you have anyone in mind?" He brushes his hands on his black button-down shirt, and I cock an eyebrow, knowing he only pulls that shirt out of his closet for special occasions.

I chance a look at Vada. She sits in her corner and leans against the wall, partially turning her body toward me, but she's more in a position to get a view of the whole table. I can't read her thoughts.

"I just figured you might bring one since you're done with school now and you have a bit more free time," Dallas says.

"Wow, you finally finished?" Her lips separate as she quietly breathes in. She hasn't touched the drink sitting in front of her.

But neither have I. My new beer still sits in front of me, the foam slowly starting to disappear on the surface of the amber liquid.

"Um, yeah." I clear my throat and touch my fingertips to my glass. The condensation building up on the outside soaks into my skin. "I finished the other day."

"Congratulations."

Guilt knots in the bottom of my stomach—guilt for not telling her.

When I swing my gaze back up to her, her green eyes are swimming with sincerity. There's truth in her words.

"Thanks."

"How was the graduation ceremony?" Vada's expression is fairly neutral given the tone of her question. I can tell she's trying to hide the fact that I haven't told her I finally finished school or that I graduated. If I tried hard enough, I know I'd be able to see the bitterness she feels about me not telling her.

"I decided not to go," I tell the table. "I didn't want to make a big deal of it. I'm just grateful to finally be done."

The three of them frown, clearly surprised by my decision to back out of the ceremony, but just because I spent far too many years buried deep in statistics and thirty-page research papers doesn't necessarily mean I wanted to walk across the stage in a cap and gown. I leave out the part where I decided not to because of Ryan.

"Huh," Dallas says. "Well, it's still pretty fucking awesome you got your master's."

I give him a smile of appreciation.

"Does that mean you're thinking of bringing a date?" Sloan asks.

I still don't know how much Vada has told Sloan about us. I don't know if Sloan knows about our secret or the night I showed up outside her apartment.

Sloan's eyes move back and forth between me and Vada, and part of me thinks she might know our secret. The transparency between the four of us is more blurred than I thought.

"I was thinking about it." Vada answers her even though Sloan's question was directed at me.

"Really?" Sloan asks, clearly just as surprised as me.

A burning sensation sparks in the center of my chest at the thought of Vada bringing a date. It's an irrational feeling and one I have absolutely no business having.

I raise my eyebrows, surprised she was so quick to answer Sloan. I clear my throat and pretend to look down at the dinner menu still in front of me. This dinner hasn't even fully started, but I already feel like I'm drowning in our conversation. When I turn my attention back to Vada, the realization of just how far we've separated ourselves hits me.

"Yeah." She crosses her arms over the edge of the table in

the same way she did before. She sticks out her chin a bit and shrugs one shoulder as she looks at Sloan. "I was thinking of asking Levi from work, but I wanted to check with you first to see if it was okay to bring one."

"Of course," Sloan says, blinking several times. Her eyes move between me and Vada before she looks down at her menu.

Dallas picks at the label on his beer bottle. "Is that one of your new copy editors at *The Chronicle*?"

"*The Chronicle*?" I ask. Last I knew, Vada was still working at *The Daily News*. I never did find out what happened after her boss disappeared. I didn't think to ask the night of Dallas and Sloan's engagement party. "When did you leave *The Daily News*?"

"Oh..." Vada absentmindedly swirls her straw around in a circle. The ice has completely melted. She hasn't touched her drink just like I haven't touched mine. "I only stayed a few more weeks after I found out Randy left."

"Oh, well congratulations on the new job then."

It's been months since Vada and I have had an actual conversation. I hadn't realized how drastically our lives have changed in the nearly five months since Ryan's death, since I cut myself off from her completely, drowning in my grief. Somehow, I've managed to pull myself out, and as I sit in front of her now, I can't understand why I shut her out for that long.

The way her eyes light up as she listens to Sloan and her brother talk causes my heart to skip a beat. The way she tucks her bottom lip under her teeth without even realizing it makes my cock twitch. Everything about her is beautiful.

Even still, the thought of her with another man causes my muscles to tighten and my chest to swell.

"Thank you," she says, giving me a weak smile. The more her weak smile starts to fade, the more the cracks between us widen. I know we're in this position because of me, but it doesn't change the fact that it still hurts, in one way or another.

The cracks widen even more the longer we sit through dinner. By the time we've ordered our food and I've pretended to have an appetite for anything other than Vada, I realize the distance between us is further than I realized.

CHAPTER SIX

Vada

"Wʜᴀᴛ ᴛʜᴇ ʜᴇʟʟ ɪs ᴡʀᴏɴɢ ᴡɪᴛʜ ᴍᴇ?" I ɢʀᴏᴀɴ ᴀɴᴅ sʟɪᴅᴇ the palm of my hand down my face, still mulling last night over in my brain.

"There's nothing wrong with you." Cassidy doesn't move her eyes away from the floor of trampolines set behind the net we're standing in front of. She searches the entire floor, sifting through the dozens of kids jumping up and down until they land on the boy in the back corner.

Jonah's steps are dramatic as he walks over to pick up one of the balls. He tries to run then jump, throwing the ball in the air toward one of the baskets hanging on the back wall.

"These places make me nervous." She brings her hand to her mouth and presses her thumb against her lip, biting down on her nail.

"It looks like he's having a blast to me," I tell her, hoping to ease her anxiety.

It doesn't work.

"He's been begging me for months to bring him here, and now that he's finally old enough, he hasn't wasted a second reminding me. I'm just afraid he's going to break a bone or get a concussion, or some kid might accidentally step on him."

"He's having fun, Cass. Look." I nod as he jumps, attempting to throw the ball into the hoop again. He misses again, but when he lands, he catches Cassidy and me watching him.

He waves then spins around to pick up one of the balls that have rolled behind him. His brown hair bounces with his movements, and his light honey brown eyes flicker with the bright lights of the trampoline park.

I only met Jonah a few weeks ago, but there's a familiarity to him that I haven't been able to put my finger on. He's incredibly kind and way too smart for his own good.

"Aunt Cass, did you see that?" Jonah yells across the trampoline park, and his mouth spreads into a wide grin. He's missing one of his front teeth and several of his bottom teeth. He doesn't shy away from grinning with pride for finally making it through the basket on his last shot.

"I did!" Cass yells back. "Great job, buddy."

Jonah moves on from the basket and starts jumping from one trampoline to the next. It doesn't take him long to make it from one end of the park to the next before turning around and doing the same again.

"Sloan was going to reach out to you, but I figured I'd mention it to you first."

Cassidy turns toward me, the lights catching the dark golden strands of her hair. "What is it?"

"She said she loves your work and wants to hire you to be the photographer at the wedding."

"Really?" She places her hand on her chest, and her eyebrows arch across her forehead in shock. "She wants to hire me?"

"Yeah." I give her a smile, my chest warming with the

expression on her face. She's clearly surprised, but knowing how flattered Cassidy feels to have Sloan wanting her to photograph her wedding pushes my uneasiness about the Colton situation to the side, even if it's only for a brief few minutes.

"I would love to."

"Great. Thank you." I gently place my hand on her arm, allowing her sheer joy to fill the air. "I'll give her your phone number so she can get in touch with you," I add.

"I really appreciate it, Vada. I haven't photographed any weddings before, but I did do a few graduations back in college. It'll be fun."

"It will be." I give her a smile and turn my attention back to the endless rows of trampolines in front of us. Jonah is still hopping around aimlessly with a grin that seems to be permanently stuck to his face. I love it.

"So, are you actually planning on taking Levi to the wedding?" Cass asks me. She keeps her attention on her nephew even through her shift back to our earlier conversation about my date dilemma. Before our detoured conversation about Sloan wanting to hire her, I spent the past thirty minutes giving her a play-by-play of dinner last night. It wouldn't have taken as long if it wasn't for the fact that I had to explain my background with Colton and why I blurted out that I was taking Levi as my date. I left out the part about our one night. Our secret might be long gone and buried, but that doesn't mean I'm not still keeping up with my end of the bargain. I usually talk to Sloan about these things, but our schedules haven't exactly lined up long enough for me to discuss it with her.

For now, I'm comfortable enough to talk to Cassidy. After moving to Austin a few years ago, I've kept only a few friends close to me. Sloan has stuck around longer than any other friend I've ever had.

I need to get this off my chest and speak the words out loud. I need to let this feeling go and think of another solution.

"Ugh," I groan. "I don't know. I haven't thought about it. For all I know, Levi wouldn't even be able to go. I just sort of said it without thinking." I drag the toe of my sneaker across the carpet. It's a deep shade of blue with white specks scattered across it. It reminds me of a night sky consumed with stars.

"I'm sure you can talk to Sloan about it." She pauses then abruptly holds her finger up with an idea. "Or you can take someone else."

"True." I twist my mouth and chew on the inside of my cheek, thinking about what to do. Luckily, I still have some time to figure it out. I shrug. "I mean, it wouldn't be terrible if I brought Levi. I just don't know him very well—it might be a little awkward."

"Is Colton taking a date?" she asks. Her eyes move past me, catching Jonah hopping the last few jumps out of the trampoline arena. He lands on the platform and starts heading toward us.

"I don't know," I tell her. "I blurted that I was wanting to ask Levi before he even had a chance to respond about whether he's taking a date or not. Afterward, Dallas and Sloan started talking about other wedding plans, so it was never brought up again."

A small part of me believes he wouldn't be taking a date. As long as I've known Colton, he's never made his love life a priority. Other than him mentioning a few one-night stands he had back in college, Colton has never talked about those he's slept with—including me.

That's probably one of the reasons he's been able to dig a hole so deep to bury our secret. He simply exists as if it never happened. That's how he's always existed.

Colton has never been able to put anyone ahead of himself.

Even though I wish we could have been more, I don't hold

resentment toward him for it. His life is built upon the idea that you can't achieve success unless you do it by yourself. If I've learned anything about Colton in the past few years, it's that he values how the world sees him, even if it means sacrificing his own happiness to get there.

On the other hand, I start to wonder if Colton will take someone. Maybe he's changed. Maybe his newfound freedom after finishing school has opened him up to the possibility of dating, only now he doesn't consider me an option anymore since we've drifted apart. After all, it was his choice to cut me out after Ryan's passing.

I don't necessarily blame him. From experience, death can make you do things you never thought you were capable of. But I can't deny the sting that pricked at my chest the moment he said he finally graduated. I feel so detached from his life.

Maybe he doesn't care if I take a date to the wedding. Maybe he does.

Either way, it shouldn't matter to him, or to me.

"Aunt Cass! Aunt Cass! Did you see me jump into the ball pit?" Jonah comes roaring toward us at the end of the ramp coming from the trampolines. His hair is disheveled, and sweat drips down his smooth, round cheeks.

He's trying to catch his breath when he sidles up to us. He's still beaming with excitement as his eyes move from Cass to me then back to Cass.

Cassidy laughs, clearly relieved to see he's come back down to her in one piece. "I did, buddy. That was a killer jump."

"I tried to do it like those guys I see in those videos on YouTube."

Cassidy rolls her eyes. "I hate that Pop-Pop lets you watch those kinds of videos."

"I don't watch them all the time." Jonah shrugs, popping out his bottom lip. "Only when he ends up falling asleep watching those shows about old stuff from a gazillion years ago."

"A gazillion, huh?" I ask him.

"One time he was watching this episode where a guy dug up an entire human skull." He dramatically turns to me and widens his eyes as much as he can. I'm not sure if the excitement pouring out of him is from his thirty-minute jumping spree on the trampolines or if it's because he clearly remembers this human skull as if he just saw it today.

He scrunches his nose and shakes his head. "It was disgusting. Pop-Pop watches stuff like that all the time."

"You're right on that one, buddy," Cassidy says, placing her hand on his back. She immediately pulls it back with a face of disgust. "Wow, you really worked up a sweat. We should probably get going. We don't want to be late for dinner."

Jonah turns to Cassidy, clasping his small hands. His knuckles fade to white. "Oh, please can I jump for a little more?" He points to the screen on the wall, where three different colored dots are displayed in rows, a timer counting down beside each color. "See?" Jonah explains, pointing to the TV then the bracelet wrapped around his wrist. "It says green bracelets have more time."

"Sure." Cassidy sighs. "The timer says you have ten more minutes. Go ahead."

"Yes!" he yells, a grin spread wide across his face. "Oh, wait." He digs his small hand into his pocket, pulling out a metal keychain. "Can you hold on to this for me? I don't want to lose it."

"Of course," Cassidy says, wrapping the keychain up in her hand.

He jumps up and down before racing back up the ramp to the trampoline area.

Cassidy crosses her arms and tilts her head to the side as she keeps an eye on Jonah the whole way. "I can't believe my dad still watches those boring archaeological shows. No wonder he falls asleep watching them."

I laugh. "They aren't too bad."

"You two can watch them together then." Cassidy scoffs, teasing me. Her face relaxes and she watches Jonah with a slight frown. "Jonah means the world to my dad though."

"He lives with your dad, right?"

"Yeah." Her frown deepens, the corners of her mouth creasing. She blinks several times, inhaling a deep breath. "My sister got pregnant with Jonah her senior year of high school. She was barely eighteen, and for a while, she wasn't sure she even wanted him, but our father convinced her to have him. And then..." She pauses, her throat thick with the words she hasn't yet said out loud. "She had him, but she simply wasn't the same after she brought him home. She never wanted to hold him or feed him. It was like she'd changed into this completely different person. Then one morning, she was gone. She just wasn't there." She looks down at the ground, holding back her tears. "We haven't seen her since."

I shift my gaze up to where Jonah is trying to throw the ball back into the hoop against the wall. Cassidy is watching him too.

"I have no idea where she is or if she's even still alive," she continues. "It's been seven years. After a while, I just stopped waiting, and I promised Jonah I would never do that to him. My dad and I are all he has."

"What about his dad?"

She shakes her head. "I don't know who he is. Neither does my dad. My sister never talked about him, and the only time I heard her mention anything about him was the night she said she slept with him. It's the same night she got pregnant with Jonah. She said she met him through some of her friends at a football game. He went to the school we were playing against. I guess they met up sometime after the game and ended up sleeping together, but that's all I know. My sister and I may only be two years apart, but we were never close—not in the way sisters usually are. I don't even think he knew she was pregnant. This is the only thing we have of his."

She opens her hand, showing me the keychain Jonah gave her before going back out to jump. It's simple with a blue star etched onto one side.

"She told me he left this in her car the night they slept together. She didn't take it with her when she left, so I gave it to Jonah to hold on to. I told him it belonged to his dad, and now he carries it with him everywhere." Cassidy folds her fingers back, covering the keychain. She holds it as she finds Jonah jumping in the same spot as before.

"I'm sorry your sister left." A dull ache pounds in my chest, thinking about Jonah's circumstances.

"I miss her, but I don't mourn for the person she became after Jonah was born. I mourn for the sister she used to be, but I know that version of her left the day she had Jonah. If I had to choose, I'd choose him...over and over again."

"You're an amazing aunt, and Jonah is lucky to have you."

She turns her head toward me and sniffs. Tears line her eyes, but they haven't spilled. "Ridiculous," she says. "I didn't expect to get into a conversation of this depth at a fucking trampoline park."

We both laugh, and I wave her off. "Totally fine. Jonah's going to be a stronger kid for having gone through that, and because you and your dad are there for him. Plus, it was nice to get my mind off my life for once."

"About that..." Cassidy rolls her neck, tilting her head back to me. Her mouth spreads into a devious grin. "Have you figured out what you're going to do?"

I watch Jonah inch his way to the ledge over the ball pit. The jump isn't very high, but still, he squeezes his eyes shut and jumps off the edge, lifting his legs to his chest. He cannonballs into the pit of plastic, disappearing underneath them before climbing his way back out.

"I don't know." I shrug, figuring it's about time to move on. "Maybe I will take him. Either way, this wedding should be interesting."

CHAPTER SEVEN

COLTON

I'VE ALWAYS HATED THE DRIVE OUT TO MY PARENTS' HOUSE, not because it's long, but because I fucking dread the feelings that boil inside me when their house comes into view. As soon as I drive through the black wrought iron gate surrounding my parents' ranch, I immediately regret coming here.

Eight years.

It's been eight years since I lived here, yet the feeling this place gives me hasn't disappeared with time. Amazing how a place can do that to you.

On top of that, I haven't been here since the day of Ryan's funeral. For my mental health, I had to stay away. It had more to do with my father than it did with my mother, but I can't help the need inside me swelling, the need to turn my truck around and drive as far away as I possibly can.

As I get closer, I decide to just stick it out.

The dirt driveway leading to their mansion in the middle of nowhere crumbles under the large tires of my truck. The sound fills the silence of the vast countryside surrounding me.

I keep one hand on the steering wheel and dig the other into the center console, pulling out a piece of gum, a habit I've acquired whenever I come over here. It's healthier than ciga-rettes or alcohol, and certainly cheaper. I pop the small minty rectangle into my mouth and start chewing on it the second I pull around the large circle at the end, stopping in front of the front door.

When I step out of the truck, the dry country air slaps me in the face. It feels different here than out in the city. Somehow, I feel the sun's rays touching every inch of me. There's no escaping it out here.

I nudge my glasses further up the bridge of my nose, inhaling a deep breath.

My feet drag against the dirt as I take in the endless expanse of field surrounding me. In another location, my parents' house might be considered a mansion. Out here, it looks like it could easily be swallowed whole. Round bales of hay are scattered across the wheat fields. I remember hiding behind them as a kid, wishing I were somewhere else, anywhere else that didn't involve the pressure from my parents to be perfect in every aspect of my life.

The two-story mansion I grew up in sits about thirty minutes outside of Austin. It's hard to believe how Texas can have so many different faces. It's a completely different world out here, different from the life I've built away from my family.

I shove my hand into the pocket of my jeans and take another deep breath as I step up onto the front step. I stand in front of the door and press my finger to the doorbell. I can hear it ringing from where I'm standing, but it takes several minutes before someone finally answers.

I only stay out here that long because it doesn't surprise me. My parents don't rush for anyone, not even their son.

My mother appears behind the large rustic wooden door. A substantial wooden wreath hangs from the door, and it bounces against it with how far she swings it.

"Oh, Colton," she says, giving me a warm grin and holding her arms open for me. Her hug isn't strong when she wraps them around me. Her embrace never has been, but my mother isn't one for showing much emotion. It's probably the reason she's been able to put up with my asshole of a father for as long as she has. "I almost forgot you were coming today."

She releases me and quickly shuts the door.

"Are you disappointed?" My question is a jab I shouldn't have taken, at least not at my mother.

"No." Her simple answer is unconvincing.

My mother may not have been the most affectionate growing up, but I'm thankful to look more like her than my father. Her brown hair is pulled back into a tight high bun, and a few strands frame her rounded cheeks. Her favorite gold-framed glasses are perched on her nose, and she pushes them up the bridge of her nose using her perfectly manicured finger.

"Your father is in his study arguing with one of his clients again."

"Why does this not surprise me?"

My eyes immediately move to the picture hanging on the wall near the front door. It's a picture of my brother. The image of his face, so similar to my father's, makes my stomach turn. The pain of his loss still hits me the same way it did four months ago.

I can tell it's done the same to my mother. The dark circles under her eyes have darkened since Ryan's funeral. Time doesn't appear to be healing her wounds.

"What's he arguing about this time?" I ask her, walking further down the hallway leading to the kitchen.

"Oh, you know." She waves her hand flippantly. "This and that—negotiations. I think he said something about how a client hasn't paid him what he's owed."

My father's voice echoes throughout the first floor, which

says something about the volume he's using. This house is massive, with a total of thirteen rooms on the first floor alone. The fact that you can hear my father's voice booming from his office to the kitchen is a testament to the kind of man he is: inconsiderate and scary as fuck.

My mother saunters around the large granite island. She grabs a short glass from the cabinet above the tray of liquor in the corner, reaches into a bucket beside the bottles, and drops three ice cubes into her glass. She then fills it halfway with scotch. The dark, amber liquid sloshing around causes my stomach to twist more than it already has since I walked through the front door.

My mother holding a glass of scotch in her hand at this time of day has become the norm. She leans against the island and brings the glass to her mouth. She takes a sip then swallows before she strikes up conversation.

"I'm having our chef make us some barbecue for lunch." She uses the hand holding the glass of scotch to point toward the back yard. "How does that sound?"

I follow where she's pointing and look through the floor-to-ceiling windows. The large, paved patio expands about twenty feet. Beyond that is the inground pool and hot tub overlooking the ranch. Situated in the corner of the patio sits a large flat top grill and smoker. They look like they haven't been touched.

"Seriously, Mom?" I can't help but look at her with utter confusion, but none of this should shock me. Her care and social awareness haven't existed for a long time, even before losing Ryan. But I think his death only caused her to pull away even more.. Either way, her disregard for me still stings.

"What?" she asks, still unaware. "I thought you might like it."

"I do like barbecue, Mom." My tone is even and a bit clipped. I can't help it. "That's why I make it for a living."

I know I shouldn't put expectations on others, especially when it comes to my family, but I can't help the sting that continues to prick at my chest at the idea that my mother wouldn't even consider me bringing over food from my restaurant. She's never eaten my food, much less stopped by the restaurant. I opened a fucking barbecue restaurant and she's having her personal chef make barbecue over having her son's. The whole situation just feels like shit. It's another stab at how they preferred my brother over me.

As if on cue, a man wearing a black and white striped apron appears from behind the door to the large butler's pantry. He's carrying a large metal pan filled with vegetables speared onto skewers. Beside that is a mound of uncooked smoked sausage and halved chickens.

The chef doesn't speak a word as he makes his way through my parents' kitchen. My mother doesn't speak to him, and he only gives me a courtesy nod of acknowledgment as he steps outside. The large French doors are propped open. At first, I wonder why in the hell they would keep them open when it's nearly one hundred degrees outside, but the patio has three large ceiling fans mounted to the barnwood ceiling. At least it'll offer some reprieve when outside.

Still, this entire situation is fucking awkward, and I wish I could leave. I'm already trying to come up with an excuse when the door to my father's study slams shut and the sound of his loafers hitting the shiny concrete floor prevents me from finding a way.

He rounds the corner into the kitchen and heads straight for the bar like my mother. They're one and the same: oblivious to the outside world, too consumed with their own lavish lives to care about anyone else.

"Colton." He keeps his back toward me the entire time he makes his drink. "You're a bit late."

My father has always believed everyone is late if he isn't the first to be in the room. I don't refute his comment or argue. I simply ignore it.

"How's business?" Deflection—I've perfected the art when it comes to him.

He's living his life the same way he did before Ryan died. He pretends as if it never happened.

"Oh." He sighs, turning around. He shoves one hand into his khaki slacks and walks over to the open French doors. He surveys the ranch as if he's taking inventory of what's possibly out of place. "Business is steadily growing. We're up three percent in profit from last year."

"That's great," I tell him, pretending to be interested at all.

My father is the CEO of a multi-million-dollar engraving company. At his factory, he produces engraved metal and metal signs for various companies around the country. He inherited it from his father, and at one time, the business was promised to Ryan. Now my father knows all of that has gone down the drain.

By the time the offer was set to be handed down to me, I already had my heart set on opening my own restaurant. I decided to move in a different direction, and in my father's eyes, I became a disappointment.

My father's ranch holds no connection to his metal company other than the tall metal arch at the foot of the driveway when you turn onto the property. Even though there's no connection other than that, my father treats the ranch as if it's producing the bulk of his profits. He sells a few bales of hay, and from time to time my mother will buy horses then decide to sell them once she's trained them. But my father's metal business is his sole income and the one branch of business that makes him feel the most powerful.

It's a life I'm glad to not be a part of. My father, however, hasn't seemed to let go of the fact that I decided to take a different path.

I walk over to the cabinet and grab an empty glass before filling it with water from the sink.

"How's your business going? The restaurant."

The pit in my stomach grows, and my eyes shift to my mother, who is now sitting on one of the wicker chairs situated on the concrete patio. Her legs are crossed, and her drink is dangling from her fingers as she relaxes her arm over the armrest.

I know my father isn't asking for personal reasons. He wants numbers and statistics. He wants the holy grail of business answers.

"It's going well." I inhale a deep breath. "Sales are up five percent from last year since we started our live performance nights."

Despite my positive news, he still shakes his head. "I still can't believe any son of mine would decide to open a barbecue restaurant in the capital of Texas. Despite the fact that you started a business in an already saturated market, I will say those numbers are good. I still wish you had gone into business by yourself and not split it with Dallas Beckett."

"Dallas has been an incredible business partner, Dad. In fact, he's the reason sales have gone up this past year. He performs almost every weekend and changes the menu constantly to keep up with the trending market."

I hate that I feel the need to defend myself or Dallas to my father. I'm no longer a child, but in his eyes, it doesn't matter how old I am. He'll always treat me as if I'm incompetent.

"Is that sister of his still helping you out down there?"

"Oh yes," my mother chimes in. "What was her name? Vada?"

I swallow, the feelings of last night still weighing on me.

Unsure of what to think about how the dinner went, I've been trying to put it out of my mind. The silence I'd given Vada after Ryan's death is solely on me. I was buried too deep in my grief to think about the pain it would cause once she came back into my life. I wasn't naïve enough to think she never would.

She's my best friend's little sister.

It's impossible for me to stay away from her. Even if I wanted to.

But now, a significant amount of time has passed, and she's bringing a date to the wedding, someone named Levi.

"Yeah." I clear my throat. "Her name is Vada."

She grins, and the expression looks foreign on her, but I like it. I wish she would make it more often.

It quickly fades, and I turn to my father, following him out to the patio. I sit in the wicker chair opposite my mother. My father remains standing.

"No, she went back to work at the newspaper," I answer him. "Well, actually she's working at *The Austin Chronicle* now." Although it's been months since I've seen Vada and I only learned that bit of information last night, I pretend it's something I've known all along.

I think it's ironic how even though I've been coming here every Saturday for years, they decide to bring her up today, the day after our dinner last night.

"Huh," my father says, pouting his lips in thought. The wrinkles around his eyes deepen. "*The Austin Chronicle.*"

"Yep." I exaggerate the word as it falls from my lips. I can see my father's thoughts oozing out of him.

He's wondering why in the hell I associate myself with people who, according to him, aren't as distinguished as him. He's wondering why I haven't taken the same path as him and associated with artificial people with endless amounts of money stuffed into their pockets.

He shrugs, frowning in thought. "*The Austin Chronicle* is one of the most successful newspapers in the state, not to mention their net worth."

Like it matters.

I'm not surprised my father knows what Vada's newspaper is worth. He keeps up to date on all sorts of shit like that. He's the poster child for what a Fortune 500 devotee looks like.

"Still…" He sighs. "It's like I've said all along: it's best you stick to finding someone with the same social standing as us. Journalists live messy lives. They're unorganized and don't get paid nearly enough."

"According to whose standards?" The words spill out of my mouth faster than I'm able to comprehend the gravity of my question to a man such as him.

The palms of my hands are hot, and the muscles of my hands and arms are clenched tight. I don't realize I've tensed up, listening to my father spout off the same old bullshit.

"I'm not sure what you mean." His thick greying eyebrows slant over his piercing stare. His eyes are an intense shade of chocolate brown. They're dark, so dark they used to scare me when I was younger. Now all I see when I look at him is a coward.

"Money is all relative, Dad." I lift one shoulder and place my glass of water on the table in front of my mother. It lands firmly, the sound echoing in the silence. "To someone homeless, a person making minimum wage is wealthy. Either way, it doesn't matter."

She simply stays where she's sitting, staring out at the field. It's as if she's stuck in a trance, but I know better. She's staying silent in order to avoid the whole conversation.

My mother's trained herself to stay out of my father's conversations, especially when those conversations boil into conflict, but I can't sit here and listen to my dad's complete and utter bullshit.

"Did I not teach you anything?" He steps closer. He's now standing on the other side of the table from me. His brown eyes narrow into two thin slits. "It's just like I told you when you were younger—you *will* make something of yourself, and you will *not* disgrace the Adler name." He lifts his glass to his mouth and takes a long sip, curling back his lips as he swallows. "You're lucky I kept you and your brother away from too many distractions. If it weren't for me, you would have wasted your life with some girl who wasn't even worth it. Ryan never had issues focusing on what to do with his life, and he never allowed himself to be influenced by a woman. You two were only a year apart, so I never understood why you couldn't be more like him. Luckily, after he died, you kept your act together—finally. You worked hard and put your head where it really matters." The corners of his mouth turn down as he tilts his head to the side. "I can't say much for that barbecue restaurant you insisted on opening, or for that business partner of yours and his sister..." His words fade as his eyebrows arch across his forehead, and he lets out a sharp hiss between his clenched teeth. "Well, that's another topic in itself. I could go on, but there's no point. She's not worth it, son. At least you got your master's at UT like I suggested you do. Right, Faye?"

He turns his attention to my mother, dipping his chin and looking at her with a heavy expression.

She turns her head high enough to look up at him. "Of course." Her voice is small and hushed. She swings her saddened eyes to me, offering me a weak smile before going back to staring out at the nothingness in front of her. "I'm proud of you for finishing your schooling, sweetheart."

My heart aches for my mother and the woman she used to be. I feel like I'm talking to a robot. I know my mother's pain comes from losing Ryan, but I know it also comes from the constant pressure and strain put on her due to putting up with my father for so long.

A strong, bitter metallic taste hits my tongue as I stare at the man standing before me. I'm biting the inside of my cheek so hard I've broken the skin, a small bit of blood filling my mouth. I thought I was biting down on the piece of gum I popped into my mouth before coming in here. This is precisely the kind of moment I use it for, but this time it didn't stop me from drawing blood. I swallow back the taste, but I don't swallow my father's words. I can feel my jaw ticking and my heart beating harder with every agonizing second that passes.

The greedy, selfish bastard has the nerve to stand in front of me and shit all over my life and the people I've decided to allow to be in it, not to mention bringing up my past and Ryan. Ryan wasn't as perfect as my father is making him out to be. Don't get me wrong, he was a saint compared to me, but I know there were parts of his life he never allowed our father to see. He'd only let me in.

I press my lips together, swallowing the last bit of blood lingering on my tongue. Narrowing my own eyes, I squint as I look out at the field the same way my mother is. She still hasn't moved, but I don't miss how her fingers are clenched around her glass, her knuckles fading to white.

I hate that my father's words have made her uneasy, but I can't ignore how a part of me is relieved to see a sign that she still cares. In what capacity, I don't know.

My attention shifts to the chef my mother hired to cook lunch, and I watch as he loads the skewers onto the grill. Fire sparks in my chest, and I swing my attention back to my father. There's a ring of sweat around the collar of his pressed button-down shirt, and he rattles the ice in his glass, sipping the last bit of alcohol collected at the bottom.

The truth is, I'd rather be any place other than here in this moment. I remember exactly why I hate coming here and why I've removed myself so far from this life. It's because I've never wanted to be my father. I never want to live a life where my family fears me. I never want to live a life as miserable as the one he leads.

It doesn't matter what I do. I will always be a disappointment. I will never be Ryan.

And that realization settles deep under the fire growing in me. I don't know whether to feel sorry for him or hate him.

"Well?" he asks, arching his eyebrows. He stuffs his hand into his pocket as another drop of sweat drips down his cheek and soaks into his shirt. "What are your plans now that you've finished? I hope you'll go for your PhD—then you can leave that godawful restaurant you've created. It would be a shame to waste that education."

I catch myself turning the corners of my mouth into a frown before it transforms into a humorless grin. I'm laughing, but not out of humor. I'm laughing out of disgust. "You know what?" I swipe my hand across my mouth and take a deep breath. I curl my fingers into a tight fist and shove my hand into my pocket before I find myself placing it elsewhere. "I think I've just lost my appetite." I nod toward the chef who's still babysitting those fucking skewers. "Enjoy your lunch."

I leave them on the back patio, not caring if my father comes after me, to listen to what he has to say. I make my way back inside, heading straight to the front door. When I make it to my truck, I spit out the piece of gum I've been keeping pressed against my cheek. My boots kick up dirt as I climb into my truck, covering it up. I slam the door and jam the key in the ignition knowing there is no way in hell I'll ever be able to leave this place fast enough.

SECRET #2

*No matter how hard you try, some secrets are
impossible to forget.*

CHAPTER EIGHT

Vada

"I NEED YOUR HELP." SLOAN SIGHS THROUGH THE SPEAKER pressed against my ear.

I wedge my phone between my cheek and shoulder as I pull the strap of my seat belt across my chest, snapping it into the buckle.

"What's going on?" I glance over my shoulder, making sure Jonah's buckled himself in as well before I even bother starting the engine. It's a habit I've developed since deciding to start helping Cassidy out with her nephew. Although Cassidy's father has full custody of Jonah, she still takes care of him on the weekends. Now that her photographs have started getting more attention around the city, she's been booking a few photo shoots on the weekends to bring in a bit more money.

Once her schedule started to fill, she asked if I'd mind pitching in by taking Jonah to his T-ball practice on the weekends. . I didn't mind agreeing since the kid has kind of grown on me.

The space above his top lip is stained a bright red from the juice he drank before we jumped into my car, and there are dark green and brown smudges smeared across his knees. I give him a smile and turn back to face the front.

I keep the car in park while I talk to Sloan. She sighs into the phone, sounding exhausted.

"Why do you sound out of breath?" I ask her.

"I've been—" She swallows before breathing in slowly. "I've been going on morning runs with Dallas."

"Oh, good god." I laugh. "What on earth made you want to do that?"

"I don't know. I'm blinded by my love for him, I guess."

"Love can do that." I let out another laugh. "Well, kudos to you. He takes those runs pretty seriously. I couldn't imagine."

"He's hard to keep up with, but I think he purposely slows himself down so he doesn't feel bad if he ends up leaving me behind."

"Miss Vada?"

"Hang on a second, Sloan." I'm still holding the phone against my ear when I turn to look at Jonah. He's patiently waiting in his seat with his hands crossed in his lap. "I'll be off in just a minute and then we can head out."

"Are we still stopping to get ice cream on the way?" He straightens his back and the backs of his cleats hit the bottom of his seat. The grin on his face is priceless.

"For sure, buddy. Don't we always stop on the way home?"

"Yes!" he yells. He curls his fingers into a tight fist and jerks his arm down as if he's just won the T-ball championship.

"I'm sorry," Sloan says. "I forgot you were with Jonah today."

"That's okay. He just got done with practice and we were about to head out. We've sort of made it a tradition to grab ice cream before I take him back home. What did you need help with?"

"Oh, yeah, about that." Her voice ticks up a notch as she

remembers why she called me in the first place. "I completely forgot that this week is parent-teacher conferences. Even though the students only have half a day, I'll be in meetings with parents until six in the afternoon, at least. Dallas is pulling double shifts at the bar since Erin broke her ankle last week. Anyway, the florist said the centerpieces for the wedding are available for pickup on Monday at two in the afternoon."

"I can do it."

"Really?" She sighs with relief. Either that or she's still struggling to catch her breath. " I didn't even finish asking you yet."

"That's okay. I knew that's what you were getting at." I grin. "Isn't that the job of the maid of honor, anyway? To help in times of crisis?"

"You have a point."

"I do." I smirk while shoving my key in the ignition, knowing if I don't start backing out of this parking lot soon, I won't have time to stop and get Jonah ice cream like I promised.

"Thank you," Sloan adds.

"You're welcome," I tell her, knowing I would do it even if she wasn't in a bind. "But the wedding isn't for another nine days—why are they ready so early?"

"Well, I decided to go with the chrysanthemum centerpieces. They typically stay fresh for three weeks, and the florist asked if we might be able to pick them up early to make room in her storage. I told her we could without thinking about it. Dallas and Colton said we could keep them at the restaurant until the wedding."

"Oh, that's nice of them to do that."

"Yeah. So, is it okay? Are you able to pick them up?"

"Of course."

"Thanks." She sighs. "I'll text you the address and let the florist know you'll be picking them up at two."

"Okay, I'll talk to you later, and good luck if you insist on keeping up with these runs with my brother."

"Thanks," she mutters, following it up with a groan.

When I hang up the phone, I look over my shoulder one last time before putting the car in reverse. "Alright, buddy. You ready to get some ice cream?"

"Yep." He pops his lips and taps his fingers on his knees in excitement. "Can I get extra sprinkles this time?"

I'm not going to lie...I might be just as excited to get ice cream as Jonah.

WHEN I PULL into the parking lot, using the address Sloan sent me, I find Colton sitting on the tailgate of his truck, and my heart sinks into the pit of my stomach at the sight of him. Aside from the wedding planning dinner, it's been entirely too long since I've seen him, and it absolutely never fails. No matter how much time passes, he still manages to make my stomach queasy in the best way possible.

He's wearing a white Texas Longhorns baseball cap with the orange longhorn logo stitched in the center. The bill of his cap shields part of his face from the unrelenting sun. He hasn't noticed me pulling into the spot a row behind him. His phone is resting in the palm of his hand, and his thumb moves up and down the screen several times. It stops for several seconds before he swipes at it again. His white t-shirt clings to his muscles, and his long legs are bent over the end of his tailgate, casually swinging back and forth.

I swallow, nervous. I don't even know why he's here. I start to think it might be a coincidence, looking around at the surrounding shops. Other than a woman's clothing store and a pet store, I can't think of why he would be here. He looks like he's waiting for someone.

Maybe he's waiting for someone inside one of the stores. Colton's life has become a complete mystery to me.

I step out of my car, ignoring the sickness rising in my throat. It's stupid, really, the way he makes me feel.

I haven't even started making my way toward him when he looks up at the sound of my car door closing.

"Hey." He grins, shutting the screen off on his phone. He slides it into his front pocket and lays his hands on his lap. They're relaxed as his smile stays plastered to his face. The dimple in his cheek grows.

I look behind him to the flower shop before bringing my eyes back to his. "What are you doing here?"

He stretches both of his arms out, pressing his palms flat on the tailgate beside him. He pushes himself off, and his heavy boots land on the pavement. "Sloan told me you were coming to pick up the arrangements and figured you might need some help. She wasn't sure you'd be able to fit them in your car."

"Well, I don't." I swallow back my nerves, not understanding why Sloan would ask me to pick up the centerpieces without letting me know she'd asked Colton as well. "There's plenty of room in the back seat and my trunk."

He raises his eyebrows, unconvinced. "Are you sure?

"Yeah." I cross my arms over my chest. "Why wouldn't I be able to?"

I don't know why, but I push back against Colton's offer to help. Seeing as this is the first task Sloan has handed to me as maid of honor, I want to do it on my own.

She refused a bachelorette party. Instead, Cassidy and I slept over at Sloan's house, made one too many batches of my signature margaritas, and watched Netflix. It's a tradition Sloan and I have made over the course of our friendship. In a way, I'm thankful she's made the maid of honor duties easy on me, but a part of me wishes she'd given me more to do. Perhaps there will be more on her wedding day.

For now, I'm here to pick up the centerpieces, centerpieces I have yet to see. I'm wondering how big they must be if she's recruited Colton.

"Do you know how many centerpieces there are?" he asks, as if it's going to change my mind on whether or not I need his help. He slowly steps closer to me. His boots drag with each of his calculated steps. My chest tightens with a breath as he dips his head then brings his eyes back up to mine. His mouth is closed and his lips are pressed together, but I can see the ticking of the muscles in his jaw as he stands in front of me. He lifts his hand and drags his fingers gently across his bottom lip. It's as if he's thinking.

I wish I could read his mind.

I pull my bottom lip under my teeth and struggle to remember how many tables Sloan said she was planning on having. It's difficult to think about numbers—or anything, for that matter—when Colton is standing this close to me, and something deep inside my gut tells me he knows what he's doing. He's doing it on purpose.

"Six. She said she's planning on six."

"Actually, twelve, but you were close." His eyes dance between mine and my mouth, unsure of where to stop. He tips his head a fraction, nearly bringing his forehead to mine. I close my eyes, preparing myself for what he's going to do. When I open them, he's no longer standing in front of me. His back is turned toward me as he lifts the edge of his tailgate. The large metal clicks into the bed of the truck with a loud bang. After it closes, he spins around and rests his arm on top of the tailgate, leaning into it.

"Twelve?" I raise my eyebrows, shocked that Sloan failed to

mention this. Twelve tables equate to a large wedding. "How did you know this change and I didn't?"

I'm confused, and my mind struggles to comprehend how this wedding has now doubled in size. Deep down in my gut I know it's a combination of a lack of caffeine to combat my usual midafternoon slump and the fact that this is the first conversation I've had with Colton in months.

"I'm a groomsman." He shrugs.

"Not every groomsman pays attention to the number of tables, though. Or at least I don't think they do."

"I'm not just any groomsman. I'm the best man, and besides, you forget I've done this before. I'm not new to the whole planning of a wedding and helping set up." The corner of his mouth curls into a smirk, and I'm unsure if I want to use my hand or mouth to remove it. It's melting me from the inside out, and it's now that I'm realizing how natural it is for Colton. It's natural for him to pull this feeling out of me with near minimal effort. He's been doing it ever since he saw me step out of my car.

"Oh yeah," I mutter, rolling my eyes away from him. I'd forgotten he helped Dallas when he married Hailey. I press my lips together and stare off into the nearly empty parking lot. For the afternoon, I'm surprised it isn't busier.

"Actually," he says, "Sloan only mentioned it when she asked me to help. I think she was too busy with everything else and probably just forgot to tell you."

"I'll be sure to get on to her later." I smirk, shaking off Sloan's omission.

"How have you been?"

I turn back to look at him, allowing his question to sink in. The bitterness at the end of my tongue is starting to dissolve.

I inhale a deep breath. "I've been good."

"Good."

"Yeah." I nod. "And you?"

He looks down at the ground and drags the toe of his boot across the pavement. Half of his face is shielded by the bill of his hat, but when he looks back up, the sun catches the caramel-colored flecks in his eyes. I've missed the way they make my heart pound in my chest.

"I'm doing better." A slow smile creeps across his lips. One of the corners of his mouth tilts higher than the other. I've forgotten what it's like to have my mouth pressed against that same spot.

"Better? Is the graduated life not everything it's cracked up to be?"

I'm not entirely sure what he means by *better*. It could be a simple answer, one that doesn't have deeper meaning, but I ask him anyway, teasing him. For so long he made it sound as if his life would be better as long as he finished school. Grass is always greener, that kind of bullshit people spout off to sound wiser.

We haven't talked about the conversation we had at dinner with Sloan and Dallas. I don't know if Colton intends on bringing a date, and part of me wonders if he felt anything at all when I mentioned I was interested in bringing Levi. Maybe he doesn't care and that's why he's been silent about it.

I wouldn't blame him. Too much time has passed for me to expect things to be different.

He looks past my shoulder, out to the cars passing down the street. "I didn't say that." His eyes find mine again. "But yes, I'm better now." He allows his words to linger only for a second before he pushes off the truck. He leaves me standing at the back end of the parking space and heads toward the floral shop.

Even when I step up onto the curb, I'm still holding my breath. I try not to read too much into his words.

But yes, I'm better now.

He's holding the door open for me when I reach the entrance, but he doesn't look in my direction as I pass him. He keeps his head down, using the bill of his hat to shield the expression on his face.

At first, I thought he looked fucking irresistible with that hat on. I almost feel as if he's using it to his advantage, only giving me glimpses of his expressions when he wants to share them with me. His words out in the parking lot weigh heavily between us.

When we step inside and tell the florist we're there to pick up Sloan's centerpieces, she quickly starts pulling them out of the back storeroom.

My eyes widen when she pulls out the first one, handing it to Colton. My jaw drops and my lips part as I watch him carry it. I move to open the door, holding it for him as he brings it out to the truck.

"I thought this was going to be a small wedding. Why did Sloan make it seem like she wasn't going overboard?"

Colton laughs as he looks over his shoulder. The smile on his face melts my insides, heating the space between my legs. The tension from earlier has dissolved. He's not even bothered the slightest bit. "She said the wedding was going to be small, but I guess she never claimed the decorations would be."

I don't say anything as he keeps moving toward his truck. I'm afraid he's going to trip when he steps down off the curb, but he's graceful and doesn't miss a beat. I jog to catch up to him and move around him, opening the back passenger door.

"I'm glad." He grunts, stretching further through the back seat. "I'm glad she's doing it the way she wants though. She deserves this."

"She does."

I keep my hand on the door as he sets the vase down on the floorboard, sliding it all the way across. He makes sure it's snug before he steps back. I'm still holding the door when he turns around.

The space between the inside of his truck and where I'm standing isn't very big, and the moment his eyes look down on me underneath the bill of his hat, I lose my train of thought. We've caught ourselves back in the same situation as before, only this time we're standing in front of the back seat of his truck instead of his tailgate.

"Thank you for helping." They're the only four words I can think to say. Deep down I'm thankful for Colton and how he's selflessly taking the time to help move a bunch of flowers.

His caramel eyes harden to a light shade of honey. It's as if the more intense his stare grows, the lighter they turn.

"Don't mention it."

I focus in on his lips as the words drip from his mouth. They're slow and meticulous as he stares down at me. His eyes move to my face. Every shift of his eyes leaves a burning sensation across my skin. My cheeks flush and my palms sweat.

He steps closer, the toe of his boot tapping against the toe of my sneaker. He doesn't speak a word. He simply stares, only this time his eyes are shadowed by his hat, and he keeps them pinned on mine.

My chest feels like it's going to cave in from the pressure his stare is giving me.

"We should grab the rest," I tell him, feeling like I might explode unless I move. I need to move my legs to remind me I'm still rooted to the ground.

I leave Colton standing there and allow my hand to fall away from the door. As soon as I turn around, I inhale a deep breath, my lungs starving for air. They burn as if I've just kicked off the bottom of the ocean, fighting and kicking my way to the top, only making it right before my lungs burst from a lack of oxygen.

It doesn't take Colton and me long to load the rest of the centerpieces into the truck. When we're finished, I ride with him to the restaurant to unload them into the storage room. He pulls around to the back entrance, and we carry them in without a word from Dallas. From what it looks like, he's swamped with a full bar and too busy to notice we're here.

The sounds coming from the front dining area and kitchen give me an odd sense of longing. Part of me misses the fast-paced environment and the customers. It's a small part, but the feeling is there nonetheless.

After we load the last centerpiece into the storage room, Colton and I stand outside the back door. He allows it to close behind him. It slams shut, cutting off all the noise coming from inside.

"I'll take you back to your car and then I'll help them with this rush."

"I can stay and help too if you'd like." It's been nice spending time with Colton today. I can feel us starting to slip back into the way we were before. Maybe it isn't as strong, but it's still there, like blowing the flame out from a candle. The flame may be gone, but the wick still lingers with embers.

"You don't have to do that." He shakes his head as he lifts his cap off his head. He runs his fingers through his hair, pushing it off his forehead. His hair is unruly, yet somehow it looks as if it's made to stay that way. He replaces his hat then slides his hands into his pockets.

"This sounds familiar."

"What does?" he asks me.

"This conversation."

His eyebrows furrow, and it takes him a moment to realize what conversation I'm referring to. We're standing in the same spot, only this time we're different.

His thought-filled eyes are guarded by the bill of a Longhorns baseball hat, and I'm standing here remembering what it felt like to have him taste me in places I know I'll never forget.

This time we're remembering how a conversation like this led to our one-time secret.

"I know I don't have to, Colton." I grin, my body humming with nerves. "I *want* to."

I pinch the tip of my tongue between my teeth, holding back the butterflies raging in my stomach. He loosens his hands from his pockets and steps closer to me, grasping one of my curls. My hair is longer this time, his finger grazing against my chest, against the spot above my breast.

He drops the curl, and with a blank expression, he slowly backs away. His eyes are hardened like they were before, making it impossible to know what he's thinking. Without another word, he opens the door and holds it open for me, allowing the commotion of inside to drown out our silence.

But once I cross the threshold, I finally hear his voice hit the hollow of my ear. "If you insist."

CHAPTER NINE

Vada

THE KNOCK ON MY FRONT DOOR JOLTS ME OUT OF MY BED. I sit upright, clutching the sheets to my chest as if they're going to somehow protect me from whatever it is that's pounding on my door.

I grab my phone from my nightstand and see that it's already nearly seven at night. I must have fallen asleep watching one of my favorite investigative shows when I got home. Work was long and exhausting, especially after helping Colton and Dallas at the bar yet again.

Once I got home, I didn't even bother making dinner. I crawled under the sheets in my bed, and eventually, my eyes grew heavy, too heavy for me to keep open long enough to turn the TV off. My show is still playing when I move across the bed to answer the door.

"I'm coming," I yell, rubbing my eye with the heel of my hand. I probably say it too loud for someone who has neighbors butting up against three of the four walls.

The pounding pauses once I'm in the hallway, and when I swing the door open, I find Colton standing on the other side of it.

"Hey." I groan, trying to get the sound of sleep to leave my throat. I swallow and lift my hand, my fingers disappearing under my hair as I rub the back of my neck.

Colton's eyes move along my body, taking me in. "Have a nice nap?" he asks, arching his eyebrows above the frames of his glasses.

"How did you know I was taking a nap?"

"I can just tell." He says it casually, but I can't help noticing the way his eyes focus on my hair.

I move my hand from my neck to the back of my head, immediately feeling my cheeks warm. My curls have tangled themselves into some kind of bird's nest. I work my fingers through it and step to the side, allowing Colton to come in.

I'm wearing my small pair of sleep shorts, the kind that barely cover all of my ass cheeks. I'm almost one hundred percent certain if I were to bend over, half my cheeks would show, but I only ever wear them when I'm home and intend on spending the rest of the night binging investigative documentaries. Under my favorite zip-up hoodie, I'm wearing a black thin-strapped tank. The shoulder of my unzipped hoodie falls down, exposing my bare shoulder. I lift it, feeling the cool night air breeze against my skin.

Ever since the day we picked up the centerpieces for the wedding this coming weekend, I've progressively seen Colton more and more, starting with a few days ago and when I've offered to help out at the bar the past few days.

I'm more than happy with where I'm at in my career, especially since my change in jobs several months back, but I won't deny that being back at the bar and serving my old customers satisfied me in a way I hadn't realized I missed. When I'm in a groove, in the middle of a dinner rush, everything clicks into place. It feels natural. It's as if it brings this more eccentric part of me out, the bold and cheerful one everyone is used to. If you catch me outside the bar, I'm a quiet girl who spends her free time watching way too many shows about people killing each other. I like to believe I'm well-balanced.

I won't lie though—it felt great to work alongside my brother again, and Colton. It's strange how I've seen him more in the past week than I have in almost a year. Something in him has shifted. Maybe it's because he's now finished with school, and this is his way of working his way back into my life. I'm not entirely sure.

My eyes fall to the small dark green bag in his hand. "What's that?"

His eyes follow mine and he lifts the bag, looking at it. "Oh, I owe you."

"Owe me for what?" I ask him, confused. Is it bad that my mind immediately goes to sex? I imagine the bag filled with vibrators, blindfolds, and ties.

"I might be just a few months behind on mounting that TV for you."

Dammit. No such luck.

"You don't owe me mounting my TV." I shake my head, pretending not to be just a bit happy to see Colton standing in my apartment offering to mount the TV I bought almost a year ago. Oh, and pretending my mind didn't just wander to him holding a bag of sex toys. "How did you know I needed it mounted?"

"I saw the kit sitting next to your TV when I came over that night you were getting ready for your going away party."

"So, you brought your tool bag in the hopes I haven't mounted it?" I ask. "It's been over four months, Colt."

"Does that mean you already mounted it?" he asks, and my stomach dips.

"No. I haven't mounted it." I tuck a few strands of my hair behind my ear, stepping backward into the living room.

"Okay. Well, no time like the present, right?"

"I guess not." I turn on my heel and head for the kitchen.

Colton slowly follows me inside. He slides off his boots before he steps any further. His feet pad across the hardwood floor as he moves to the kitchen, setting the bag on top of the island. "Still no roommate, huh?"

"No." I head over to the fridge to grab a bottle of water. "I don't think it matters to me whether I have one or not. I'm getting used to living here by myself." A couple years ago I lived with a friend of mine from college, but when the world started to fall apart around us with Hailey's death, she split without so much as a twenty-four-hour notice. Other than the note she left on my refrigerator saying she was moving back home, I haven't heard from her since.

I slide a bottle of water across the counter to Colton. I move around the island and lean against it with my elbow. He mimics my stance, resting his on the edge as well. We're standing close, but not too close. His eyes move along my body, and again, his stare turns my insides hot and molten.

Colton has a way of making me feel as if I'm the only person standing in the room. Right now, I am the only person, but somehow, he's managed to expose me even more. Sometimes it's as if he's reading the thoughts in my mind simply by looking at me. I'm left bare and open, vulnerable.

It's entirely too much.

I try to think of anything I can to sober my thoughts and get rid of them completely. I simply want this feeling to go away because I know the power Colton has over me. He has yet to truly let it happen, but I know, without a shadow of a doubt, he would break my heart. He has the power to break it into as many pieces as humanly possible. He has the power to shatter what hope I have left that we could ever live happily.

I grab his green tool bag and move around him, heading

toward my bedroom, but he grabs my wrist, stopping me. He holds my arm against his body. My hand is dangerously close to the button of his jeans. His fingers gently press into my bicep as he holds me, pinning his stare to mine. I gasp, feeling the warmth of his touch shoot straight between my legs.

Nothing except our breaths mingle between our mouths. I tip my chin higher, catching his stare. There they are again, his honey caramel eyes.

When he looks at me this way, I'd wish he'd put us both out of our misery. I wish he'd bend me over the arm of my couch and fuck me until my entire body becomes numb and there's nothing left. At least then I'd be able to get rid of these fucking butterflies in my stomach.

"I'm not entirely sure I like the idea of you living alone."

His words stop my breathing. I can feel the blood drain all the way from the top of my head down to the tips of my toes.

I nervously swipe my tongue across my lips. "I've been living alone for the past two years, Colton."

"That doesn't change the way I feel about it."

"Should I care about the way you feel about it?" It's a bold, frightening question. I don't realize the weight of it until it's already poured out of me.

"I don't know," he muses. "Should you?"

There. There it is.

I can see it in his hardened stare. He's burning to know if I still care for him or not. He wants to know if I've let go of the idea of him, of us. He wants to know if there's anything between me and Levi and my asking him to go to Sloan's wedding.

But I don't tell him.

I sigh, allowing my shoulders to fall with a heavy breath. "We're talking in circles."

I start to move, gently tugging my arm from his grip, but he pulls me back. With his other hand, he reaches between us, sliding his hand across my stomach. The backside of his fingers graze against my thin tank top, the knobs of his knuckles creating small pressure points down to the waist of my shorts.

I'm hot and wet and absolutely ridiculous under Colton's touch.

I'm waiting for him to slide his fingers under the elastic waist of my shorts. I'm waiting for him to press his mouth to mine, finally claiming it. I'm waiting for him to tell me he's now free from the one obligation he claimed prevented us from being together.

But he doesn't. His hand moves away from my stomach and grips the handle of the bag I'm still holding between us.

"Well, then," he says, backing away, "I guess I should finally get that TV mounted for you."

CHAPTER TEN

COLTON

"There's absolutely no way."

"I'm telling you." Vada extends her arm even further, shoving the cup in my face. "This is the best flavor."

I scrunch my nose and shake my head. "It looks like it's going to give me a stomachache."

"It won't." She keeps her cup close to my mouth, moving it back and forth, urging me to take it. "Trust me."

I narrow my eyes, unconvinced. She's been trying to get me to take a sip of her drink ever since we ordered. I eye the concoction. It's a nauseating purple color swirled with glitter. To be honest, it looks like a craft project.

She nods her head toward the milkshake in my hand. "That will probably give you a bigger stomachache than mine will."

I laugh. "How do you know?"

She sticks the end of her straw into her mouth, wraps her lips around it, and sucks up some of the liquid. Her cheeks pucker, and no matter how hard I try, I can't get rid of the image of her mouth wrapped around my cock, looking the same way. I cough, hoping to tame the thoughts running rampant in my mind before my cock perks up, hard as stone.

When Vada suggested going out for a late-night snack, I didn't think she meant ice cream. I pictured us sitting in one of those old-school diners that serves the world's worst cup of coffee. But instead, after I finished mounting her TV on the wall, she was quick to suggest us leaving her apartment and walking over to the ice cream shop down the street from her apartment.

I'm not sure what had her wanting to leave so quickly, but I assume it might have to do with the way I've been testing her the past few days. I can't help it.

She answered the door in those tiny shorts, exposing those long tan legs of hers. One of her shoulders was laid bare, and all I found myself wanting to do was lean forward and press my teeth to her delicate flesh, biting down and tasting her.

I wanted to bend her over the kitchen island and fuck her like I remember. The memory of what it felt like to have my dick buried inside her so deep, giving her the best pleasure she's ever had was eating me alive.

In a way, I guess I'm thankful she dragged us out of her apartment, but I still don't know where she stands as far as me or Levi—or anyone, for that matter. The topic of us and relationships seems to be one we're both avoiding. Maybe it's because we've kept our secret between us for so long that we don't even toy with the idea of mentioning anything related to that department.

It fucking sucks though, because I can feel the itch to talk about it intensifying the more time I spend with her.

It's been several days since Vada and I met to move the centerpieces, and life has almost gone back to the way it used to be. I was stunned when she offered to help out at the bar that day. I watched in awe as she flowed naturally behind the bar as if she hadn't missed a single day. She mixed drinks without hesitation, never stopping to figure out what she needed. She greeted the customers with that same smile that makes me feel as if she's placed her lips directly over mine, depriving my lungs of all their oxygen.

It's a feeling I'm quickly learning hasn't gone anywhere. It's still right fucking here, in the middle of my chest, pumping through my veins.

She finishes her sip and holds her cup in front of her face, reading the label. "I grab one of these nearly every weekend, and I always get the same thing. Well, one version or another. This one is my favorite flavor though."

"Really? When did you start this new tradition of yours?"

"Um..." She twists her mouth and tilts her head. "Only in the past few weeks."

"Why?" I ask, intrigued. It's nice being able to have casual conversation with her, aside from the fact that I still want to touch every inch of her. "Is it a new place or something?"

We've been walking back to her apartment for the past fifteen minutes. Our steps are slower this time around, and at this rate it's going to take us nearly twice as long to get back as it did to get to the ice cream shop.

"No." She turns her attention to the row of houses lining the street and the trees blowing in the breeze. It's nice to be walking outside when the air is cool and not feel like I'm sweating my ass off twenty-four seven.

Still, I'm thankful to be standing next to Vada again, talking again. As much as I'd love to touch her skin and fuck her, I'm enjoying her like this too.

Vada inhales a deep breath, and a small smile appears on her delicate mouth. "I've been helping my friend out lately by taking her nephew to his baseball practices on the weekends. We stop at this place for ice cream after every practice before I drop him off."

"Every time?"

"Yep." She nods, inhaling a deep breath. She lowers her arm and carries her cup lazily in her hand. It swings with the motion of each step she takes. She's relaxed, and based on the way her face brightens at the mention of this kid she's been watching, I can tell she enjoys it.

"That's pretty awesome of you."

"It is, isn't it?"

The twinkle in her eye mixed with the sass coming from the end of her tongue is enough to make my dick hard.

She laughs and shakes her head. "I'm kidding. My friend needed help, and I happen to like Jonah. He's a good kid and he's fun to be around, but it's only for one more week. Then he's done with T-ball, and I won't need to give him rides anymore. I think that's why I started taking him for ice cream every time— to make it feel a bit more special."

"Does he not play any games? I thought this was the time of year for that kind of sport."

"No, he doesn't actually play in a league. This is just one of those classes that teaches the basics." She bites the corner of her mouth. "I think Cass said this is the third time he's taking practice lessons without actually having ever played a game."

"Wow."

"He doubts himself."

"I'm the same way though. Terrible at sports, always have been. That's probably why I majored in business and spent my time teaching myself how to cook."

"What?" Her voice is laced with a hint of playfulness. "You never picked up a ball or played on a team in high school?"

"No." I laugh, massaging the back of my neck. "I tried a few sports here and there, but they weren't for me. Personally, I found myself wanting to work on my father's ranch rather than playing on some shit sports team. And that is saying a lot."

"You did not." She taps me on the arm. Vada vaguely knows

the ins and outs of my relationship with my parents. She doesn't know all the details, especially not the ones where my father thinks she and Dallas don't belong in my social circle, but she knows he's a bitter man with too-high standards, knows my mother is a ghost of the woman she used to be ever since Ryan died.

Vada knows I've spent my life trying to please my father and myself at the same time. It's a battle I've consistently lost.

"You're right," I say. "Both of those sound fucking awful. I think that's why I stuck to opening my own restaurant, to get away from them and prove I can build a life that doesn't involve my father's business." I pause, and she doesn't speak another word. After a few more steps, I add, "I'm sure Jonah will join the team when he's ready."

"Maybe." She smiles.

"Has writing always been your passion?" I ask, switching the direction of our conversation.

"A little." She takes a sip of her drink. "When we were kids, Dallas used to spend hours outside with our dad working on his motorcycle when he would come visit. It was something they used to bond over since Dallas always showed more interest in it than I did. Well, actually, I'm not sure if that was the reason." She pauses in her story long enough to take in a shaky breath. "My dad never put the same effort in with me that he did with Dallas. My mom will never fully admit it, but I'm the reason she left my dad when she did. It's one thing to have a child before the age of eighteen. It's another to have two. In my father's eyes, Dallas will always be the unexpected surprise. As for me, I'll always be the second mistake that tore my mother away from him even though it was before I was even born."

I ignore the twist in my chest as I listen to her tell me the story of her father. The idea that Vada's father never cared for her the way he did for her mother or brother hits me hard. It's enough to make my blood boil and my anger nearly rise to the surface, but I hold it back, not wanting to ruin the night we're having. Vada's shared more with me tonight than she has the entire time we've known each other. I won't take it for granted.

"Where is he now?" I ask.

She turns to me, her mouth set into a frown. "Dallas didn't mention it to you?"

"Not really." I shake my head.

"He used to work for a motorcycle dealership years ago in North Carolina. Well, the night before he was supposed to take a road trip down to Florida to see my grandparents, he couldn't get his own bike to work, so he walked down to the dealership in the middle of the night and stole one of their bikes. He simply drove it off the lot as if he owned it and never bothered to let anyone at his job know he'd taken it. They caught him on camera and tracked him down before he could even cross the border to Florida from Georgia."

"What happened to him?"

"He was arrested and sent back to North Carolina. He served a couple years in prison, and he was released about two years ago. Dallas talks to him more than I do."

"Is he coming to the wedding?"

"I don't know." She shrugs. "Can I tell you something?"

"Yeah." I raise my eyebrows, curious.

"Even though I know Dallas is considering having him there, I hope he doesn't come. He's a piece of shit and doesn't deserve to be there."

"You have every right to feel that way, and I'm sorry he wasn't there for you."

"Thanks." She looks at me with appreciation, but I can see the sadness taking over her eyes. The way she looks at me anchors my feet to the pavement. I want to stop walking and wrap my arms around her, pull her to my chest. I want to place both of my hands around her face and pull her mouth to mine, washing away the pain inside her.

But I don't. I keep walking with her beside me.

We're close to her apartment complex when our conversation falls silent. The large steel fence framing the lot appears on our right as we walk down the sidewalk.

Her eyes fall to the milkshake in my hand. "Here." She reaches for my cup, takes mine from my hand, and replaces it with hers. "Trust me. Just take one sip and I'll give yours back to you."

We're now standing in the middle of her courtyard. The sky is painted a pitch-black color. There are no stars, but the golden hue of the string lights hanging above slather Vada in warmth. Her pink lips pout as she looks up at me with her blue eyes. They almost look green, mixing with the yellow reflection from the lights.

I look down at the cup of purple liquid in my hand. Half of it is already gone, and when I swirl it the same way Vada did earlier, a cloud of glitter rises to the surface. It looks disgusting.

My thoughts must be clearly written on my face because Vada says, "I'm telling you, Colt, it's not as bad as you think."

"Is it even edible?"

"Of course it is." She laughs. "I wouldn't be drinking it if it weren't. It's for show anyway. You can't taste it. Kind of like the mustard you put on your pork shoulder before you smoke it."

I narrow my eyes, remembering how I told her that the day she offered to help out at the bar before the grand opening. I told her I put mustard on the pork because it tenderizes it. You can't taste it.

The way she uses my own words against me drives me fucking insane. It isn't necessarily a bad thing.

"Fine." I almost bring the cup to my mouth then I watch her grab the straw of my milkshake, which she now holds. She pinches the end of it, moving it around in circles, stirring it. She tilts her head to the side and stares at me, shoving the straw into the corner of her mouth.

She takes one long sip, and I swear my dick twitches watching her cheeks pucker with every suck. She smiles even with her lips around it. She's still waiting for me to take a sip.

I bring the cup to my mouth and take a drink. The purple fizzy liquid hits my tongue, and I make sure I've filled my mouth enough to satisfy Vada before swallowing.

"Well?" She arches her eyebrows.

"It's not bad, I guess." It's the truth.

"No...it's not that bad," she says with a satisfied grin.

There's a small dollop of the milkshake in the corner of her mouth as she pulls the straw away. I step forward and reach out, pressing my finger to her skin.

I catch her off guard, and her chest calms as I swipe my finger from the corner of her mouth then drag it across her lips. They're warm and soft, everything I remember them to be. I'm imagining what it would feel like to have my lips pressed there instead of my finger.

I drag the pad of my finger from one corner of her mouth all the way to the other. When I've reached the other side, I pull it away and bring it to my own mouth. I drag my tongue across the pad of my finger before sticking it in my mouth. I make sure to wrap my lips around it the same way she did the straw, letting the vanilla mix with the flavor of her mouth.

The sweetness coats my tongue, followed by Vada's faded lip gloss. It's worn off as the night's gone on, but it's still on her mouth enough for me to taste it. My lips make a smacking sound as I pull my finger from my mouth.

She hasn't moved. Her eyes are wider than I've seen them all night, and her chest is now moving. Her cheeks blush red, and her chest stops moving up and down. She's holding her breath, stunned by what I've just done.

"No." I keep my expression straight. I don't want her to know what this is doing to me. "I think I like the taste of this one better."

Her chest suddenly starts moving again, slow at first then faster with every breath she takes. They're quick, shallow breaths. They aren't foreign to me. They're the kind I know she gets when her heart is racing, and I know I've struck a nerve.

Me tasting her has only furthered her thoughts about me, but all of it fades the second she backs away. She holds her cup to her chest. What glitter is left settles at the bottom. She nervously licks her lips, and her eyes roam, looking everywhere but directly at me. One second she's looking over my shoulder then the next she's looking to her left.

I'm confused because, for a moment, I can see it on her face. She's showing herself to me, letting me know she still feels the same way as the first time I touched her outside my bar that night.

The night we forged our secret.

But now, I'm not so sure. She's retreating.

Her eyes soften and her eyebrows knit together. It's a subtle movement but one that doesn't go unnoticed.

"I'll..." She clears her throat. "It's getting late, and I should get to bed." She takes another few steps back. "Thank you for mounting my TV."

"Well, I told you before—I owed you."

I take a step closer to her, and her eyes immediately move to my feet.

She steps back again.

I don't move.

"Right." She nods, swiping her tongue across her mouth

again. She's tasting the same place where my finger was. She's tasting where I touched her. "Well, I'll see you at the wedding."

"Yeah."

She backs away again; this time her back has nearly hit her front door. "It'll be good. And you'll get to meet Cassidy and Levi."

I hold my breath, and my chest burns hearing his name fall from her mouth.

"Levi?"

"Yeah," she says. Her body has eased up a bit more, and her eyes have softened. "He's my date to the wedding, remember?"

Fuck. Fuck, fuck, fuck.

"You're bringing someone, right?" she asks.

I swallow down the tightness building in my chest. "Yep."

"Okay." She gives me a soft smile, and my heart nearly spills out of my chest. "Well, thanks for mounting my TV. And for this." She raises her cup then slowly turns around. She doesn't wait for me to answer her, and I don't miss how her chest froze with my answer and her shoulders tensed. "I'll see you at the wedding," she adds.

I nod. "See you there."

She disappears behind her front door and closes it behind her, and I don't think I've ever felt more confused about us than I do now.

CHAPTER ELEVEN

Vada

I'M SITTING AT MY ASSIGNED TABLE, TWISTING THE STEM OF my champagne glass between my fingers. It's empty and has been for the past ten minutes. I've been thinking about flagging down one of the waiters carrying trays full of unlimited champagne, but I can't bring myself to stand. Dallas and Sloan decided to have their wedding in a hotel outside the city. I was thankful they decided to celebrate outside the bar, and the hotel is beautiful. A large chandelier hangs in the center of the ballroom. Each table is adorned with a white tablecloth, and the centerpieces Colton and I picked up are set in the middle of each one.

I look down at my bare feet and flex my toes, cracking them several times, releasing the tension that's built up in them all day. I fucking hate heels. Sloan told me I could wear whatever shoes I wanted since no one would be able to see them under my dress, but I didn't listen. I wanted to go all out for her wedding, and part of that required me to wear heels.

Now I'm regretting it.

"You look beautiful, you know? Sloan did a service to you by picking that color for your dress."

My mother sits down in the empty chair beside me. Her long curly brown hair is pinned halfway up, the top half set into a perfect bun resting on the crown of her head. The bottom half of her layers cascade down her shoulders, stopping above the neckline of her copper-colored dress.

Honestly, if I ever wonder what I'll look like in twenty years, I won't have to look far. Not to sound stereotypical, but where Dallas looks like our father, I'm the spitting image of my mother, a carbon copy dated nearly eighteen years apart.

The deep copper tone of her dress highlights the golden tan across her skin. She looks beautiful, but I also don't ignore her sideways compliment about my dress.

I resist the urge to roll my eyes and lean on the table, resting my chin in my hand. She mimics me by doing the same.

"Is that your way of telling me I look good in this color?" I ask her, scanning the ballroom we're using for the reception.

"I did tell you that."

"No, you didn't." I shake my head. "You said Sloan did me a service."

I rest my other hand on my leg, feeling the smooth fabric under my palm.

My dress is a dark green-blue color. Sloan told me she picked it because green is her favorite color and dark blue is Dallas'. Considering I'm her best friend and Dallas is my brother, she thought it would be appropriate for me to wear a color that represented both. I may be the maid of honor, but I'm also the only bridesmaid. It wouldn't have mattered what color Sloan picked; I still would have worn it regardless, but I do love this one.

"You know what I meant though." My mother sighs, giving me a light smile. She's always been a classic beauty with a bit of an edge to her. I guess that's the kind of woman she was forced to become when she got pregnant at sixteen.

Her eyes move over my shoulder, causing me to move with her to see what she's looking at. When I turn around, we watch as Dallas and Sloan stand in front of the table of cupcakes, picking which one they're going to use to stuff each other's face with. Colton's standing behind them, talking to a woman in a short black dress. I've never seen her before, but my best guess is that she's one of Dallas and Sloan's friends. Colton's been talking to her nearly all night. Every now and then, she reaches out, touching her fingertips to his arm. Then, as if on cue, she tilts her head back in laughter as if every word out of Colton's mouth makes her giggle.

It's enough to make my stomach flip upside down.

He's wearing a black suit that's perfectly tailored to his body. His hair is pushed back off his forehead, not a single strand out of place. He's traded his glasses for contacts, a rare sight with Colton. His short beard is trimmed but not completely gone.

I've avoided him since this afternoon when we met here at the hotel for the wedding. Before that, I haven't talked to him since the night we walked down the street to get ice cream, when I left him standing outside my apartment. An intense bolt of electricity hit me that night when he dragged his finger across my mouth then tasted me afterward. When I walked back inside my apartment, I pressed my back against the door and struggled to catch my breath. I still felt the heat across my lips as I tried to discern my feelings. As much as I loved the way he touched me, I realized a part of me still holds resentment that he's never vocally shared his feelings with me. Instead, he pulls out these moments where he's touching me in ways he shouldn't be touching a friend. Then other times, we go through long periods of silence. I guess we're back to the silence because I haven't spoken to him since that night, and he's made no effort. Neither have I.

I guess I now see the reason standing in front of him, hanging on his every word.

"Your brother looks happy," my mother says, pulling my attention from Colton and his date.

I turn back around to face her. "He is, Mom."

"He clearly isn't missing your father here," she mutters, bringing her glass to her mouth. She takes a sip then places it down in front of her.

I try to rein in my anger, playing off my father's absence coolly. I shouldn't give a fuck about that man when he's never given one about me.

"I don't think anyone is. Did he even invite him?" I don't know why I'm asking her. I wouldn't expect her to know the answer.

"I'm not sure." She frowns. "When was the last time you talked to him?"

My mother doesn't usually pry for information from me, knowing I hardly ever talk to my dad. Why invest in someone if they aren't willing to invest in you?

"I don't know." I breathe out, twisting the stem of my glass. "It's been too long for me to count."

"I won't give you any advice on your relationship with him. It's understandable why you don't want to talk to him. You're a grown adult and can make your own decisions, but if you do talk to him, make sure you continue to guard that heart of yours."

She looks past me again, watching Dallas. Her eyes line with tears, just like mine. They threaten to spill, and my heart cracks with her words. It cracks simply with the realization that despite my mother getting pregnant at sixteen by an asshole she met at an R.E.M. concert, she was a great mother. Dallas and I turned out okay.

"I thought he died right along with Hailey when she passed," she says, her voice wobbling. "But Sloan has brought him back to life, and I will forever love her simply for that fact. He deserves this."

"I agree." I stare at my empty champagne glass.

"What about you? Are you happy?"

When I look into my mother's eyes, I try not to let my emotions show. She's always been good at spotting them.

"Yeah, I'm happy." I don't even convince myself the words are true the moment they leave my mouth, and I know my mother will see right through my lie when I look over her shoulder.

Across the dining room, I find Levi and Cass standing together. Well, not exactly together. Her camera is strapped around her neck, and every few seconds she lifts it to take a picture of a few of the guests.

Beside her is Levi, waiting to grab a drink from the open bar. He moves up in line. Cassidy has the camera pressed against her face and doesn't notice how close she is to Levi until she bumps into him, causing him to stumble forward. Once he's righted himself, he spins around, giving Cassidy a scowl.

I turn my attention back to my mother as soon as they start up a conversation. "How long are you staying?"

"Oh, I drive back to Texarkana tomorrow. Rob and I are supposed to meet up for our third date."

"Really?" I ask, intrigued to hear more. She mentioned him the last time we spoke on the phone, but I haven't heard how their first date went. "The whole online dating thing seems to be working out then, huh?"

She winces then shakes her head, giggling. "I guess so."

"You guess what?" Warm arms wrap around my neck from behind, and Sloan's face presses against mine. She tilts her head against my cheek as we both look at my mother.

My mom laughs as she looks between me and Sloan. Sloan

gives her arms a quick squeeze around my neck before sitting down on the other side of me.

"I was just telling Vada about Rob."

"Oh." She nods, her purple-dusted blue eyes widening. "Your new boyfriend. I knew you guys would hit it off."

"Stop," my mom says. "It isn't serious, but from what I've seen of him so far, I like him."

Sloan glances over her shoulder. "The real test is getting Dallas to approve."

My mom scoffs. "I don't need Dallas to approve of anyone." Her southern drawl hits every word, and it makes me realize just how much mine sounds like her. I don't usually notice it until I hear hers.

They both start to laugh, and a warmth spreads over me. This is the first time I'm realizing that not only is Sloan my best friend, she's also my sister-in-law. She's part of the family.

My mother and Sloan continue on with their conversation, and I catch Colton out of the corner of my eye. He's making his way over to the bar, standing in line behind the couple behind Levi. Levi is now standing at the bar, ordering fresh drinks from the bartender. Cass is no longer in sight. She must have moved on to take pictures of the reception going on around us.

The hotel ballroom is decorated with eucalyptus leaves and small white flowers. The decorations are subtle and perfect for their style. Even though Dallas and Sloan added more guests the closer it got to the ceremony, it still worked out perfect for them.

After Levi collects the drinks from the bartender, he walks back over to our table. He catches Colton's attention as he passes him. Colton keeps his expression blank, much like he has every time he's looked at me today.

His expression is flat, but the muscles of his jaw flex as he shoves his hands inside his pockets. The sleeves of his suit stretch over his biceps. I press my thighs together, not wanting to lose myself in thinking about a man who clearly shows no interest in me outside of being his friend.

"Sorry it took a while. I saw your drink was empty while I was in line, so I got you a new one." Levi sets a full glass of champagne in front of me then sits down in the chair next to Sloan since she took his seat. He unbuttons the jacket of his dark blue suit.

"Thanks." I give him a smile of appreciation, not wanting to look in Colton's direction. No matter how hard I'm trying to avoid it, I still can't help but feel the invisible thread connecting to him. There's a tug on my chest, willing me and urging me to look in his direction, but I don't.

"Thanks for coming, Levi," Sloan says. Her lips are painted a rich, dark purple. They complement her lilac-colored eyes perfectly.

"Thanks for having me, and congratulations." He gives her a smile and leans on the table with his forearm.

"Thank you." Sloan tips her head to the side and smiles, her cheeks warming.

A new song starts on the overhead speaker, the subtle piano music switching to a faster-paced song. Dallas stands between me and our mother.

Colton stands on the other side of her. He still has one hand shoved into his pocket, the other wrapped around a glass of beer. We're already at the end of the reception. All of the formal photos have been taken, and we've just finished dinner. Colton and I have already both delivered our speeches. I had tears in my eyes while giving mine, and I couldn't take my eyes off Colton when he gave his. He looked delicious in his perfectly trimmed dark suit. There was something about him that looked different. He appeared tougher somehow, stronger...like I wanted his body all over mine.

"Oh, honey," my mother says to me. "Did you decide to stay in the hotel, or are you driving back into the city?" Her eyes move to the full glass of champagne Levi put in front of me.

"I got a room for tonight. It was just easier that way."

"Okay, I just wanted to check." She gives me a relieved smile.

"What?" Dallas asks. "You aren't worried about me or Sloan?"

"Why would I be?" She looks up at Dallas towering above her. "Sloan told me you booked the honeymoon suite months ago."

"Of course she did." Dallas sighs and looks over at Sloan. Their love is sickening sometimes, but I also love it at the same time.

I look over at Colton to see what he might be thinking, but his expression is blank as his eyes move over the table.

"Would you care for a dance, Mom?" Dallas holds his hand out to her.

"You're kidding." I smirk in disbelief at my brother. "I don't think I've ever seen or heard of you being the first one to initiate a dance."

"What can I say?" He grins. "I'm a changed man."

"Wow." My mother turns to Sloan with a sparkle in her eye. "I love the influence you've had on my son."

Sloan shrugs and waves her comment off, bringing her drink to her mouth. "I've done absolutely nothing. He's always been in there—he just doesn't like to show this side of himself very often."

"Now *that* is true." I point to Sloan, and both of us giggle. Dallas rolls his eyes, ignoring us. My mother finally takes his hand and stands.

They head out to the dance floor, and Colton sits down in my mother's empty chair. He doesn't say a word. He relaxes back in the seat and rests one hand on the table, keeping his fingers loosely wrapped around his beer.

I haven't seen the woman he was talking to earlier. I've noticed he's been by himself since he was standing in line at the bar.

"Oh, Levi," Sloan says, "I don't believe you've met Colton yet. He's Dallas' business partner and best man."

"Oh yeah," he says. "I saw you in the ceremony. It's nice to meet you." He reaches across the table, extending his hand to Colton.

"You too."

I avoid Sloan's stare. I can feel her eyes on me, knowing this must be awkward to some degree. I still haven't told her about Colton's and my one-time secret. That happened before I met her, before she had even moved here. However, she does know about my feelings for him and how, despite the fact that he's been finished with school for the past month, I'm fairly certain he has no desire to move me out of the zone he's put me in, the friend-slash-brother's-little-sister zone.

Colton lifts his chin a bit higher but falls back against his seat. I can't quite get a read on what's going on in his mind. He hasn't acted any sort of way toward Levi.

"Vada mentioned you and her work together." It's a statement more than it is a question. Levi responds anyway.

"Yeah." He nods. "Technically, she's my boss. I'm just a lowly columnist." He leans forward on the table, crossing his arms over the edge.

"You are not," I say, hating how he makes our respective positions sound. I'm not much older than Levi.. I have yet to know his exact age, but I do know he graduated college a few years after I did.

Levi shrugs and playfully shakes his head. "Regardless, I

enjoy working at the paper. Eventually, I hope to work my way up like Vada has. Maybe then I'll be *her* boss."

I let out a hollow laugh. It falls on a breath at Levi's joke, but Colton's burning stare heats my body. I can feel the tension filling the space between us.

"I bet."

It's only two words, but the sarcasm dripping from them washes over me.

I quickly shift my eyes to Colton. If Colton meant for those two words to come across as bitter, Sloan didn't notice. Levi didn't either, but I did.

His caramel eyes have shifted to that all-too-familiar amber honey shade, and I can't help but feel a twinge of excitement spark inside my chest—but it isn't the good kind of excitement. It hits like a barrel to the chest, catching me by surprise.

He clears his throat then closes his mouth. I can see the muscles ticking in his jaw.

I press my lips together and hold in a breath, urging Colton not to press Levi. He's still staring at him, letting awkward silence descend upon the table.

"Where's your date?" I ask Colton. My question is for two reasons. One, in the hopes it will stop him from interrogating Levi. I'm unsure of how he feels about him being here, but the longer we sit here, the more I get the feeling he doesn't exactly like him. Reason number two: because curiosity is getting the better of me.

I'm nosey; what can I say?

I can feel Sloan's surprised gaze fall on me, but I ignore her and stare at Colton. He doesn't miss a beat.

He nods his head behind me, and I turn around, spotting his date over in the corner talking to the DJ. She's in full-on conversation mode, waving her hands around dramatically.

"Um..." Sloan clears her throat and stands. She fixes the bottom of her long white dress, smoothing out the wrinkles. It's a flowy ball gown with just the right amount of fabric fanning out from her waist. She adjusts it then places a hand on my shoulder. "I'm going to see if I can steal Dallas away from your mom."

I give her a soft smile before she walks away, leaving me with Colton and Levi. I'm about to open my mouth to strike up a conversation when Colton's date suddenly appears beside him. She leans into him, shoving her hand into his shoulder, pushing him.

"Hey, Colt. What's up?" she asks. She's clearly had a little more than the rest of us to drink. The wine glass in her hand jerks back and forth with her movements. The dark red liquid almost spills out, but she manages to catch it before it splashes in my direction. She rests her hand on Colton's shoulder, and my chest tightens the same way it did when I saw him standing in line. He doesn't answer her question. He simply stares at me, and I feel like I might explode.

I'm ready to leave the table, but Levi catches me first. He stands, offering me his hand the same way Dallas offered his to my mother.

"Do you want to dance?"

"Sure." I give him a tight smile and down the entire glass of champagne he brought me only minutes ago. The bubbles burn and fizz on their way down, sparking against my tongue.

I stand up and grab Levi's hand, letting him lead me out to the dance floor. I don't even bother looking back at Colton and his date.

CHAPTER TWELVE

COLTON

"Isn't that chick the maid of honor?"

I don't look away from Vada and Levi swaying out on the dance floor as Trinity stumbles over her words.

"Her name is Vada, and yes," I mumble, "she's the maid of honor."

I'm already annoyed with her. Apparently, she's a girl Dallas met a few years back when he and Hailey used to travel around to some local bars in the area to perform. Up until this morning, I'd never even fucking heard of her, much less met her.

"Whatever," Trinity says, waving me off. She sits in the seat Vada was sitting in and halfway turns, resting her arm over the back. "I can't say much about how she was at the table, but her mood has certainly perked up now that she's out there dancing." She rolls her gaze to mine. "Do you want to dance?"

Her eyes are hazy with alcohol, and I can practically smell the wine radiating off her breath with every word she speaks in my direction. She's sloppy and messy. I'd say it's because she's had one too many glasses, but she was like this even before she put alcohol in her system—as far as I know. Hell, she could have been drunk even before she got here.

"No." I answer her then turn my attention back to Vada. Vada and fucking Levi.

The edges of my vision burn with red every step they take. One of his hands is wrapped around hers, the other resting on the small of her back. His fingers are splayed out, his fingertips dangerously close to the curve of her ass.

I clench my fist under the table, forcing myself to take deep breaths. My knuckles tense and stretch every time I curl my fingers.

"I'm not going to lie," Trinity says. "It looks kind of fun."

"Then, by all means, go out there." I unclench my fist and wave my hand toward the floor. I'm probably being an asshole, but it doesn't necessarily matter to me. Trinity isn't my date, and I owe her nothing. She simply chooses to hang around me for the sake of having company.

I take a swig of my beer as Trinity shrugs. The song has shifted to a more upbeat one, and for a moment, I'm thankful. I figure Levi and Vada might spread out, giving each other more space, but I'm dead wrong. He pulls her in, pressing her chest to his. They start moving faster, and it's as if everyone around them is oblivious to it. In fact, it looks as if Dallas and Sloan are encouraging it.

Vada is the most beautiful I've ever seen her. It's not that I don't think she's beautiful every other day, but there's something about her tonight. Her long teal dress fits around her curves like a glove. It's as if the designer took one long sheet of fabric, wrapped it around Vada's body, and stitched it in all the right places. Her neckline dips between the swells of her breasts. It's incredibly sexy yet classy at the same time. There's a long slit that runs down the side of her left leg. The opening at her ankle slithers up and along her smooth skin. It's an incredibly high slit, stopping just below the very top of her thigh. It's been driving me crazy all fucking night, and if I stare at it too long, my thoughts start to go in a million different directions—definitely thoughts that aren't appropriate to be thinking at my best friend's wedding, the same best friend whose little sister is the one I'm having those thoughts about.

Vada and Levi get swallowed up by the crowd, including Dallas and Sloan. On the outer edges, Cassidy is taking pictures. Every now and then she lifts the camera to her face, snaps a few photos, then stands upright again. She moves a few feet then takes more pictures. Her focus tries to stay on Dallas and Sloan, but she struggles to keep up with them as more guests surround them on the floor.

Before the ceremony, Sloan introduced me to Cassidy. I've never met her before, but she's vaguely familiar to me, as if I've possibly met her before, or someone who looks like her. Her long blonde hair drapes down her back in waves. The top half is weaved into a braid like a crown on her head. When I spoke to her earlier, she seemed kind, but I didn't learn too much about her other than that weddings are out of her realm of expertise. Nonetheless, she has been taking pictures non-stop.

I can't place where I know her from. It's annoying, but I turn my attention back to Vada.

Dallas lied when he said he and Sloan were planning on this being a small, intimate wedding. It's not nearly as large as some weddings, but it is bigger than anticipated. The dance floor is now crowded, and when I look around the dining area, I'm one of the only people left sitting. Aside from Vada's mom over at the bar and two of my employees from the restaurant, I'm the only one not on the dance floor.

Except Trinity. She finishes off her glass of wine and stands, adjusting the neckline of her dress. Her lips are pursed as she glances over her shoulder to the dance floor. "Well, if you aren't going out there, I am. I'm too buzzed to care but not too drunk to go out there and enjoy myself."

"Okay." I scratch at my chin, fighting the urge not to laugh. She might be obnoxious, but she seems like she's a good person deep down.

Without another slurred word, she heads out to the dance floor, joining a group of people near the DJ booth.

I'm watching the dance floor, still waiting until I see Vada again. I haven't seen her since she was swallowed up by Dallas and Sloan, but just as I'm thinking it, she pops out from the crowd. She's still dancing with Levi in the same way they were before. The lights have dimmed as the night has passed. What once was a quaint wedding reception now looks like a nightclub. Cassidy is no longer standing on the outer edges taking hundreds of photos. I figure she's probably joined in on the party.

The part of the dining area where I'm sitting is still slightly lit, the other half covered in black. A few strobe lights flash over the dance floor. One minute Vada's gone; the next she's a flash of white light.

Watching Levi's hands wrap around her waist brings an anger coursing through my body unlike anything I've ever felt, even more so than when I listen to my dad complain about how I'm a failure compared to my brother, Ryan. It's even more than the anger I felt when I realized I could never truly have Vada when we first met.

But the more I sit here and my vision ebbs from black to red, I realize there's nothing stopping me from moving ahead with her. Maybe it's been fear holding me back. Maybe I've felt too much time has passed since the last time I placed my mouth on hers. Maybe it's the fear that both of us have held onto our secret so tightly, eventually we allowed it to dissolve under the pressure of time.

I clench my fists again, only this time I can feel the muscles in my hand tightening all the way up to my forearms. I bounce my leg under the table, watching as she leans into Levi. His hands are touching her body. His mouth is dangerously close to hers. There's a smile that's been permanently plastered to her face ever since she stepped onto that dance floor with him. She tips her head back in laughter. When it subsides, he leans forward, bringing her face next to his. He says something in her ear, and heat rises up my chest around to the back of my neck. I bite down on my teeth, clenching them so hard a pounding pain beats through my temples.

Every piece of me is on fire, watching as she smiles with her face pressed against his. My stomach flips and my heart pounds with every flex of my fingers and every bounce of my leg.

Flashes of light continue to pulse over the crowd. Levi turns in the other direction and starts pushing his way through, leaving Vada behind.

The second I see him disappear behind the wall, I rise out of my chair, and my feet are suddenly carrying me across the ballroom.

CHAPTER THIRTEEN

Vada

My heart is pounding in my chest, beating to the same rhythm as the music floor. I haven't danced like this in a long time. It's surprising and incredibly liberating. Ever since I stepped foot on this dance floor, I've used it as a way to drown out my thoughts of Colton.

I haven't been able to stop.

I haven't been able to stop thinking about the way his jaw ticked as he stared at Levi. I can't stop thinking about the way his eyes seem impossibly richer now that he's wearing contacts instead of his glasses.

I don't know how many songs Levi and I have danced to by the time sweat is dripping down my back and the front of my dress. I can only imagine how my dress looks or how my hair has now fallen out of its place, but I don't care.

I've needed this. I've needed a way to forget about Colton and where we are or aren't. I don't understand him and how he can go on with his life pretending as if we're nothing more than friends, but since the moment Levi even looked in his direction, he's been acting like an asshole.

Poor Levi never stood a chance.

I'm still moving to the song playing in the ballroom when Levi pulls me toward him, bringing my face next to his, close enough for him to speak in my ear.

"I should probably start heading home. Don't want to get stuck in traffic."

I nod with him still leaning into me. "Okay," I yell, unsure how well he can actually hear me over the bass pumping through our bodies. "Thanks for coming."

"Thanks for inviting me. And tell Dallas and Sloan I said thank you."

When he pulls away, I nod, feeling sweat drip down the back of my neck. I watch as he elbows his way through the crowd and then disappears. As soon as I can no longer see him, I spin around, looking for Sloan or Cassidy, anyone I can dance with now that Levi is gone.

Levi wasn't my date. In fact, I asked him if he wanted to come to the wedding simply for an assignment. After Levi heard about Cassidy being asked to photograph it, he came to me with a story idea: to write an article on how the couple famous for their performances around the city were getting hitched. They took him up on the offer of writing an article about them and agreed to have it published in the paper. I gave him the ultimate green light on the story as his managing editor, and in exchange, he was invited to the wedding to see it firsthand.

Although Levi technically wasn't my date, part of me is lonely on the dance floor. Ignoring the urge to leave, I stay and dance out of principle. The song changes once again, this time to a faster song. I recognize it from a few years back, and after several seconds, I start moving my hips. I tilt my head to the ceiling and close my eyes. I move from side to side. I'm dancing barefoot, but I don't care. The wood floor feels good on my aching feet, and with every move I make, it's as if I'm working those pains out of my muscles.

The ballroom is nearly pitch black. Bright flashes of white and green pulse across the crowd, and it's hard to make out who's surrounding me. I don't see Sloan, and I don't see Dallas. I close my eyes again, swaying to the music and allowing my two glasses of champagne to flow through my veins.

My thoughts weave with the music, and my heart bubbles in my chest. I feel good and free. The music and dancing feel so good I almost don't notice the two hands sliding across my waist from behind. A large wall of muscle presses against my back. Despite the intense amount of sweat surrounding me, all I smell is mint and a subtle hint of burning wood. It's a scent I find myself leaning into. My head tips back into the body behind me, allowing that scent to swallow me up. I'm still swaying my hips from side to side, slowing down enough to allow our bodies to fall into the same rhythm. The two large hands slide further along my waist, dipping down to my hips. Long fingers press into me, keeping my movements in line with the beat. I keep dancing because I want to feel free. I want to forget about Colton and the pain I get every time I look into his eyes, knowing our timing will never line up.

For a moment, I wonder if the man I'm dancing with is Levi. Maybe he decided not to leave after all and feels bold enough to dance with me this way, my ass pressing into his hips, his chest pressed against my back. But my assumption is completely shut down as his hands run down my hips to the top of my thighs. His finger finds the opening of the slit of my dress.

Part of me is relieved when I realize it isn't Levi. I don't need an awkward boss-employee relationship or even an awkward encounter, as this one would certainly be.

The man's finger dances on the seam, circling my flesh as he lowers his face, pressing his mouth to my ear.

"I want you to know…this has been driving me fucking insane all night."

I gasp and stop moving the second his breath hits the hollow of my ear. His voice sends a shiver down my spine, and I'm immediately wet for him, completely fucking soaked.

Blood drains down to my bare feet. I'm tingling all over, from the tips of my fingers down to my tired, aching feet. I want to stay where I am and revel in the feeling he's giving me. As soon as his hands were on me, I was living in a fantasy world, one where I savored the moment of having someone else's hands caressing and appreciating every inch of me. But then reality set in, and it was like I was waking up from a deep dream. I want him to keep going, but I'm also tired of the constant back and forth he's been giving me for the past week.

Now grasping my current situation and the man behind me, I stop dancing and abruptly turn around.

Fire burns in my chest at the sight of him. The top button of his shirt is undone, and the front of his hair is no longer styled impeccably. A few strands hang loose over his dark, brooding eyebrows. I hate it. I hate the way the lines of his face are high-lighted by the pulsing lights streaming down over us. It turns my insides to hot, molten mush.

"What are you doing?" I ask him. I cross my arms over my chest and narrow my eyes. I don't care that there are about thirty people surrounding us, all dancing and shoving their bodies into ours.

"What do you think I'm doing?" A devious, smartass smirk spreads across his gorgeous mouth. My insides burn up even more. "I'm dancing with you."

I'm not sure why, but his words strike a chord within me, mixing with the fire that's burning for him as anger rises to the surface. I unravel my arms and clench my fists at my sides. Colton's constant back and forth, playing both sides of the line is too much for me. It's definitely too much for me to handle when I've had a few glasses of champagne and we're dancing at my brother's wedding.

"I think I'm done dancing for the night." I make sure to pin him with my narrowed gaze before spinning on my heel. I push and elbow my way through the crowd, aiming for the lobby. I want to get to the elevator and to the hotel room I booked for the night.

When I'm free from the dance floor, I inhale a deep breath. Realizing I don't have my shoes, I spin around and walk back to my table on the other side of the ballroom. Once I've snatched my shoes back up, I turn and slam into Colton's chest.

His frame towers over me. His hands are shoved into his pockets, but the look in his eyes tells me everything I need to know.

"We're not doing this," I tell him. I take a step back then make my way around him.

My feet carry me toward the lobby like I originally planned. I don't even care if Colton is following me. My heart races and heat trickles down my throat and into my stomach. The truth is, I want him to touch me. My body burst into flames when his hands slid across my waist on the dance floor. My stomach fluttered as he lowered his mouth to my ear, ghosting his lips against my flesh as he said those words out loud.

We're walking toward the hallway leading to the elevators. I can hear Colton's feet tapping against the tile.

"Vada, stop."

I shake my head in disbelief. I let out a fake laugh, allowing the frustration of the past two years to pour out of me. It's as if the wall of a dam has broken and all the water is flooding out in one large sweeping wave. It's messy, crushing, and reckless.

So are my feelings for Colton.

"You're impossible."

"Just stop," he begs again. "Listen to me for a minute."

I'm standing in front of the elevators, and I reach out to press the call button. Colton's hand wraps around my wrist, stopping me.

"Listen to what?" I jerk my hand away. I'm breathless, and my chest caves with the pressure. "Are you going to tell me what in the hell made you think it was okay to do that?" I point behind him to the dance floor.

He takes a step closer to me, bringing his face close to mine. His eyes spark without his glasses. I've never seen them as bright as they are now. They're clear and raging with fire. It feels as if in this moment, he's giving me permission to see inside his soul.

He clenches his jaw, and his eyebrows deepen with his stare. His eyes pierce mine, and I hold my breath as the words fall from his mint-scented mouth. "Because I couldn't fucking sit there and watch his hands touch you in places I've touched you. I couldn't take it for one more goddamn second."

The elevator dings and the doors slide open. I don't move my eyes from Colton's, but suddenly my feet are carrying me backward. I'm stepping into the elevator, but I can't decide if it's me who's moving them or if it's Colton leading me in. My back hits cold metal, and I gasp. The doors close behind him, but he makes no move to choose a floor.

He's towering over me as I tip my chin higher, refusing to give in so easily. It's hard to believe after this long, Colton would still want me, or that he would get this frustrated over me and Levi dancing.

It's stupid. It's also turning me on with how angry this is making him.

His gaze roams over me, his eyes indecisive about what to focus on. They flick back and forth from my mouth to my chest then back up to my eyes.

"Why should that bother you?" I stare up at him, sticking out my chin. My throat swells with nerves, and my thighs clench when his body presses against mine. "You have a date. Shouldn't she be the one you're dancing with and interrogating in elevators?"

"She's not my date." He says it so factually, so directly, as if she holds no meaning to him whatsoever.

"Oh, really?" I press my lips into a flat line. "Didn't look that way to me."

"I'm serious, she's not. I didn't even meet her until earlier at the ceremony."

"But she was all over you, and you said you had a date when we were outside my apartment the other night."

"You assumed she was my date. I never said she was. I told you that because you said Levi was your date."

"So...what? Seeing me with Levi pissed you off and that suddenly makes it okay for you to make up your mind about me? I had every right to bring a date if I wanted to. That shouldn't bother you."

"Well, it did." His voice is direct and even again, as if that is the only correct answer. "I can't even begin to tell you the thoughts I had while watching him touch you."

"You've had months, Colton." I narrow my eyes, unwilling to give in to him so easily, no matter how bad I want to. "I find it odd that now all of a sudden you want to touch me when you see another man all over me."

"You're right." He tightens his jaw. "I have no right to claim you, but I can't explain the fire I felt inside watching him all over you. Touching you in those...same...places...I...did..." He inhales a breath between each word.

"That was two years ago."

"Doesn't feel like it to me," he confesses.

"Well, it has been."

"Huh." He breathes out. "It's been that long."

"Yep." I narrow my eyes, allowing him to read the thoughts

clearly on my mind. I want him to see how frustrated I am about him not taking this initiative sooner. I want him to answer as to why he hasn't made a move until now. "You said you were angry watching Levi touch me. Why?"

"Is that a serious question?"

"Yes." I steel my face and pin him with a glare, letting him know how serious I am.

"I know I have no right to get jealous, but I don't think I realized just how angry it would make me to see his hands all over you." He swallows, swiping his thumb across his lip in thought. "I should have known, though. I've been angry about it ever since you told me he was your date."

"He wasn't my date." My confession spills from my mouth before I even realize I'm saying it.

"What?" His eyes light with intrigue and a bit of anger.

"Yeah." My cheeks blush. "I kind of sort of lied about it."

"Kind of?"

I lift one shoulder, brushing it off. "At first, I considered it, but Levi is just a colleague of mine, and a friend."

He clenches his jaw and looks down at the floor. I can't tell what he's thinking, but he's at least giving me more than he has in the past few months. As horrible as it is, he's showing me that me being with someone else other than him bothers him to some degree.

He's still looking at the floor, but he has yet to move away from me.

I hold my breath, nervous to ask him my next question. "It bothered you to see his hands on me...where exactly did you mean?"

I ask him this because I'm still not completely convinced he's in this with me. I'm still not convinced he's been thinking about me.

He snaps his head up, lining up his gaze with mine. "Here,"

he whispers. He reaches behind me, sliding his hand across my lower back. His large palm shifts across the fabric of my dress, stopping at the curve of the base of my spine. He pulls me toward him, slamming my hips into his. He's already hard for me, and I gasp. His erection presses between my thighs.

My eyes flutter with the motion, reveling in the feeling I'm getting from it. It's exactly as I remember it.

"And here." He growls, lowering his hand and spreading his fingers across my ass cheek. His voice trembles against my body, and I swallow down the thickness of it.

His other arm is bent above me, caging me in, and I shift my gaze to his side, wondering if the elevator has decided to move. It hasn't. Instead, the door is shut, but the lift isn't moving. We've just been sitting here on the first floor.

"Twelve," I say.

"What?" he asks. I've pulled him out of his moment, but if I don't tell him which floor my room is on, someone will see us in here, or worse, join us.

I urge him with my eyes toward the button panel. He glances over his shoulder, but only long enough to reach behind him and press the number twelve. He taps the button, and then he's on me again. His arms are at either side of me, pressed against the wall. He's caging me in.

"It's been almost two years that we've kept our secret," I tell him. "I thought you would have forgotten enough by now to not even care that Levi had his hands on me. I wouldn't expect you to remember it anyway."

"Wow, Vada Beckett." He drags his finger down the center of my chest, drawing a line past my neck. He connects it to the start of the slit on my leg, placing his finger where he drew a circle on my skin on the dance floor. "I'm shocked you would think I could *ever* forget how it felt being with you. I haven't forgotten."

"Well, considering you've kept me away because of our deal and then what happened with Ryan..." I let my statement fall away. I hate that I'm even bringing this up right now, but his need to keep me at a distance has always been a point of contention for us, and I can't help the insecurity I feel surrounding the way Colton left things when Ryan died.

The ball has been in his court the whole time. It simply feels like he's placed it on the floor and walked away, leaving it to sit there untouched.

"My life is different now than it was then." He swallows, our breaths the only sound between us. I can see the sadness still in his eyes over losing Ryan so suddenly. "I'm sorry I disappeared after Ryan died."

"Don't." I lift my finger, pressing it against his mouth. I search his gaze, hoping I'll be able to find truth in his words.

I bite down on my lip, anticipating his reaction. Knowing he was jealous of Levi sparks a new sense of excitement in me. Knowing he's speaking the truth when he says his life is different than it was four months ago causes my stomach to flutter and my heart to nearly leap out of my chest. Maybe he is ready to move on.

I want to stand my ground and tell him he needs to decide. It's either all or nothing.

But now that he's standing here in front of me, I don't want him to disappear. He's real and he's here. His chest is against mine, and my legs are pressed between his. I don't want this to end before it's even started.

I loosen my hold on my bottom lip, and Colton's eyes move to it, watching my mouth as the next two words come out of it.

"Prove it."

With minimal effort, he returns his fingers to the slit of my dress and grins. "Challenge accepted."

CHAPTER FOURTEEN

Vada

Colton's hands have a way of bending me and molding me to whatever he wants me to be. I feel like a hardened piece of metal over a bright, hot flame. Once it reaches the right temperature, it can be made into just about anything. That's what Colton's hands do to me.

I always say I'm going to walk away, but I never do. I'm tired of fighting this. I'm tired of fighting the burning need that grows inside me for Colton.

His fingers slide under the fabric. I hold in a gasp as they work their way along my inner thigh. He shoves my dress aside. It bunches between my legs, and the second his hand touches the space between my thighs, I know he'll be able to feel exactly just how wet for him I am already.

The thing is, I want him to touch me. I hadn't realized just how much I've missed it, how much I've craved it. My need for his touch has been hiding in the dark, waiting for the moment he'd draw me out with the light.

Now here I am, panting and dying for him to kiss me.

We ride the entire twelve levels without him claiming my mouth with his. He's keeping me begging. I stand on my toes, pressing them into the cool tile. I tip my chin higher, attempting to bring my mouth closer to his. He stops me. A devilish smirk spreads across his mouth as he presses his finger to my lips. He clicks his tongue in disapproval, and my stomach skips a beat.

The moment is finally here, the moment I've imagined reliving for the past year and a half. Only this time, he's different.

Before, when Colton and I were together that night at the bar, we forged our secret, coming together in our grief. We were grieving the loss of my sister-in-law Hailey. We were grieving the ghost of a man Dallas had become. Colton wasn't gentle that night, but there was a vulnerability to him.

Tonight, he's different. He's vicious and primal in his movements. Darkness fills his eyes, jealous of what he watched Levi do to me. Overall, I didn't think Levi had pushed the boundary, but with the way Colton's body has reacted to mine, he believes a line was crossed.

We're nearly to the twelfth floor. I look over his shoulder at the ascending numbers, watching as it moves from nine to ten.

"Do you trust me?" he asks.

When my eyes move back to him, he's reaching up to his neck, unraveling the knot of his tie. His eyes soften a bit, and I can tell he's hoping for me to say yes. My heart is hammering away in my chest.

"Yes," I whisper. My voice wobbles with nerves. I completely and one hundred percent trust him. It's the anticipation of what he's planning that has my nerves all jumbled.

He removes his tie, sliding it out from under his collar in one move. It's teal, the same shade as my dress.

He grips both ends and raises it up to my face, placing it over my eyes. He gently pulls my head forward, tying it behind me. My vision shifts to nothing but darkness, and suddenly every other sense is on high alert.

Colton's scent fills my nose as I breathe him in. The burnt wood is stronger. His minty breath is more intense. Every single breath is louder than the one before it.

I'm listening for what he's going to do next. I can still feel him in front of me.

He rests his mouth near mine, ghosting his lips along the corner. I breathe in and hold my breath as he whispers against my skin. "I've had a long time to think about this."

The elevator chimes, and I hear the doors glide open. I wait for Colton to direct me where to go, gasping when his arms wrap around me and he lifts me over his shoulder.

His thick arms are wrapped around my legs as he carries me out of the elevator. His feet are muffled by the carpet. He stops after only a few steps, but he doesn't put me down.

"What room number?"

"Forty-three twenty."

He pauses for another moment then starts walking in the direction of my room. We don't talk as he carries me down the hall. My stomach is still bubbling, and there's a part of me that's thrilled by the idea of not knowing what his plans are. The sound of the hallway is intensely quiet. There's no other noise aside from our breathing. I grip Colton's suit jacket, fisting the fabric between my tightened fingers.

He suddenly stops then slowly lowers me. My back hits what I'm assuming is the door to my room.

"Where's your key?" His voice is smooth and deep.

I smirk and give him a small chuckle. I can't see where he is or if he's even still standing in front of me, but I lift my hand and drag my finger down the center of my chest. "You'll have to find it."

A loud sound pounds above my head. I can only assume it's Colton's hand pressed against the door because his other hand is quickly on me. He uses the tip of his finger to trace the neckline of my dress, a deep V that cuts down past the swell of my breasts.

"A scavenger hunt?" he asks. I don't answer him out loud, allowing him to explore me without any reservations. I nod as he lazily drags his hand across my chest, drawing a line from one breast to the other. His finger catches the corner of the key card I stuffed under the fabric of my dress. He grabs it, and I feel it get slowly dragged out.

"It's interesting," he says, "that you decided to keep it here all day."

"No pockets."

"Where's your phone?"

"In my room."

"Smart."

It's the only word he says before I hear the beep of the key card swiping in front of the lock on the door to my room behind me. I hold my breath, unsure of what he plans on doing next. So far everything has been completely unexpected.

I didn't necessarily imagine my night turning into a situation where I'm standing in the hallway blindfolded, completely at Colton's mercy.

I gasp when I feel his hands at my waist. He starts leading me backward into the room. I'm unsure where he's leading me. After a few more steps, he suddenly stops me. I try to imagine where we might be standing, but my thoughts are cloudy, blurred by thoughts of Colton.

"Do you still trust me?" he asks.

"Yes." Three deep, husky breaths are pressed from my chest. My skin is on fire. I can feel his eyes on me, deciding what to do.

"Good," he says into the hollow of my ear. Only this time, he's standing behind me. "Because I intend to punish you for your little lie about Levi."

Goosebumps break out across my skin, and I can feel myself getting more wet with every word he speaks into my ear.

"But don't worry," he adds. "I'll make sure you enjoy it." His chest is pressed against my body. He wraps a hand around each of my arms, sliding them down as far as he can reach, urging me to bend forward. "Place your hands here," he orders. "I want your palms flat."

I do as he says. The cold marble hits my hot, damp skin. I know exactly where we are now. My heart skips a beat realizing where.

Cool, crisp air hits my bare back as he steps away from me, and goosebumps break out across my skin as he unzips the back of my dress. He's slow and meticulous, a sharp difference from how I remember being with him the first time.

"I considered taking this at a different pace." He smooths his hand across my back as he allows the straps of my dress to slide off my shoulders. The fabric pools at my feet, and I'm left in nothing but my lace thong.

It sounded as if there were more to his statement, but his hand stops caressing my back and he hisses between his teeth. I'm assuming it's because I decided not to wear a bra underneath my dress. It didn't really go with this dress, and I figured I could pull it off without one.

Apparently, Colton agrees.

His hands wrap around my back. He flattens his hand and slides his palm under my arm, around to my breast. He finds my nipple and pinches it between two fingers. Now it's my turn to hiss.

I gasp and arch my back, pressing into Colton. I'm already looking for relief. My thighs tremble, and I can feel myself growing more wet for him the longer he drags this out. I both love it and hate it at the same time.

"You know, I'd have to guess you were hoping for this

tonight, with me. I mean, look at you." He slides his hand across my breast one more time, making sure to pinch my hardened nipple before dipping further down. He moves it all the way down my stomach before sliding under the waist of my thong. He teases my folds once with his fingers before parting me, finding my soaking-wet clit.

I gasp out a heavy breath and push back against him. His hardened cock is pressed against me. He's full and ready for me.

But he still takes his time. His hand starts working slow circles over me, and I start to curl my fingers onto the counter. I stand on my toes, searching for any sort of relief. It's as if I haven't been touched since that night with him two years ago. I mean, I've touched myself, imagining my hand was Colton, but it hasn't felt anywhere close to this.

He keeps his fingers pressed against my clit, his circles growing faster. With his other hand, he reaches up and slowly unravels the tie. He allows it to fall away from my face. It drops to the floor, and I look down, watching his hand on me.

"Oh, god," I say, digging my fingers into the counter. "I'm going to come."

"Look up." He grips my chin, forcing me to look up. "Not yet. Don't come yet."

"But I—" I inhale a shaky breath. "I need you, Colton. It's been too long."

Above the counter I'm leaning on, there's a tall mirror that nearly reaches the ceiling. My hotel room is quite modest for this hotel. It's not as fancy as the room I know Sloan and Dallas booked, but it fares nicely compared to some others I've stayed at in the past. This one includes a complete mini bar situated between the bedroom and bathroom. The counter isn't as tall as a kitchen counter, low enough for Colton to bend me over, like he has me now.

It takes a few seconds for my eyes to adjust, but when they

do, all I see is Colton standing behind me. His hand is between my legs. My arms are spread out and my palms are pressed flat against the counter, steadying my quivering legs. I'm weakening by the second, and if Colton doesn't stop soon, I'm going to fall apart all around him. He's everywhere, and I can't escape him, couldn't even if I wanted to.

I don't.

I'm still riding his hand when he moves his other one down to the waist of my thong. His eyes have darkened to a light shade of brown as he stares at my reflection in the mirror. I have a clear view of his face, and within seconds, his expression shifts into one of impatience. I can see the spark flaring up inside him. He can't wait any longer.

"Do you want to know why I removed your blindfold?" he asks.

I swipe my tongue across my lips and take in a deep breath, wondering how in the hell I'm supposed to carry on a conversation when his hand is holding me against his hardened cock. I roll my hips into him. "Um, I don't know. Why?" I squeeze my eyes shut, feeling myself starting to fall off the cliff to oblivion.

"Open your eyes," he orders.

My eyes snap open, and I find him staring at me.

"Because after two years, I wanted you to watch me fuck you. Now that I have you, maybe this time you won't forget so easily."

"I didn't forget." I pant and swallow a breath, hoping he feels the weight of my words.

He does.

"Well..." His lip curls. "For good measure, let's just make sure of it."

I bite down on my bottom lip and watch through the reflection in the mirror as he quickly wraps his fingers around the waist of my lace thong and slides it down my legs. It's now joined my dress at my feet.

I gasp, feeling the absence of his hands on me. A tingling sensation breaks out across my body.

He stands and removes his suit jacket then undoes the buttons to his shirt. He quickly removes it and tosses it off to the side of the room. He unbuckles his belt and his slacks. Once he has both of them undone, he removes his pants and boxer briefs in one smooth motion. His erection springs free, pressing against me from behind. Feeling his skin against mine lights my soul up.

I'm a firecracker ready to explode. I'm missing his fingers on me, but as I watch him center himself behind me, I'm missing the way it feels to have him inside me.

He grips the back of my hair, lifting my chin up to face him through the mirror. He leans forward and presses one soft kiss to my back before wrapping my hair around his fist. His kiss is like a mark on my skin. I can feel it long after he pulls away.

"That's the last time I'll be gentle."

I swallow, allowing his gaze to shoot straight for my chest. My eyes are pinned to his when he pulls back. He grabs his cock and pushes into me in one quick motion. I grip the edge of the counter as he suddenly fills me. He's thick, and the sensation is nearly too much for me when he pulls back out, slamming into me again.

A raspy groan escapes my throat and I tilt my head back, watching Colton move behind me. Every thrust I watch him make behind me feels as if he's burying himself impossibly deeper inside me.

This time it's completely different than the last.

With one hand, I reach behind me, gripping Colton's waist. My nails scrape against his skin before I place it back on the counter. "I need you, Colton."

"You want more?"

"Yes." I moan, biting down on my lip, stifling a cry that's most likely going to come out if I don't try to temper it.

"Well," he says breathlessly, "I did say I wasn't going to be gentle."

He pulls out then pushes back in.

Out.

In.

Harder.

Deeper.

I start pressing my hips back, slamming them against his. His body is damp and hot as he works me. The loud clap of our bodies meeting with every thrust echo across the otherwise quiet hotel room. My toes start to go numb, the promise of an orgasm on its way. I tilt my head up and stand on my toes, making sure to catch Colton's gaze in the reflection. I tighten around him. My breasts bounce with every thrust, and the more I stare into his eyes, the faster we move. We start to move together as one. My hips roll into his waist, and his body molds to mine, pinning me against him.

Now, in this moment, I'm thankful Colton decided to wear contacts. For the first time, I feel like I can truly see what he's feeling inside.

His thoughts about me are clear. He's burned for me just as much as I have for him.

One.

Two.

Three more thrusts. Tiny explosions burst across my skin as I reach my orgasm. I press my chest to the counter, keeping my hands pressed to it. Colton continues moving inside me as my body quivers, riding out my orgasm.

"Come on, Colton," I tell him, feeling his cock swell within me. It only makes my orgasm that much better.

"Fuck, Vada. I'm coming." His thrusts suddenly stop, and

his hands are on my waist, holding me as his cock throbs inside me.

Once he's finished, he pulls out of me. I still haven't moved from the counter. When he places his hand on my back, I realize I haven't moved. My arms and legs feel like Jell-O. They're also completely numb.

I stand, and Colton gently turns me around. His soft touch is a nice relief from how we both were just now.

He grabs my hand and leads me over to the bed. I fall backward, the soft fluffy sheets billowing around me. He climbs over me, hands beside my head, caging me in. He leans down, bringing his face close to mine.

His lips are dangerously close, and when I think about it, he still hasn't kissed me. Not once.

But that notion doesn't last long when he ghosts his lips across mine. "Now, this is one thing I haven't forgotten."

He leans down and presses his lips to mine. At first, he's soft, possibly making up for what he just did to me against the mini bar. Then he leans in deeper, claiming my mouth with his. He tastes like mint but sweeter.

He coaxes my mouth open with his tongue, sliding it along my lips. I reach up and wrap my hand around the back of his head, willing myself to never forget this moment.

SECRET #3

Secrets always have a way of revealing themselves.

CHAPTER FIFTEEN

COLTON

It's impossible to remember every single solitary moment in your life. As humans, we typically tend to only remember those that define our lives, like when we graduate high school, when we lose our virginity, or when we fulfill our dream of opening our own business.

Those are the moments we remember the most, and I just added one more to that list. It's been impossible for me to forget the night I had with Vada two years ago, but I have to say this night has miraculously topped that one.

It was a foolish move to come up behind her on the dance floor after Levi walked away, but something came over me. It was as if someone else hijacked my body, willing it to take the steps forward to claim what I've wanted for so long.

Watching Levi with Vada was enough to set my heart on fire, but then when I confronted her in the elevator and she told me he wasn't her date just as much as Trinity wasn't mine, all bets were off.

I was ready to make her mine, finally—regardless of my parents' disapproval.

I'm twenty-six years old and don't necessarily need it, but I can't deny that I've had a habit of seeking it out all my life. I only ever wanted to please my dad, regardless of what it cost me. I know he doesn't approve of me having Dallas as my business partner, and he already warned me to stay away from Vada for whatever fucking reason.

But I no longer care. Being with Vada makes my heart want to jump out of my chest. She gives me tunnel vision. Nothing else matters when I'm with her.

We're still lying on top of the bed in her hotel room. We haven't even bothered getting under the sheets. My dick twitches at the memory of being inside Vada only minutes ago. Her arms are wrapped around me, and her cheek is pressed against my chest.

At first, I think she might be asleep. Her hushed breaths are slow, moving with the steady rhythm of her body, making me think she could be, but now I know she isn't. She's drawing invisible lines across my chest.

I tilt my chin up and stare at the ceiling.

"What are you thinking about?" she asks.

I frown in thought and thread my fingers through one of her curls. "Nothing in particular."

"I don't know why, but I find that hard to believe." She laughs.

"It's stupid." I groan, turning to look out the window. In the distance I can see the lights of downtown Austin. Even though we're just outside the city limits, it still feels like a world away.

"Now, I definitely find *that* hard to believe." She sits up, resting her chin against the back of her hand. Her palm is pressed against my chest, over my ribs. "Why don't you try me?"

Her eyes are tired, but I can tell she's satisfied. This is the first time we've ever been this way, lying naked in a bed together, just talking. We've never been able to do this before.

I squeeze my eyes shut and raise my free hand, rubbing my

eyes with my fingertips. I then run my palm across my forehead, pushing my hair up. I leave my fingers threaded through the strands as I stare at the ceiling.

I run my other hand along the smooth curve of Vada's back. She's still staring at me, waiting for me to answer her.

For a moment, when I catch her gaze, I spot a hint of fear in it, or maybe it's worry—worry that I'm questioning what we've just done, worry that I'm regretting it. I gently press my fingers into her flesh, willing her to stay, a silent promise that it isn't what she thinks it is. Her body molds to mine perfectly, as if she was meant to be next to me all this time.

She sighs and closes her eyes briefly, allowing herself to savor my touch.

"I went to see my parents for the first time since the funeral," I confess.

I hate that I'm thinking about this right now. I hate that my mind has wandered to the main reason I've kept Vada away from me all this time. It was a stupid and foolish decision. I allowed it to cloud my mind for so long, never quite understanding that they had a big part in it. My own grief and fear of disappointment nearly drowned me.

"Oh," she says, surprised by me bringing them up. I can't deny how it's been weighing on me lately, as much as I fucking hate that it is. "Don't you usually go to see them every weekend?"

"I do." I sigh, thinking back on the last time I was there, my mother's vacant eyes and my father's disapproving stare. "But I haven't been since then."

"Do you want to talk about it? It's obviously bothering you if you're bringing it up now."

I've only talked to Vada about my parents in vague terms. I've never told her about my father's shady business dealings, how he's always been the one to pressure me into finishing business school, or how he feels about her and Dallas.

She does, however, know about the loss our family has felt from Ryan's death. She also knows how, in many ways, it's part of the reason there's tension between us.

"Not really," I tell her. It's the honest truth. I don't want to talk about my parents when I have Vada lying next me. I swallow down my thoughts and push them to the back. I tie them to a cinder block and toss it into the ocean of thoughts filling my brain. I shouldn't have brought it up in the first place.

"Okay," Vada says. There's a hint of disappointment in her voice, and I know why. She was hoping I was going to open up to her. She was hoping I was going to share more with her, but it's hard to share their opinion of her when I know all it will do is hurt her.

"I shouldn't have brought it up." I'm quick to recover. "I don't know why I said it just now."

"Because you were thinking about it." Her mouth curls into a devilish smirk, and I resist the urge to lean forward and smother it with my own mouth.

Instead, I reach down and playfully smack her ass. My palm stings, and she yelps as her eyes spark with excitement. She likes it when I play with her. She likes it when I'm forward. Her smile fades, and so does mine.

"Basically, they pulled the same shit they always do." I sigh. "My father was condescending, and my mother was oblivious to the entire world around her, including me. I just decided I wasn't going to take it anymore, so I left."

I can feel Vada's expression change against me. She winces, knowing my mother's rejection stings worse than my father's.

"I don't think it's your mother's intention to be the way she is. Maybe she can't help it."

"You're probably right." I resist the urge to roll my eyes. "She never does anything intentionally."

"I'm sure she's still in there. She probably lost her way and just needs to be found again."

I want to smile. Vada always has a way with words. She always has a way of taking on a different perspective, even if she has a smart mouth half the time. "You might be right. Again."

We lie in silence for a while, allowing it to settle in our bones.

"I should shoot Sloan or Dallas a text," Vada says, cutting our silence. "Don't you think they're wondering where we are?" She presses her mouth to my skin. She doesn't move, simply keeps it pressed there, soaking in the warmth of my body touching hers. She rolls to rest her cheek on me. "We kind of dipped out without telling them."

"You're right. We did." I think back to when I pinned her against the wall in the elevator and used my tie as a blindfold, the way her bottom lip separated from her top as she breathed me in. She enjoyed being blindfolded, and the thought that she put her trust in me completely made my dick grow even harder. She looked fucking sexy in that tight dress with my tie wrapped around her.

"What time is it?" she asks.

I glance up at the clock hanging on the wall across from the bed we're lying on.

"Ten o'clock."

"Well, shit." She laughs. Her body quakes against mine, and the feeling it gives me shoots straight to my dick.

"What?"

"They're probably still partying down there. I thought it was later than it is."

"Nope," I tell her, threading my fingers through her hair. "It's definitely not."

"Do you think they've noticed we're gone?"

I frown, thinking on it. "I'm not sure. I would normally say yes, but from the way they appeared, they looked like they'd had quite a bit to drink already, and they might be eager to get to their own hotel room."

"Well." She sits up and licks her lips. "I'm not exactly eager to get back, either."

"You aren't?"

"No." She shakes her head then attempts to roll off of me, reaching for her phone on the nightstand. "But I should probably text them anyway."

I grab her waist, pulling her back. "Not so fast."

She wraps her bare leg around my body and crawls on top of me. She pins both of her legs against my waist and stares down at me. My dick hardens, taking in the sight of her above me.

Her warm center presses against my stomach, still wet from me being inside her. Her ass rocks against my dick. She isn't realizing just how much she's teasing me with the tiny flicks of her hips.

I press both of my hands onto her hips. The longer I hold them there, the more dramatic her movements become until she's fully rocking her hips back and forth over me. She bites down on her bottom lip.

"Can I ask you something?" she asks.

"Always." I fight back a groan as I take in her body. Her breasts are on full display for me, gently bouncing with her movements. Her nipples are hardened into two pebbles.

"Did you ever think about our timing?"

I stare up at her with confusion. "Timing?"

"Yeah." She tilts her head back and closes her eyes before rolling her head back to look down at me. Her breathing is starting to pick up, every word heavy. "I mean, do you ever wonder what could have been between us if the timing had been better? Like with my career and your school?"

I swallow, feeling her words shoot straight to my chest. She's beautiful as she sits on top of me wearing nothing but her emotions. She's revealing her deepest thoughts to me, and I'm wondering if she's even noticed just how vulnerable she is right now. Her words cut me deep. My chest twists with an ache for a life we haven't been living these past two years.

The constant back and forth, the fear of disapproval from a family who will always disapprove no matter my circumstances...

"I have."

Her eyes stare right into mine, and her hips slow as she digests my words.

"I'm sorry I couldn't before," I continue, "but I'm trying to do better. I'm trying to live the life I want to live. Not for others, but for myself."

She bends, bringing her face closer to mine. Her curly hair falls to the side of her face, the ends dancing across my ribs. Her long brown hair combined with her smooth tan skin and the city lights in the distance is doing something to me.

"Good answer." Then she leans even further, bringing her mouth close. She presses her lips against mine, and the longer she holds them against my mouth, the harder she presses. I lift my hand and hold it against the back of her hair, keeping her pressed against me. She tastes sweet and exactly how I remember. I part her lips with my tongue and entangle it with hers.

I moan against her mouth, my dick growing even harder for her. I wrap my arm around her, keeping her pressed against me as I roll her over. She lands against the mattress with her legs wrapped tightly around my waist.

She loosens them enough for me to pull away from her. I bite on her lip once before sitting up. My knees are bent between her legs, and I drag my fingers across her jaw, drawing invisible lines down her neck to her collarbone. Her eyes flutter closed, and her chest rises as I go deeper. The white light from the moon and city lights in the distance highlight the curves of her body. Her skin glows and my chest expands with warmth.

It's absolutely terrifying.

After I trace lines across her collarbones, I lazily drag my hands to the round curves of her breasts. Her nipples pebble under my fingertips, and her back arches off the mattress. She swipes her tongue across her swollen lip and inhales a sharp breath, reacting to my touch.

Chills prickle across her skin as I circle around her nipple one more time before sliding my hands down to her thighs. Her pussy is wet for me again the second I press my dick against her. I don't push myself inside. Instead, I rock myself against her folds, teasing her.

My hands are on her knees, holding her legs up for me. She clamps them around my ribs, wanting to keep me close, but I have other plans.

"Does that feel good?" I ask her.

"Mmm." She nods, pulling in her bottom lip. She raises her hands to her chest and starts to massage her breasts. Using her own fingers, she pinches her nipples, moaning as she tugs on them before letting them go. "I want you inside me," she says.

"In a little bit," I tell her, lowering myself. I lift her legs over my shoulders, bringing my face closer to her pussy. She opens her eyes and stares down at me as I look up at her with hooded eyes. "I want to taste you first."

CHAPTER SIXTEEN

Vada

Work is the last place I want to be.

Ever since the night of the wedding two weeks ago, I've had trouble staying here for my usual nine to five. The newsroom has been busy gearing up for the summer.. In combination with it being an election year, the city is also hosting multiple music festivals, as it does every year.

My boss, Nate, has been on edge, asking us to stay late nearly every day and calling large whole-office meetings every day. Those days run especially long.

I'm sitting at the opposite end of the table from Nate. He's standing in front of his chair as usual, going over everyone's assignments. The sleeves of his white button-down are rolled up to his elbows, and there's a small stain near the collar. He's a mess, but surprisingly he hasn't missed a beat. He's stressed, but it isn't unusual for someone in his position. Editor-in-chief carries a lot of weight in our industry.

A weight I wish to carry.

Levi is sitting beside me, intently taking notes. He hasn't looked up much since our meeting started. Three seats down from him, Cassidy is scrolling through her phone. From what I can tell, she hasn't been paying much attention to our boss' speech on why we need to be the first to scoop the story on the upcoming state senator.

In between my own notes, I've been scribbling circles on my notepad, waiting for the meeting to wrap up before our lunch break. I'm hoping to see Colton at some point today.

Since Sloan and Dallas have been away celebrating their honeymoon in Nashville, Colton has been pulling double shifts at the restaurant. I offered my own help, but aside from one day, my boss hasn't given me much time. I've simply stretched myself too thin. By the time I'm out of here, I'm exhausted.

My phone vibrates across the table. Levi looks up from his notepad long enough to give me a curious eye before turning his attention back to his notes.

Colton: Are you still able to meet for lunch?

Another text comes in as I'm reading the first.

Colton: I'm hungry.

He follows his text with a wink face emoji.

I fight back the urge to laugh at the same time the space between my legs heats. My cheeks blush, thinking about his mouth on me. I clench my thighs together and look out the conference room window. The sun is blocked by the building across the street, but some of the rays filter through. Half the room is filled with bright yellow and white light.

I swallow and pick up my phone, responding to Colton.

Me: Hungry, huh?

Colton: Starving.

Colton: I'm free for lunch for about an hour before I need to get back.

Me: I'm not sure I'll be able to leave. I have several articles I need to go over.

Me: If you're up for it, you can meet me here in the office for lunch.

I set my phone down and pick up my pen, tapping it against my notebook. I half listen as Nate wraps up the last of the meeting. My phone vibrates on the table again.

Colton: Be there in thirty.

"Alright, everyone. That's all I have for you right now." Nate claps his hands together and inhales a deep breath. "I want all of you to have your work turned in to Vada by tomorrow. I know there's a lot going on right now, but the news never sleeps, so neither do we."

Everyone rolls their eyes and groans, standing from their chairs. They're quick to rush out of the meeting room, pouring out through the tall glass doors.

I grab my notebook and pen, pushing myself out of the room as fast as possible as well. If I want any free time to talk to Colton while we eat, I'll need to check my emails before he gets here. I push through the doors and am heading to my office when Cassidy sidles up beside me.

"Oh my gosh, I thought that meeting would never end."

"Me either." I laugh.

"You seem to be in a good mood today."

I look over at her, keeping up with my steps. I didn't realize how much I've been smiling, but now that Cass has mentioned it, I know what she's talking about. My steps are quicker, and my entire body feels lighter.

"I am in a good mood." I give her another smile.

We reach my desk and I sit in my chair, refreshing my computer and pulling up my email.

"I take it you and Colton are doing good then."

It wasn't until a few days ago that I filled Cassidy in on what's happened between me and Colton. She hasn't said much about it since I told her.

"We are." I can't help it. I grin like I haven't grinned in over two years.

"Good." Her eyes sparkle with happiness for me.

She gently leans against the door frame to my office. Since I've been here for more than eight months and proven my loyalty to Nate and the paper, I moved my desk from the news floor to a full-size corner office. Other than getting a nice view of the city, I also have a new computer. Even my chair has been upgraded.

"How's Jonah doing?" I ask her. I haven't seen him in over two weeks, ever since his last T-ball practice. Cassidy said I could see him whenever I had a chance, but I haven't hardly had a free moment. My life has become a constant flow of article after article, edit after edit. I miss the buddy I made over the past few months.

"He's doing great. He's been talking about how he misses you and the little ice cream trips you would take together."

"Oh no." I scrunch my nose. "He spilled the beans? It was supposed to be our little secret."

Cassidy giggles. "He definitely did. You should know better. That kid can't keep a secret for anything, especially when it comes to ice cream."

"Right." I sigh, leaning back in my chair. I start sifting through my emails, tossing out any that are obviously junk. I glance at the time displayed in the corner of my screen. Colton will most likely be here any minute.

"Speaking of Jonah," Cassidy says, "I've been meaning to ask you."

I shift my attention from my computer to her. "What's up?"

"Well, a couple out in Waco wants to hire me to take pictures of their wedding."

"Really?"

"Yeah." She chuckles. "I had a ton of fun shooting your brother's wedding and put a sample picture on my Instagram. The couple reached out to me because they saw it and loved it.

Their original photographer had to cancel, so they asked if I could fill in last minute. They're offering to pay me a good amount, and I could use the money since my dad needs his knee surgery. We've been kind of short, so I couldn't turn it down."

"Of course." I shake my head, understanding where she's coming from. "I get it. That's awesome that you're finding freelance work on the side."

"Thanks." She gives me a relaxed smile. "My dad can't get around as much until the surgery because of his knee and I'll need to stay through the weekend, so I was wondering..." She winces as if she's nervous to even ask. "If Jonah might be able to stay with you. It would just be for the two days."

"Are you kidding?" I don't hesitate. "Of course he can stay with me."

Her shoulders fall, and she sighs with relief. "Thank you so much. I was hoping you wouldn't mind. Jonah loves you."

"Aw." I grin, my chest warming at the thought. "I love that kid, too. I'll make sure he has a ton of fun."

"Great. I'll let my dad know."

"Okay." I start to click on my mouse, resuming sifting through my emails.

"I meant it," Cassidy says. "You do seem happier."

"Thanks." I stop clicking and give her a genuine smile. It's true; I am happier. It's as if the pent-up feelings I've had for Colton have now been released and I'm able to show them.

I haven't talked to Dallas about where that leaves me and Colton. I'm not entirely sure how he's going to take the news of whatever it is that's going on between Colton and me. As far as I know, he'd be happy as long as I am. But even if I were to tell my brother I was falling for his best friend, I wouldn't even know how to describe it because I don't know where Colton and I stand.

In the elevator at the wedding, he confessed he's changed

since the last time we visited the topic of being together. I gave him an ultimatum then: either give me all or give me nothing. I wouldn't settle for any less. But I guess with time, my strength when it came to Colton weakened.

Worry settles in my chest, directly behind the delight at how great things have been going for us lately. Even though we've both been incredibly busy with work, Colton has still managed to carve time out for me, and that means a ton coming from him. For the first time, he's managed to make me a priority, and the fear of losing him before I've truly had him is the one reason I haven't brought up the subject of where we stand.

"Hey, Vada. Can I talk to you for a minute?" Nate appears in the doorway to my office, standing beside Cassidy. She raises her eyebrows at me before giving Nate a nod and heading back to her own office.

"Sure." I click out of my emails. My phone vibrates across my desk, but I ignore it, wondering why Nate has decided to come to my office.

"I've just put Gallagher on a story about one of the local vape shops that started selling CBD products. It's a big controversy with the state right now, and every newspaper, reporter, you name it are after this story. Anyway, I told him to get it to you by this afternoon. I know you already have a ton going on, but I'm going to need you to stay and have this polished by tonight. I want to have the story posted and running tomorrow."

I bite the inside of my cheek as my stomach sinks. My eyes are sore and my head pounds as I stare at Nate standing in my doorway. I'm wondering how in the hell I'm going to have the energy to stay late tonight editing an entire fucking article. I hope to hell Gallagher doesn't take his time getting his story to me.

I tighten my grip on my mouse but give my boss a reassuring

smile. As much as I hate how much work Nate is putting on my plate, he still beats my last boss. At least he's kind.

"Sure thing."

Nate taps his fingers on the door frame before walking away, happy to have me agree so easily.

I sigh and fight back the urge to ball my hands into fists. I grab my phone from my desk to see why it vibrated when Nate showed up at my door. My stomach sinks even further and my chest twists when I see Colton's name above a text.

Colton: Shit, I'm sorry, babe. I won't be able to meet you for lunch. We just got a major lunch rush, and I can't leave the kitchen understaffed. I promise I'll make it up to you.

I drop my phone to my desk and put my head in my hands. As much as I try to ignore the familiar pit growing in the bottom of my stomach, I can't stop the thoughts running through my mind.

Colton's text has me feeling like I've spoken too soon. Maybe he isn't ready to fit me into his life. Even though I know his work has been consuming him just as much as mine has me, I can't stop the fear that maybe it hasn't. We spent too long with Colton holding me at a distance. I've always said I would never settle for second best, but before the night of Dallas' wedding, I wasn't even second.

And the more I let that thought sink in, the more I start to wonder if that fear will ever go away.

ALL THE LIGHTS on the entire office floor are turned off with the exception of my office. City lights pour in through my blinds. I don't have them completely open, but I kept them set in a way that still offers some outside light aside from the one in my office.

Cassidy offered to stay and keep me company while I edit Gallagher's article, but I told her not to bother. I wasn't entirely sure how long it was going to take, and I didn't want her staying too late, not when she has her dad and nephew to help take care of.

I'm near the end of the article when I hear the elevator doors open. A pinging sound echoes across the empty space. They're located on the opposite side of the floor from where my office is. A chill prickles its way down the back of my neck, and my heart drops.

I don't know why I get so nervous. My mind automatically goes to the most dramatic scenario. Actually, I know exactly why it does: all those fucking investigation shows I watch. Murders, people who go missing—it's awful yet addicting.

I inhale a deep breath, telling myself it's probably someone from the office or one of the cleaning crew members. I lean to the side, looking around my computer and through my open office door to see who it is. I don't see anyone. The entire floor is silent and empty.

I stand and walk over to the door, peeking out to see if anyone is sitting in their office or cubicle. When I don't see anyone, I turn back and head toward my desk. Only a few more paragraphs to go over and I'll be able to leave.

I nearly make it to my chair before two arms wrap around me, pulling me to their chest. I scream, the blood draining from my face. A hand covers my mouth, stifling my voice.

When the other hand spins me around, I want to cry with relief.

He lowers his hand and laughs, showing me his delicious grin.

"What the fuck, Colton? You scared the shit out of me."

"I know." He laughs. "I'm sorry, but it was too tempting. This place is a ghost town."

"Whatever." I straighten the waist of my skirt. I'm wearing my favorite pale pink button-down tucked into my black leather skirt. I'm wearing a matching pair of black heels, but I took them off near the end of the day. I couldn't stand wearing them after moving all over the floor today.

My bare feet pad across the tile floor as I move to go back to my desk, but Colton stops me. His hand wraps around my arm, pulling me back to face him. He's still wearing his Dallas' t-shirt and faded, torn jeans. His hair looks like he's run his hands through it several times today, yet the ends still rest perfectly across his forehead. My eyes meet his, taking in the warm honey color that seems to shoot straight to my chest, connecting every cell in my body. He isn't wearing his glasses again, opting to wear his contacts instead. Him choosing those over his glasses seems to be happening more frequently.

His glasses haven't bothered me in the past, but I've grown to appreciate him without them. It's as if he's giving me access to a deeper part of himself that I can't see when he's wearing his glasses. He's more vulnerable this way.

"I'm sorry I had to back out of lunch." His eyes sadden with regret as he lifts his hand, tracing the line of my cheek with his finger. The fear I have of Colton disappearing at any time still rests in the back of my mind, but his apology soothes my worry for now, pushing it further back.

"That's okay." I swallow the tiredness threatening to overtake my body. "I've had a lot of work to do anyway. I've been going over this article for one of my reporters. I'm almost finished."

"Okay." He gives me a soft smile and wraps his hand around

the back of my neck, threading his fingers through my hair. "I'm also not sure how I feel about you being here all by yourself this late."

I twist my mouth into a smirk and nudge him with my hand. "I'm fine. Besides, you and Dallas are the ones always teasing me for being paranoid. Now you're the one who is worried?"

"I do worry about you." He lets out a small laugh. It's barely above a whisper, but I don't miss how, despite the lightness in his voice, his body has turned rigid and tense. He stiffens his shoulders and flexes the muscles of his arms as he presses his fingers into the back of my neck.

His words shoot straight through me. He's genuinely worried about me, thinking of how I'm spending my evening holed up in my office alone. I realize Colton has made me a priority, something he couldn't have done before.

He pulls me forward, claiming my mouth. His lips press against mine. He isn't gentle, pouring his kiss into me as if he's making up for every minute he missed seeing me today. He's making up for backing out on meeting me. He's making up for the fact that I'm here in my office, alone, scouring an article.

Every bit of my fear from earlier is dissolved the second he parts my lips with his tongue. He tastes like mint and smells like burning wood. He smells like home. The scent alone warms my stomach, shooting straight between my legs. I clench my thighs, heat spreading across them.

I'm already wet for him, and he's barely touched me.

His other hand slides down my back as he continues kissing me. He grips my waist and moves me backward until my lower back hits the edge of my desk.

"Seriously," I say against his mouth. "I'm almost done and then we can head out."

"You know..." His lips move against mine as he pushes me

back. I'm sitting on the edge of my desk when he stands between my legs. "I never did get to eat lunch."

"Is that so?" The bottom of my skirt rides up my thighs, digging into my flesh. Colton smooths his hands across my bare legs, working his fingers under the leather.

"Yeah." He nods, still keeping his mouth against mine. I drag my hands across his arms, savoring the way my fingers move over the subtle curves of his flexed muscles.

The hand he's kept around the back of my neck moves to the front. He presses his palm against the delicate flesh as I tip my head back. He's rough and gentle at the same time, a signature I've learned.

He keeps me on the edge of the desk but uses his hand on my neck to push me backward. I lean back on my hands, straightening my arms at my sides. Dragging the hand on my neck down, he pops open the first three buttons of my shirt. I gasp as his fingers ghost along my skin, causing goosebumps to spread.

"Colton." I swallow and try to keep up with my thoughts. "I need to tell you something."

"What is it?" he asks, drawing invisible lines across my skin.

"I need you to know that your touch..." I lick my lips again, feeling his hand drift over my breast, teasing my nipple. "Sets me on fire."

Fisting the end of my skirt, he pushes it up my thighs, revealing my entire legs. The cool air of my office teases at my hot center, begging for Colton to keep me warm. He doesn't waste any time. I lift myself off my desk high enough for him to remove my panties. After I sit back down, he slides them down my legs. He balls them into his hand and shoves them into the pocket of his jeans.

"Did you just—" He presses his finger to my mouth, stopping me from finishing.

"Sshh."

My heart thrashes inside my chest at the thought of him keeping them. I've never had a man do that before, and surprisingly, it turns me on even more.

Fire grows in my belly as he kneels on the floor. He looks up, pinning his stare to mine. They're steeled and firm as if he's on a mission, knowing exactly what he wants to do.

He's still kneeling in front of me when he lifts my legs, resting them on each of his shoulders. With his eyes still on mine, he lifts his hand and drags his index finger between my folds. He doesn't put any pressure on me, which makes me pull back due to how sensitive his skin feels against mine. He might as well be dragging a feather across my skin.

He leans forward, blowing a small amount of air on me, teasing me. I writhe above him. I press my legs into his shoulders and his neck, begging him to keep going.

I moan, arching my back on the desk, and let out a low hiss between my teeth. My nipples are taut against the cold air rushing over them, and I lie flat back onto my desk. I pinch them between my fingertips, a tingling sensation creeping down my entire body.

My heels dangle as they hang behind Colton, but once he presses his lips to me, I clench my legs, pressing my calves against his back.

"Oh, fuck." I cover my mouth and moan against my fingers, remembering we're in my office. There's no one here other than us, but the idea that we're somewhere usually driven with madness makes me more cautious. The city lights from afar shine down on Colton's brown hair. I grip the ends as he slides his tongue between my folds, tasting me.

He moans, sending a shivering vibration through me. His mouth is warm, and the tip of his tongue circles my clit several times before he sucks on me. He's both sharp and soft in his movements. The bit of pain that comes with his sucking is quickly soothed by the lapping of his tongue. He pulls away.

"You're delicious, Vada." He comes back, sliding his tongue again. Up and down. Down then up before circling again.

My neck heats and my muscles tense. I'm already nearing my orgasm. I try to pull away from Colton, wanting him to be inside me. I start imagining his dick filling me, pumping in and out, taking me for all that I am on my own desk amongst Gallagher's fucking article.

My computer screen comes to life, shining a bright blue-white light across us. Colton's tan skin pales in it, and the vision of him looking up at me with hooded eyes as he works me with his tongue sends me over the edge. Every single fiber of my being ignites into tingles, and sparks burst across my body.

"Colton." I breathe out his name. My chest expands, and it feels as if my heart is going to explode right out of it. I tug on the ends of his hair harder and push his mouth against me. I'm slick and wet and hot.

Then it happens. My legs shake and quiver against his sturdy frame. His muscles contract as he places his hands on my thighs, keeping me pressed against him as he works out the last bit of my orgasm.

When I'm finished, my legs fall slack against him, and my chest works harder to catch my breath. Rising to stand, Colton hovers above me. His smooth lips glisten in the computer light. He hasn't attempted to wipe his mouth. Instead, he leans over me, bringing his face close to mine.

Only then does he lean forward all the way, pressing his mouth to mine. It's the first time I've ever tasted myself. It brings heat to my cheeks and a slow burn to my chest. I smile against his lips.

"Are you full and satisfied now?" I ask him.

He pulls away and considers my question, but only for a

moment. "Not exactly." He shakes his head. "That was only the appetizer, babe."

I wrap my legs around the back of his legs, pressing my calves against him. He starts to unbutton his jeans, freeing himself from the constraint. His erection springs free, standing perfectly straight. I sit up. My breasts fall free from my shirt, but I don't care. I wrap my hand around his length, stroking him up and down. He tilts his head back, up to the ceiling, inhaling a sharp hiss like I did a few minutes ago.

"Fuck, Vada." He grinds his hips into my motions. He starts moving with me, but I'm caught off guard when he bends down and possesses my mouth with his. His kiss is hard and rushed, as if he's pouring every thought he's ever had about me into it. "I need you now."

He quickly pulls away from my mouth and gently presses against my chest, urging me to lie back to give him access. I stare up at him with hooded eyes, anticipating his next move.

He pulls back, centering himself in front of me, then pushes into me with one thrust. His thick length fills me completely. He pauses for a few seconds, and his eyes meet mine. They're soft as they roam over my features, as if he's working to memorize them, or maybe he's trying to memorize what my face looks like when he's inside me.

I inhale a deep breath as he pulls back until the tip of his cock is the only part still inside me. He pushes back in, and a tightening sensation pulls at the bottom of my stomach with pleasure.

He doesn't take his eyes off me as he moves his hips back and forth, slamming into me over and over. I open my eyes and allow him full access to me, every part of me.

The more he pushes into me and the closer we both get to reaching our orgasms, the more I start to wonder when it all changed for us. I try to pinpoint the moment that made Colton decide to give us a chance, but when I finally do fall apart underneath him, I can't come up with a cohesive thought, at least not one that doesn't involve the feeling I get when he places his lips against mine.

This is perfect.

CHAPTER SEVENTEEN

COLTON

"How was it?" I lift one of the cardboard boxes from the back of Dallas' truck and walk it into the back of the restaurant. We decided to close today for inventory and to fully replenish our stock, buying several boxes of produce from the local farmer's market. It probably isn't the best move financially, but the business needed it. I also haven't spent time with Dallas one on one in what feels like forever. Between his wedding and honeymoon and the running of the restaurant, we haven't seen much of each other unless it's to talk about work.

"Honestly, man, I didn't want to come back."

"Really?" I scrunch my nose and dip my eyebrows. "You just went to Nashville—how different could it be from here?"

"Oh," he says matter-of-factly, "it's different. The music scene is incredible out there, and the barbecue is pretty good."

"Not as good as ours though, right?" I give him a fake scowl, not caring that he dared to try another place's barbecue.

"Of course not." He chuckles and sits at the end of his tailgate, wiping his hands across the top of his pants. The sun reflects in his blue eyes as he stares up at me.

I still haven't told him about me and Vada. Guilt settles in my bones, realizing I've never mentioned it to him. For all I know, Dallas has no clue I've had a thing for his sister since the moment he introduced me to her, or that I've been sleeping with her for the past three weeks.

I never even told him about the secret we've kept for the past couple of years.

"I will say though," he continues, "it isn't as weird as Austin. You can't beat this place."

"No." I laugh, shaking my head. "You can't."

I grab another box from his tailgate and carry it over before coming back. He's still sitting on the edge, resting his arm over the side of the bed. His black metal ring glints in the sunlight.

"How does it feel?" I nod toward his ring. Dallas and I used to never discuss our relationships. When I first met him in college, he was already dating his first wife, Hailey. They weren't married yet, but they were inseparable. As for me, I wasn't in a relationship as serious as Dallas and Hailey's, but I was hardly ever alone. For me, it was more about sticking to one woman, committing to her long enough to fulfill what I now know are my father's dreams and ambitions. They were never mine. I drove out all possibilities of caring about someone more than myself because of my father.

Where I've lacked in doing that even once until now, Dallas has managed to do it twice.

He looks at his hand and lowers it to his lap, twisting his ring between his fingers. "It's great. I know people always say this kind of shit, but it's true—I don't know how I got so lucky."

"Me either." I give him a smirk and sit beside him on the tailgate. It's eerily quiet inside the restaurant since we're closed. The door is propped open, and the music from inside is hushed. Faint sounds of country music filter out to where we're sitting on the back of his truck. "I'm just messing with you. You know we all love Sloan. I don't know how she did it, but she inserted herself into our lives fairly effortlessly."

"She really did." Dallas nods, looking down at his hands with a grin. "Vada did a great job suggesting you hire her when you did. Otherwise, I probably would have avoided her every chance I got when I left my house. Actually, for a while there, I did."

Silence grows between us, and I can tell he's thinking back to that day, the day Vada convinced me to hire Sloan, not to mention Sloan herself.

"What about you?"

"What about me?" I play it off as if I don't know what he's getting at.

"Come on." He grunts, pushing off the tailgate. "You used to try to talk to me all the time about my dating life after Hailey. I think it's only fair I give you the same shit." He drags a few logs of wood out from the bed, behind where he was sitting on the tailgate. He carries them over to the smoker, setting them in the bin beside it before walking back over to grab another few logs.

"I guess." I shrug, helping him with the wood.

I've never been nervous about Dallas finding out about me and Vada. I've never been nervous to tell him, but it's true that there's a small part of me that's scared as fuck to tell my best friend I have a thing for his sister, to tell him I'm sleeping with her. We may all be in our twenties, but you can't put an age limit on a brother's instinct to protect his sister.

"I'm concerned," Dallas says, grunting as he carries over another set of logs. "You claimed you were too busy before to have a relationship with anyone. What's your excuse now?"

I pause, wincing. This is an uncomfortable conversation, and I'm not sure the best way to outright tell him about me and Vada.

"Um..." I inhale a deep breath and hold it as I pick up

another stack of logs. It's the last one, and I'm thankful to be done. It's fucking hot out. "About that." I scratch at my chin then spit it right out. "I've been talking to Vada, and..."

He stops loading the logs onto the stack he's been building beside the smoker and pulls himself to a full stand. His expression is blank, and I can't fucking read him from where I'm standing at the end of the truck.

He pauses before dropping the last log. He makes his way over to where I am and puts his hands on the end of the tailgate, lifting it up to close. It slams shut, and then his arms are crossed over it. His eyes narrow as he looks at the road behind me. He shifts them to me, pressing his mouth into a firm line.

Then that firm line curves into a smirk. "I've noticed she's been happier, and I wondered if you might have anything to do with it, considering you've been acting the same."

"What?" I ask, surprised.

"Yeah." He laughs, wiping his hands on his jeans. He adjusts his hat and squints toward the sun. "Sloan and I have had a feeling for a while now. We didn't know the extent of what's been going on with you two, but I won't lie—I've been trying to pry it out of you for a long time now."

"You're an ass." My shoulders relax with a chuckle.

He taps my arm then backs away, moving around to the driver's side of his truck. "I know brothers are usually overprotective when it comes to their siblings and whoever they're dating, especially when said person is their best friend." He stops before he opens his door, squinting up at the sun as he looks at me across the bed. "But I never understood that notion. Wouldn't you think you'd rather have your best friend date your sister? You know them better than anyone else."

"I guess you have a point." I give him a smile.

Dallas opens his door and holds it. "Yeah, I do. But one more thing, Colt." He taps the top edge of the bed with his fingers. "Break her heart, and I just might reconsider that notion."

I laugh even as my chest twists and aches with his words. "I wouldn't expect anything else."

I LIFT the top of my center console and pop a piece of gum into my mouth, anxious to get to Vada. I haven't seen her since that night at her office, and the thought of seeing her in just a few short minutes has my cock hardening and my heart racing on the drive over to her apartment.

It's stupid, really, how my body reacts to just the thought of seeing her. Being around her is like breathing in fresh air.

It's addicting.

She's addicting.

Not that I needed it before, but having Dallas' approval of us being together only adds to my feelings for her. It's odd that, although I didn't need his approval, I somehow feel better about moving forward with Vada now that I have it. Maybe I took Dallas' opinion into account more than I was willing to admit.

When I park outside the courtyard at Vada's apartment, I toss out the piece of gum I've been chewing on and slide my phone into my pocket. I didn't tell her I was stopping by today and we made no plans for this weekend, but with how our friendship and distance has affected us these past two years, I find myself wanting to show just how invested I am in her, starting with surprising her for lunch.

I run my fingers through my hair, pushing it off my damp forehead. The sun isn't as bright as it was earlier when Dallas and I were moving the logs out of the back of his truck, but the heat is just the same.

I open the wrought iron gate, cross the courtyard to Vada's apartment, and knock on her front door.

It takes her a moment to answer, and her voice is muffled from the other side as she yells, "No. Don't put your cleats on until we get to the park."

I arch my eyebrows, wondering who she's talking to as she opens her large wooden door. She stands on the other side wearing a pair of jean shorts and a light purple t-shirt. Her shorts are frayed at the ends, displaying her smooth, tan legs.

"Hey." She grins, leaning against the door. She's still happy to see me despite the fact that she has company and I'm obviously interrupting. "I wasn't expecting to see you today."

I smile at her, allowing my eyes to roam over her whole body. I stop on her eyes and clear my throat. "I thought I'd surprise you for a late lunch, a sort of makeup for the other day."

"Oh." She quickly frowns, her eyes turning down. "I'm sorry, I should have told you—I'm watching Jonah all weekend while Cass is out of town. She's photographing a wedding in Waco and asked if I could watch him for a few days."

"I'm ready, Vada." Jonah comes racing down the hallway, appearing from the doorway to Vada's guest room. His brown hair flops as he runs before stopping beside her.

My heart sinks into my stomach when he peers up at me with his brown eyes—the same eyes I remember peering up at me from the bar that night six months ago.

"You're Jonah?" I point to him and look up at Vada for clarification.

Jonah tilts his head to the side and studies me. I can tell he recognizes me in some way. How much, I'm unsure.

Vada's gaze switches back and forth between us. She's still holding the door open, her confused expression just as strong as mine.

"Do you know Jonah?"

I smile and shove my hands in my pockets. "Sort of. Do you remember me, buddy?"

He twists his mouth, covering the two gaps where teeth used to be. He taps his finger against his chin as he thinks about it. "I think so. What's your name?"

"Um, I don't think I told you before. My name is Colton."

"Colton." He scrunches his nose. "I like it."

I laugh. "I'm glad I have your approval."

"How do you know Vada? Are you her friend like I am?" he asks me.

I flick my eyes to Vada, unsure of how to answer him. As much as I'm falling for Vada and I can't ignore the way she makes me feel, we haven't put a label on whatever this is. We haven't had much of a chance to talk about it.

I turn back to Jonah. "Oh, well, I'm her brother's best friend."

"Dallas?" he asks.

"Yep." I look back over at Vada. "Well, actually, I'm Vada's friend too."

Her smile falters, and it's hard to miss the flicker in her eyes. I've hurt her. Her face falls flat and I hate that I'm the one who put that expression there, but I don't know how else to describe our relationship, at least not to a seven-year-old kid.

She inhales a deep breath and swipes her tongue across her lips.

"Where do you know him from?" she asks, clearly pushing my comment to the side.

"I met him a few months ago at the restaurant. Well, technically he was sitting at the bar." I grin, remembering the way he shrugged as if it weren't a big deal that a seven-year-old was sitting at a bar watching a baseball game with no supervision.

"At the bar?" Vada's eyes widen in shock, her eyebrows arching above her blue-green eyes.

"Yeah." I lift my hand and scratch the back of my head, attempting to come up with the words to explain it. "It was the night we had dinner with Dallas and Sloan to talk about the wedding. I was on my way out when I caught Jonah sitting at the bar."

"What?" She turns to Jonah, her eyes widening even more. "You were sitting at a bar by yourself? Was your Aunt Cass with you?"

"No." He shakes his head nonchalantly. "We were leaving when she got a phone call, so I went back in and sat down at the bar." He looks up at Vada, his brown eyes rounding with even more innocence than before. "There was an old Rangers game on."

"Oh my gosh." Vada places her hand to her forehead, a ghost of a smile appearing on her mouth.

It may have been illegal, but I agree that looking back on it now, it's pretty funny.

It's then I realize the Aunt Jonah is talking about is Cassidy, the same Cassidy Vada works with at the newspaper and the same Cassidy who was taking pictures at Dallas' wedding. That must be why she looked so familiar to me.

Maybe.

I'm not entirely sure I saw her face that night outside the restaurant, but there's no other reason I would think I've seen her before. I didn't meet her until the night of the wedding; that I know for sure.

"It's all good," I tell Vada, not wanting her to worry. "He wasn't sitting there for long, and we talked about why he isn't allowed to sit there."

Jonah rolls his eyes dramatically and his arms fall slack in front of him. "Because it's legal."

"*Illegal*."

"Oh yeah, *illegal*." Jonah nods once at me then looks up at Vada. "Is it time for us to go yet?"

"Yeah, buddy. I just need to get my purse." Vada ruffles his hair then walks over to the kitchen to grab it from the island.

I find myself fully looking at Jonah's outfit to see where they're headed. He's wearing a striped button-down shirt with large red letters printed across it: *Austin Stars*. His shirt is tucked into his striped pants, and he's wearing a red belt.

"Baseball practice, I'm guessing?" I point to Jonah's outfit, and he instinctively looks down.

He eyes the scripted letters on his shirt before looking up with worry etched into his innocent face. "No, not practice."

"Jonah made the team," Vada says, walking back over to where we're standing near the door. Her purse hangs over her shoulder, the strap resting between the swells of her breasts. "Today is his first game."

"What?" I can feel my eyebrows shooting up my forehead in surprise. I remember the night Vada and I went out for ice cream, she told me about Jonah's hesitancy to join an actual league. He didn't think he was good enough. "That's amazing."

Jonah frowns and looks down at his hands. He draws his finger down one of the lines on his palm. "I guess."

"Why do you say that?"

He shrugs then looks up at me. "I don't know. I'm just nervous I'm not going to be as good as everyone else."

I fight the urge to wrap this kid up in a hug. He reminds me of when I was little and my mom would drag me to try out for every sport she could think of. One day I was trying out for soccer; the next I was attempting to learn tap dancing. She was all over the place, and so was I. All I wanted to do was hide out in my room and read comic books.

"I told you," Vada says to Jonah, wrapping her arm around

his back. "As long as you try your best, you'll do great. That's all that matters."

"She's right, you know." I lean forward and cup my hand around my mouth, pretending to block Vada from listening as I whisper to Jonah. "And take it from me—she's hardly ever right."

Vada's mouth pops open, and she playfully pushes against my shoulder with the tips of her fingers. "You're seriously the worst. You know that, right?"

We both laugh as I pull myself to stand. "If you truly believe that, it's news to me." I make sure to look her straight in the eye, knowing she hasn't been treating me that way. If anything, we're closer than we've ever been.

I'm finding myself thinking about Vada all the time: when I'm at work tending to the smokers out back, when I'm at home and in the shower, jerking off to thoughts of what it feels like to be inside of her. Fuck, I used to even think about her in my statistics class when I was working on my master's during my last semester.

Vada sighs. The ends of her curls dance across her shoulders as her chest deflates. "We should get going."

"Yeah." I nod once. "We can talk later and figure something out."

"Okay." She offers me a soft smile, one that makes my dick twitch and my heart beat against my ribs like a drum.

I'm falling for her. It isn't fast, and it isn't hard; it's slow and smooth. The feeling seeps its way into every cell and every inch of my body.

I push it aside, pulling my keys out of my pocket. "Well, it was good to see you again, Jonah."

"Come with us!" he yells, bouncing on his heels in excitement.

"What?" I ask him.

"Please?" he asks, a smile spread from ear to ear. Now he's showing those gaps between the few baby teeth he has left. He snaps his head to Vada. "Please, Vada? Can Colton come?"

"I don't know, buddy." She shakes her head. "I'm not sure if—"

"Please? I might play better if he's there."

"Really?" she asks him before turning to me. She giggles, and her cheeks blush with pink. "Well, how about it? Do you want to come and help Jonah play better? You might just be his lucky charm."

"Please say yes, Colton," Jonah begs. "Be my lucky charm."

The more I stare into his brown eyes, the harder it is to tell him no. I've only met the kid two times, but my heart warms with the idea that he wants to spend more time with me.

"Alright then. Let's go play baseball."

CHAPTER EIGHTEEN

COLTON

I NEVER THOUGHT THERE'D BE A DAY WHERE I SAID I enjoyed watching a game of baseball, but today is that day.

Ask me to watch a single Rangers game—or any team, for that matter—and I couldn't do it, but for some reason, watching Jonah attempting to hit a ball sitting on top of a stick is one of the best things I've ever seen.

Maybe it's because little league baseball isn't as serious. I'm enjoying the genuine laughs and smiles on the kids' faces as they race toward a plate before the ball reaches it or when they feel the bat hitting the ball, scattering it across the dirt.

The look on Jonah's face is priceless; his smile as he jumps up and down in excitement in front of me and Vada is even better.

We're sitting on the metal bleachers directly behind the fence around the field, watching as Jonah makes it around to all three bases before jumping onto home. After he makes it, he jumps up and down, running over to the fence. He grasps the metal with his small hands.

"Vada, Colton, did you see that? I made a home run!"

"Of course we did!" Vada yells. She's wearing a grin, stretching it as far as she can.

"See?" I say. "We knew you could do it."

"I guess," Jonah says. "Vada, can we get ice cream after this? From that one place?"

She quickly looks over at me then turns to Jonah. "Sure."

"Awesome." Jonah runs off to join his coach and the rest of his team in the dugout.

The field isn't very large, set behind what used to be an elementary school. The three rows of bleachers are filled with parents and grandparents, and even the lawn space around them is scattered with people sitting in foldout camping chairs.

I turn to look at Vada as she watches the teams switch positions. Jonah stays in the dugout to get a break, yet she still doesn't look away.

"Thanks for inviting me," I tell her.

My words grab her attention, and she spins her head in my direction. Orange and yellow rays of sunshine shine behind her brown curls. Hues of red peek through her brown strands, contrasting the blue in her eyes. She's a palette of color.

A slow grin spreads across her mouth. "You're welcome."

I place my hand on her thigh. Her skin is damp from the heat and humidity in the air. My palm immediately sticks to her, molding with her flesh.

Her thigh tenses with my touch. She leans into the feeling, tilting her head to the side as she stares back out at the field.

"You better behave yourself," she mutters. "We're clearly not alone."

I laugh, sidling up beside her. I scoot across the hot metal, pressing my side against hers. She covers my arm with hers, hiding where my hand is sitting on her thigh. If people were to walk by, it'd be difficult to see. I slide my hand across toward her inner thigh.

"I promise I won't do anything that'll get us in trouble." I lean into her, bringing my mouth to the hollow of her ear.

She clenches her legs together, and my hand gets wedged between them as I breathe against her ear. Her skin prickles with goosebumps, and again, I love drawing this type of reaction out of her.

"I wanted to apologize."

"For what?" She keeps her attention on the field despite the way her body has changed with what I'm doing to her.

Her breathing has picked up. They're quicker and shallower. For every breath she was taking before, she's now taking two.

"For telling Jonah I was just your friend."

She's not as quick to respond to me as she usually is. Vada is typically filled with quick wit and comebacks. She's a spitfire, hurling herself at you even before you realize she's hit you.

It's what made me fall for her in the first place.

"Are you telling me I'm not your friend?" She dips her eyebrows, knitting them between her piercing eyes.

"No, you are." I clear my throat, nervous to start this conversation. I certainly didn't expect to be having it sitting on scorching-hot metal bleachers in ninety-degree heat watching a handful of seven-year-olds play T-ball.

She rolls her eyes and scoffs, working her tongue around in her mouth. I can tell with the way she twists her lips.

I hook my finger under her chin, forcing her to look in my direction. "I just mean you're my friend too, but you're also more than that."

She pulls in her bottom lip, tucking it under her perfect teeth. "I am?"

"Of course you are." I search her face, taking in her features, everything from the smooth curve of her nose to the pink blushing her cheeks to the way her mouth constantly moves.

One minute she's biting her bottom lip, the next she's sticking it out in a pout.

I lean further in and rest my forehead against hers. I press my lips to hers, holding them there.

My heart pounds in my chest as she leans further into me, pressing her shoulder into mine. Her mouth is warm, and I want nothing more than to tell her I'm ready to move forward. I want us to figure out where we are in our lives. I want to start working toward a life with Vada, one where I'm not solely relying on a few stolen nights with her and a night we still keep between us.

I'm still holding my mouth to hers when she moans against me, wrapping her hand around the back of my neck.

"I didn't know friends could kiss. Gross!"

Vada immediately pulls away from me as I jerk my hand back, tearing it from between her thighs. My fingers are hot and sweaty. I flex them as we both face Jonah standing before us on the other side of the fence, same as before.

Vada wipes her hand across her mouth and squeezes her eyes shut, holding back a laugh, but she can't hold it in for long. Her shoulders start to shake as she sputters against her hand.

I rest my arms on my legs and lean forward, trying to avoid looking at Jonah in embarrassment. I shift my gaze out toward the edge of the field, focusing on absolutely nothing. I don't know why I feel embarrassed for kissing Vada in front of him. I'm sure he's seen plenty of adults kiss.

Right?

"JONAH'S EXHAUSTED. He's already passed out."

"I bet," I tell Vada. "He had a long day. We all did."

"He seems to love you." She grins and raises her eyebrows. Her expression melts me from the inside out.

"He's a good kid."

"He is when he's not sitting at bars watching TV by himself."

A chuckle rumbles from my chest. "You're right, but at least I saw him when I did and nobody got in trouble."

"Good. I'm glad you were there to talk to him."

"I am too."

I'm sitting on the couch in her living room as she stands at the end of the hallway. She's still wearing her shorts from earlier, the frayed ends dancing across her bare skin with every step she takes. All fucking day, it's been driving me mad.

After Jonah caught me kissing Vada on the bleachers, he finished up his game with the winning score. To celebrate, I treated the two of them to ice cream at the shop down the street from Vada's apartment. Then we went out for lunch. It was a backward way of eating, but we were out to celebrate, telling Jonah he could pick whatever he wanted for playing so well.

"You know," I say, standing up, "I've had a hard time looking away from those legs of yours all day."

"Yeah?" She looks down, grabbing the ends of her shorts, holding them out to inspect them. "What about them?"

I pout, shaking my head as if I don't have an answer. "I don't know, I can't explain it. They've just been distracting me all day." I cross the room, closing the distance between us.

Her back is pressed against the wall as she looks up at me with hooded eyes. She's tired and so am I, but I don't let her know. Instead, I press my hips into hers, pinning her to the wall.

I lean in, bringing my mouth close to her ear. It's one of my favorite ways to tease her. Her skin never fails to break out in goosebumps, and her body never fails to react.

"It's taking a lot for me to not rip those shorts off those pretty little legs and fuck you right here in your living room."

She leans into my whisper, rubbing her legs back and forth

as a low, hushed whimper squeezes from her throat. I know she's already wet for me, but I'm not sure how I feel about taking this further with her when there's only a wall separating us from Jonah.

I just wanted to let her know how bad I want her, how much I'm falling for her. I've never felt this way about anyone before. I've never been as bold with a woman as I am with Vada. She brings out this side of me, the side I've buried deep inside, saving it for the right woman.

And Vada is that woman.

I pull away from her, and when I catch her gaze, there's disappointment filling her eyes at my absence.

"Then why don't you?" she asks me.

I lift my hand and drag my thumb across her smooth lip. It moves with me, and her hot breath brushes across my skin. My dick is straining against my jeans, begging to be freed, but I can't.

"Not tonight," I tell her, my eyes moving past her shoulder.

She swallows and her eyes flutter closed. "I get it."

"But trust me," I tell her, stopping her thoughts from digging into my decision to not sleep with her tonight, looking for more meaning. "When I do get you alone, I'll make sure you don't forget it."

"Impossible."

"What's impossible?" I drag my finger across her cheekbone, drawing an invisible line down her neck to her collarbone.

"Me forgetting all the times I've been with you." She reaches forward and lifts the end of my shirt, sliding her hand underneath. She grips the waist of my jeans and jerks my hips forward. My hardened cock slams into the space between her legs, and I let out a deep groan. "Your touch is like an invisible tattoo, Colton. You're etched into every inch of my skin. It never disappears."

The last word has barely left her mouth when I slam mine to hers. I drink her in, allowing her words to fill the hole that's been inside my soul ever since I laid eyes on her.

When she parts my lips with her tongue, I'm cursing myself for not fucking filling that hole sooner.

CHAPTER NINETEEN

Vada

"What would you say is your favorite comic book?" Jonah's standing beside Colton as they flip through several comic books on the shelf in front of them.

"Um..." Colton replaces the one he just had in his hand. He turns to Jonah. "It's hard to pick just one. Everyone usually chooses *Watchmen,* but I like to stick to an even better classic."

"Which one's a classic?" Jonah asks.

Colton walks a few shelves over, searching for a particular one. He waves his finger over a few then leans forward as he sifts through the stacks. When he finds what he's looking for, he grabs it and hands it to Jonah. "*Spider-Man.*"

"I love Spider-Man!" Jonah bounces in excitement and opens the comic book, skimming through the pages. "Will I be able to read it? My teacher last year said I was doing great reading books for my grade."

"What grade are you going into when the summer is over?"

"Third grade."

Colton scoffs. "These are perfect for you then."

"Cool." He hugs the book to his chest and spins around to

face me, looking up at me with brown doe eyes. "Can I get it, Vada?"

I open my mouth, ready to answer him, but Colton chimes in. "I'll get it for you, buddy, if you really want it."

"I do." He grins. "If you like it, I know *I* will. What made you start reading comics?"

Colton sighs, a ghost of a smile appearing on his mouth. "My brother, Ryan, used to play football. On the days he'd practice, I'd have to hang around and wait until he was done, and there was this comic book store down the street from the field that I'd always sneak down to. I'd sit there and read them forever until he'd come and find me. Eventually, he started staying with me and reading one himself. Spider-Man was his favorite."

Colton's eyes line with unshed tears, swirling with the memories of long afternoons spent with his brother. He hardly ever talks about Ryan. To hear him talk about him to Jonah is enough to provoke tears of my own.

I watch Jonah and Colton walk all the way to the register, admiring how they've taken a liking to each other these past two days. They walk ahead of me, eager to check out. I catch how their walk is nearly the same.

Even though Jonah isn't my kid, I've grown to love him. He truly is a joy to have around, and I haven't minded him staying with me over the weekend, despite the incessant emails and phone calls I've been getting from my boss. I've been able to answer most of them on my own time, but there are a few where he's asked me if I can take the time to look over an article for him or message another one of our reporters.

Aside from that, I haven't had much alone time with Colton. It was sweet of him to surprise me by coming over yesterday and spending the whole day with us, cheering Jonah on for his first T-ball game, but I can't deny how disappointed I was when he left last night. I completely understood his reasoning, but I can't help it. I've fallen in love with his company, and the more time we spend together, the more I'm finding myself falling even further.

Even though he left and went back to his own place, he was texting me all night until one or both of us fell asleep. I'm not sure which one of us fell first. Then when I woke up with Jonah, Colton was already calling to see if he could take Jonah to his favorite comic book store after his morning shift ended.

Colton pays for Jonah's comic book, and when we step outside, we start heading in the direction of the park across the street. It's a beautiful day outside. The sun is shining, but it isn't too hot. The sun warms my skin as I tilt my head up toward it and close my eyes for several steps, drinking it in.

"Did you always want to make barbecue?" Jonah asks. He's walking between me and Colton. His comic book is tucked under his arm, and he's staring at the ground as he walks, being careful not to step on the cracks in the sidewalk.

Colton frowns as he looks off toward the park coming into view when we turn the corner of the square. His eyebrows dip as he scratches at the stubble lining his jaw. "No."

"If you didn't want to cook, what did you want to be when you grew up?" Jonah asks.

"Well, my parents own a ranch outside of the city, and I would always spend time with the animals. I used to want to be a veterinarian."

"Wow. You grew up on a ranch?"

"Yep." He grins.

"What kind of animals did you have?"

"Well, for a while we used to have cows and chickens, but eventually my parents decided to only keep horses. That's all they've had for the past fifteen years."

"Have you ever ridden one?" he asks, but he doesn't leave Colton much time for a response before he continues. He starts walking backward, scraping his toes across the pavement. "I've always wanted to ride a horse, but I'm scared."

"Why would you be scared?" I ask him.

He shifts his attention to me, still walking backward. "Are you kidding, Vada? They're huge. Like massive." He lifts his arms, dramatically spreading them wide. His brown hair glints in the sun, golden strands peeking through the otherwise dark shade.

"They are, but I've heard they're super sweet and gentle."

"What?" Colton looks at me, cutting his attention to my comment. He keeps his steps in line with mine. "You've never ridden one either?"

I shake my head.

"Come on." He tilts his head back in disbelief. "You, Vada Beckett, have never ridden a horse?"

"No, Colton Adler, I have not." I roll my eyes then bite my bottom lip, fighting back a grin.

He laughs, muttering under his breath. "And you call yourself a Texan."

"Hey, it's not a requirement, and besides, I grew up in the city. I didn't grow up on a ranch like you." I give him a smile and look up just in time to see the brown in his eyes lighten from the sun.

"Can we go sometime?"

"What?" Colton's eyes move to Jonah. He's now facing the right way. We're almost to the park, so I quickly snap a picture of the three of us walking down the sidewalk to send to Cassidy. She's been checking in a few times a day. I figure she'll like it if I let her know we're taking Jonah to the park. She's supposed to be picking him up tonight, assuming she gets back home when she says she will.

I'm typing up my text to Cassidy when Jonah asks his question again. "Can we go to your ranch and ride some of the horses?"

I stop typing, eyeing Colton to gauge his expression.

He hesitates, looking out toward the park. His jaw ticks with concentration, the corded muscles of his arms tightening as he shoves his hands into the front pockets of his jeans. "Um, maybe. I think we'd have to talk to your Aunt Cassidy about it first."

"It would be awesome if we could," Jonah says. "You're the coolest, Colton."

He laughs, his cheeks warming. He attempts to hide the tension simmering under his skin, but I still see it. "Thanks."

We finally reach the entrance to the park, and Jonah removes his comic book from under his arm and hands it to me. "Can you hold this for me, Vada? I don't want to ruin it."

"Sure."

And then he's gone. He races toward the jungle gym, climbing up the steps and running across the bridge to the slide.

Colton and I make our way over to a bench outside the play area. I set the comic book beside me and watch Jonah until he goes down the slide and runs over to the swings. I turn to look over at Colton sitting beside me. He's been quiet ever since we got here.

"Everything okay?"

He bends, resting his arms on his legs. He looks down between his feet before glancing over at me. He squints against the sun, the corner of his mouth curling. "Yeah. I'm fine."

"Remember what they say about the word fine, Colton—it *always* means the exact opposite."

"I shouldn't have brought it up."

I give him a confused expression even though I know full well what he's talking about.

The ranch. His parents.

I'm not sure the extent of Colton's rift with them, but it must be big enough for him to be reacting this way.

"You don't have to take him if you don't want to."

"That's the problem though—I want to, and I'm afraid of what that might mean when it comes to my parents."

"I know I don't know exactly what was said that day, but maybe you should give it a shot. Maybe try reaching out to your mom first?"

I knit my eyebrows and look into Colton's eyes with empathy. I may not know the rocky relationship he has with his parents, but I do know what it feels like to have a contentious one. I still haven't spoken to my father about not showing up to Dallas' wedding. I still haven't asked my brother if he bothered to invite him, but I haven't wanted to dredge up family issues when Dallas and Sloan are still basking in their newlywed bliss. I didn't want to stir a pot that has no business being stirred.

Colton's watching Jonah swinging. He kicks his legs back then swings them forward, getting higher and higher. Colton's face is flat, but his eyes tell a different story.

"He's great, isn't he?" I ask Colton.

He keeps watching Jonah. "I admire his innocence. He's seriously the happiest kid I've ever met, not that I've been around a ton of them."

He laughs under his breath, and I find myself smiling. I shift my attention to Jonah as well. I keep my mouth shut about Jonah's past with his mother and how she abandoned him. It's not that I don't want to tell Colton, but I don't know if Cassidy wants everyone to know the story of how her sister simply disappeared because she couldn't handle the life she'd carved out for herself and the decisions she'd made.

We sit in silence for a while, allowing the sound of squeaking metal and Jonah's laughter to fill our ears.

The sun is blanketed by a cloud, and the entire park is covered in a light grey shadow. The air cools slightly as Colton decides to cut into our silence.

"I'll think about talking to my mom." He turns his head so he's facing me. "If only for Jonah."

CHAPTER TWENTY

Vada

EVEN THOUGH IT WAS HARD TO SEE JONAH LEAVE WHEN Cassidy picked him up a few hours later, I'm thankful to have peace and quiet again. Colton and I are standing on my back patio, watching as the sun sets and the moon awakes, dragging the night sky with it.

We're both sitting on the wicker chairs, watching the fire in my miniature fire pit burn. Although I live in a small apartment complex, the area in which my apartment sits feels secluded. There's a wrought iron fence, similar to the one surrounding the entire complex, outlining my yard. A small wood-planked wall divides my space from my neighbor's. If anyone were to ever come back here, they wouldn't be able to see into my yard unless they walked around the wall. Not once in the past two years I've lived here has anyone bothered me though. I live in the back corner of the complex. It's quiet and peaceful out here, despite me living in the city.

Colton and I are alone. I'm staring at the flames when Colton leans into his chair, resting his elbow on the arm.

"I've been thinking about Jonah's question earlier today."

I roll my eyes and give him a smirk. "That kid asks a million questions a day. Which one are you talking about?"

He pauses, lifting his beer to his mouth. He presses his lips to the glass, and he takes a swig. I watch as his Adam's apple slides across his neck. When he swallows, he sets the beer down on the arm, but he still keeps his hand wrapped around it.

"He asked me if I always wanted to cook barbecue. Did you always want to write and edit stories?"

I smile and sit back in my chair, staring as the orange and yellow flames flicker. "I feel like when writers are asked this question, they always say yes."

"But?"

"But..." I inhale a deep breath and blow it out. "But no, I didn't. I used to want to be an actress."

"Really?" he asks, surprised. His eyebrows arch across his forehead, and his brown eyes warm in the glow from the fire. He's wearing his contacts again, making it easier for me to see what he's thinking.

"Yeah." I laugh, thinking back on it. "I used to do these skits in the mirror and act out these little scenes. As I got older, I joined a few theater classes and groups in high school, but it ended up not working out." I frown and take a sip of my own beer.

"Why not?"

I swallow, placing my bottle beside me on the ground. I look over at Colton. "Because I realized I enjoyed working for the school newspaper more."

"Ah, okay." Colton nods, a smile growing on his mouth. "Of course you did."

"Yeah, I did."

"I was also thinking about how he wanted to go horseback riding at my parents' ranch."

I tilt my head to the side. "You don't have to, Colt. I would understand if you weren't comfortable."

"No." He sighs. I can tell this is weighing on him. "I've been thinking about how sad my mother's been, and even if she doesn't realize how much she's hurting me, I still want to be there for her. She's hurting, and I'm sure my absence and silence aren't helping, especially when she only has my father for company."

"You're a good son. You know that, right?"

He gives a humorless laugh, his shoulders moving as he leans on his elbows, staring at the fire. "There are some who would disagree with that statement."

I already know he's talking about his father.

"Anyone with that kind of opinion doesn't truly know you."

He gives me a reassuring smile across from the fire. His face warms as his mouth lifts into a smile, a small shadow of a dimple pressing into his cheek.

We sit in silence, watching and listening to the fire flickering, then I catch Colton pulling himself to stand out of the corner of my eye.

"Well..." He clears his throat, grabbing his empty beer bottle. "It's been a long weekend, so I'm sure you want to—"

I don't allow him to finish his sentence; I stand up and walk over to where he's stopped just in front of the back door.

I can't help it. I don't want him to go. He's standing in front of my sliding glass door. His reflection is only visible due to the fire light behind him. I see myself walking toward him in the reflection.

The pull of the fire flickering across his body draws me to close the gap between us. His tan skin is highlighted against the flames, accentuating every single pulse and tick of his muscle.

I want to be near him. I need him near me. My lips crave to press against his.

When I'm standing behind him, I lift my hand and gently ghost my fingers along his arm. My nails barely graze his skin, like a whisper against the hollow of an ear. I pull him to turn around and face me. Without breaking my gaze from his, I grab the bottle dangling from his fingers and twist to place it on the arm of the chair I was sitting in.

My chest is pounding with the rhythmic beat of my heart, begging me to give in, to soothe it with what it's craving. Colton holds his breath and wraps his hand around the back of my head, threading his fingers through my long brown curls. He brings my face close to his, claiming my mouth. His warm lips press against mine, and a moan squeezes itself from my chest. My heart sighs in relief.

He bites down on my lip, and it takes everything in me not to lean into it. I'm used to him taking control, but tonight, I want to be the one. I want to show Colton just how much he means to me.

I still don't know where we're going in our relationship or where we stand. Yesterday when we sat on the bleachers at the ball field, he almost said as much, but I still haven't heard the words fall from his mouth.

He tugs on my lip, pulling it with his teeth. I start to pull away and he lets me go, but not without hesitation. I curl my mouth into a smile before pulling my bottom lip under my teeth. I can already tell it's slightly swollen and red from his gentle bite.

He releases a heavy breath from his chest, watching me as I lower myself, kneeling in front of him. His eyes flicker with curiosity and an insatiable need for me.

Usually, Colton is commanding when it comes to us being together. It's one of the things I'm learning I love most about being with him. He makes me feel powerful, and in turn it makes being with him a thousand times more exciting. But this, me kneeling in front of him—I've flipped the tables.

Now I'm the one who's giving the orders.

I reach up and slide my hands along the tops of his thighs, starting at his knees. At first, I watch my own hands as my fingers mold around his tight muscles. I move them along his thighs, around to the back then the front again. Once I've reached his waist, I flick my gaze up to his, looking up at him with hooded eyes. His face is set on me, watching and waiting to see what I do next.

I slide my hand over the bulge growing underneath his jeans. The silhouette of his erection causes me to go wet myself, just thinking about how it feels to have it between my own legs. I move my hand across his front and reach for his hand where it's relaxed at his side. I grab his finger and press it to my lips. He holds his breath as I use it to pry my mouth open, wrapping my lips around it.

Once I've licked it a few times, swiping my tongue over it, I pull it out and smile against it. "You're always the one to taste me," I tell him, dropping his hand and reaching for the button to his jeans. "Now it's my turn."

The heat emanating from the fire behind me warms my neck. Beads of sweat dot my skin, dripping down. The heat radiates across my back, filtering out to my belly. Butterflies rage inside as I unbutton his jeans. His cock only moves slightly, still contained by his boxer briefs. Once I've unzipped his pants, I slide them down his legs and reach for the waist of his underwear. I slide those down too.

His cock springs free, standing erect before me. I've yet to be with Colton this way. He's only ever been with me like this or taken me all the way. I grab his length, swiping my thumb over his mushroomed tip. He lets out a sharp hiss before closing his mouth. His jaw ticks as I bring my lips to him, pressing them to the tip. I blow on it, teasing him before opening my mouth and wrapping my lips around him.

I slide and swirl my tongue across his thick length, pushing as far as I can go. Once he reaches the back of my throat, I pull away, but not completely. I swirl my tongue around him again and again. I repeat the same thing, only this time I let out a moan. I open my eyes and look up at Colton as I work his length. He feels the vibration reverberating through him.

We're outside, and at any moment, someone could see us. My nerves hum through my veins and my heart races, but the thrill of getting caught is pushed aside when Colton places his hand on the back of my head, pushing me deeper. The tip of his cock presses against the back of my throat. He grips my hair, holding me tight. He moans, tilting his head back.

"Vada." My name falls from his mouth with a deep growl. "I'm going to come if you keep doing that."

"What?" I ask, pulling back enough to speak against him. "This?" Taking him back in, I swirl my tongue around his tip, tasting his pre-cum before taking his full length again. He pulls back slightly even though I try to take more of him in.

"Fuck." He groans. "Yes. I'm going to..."

I'm left breathless when he pulls back, hooking his fingers under my chin. He pulls me up to stand, and everything moves fast.

Somehow, Colton has stepped out of his pants and is walking me backward, toward the sliding glass door leading inside. Once we're through it, he shuts the door behind him without taking his eyes off me. The fire is still going strong outside, casting my living room in a rich, orange and red glow. Colton's a silhouette as he grabs my hips and spins us around. He pins my back to the glass door, switching up our positions.

He's standing in front of me with no pants and no underwear. He removes the only remaining piece of clothing he's still wearing. He tosses his shirt over his shoulder and drags his finger across my mouth. He leans forward, keeping his thumb pressed against my lip and his hand on my chin. He kisses me, keeping his thumb pressed between our flesh.

He keeps his kiss brief then he pulls back. His hand is still holding on to me. "Get undressed."

I do as he says, the heat growing in my stomach. When I've removed my shorts and t-shirt, I already know my insides will be as molten as the fire outside once he's done with me.

I'm completely naked standing in front of him. I'm pushed up against the glass of the sliding door. It's cold and hard along my back. I lean against it and start to drag my hand along my stomach, dipping my fingers between my folds. Colton watches me with hunger, and I start to circle my fingers, ignoring the look of jealousy in his eyes.

My decision to touch myself has left him feeling conflicted. I can tell he's enjoying it, but at the same time, he's wishing it were him instead of me.

"Do you like it when I touch myself?" I ask breathily. I fight back the moan climbing up my throat.

My gaze roams over his broad shoulders and the toned muscles on his chest, all the way down to the sculpted V of his hip bones.

My toes start to tingle, the sensation building its way up my legs. Colton starts to stroke himself, grabbing his length as he watches me. He only moves his hand a few more times before he leans forward, pressing his body against mine. My hand stops once his fingers wrap around my wrist.

"I fucking love watching you touch yourself." He grits his teeth. "But it's only me who's allowed to finish."

He removes my hand and lifts it up above my head. He pins my arm to the glass above me. He wraps his other hand around the back of my leg, hitching it around his waist. My other foot lifts off the floor as he holds me against the glass. The glass starts to warm, the cool sensation switching to heat. My skin dampens as he slides his hips back far enough to center his cock in front of me before sliding himself inside me.

My chest huffs, dramatically rising and falling as I tilt my head back. My vision wavers and everything around me starts to become hazy. The only thing in focus is Colton.

"You're mine," he says, driving himself in deeper. "Only. Mine."

"I'm yours." I pant.

"Like the first time, I want to make a deal."

His sudden need to make a deal has me slowing my breathing, but I wait, listening for what he has to say. "A deal?" I ask him, pleasure still coursing through me.

"No more secrets. No more one-time secrets. Only us."

Each word that comes out of his mouth shoots straight through my chest like an echo. I feel it building within me, and when he moves his eyes to mine, I know he means every word.

I'm his. No more secrets. Only us and the truth.

"Deal." I tilt my head back as far as it will go, my head pressing against the hard glass.

The pressure of being pressed between him and the glass nearly overwhelms me in the best way possible. Having already nearly brought myself to the edge, it doesn't take long for my orgasm to come.

"Colton." I say his name as I reach my peak, my back screeching against the smooth surface. "Oh my god. I'm coming."

"Fucking come for me, baby."

My legs quiver around his waist, my muscles contracting as I'm coming down from my orgasm. Colton slams his hips into me a few more times before he stiffens around me. His fingers dig into the flesh of my thigh as he holds me against the glass.

He buries his forehead into the crook of my neck. His hot breaths dance across my damp skin, and I wrap my arms around his shoulders, allowing them to fall slack.

When I finally gather up the strength to wrap my hands around his cheeks, I lift his gaze to mine and place a kiss against his lips, knowing he's soothed every worry I've had since the day we met with two words.

CHAPTER TWENTY-ONE

COLTON

I'VE NEVER BEEN THIS NERVOUS TO TALK TO MY MOTHER.

I pop a piece of gum into my mouth like I always do and hop out of my truck. My feet hit the familiar gravel road as I squint against the sun, taking in my parents' house. Every brick and every piece of glass is still in the same place it was the last time I saw it. Despite the constant string of company my parents have and the flow of business from my father, the place hasn't changed.

I slam the door to my truck and stalk up to the front door, not wasting any time ringing the doorbell.

I don't know why I'm so nervous. I tried to make sure this visit to see my mother was at a time when I knew my father would be gone for his usual weekly round of golf. He calls them business contacts, but I've always known better. In truth, they're a bunch of money-hungry CEOs looking to see whose pockets they can dig into.

A few seconds after I ring the bell, my mother answers the door like she did the last time I was here, only this time she doesn't already have a drink in her hand. Her light brown hair is swept up into a high ponytail, showing off her beautiful face.

Dark circles line her eyes, making her look like she hasn't slept in days.

Despite her emaciated appearance, a hesitant smile appears on her mouth.

"Colton?"

"Hey, Mom." I step around her, walking through the entrance.

I'm ready to follow her to another room as usual but stop when she pulls me in for a hug. It feels as if it's been years since she's wrapped her arms around me, and the feeling it gives me catches me by surprise.

She's warm, but I can feel the emptiness still buried underneath it. It's like suddenly remembering a moment from your childhood. Parts of it are clear, but most of it is out of focus and far away.

I can still feel my mother's love for me, even if my memory is faded.

"Your father isn't home," she says, pulling away from me.

"I know." I sigh. "I was kind of counting on him not being here. I was hoping to talk to you."

"Oh, sure." She leads me into the kitchen, and several people are lined along the kitchen island. Large binders are laid out in front of them, and they're talking amongst themselves. "I can't talk long, but I do have a moment."

"Who are all these people?" I glance around, peering down the hallway as several people move in and out of rooms carrying various items. To be honest, it looks as if they're packing the house up.

"Oh," she says, looking around with a weak smile. "These are the designers and caterers for the charity auction for your father's business next week. They're redecorating and arranging the house to be a bit more suitable for the event."

"Oh, right." I nod, knowing exactly what this is. It's my

father's way of making his business look good in front of clients and the corporate world. Every year he throws some bullshit auction, claiming to donate the proceeds to charity out of the goodness of his heart, but I know better. I've always known better.

It's just a way for him to hide the truth of what really goes on behind his deals.

"What did you need to talk about?"

I try not to dwell on the fact that she hasn't asked me how I've been or why I haven't spoken to her in months. I remind myself that my mother lives in a fantasy world, a world of her own making where it's easier to believe the world is perfect instead of the cruel one she's surrounded by.

An asshole for a husband. A son who died far too young. And another son who's only continued to be a disappointment.

One of the designers walks up carrying two different swatches of fabrics. The man holds them in front of her as my mother's eyes shift from one to the next. Without a word, she points to the one on her right, and the man walks away.

My mother is a well-oiled machine when it comes to tasks that are imperative to my father's appearance to the world.

"I, um..." I clear my throat. "I wanted to ask you if it's okay if I bring a kid over to the stables one day for a ride. He's a friend of Vada's, and he's never ridden before."

It feels awkward asking my mother's permission, but there's no way I would feel comfortable bringing Jonah over here without my mother's knowledge. I have no intention of introducing him to my father, but my mother at least deserves to know.

"Vada?" she asks, her eyebrows arching across her forehead. "Are you seeing her?"

"I am." I tell my mother the truth. As much as my parents

disapprove, it doesn't fucking matter. I'm well past the age where they should care who I'm dating.

If that's what you want to call us—dating.

"Oh." She nods. "Okay." I'm not certain, but it's almost as if I see the corners of her mouth slightly curl, as if she's attempting to smile. Even if she did, it quickly fades. It's gone before I can tell for sure.

Another one of the designers walks by, this time carrying one of the binders that were sitting on the kitchen island. My mother points to a few items on the page, and the person nods the same way the other worker did a few minutes ago.

"You can ride the horses any time you like," she tells me.

"Sounds good." I give her an appreciative smile. "I haven't asked you yet—how are you?"

She inhales a deep breath, thinking about how to answer my question. The expression on her face is the same as it always is when I ask her. She's working to sift out the most appropriate answer, hoping to fool everyone around her. She might be able to fool my father, but she can't fool me.

"I'm good."

It's a bullshit, automatic response. I'm not surprised.

"I want to say I'm sorry, Mom." An inherent part of me hates that I'm not speaking to my mother. Even if she's distant and withdrawn from me, I'll always try with her. She doesn't deserve the pain she lives in, and I hate to think she's so deeply buried in her grief that she can't see she needs help. I don't ever want her to wonder why I wasn't there for her, even if both she and my father consider me a disappointment, more so my father than my mother.

"Sorry for what?" she asks, her eyes shifting to an expression of mock innocence.

"I'm sorry I haven't come over in a while."

"It's okay." She waves me off, frowning. She's acting as if it hasn't been a big deal that I haven't been here for our usual Saturday lunches. I push the pain aside at the thought that she might not care and pull my keys out of my pocket.

"Okay, well." I sigh, heading toward the front door. "I'll let you know when we'll bring Jonah over to ride."

"Why don't you and Vada come to the auction?"

"What?" I stop in front of the door and spin around.

My mother reaches for the door handle, moving around me. She opens the door and holds it open. She doesn't offer for me to stay. She doesn't offer to talk.

I don't intend on staying anyway. I don't want to run the risk of seeing my father.

"You and Vada should come to the auction and dinner," she suggests again. "I know your father would love to see you and for you to meet some of his colleagues."

"I don't know." I shake my head as my heart sinks into my stomach.

Hours spent with my father and all his corporate cronies doesn't sound too appealing. Subjecting Vada to that kind of environment doesn't sound too appealing either.

"It'll give me a chance to meet Vada properly."

She catches my attention, staring into my eyes. It's the first time she's been able to look in my eyes in what feels like forever. It's enough to pull my heart out of my stomach and put it back into my chest.

I sigh and give her a smile. "I'll think about it."

When I get back out to my truck, I start the engine and check my phone. I left it resting in the center console because I didn't want any distractions when I talked to my mother.

Even though she seemed too involved in setting up for the charity auction, I can't help allowing my mind to wander back to the hug she gave me when she saw me standing at her front door.

Sometimes when I see my mother, I imagine her standing in the middle of a locked room, begging to be set free. Not free from life in general, more the life she's built specifically.

She's trapped in a marriage with my father who hasn't even bothered to see she's still grieving the loss of Ryan, even if it's been five years since his death. It's a pain none of us have gotten over.

I grab my phone from the center console and see I have a missed call from Vada. I dial her number, sticking my phone in the holder clipped into the vent. I pull out of my parents' driveway, watching as the gravel kicks up from my tires. I turn onto the road just as Vada answers on the third ring.

"Hey, you." She sighs loudly.

"Hey." I smile even though she can't see me. "What's going on?"

"Well, as far as work goes, it has been a nightmare."

"I'm sorry to hear that. Why?"

"Oh, man." She sighs. "Where do I begin?" She lets out a small sigh before saying, "Let's just make a long story short and say several of our stories printed wrong and the server is down so we can't post any current articles."

"Well, shit, babe. I'm sorry."

"That's okay. Did you talk to your mom?"

"I did."

"How is she?"

I sigh, gripping the steering wheel. My knuckles fade to white. I try not to think of my mother and her mood swings. One minute she's pulling me in for a hug, the next she's acting as if she's too busy for my company, ushering me out the door.

"She's good. She invited us over for dinner."

That's right, Colton. Just spit it out. Maybe it won't sound so awful when you tell Vada. Maybe then it won't leave such a sour taste in your mouth when you talk about going.

"Us?" She pauses then clears her throat. "Us for dinner?"

"Yeah." I flex my fingers. "She had all these decorators and caterers over getting ready for this huge charity auction they throw every year. I haven't been to one since I lived with them and they forced me to be there, but she asked if I could make it and invited you."

"How do you feel about going?"

I fight the instinct to immediately reject the idea. I told my mother I would think about it, leaving room to negotiate with myself.

"I want to say no," I admit. "But I told her I would think about it. What about you? Would you want to go?"

She pauses again, allowing the silence to settle into our conversation. She thinks on her answer long enough for me to turn off the long country road my parents' house sits on and onto the main road in town, heading for the highway.

"I mean, it was sweet of your mother to invite me. Maybe it won't be so bad if there's a bunch of people around to distract us."

"I don't need a ton of people to distract me. You're a big enough distraction as it is."

"Colton." She groans. "You're making it incredibly difficult for me to not want to leave right now and meet you at your apartment when you say shit like that."

I grin. "I mean, I can keep it up if—"

"No." She laughs. "Don't. I have a ton of work to get done. But if you want, you can come over tonight. Maybe for dinner?"

"I have to work at the restaurant tonight, but I can come over after we close. It'll be too late for dinner, but I'm down for dessert."

"Mmm." She moans into the phone. "I love dessert."

"Me too. It's my favorite part of the meal."

"Dammit," she whispers. "I really wish I wasn't at work right now, and it's not because of all the work I have to do."

"What is it then?"

"You have no idea how fucking wet I just got from you talking about dessert."

"Wait," I say. "Are we talking dirty when you're at work?"

"No," she says quickly. "Absolutely not."

I can tell she wants to, but I also know she's swamped. The last thing I want to do is distract her, so I change the subject.

"I'll text you when I'm leaving work tonight."

"Okay." I can practically hear the smile in her voice. She pauses again, but this time she doesn't hold it nearly as long. "I actually called you about something else."

"Yeah?"

"Cassidy asked if you might be able to go back to that park we went to yesterday. Jonah says he lost his keychain and thinks he might have dropped it when he was playing over by the monkey bars. Since we're swamped here, neither of us will be able to go by and get it."

"A keychain?" I don't remember ever seeing Jonah with one.

"Yeah," she says. "He's obsessed with this keychain, carries it with him everywhere."

"Um, okay." I tap the screen on my phone and check the time. There are still three hours before I need to head back to the restaurant. "Yeah, I have some time. What does it look like?"

"It's metal with some kind of star on it. I can't really remember what color the star is though." She pauses. "I think it was blue with a yellow outline, maybe. I only saw it one time so I can't be sure."

"Okay." I swallow the lump in my throat, remembering how I've seen a keychain like the one Vada described before. They're incredibly popular, so I push the feeling aside, wondering why

Jonah has a keychain like that one to begin with. "I'll let you know if I find it."

"Thank you. If you don't mind, could you drop it off at Cassidy's house? Her dad is there with Jonah. He's been distraught ever since he lost it, and I'm sure it'd make him happy to have it back."

"Yep. I can definitely do that."

A bit later, I pull into the parking lot alongside the part of the park where Jonah was playing yesterday. Nearly all the spots are empty. I pull my truck into the closest one and hop out while I still have Vada on the phone. I take her off speaker and place the phone against my ear as I enter the park. The monkey bars are on the far side, away from the bench Vada and I sat on yesterday. I walk along the path and step onto the bed of wood chips covering the play area.

"Hey, babe," Vada says. "I have to go—Nate's outside my office. I'll text you the address to Cassidy's. Thank you for doing this for me."

"Of course."

When I end the call, I'm already passing the swings and making my way over to the monkey bars. I'm keeping an eye out for Jonah's keychain, but I can't help it when my thoughts wander to Vada.

We've come a long way since the night of the wedding. Fuck, even before that. I start thinking about the days when I was finding it hard to get just a moment to breathe. Between school, opening the restaurant, and my best friend losing his wife, it didn't leave much room for me to be able to be anything other than on autopilot, especially when it came to my parents and the weekly visits to their house.

A weight has been lifted off my shoulders since the last time I saw my dad. It felt good to take a stand against him. I may not have told him the truth of how I feel, but at least I was able to walk out of there, unwilling to listen to any more of his bullshit. Part of me wants to believe they're so hard on me because I'm the only son they have left. I'm the only one they can rely on to leave a legacy for the Adler name. Not only did they lose my brother, they also lost any hope to build on the family name.

Either way, it doesn't change how fragile the cracks have become in our family. Now, looking back on it, it feels as if Ryan was the glue holding us together.

I push aside the twinge of pain squeezing at my chest. Maybe taking Vada to the dinner will help start to mend the cracks in my relationship with my family. Maybe my mother seeing Vada will bring her happiness again.

I stand under the monkey bars and bend over, sifting through the wood chips. A windstorm blew through the city last night, so I won't be surprised if the chips have covered the keychain, or maybe other kids have kicked them up.

I sweep my hand back and forth. I start on one end of the monkey bars, making my way to the other end. I remember how Jonah dangled from these bars yesterday. That must have been when he lost it.

I've almost given up when I see a small bit of metal peeking out. The part sticking out is a half ring of silver, glinting in the dull sunshine. Clouds have scattered across the sky, moving shadows across the ground. One second the sun is shining, the next it's gone.

I reach out and grab the keychain, pulling it out from under the wood chips. I shake off the excess dirt and turn it over in my hand, making sure it's Jonah's.

When I see the star on the front, my heart stops. It takes several seconds for my mind to catch up and process what I'm holding, the once pounding heart in my chest nothing more than a dull thud as I narrow my eyes.

The faded metal backing is covered in scratches. There are

a few dents, but otherwise it looks typical for a keychain carried by a kid every single day—not to mention the person who owned it before that.

When I look at the front of the keychain, the blue star etched into the middle is faded as well. It's a dull blue, not like the rich, navy color I remember, and the yellow outline is nearly gone.

At first, I start to convince myself there's no way this is the same keychain I know.

Maybe Jonah found it himself. Maybe he found it in a park like this one, buried under the dirt and wood chips to be stomped on by children playing.

My throat seizes and my knuckles start to bend, tightening around the long rectangle shape of the keychain. The metal digs into my skin, too dull to leave a cut but not dull enough for me not to feel a sting from it.

Then as my eyes roam over the keychain longer and I read the initials etched into the bottom, it feels as if someone's used chest paddles to jumpstart my heart. My arms and legs go numb, and I squeeze my fingers around the keychain. Before I realize it, I'm already back at my truck, jumping into the front seat.

With a shaky hand, I jamb the key into the ignition and rev the engine. Tears threaten to build behind my eyes, but I refuse to let them overtake me. I need to focus on the road.

I need to know why Jonah has this keychain.

It might be nothing.

It might be as insignificant as the dirt clinging to the bottom of my boot.

SECRET #4

Whether we want it to or not, the truth will always set us free.

CHAPTER TWENTY-TWO

COLTON

I had to pull over after pulling out of the parking lot. I forgot to check my phone for Vada's text before leaving the park, telling me Jonah's address.

I quickly type it into Google on my phone, my fingers continuing to shake like they did when I first found the keychain buried under the wood chips. I avoid looking at it as it rests in one of my cup holders. I don't know why, but I can't bring myself to look at it until Jonah confirms it in fact is not the same keychain I think it is.

Once I have the address put in, I continue driving where my phone tells me to go. When I pull into Jonah's neighborhood, I survey the houses, trying to see if any of them are familiar. The neighborhood is vaguely recognizable to me, much like how I felt when I saw Cassidy at the wedding. I couldn't place why she looked familiar to me, just like these houses.

When I pull up in front of Jonah's house, I grab the keychain and stuff it into my front pocket. I wipe the palms of my hands on my thighs and cut the ignition. I pull the key out and stare at Jonah's house for a bit, willing myself to stay calm.

The house is situated on a small piece of land, the ones on

either side only spaced a few feet away. It's a quiet neighborhood, the kind where everyone has well-maintained lawns and almost every house is identical to the one next to it.

I've always thought I was a rational type of person, always thinking before I dive head first into the deep end of any situation.

College.

The restaurant.

My relationship with Vada.

I've always taken my time, and wondered if I could be as committed as I wanted myself to be, at least in areas of my life that felt lacking. Now though, thinking about the keychain in my pocket, I question it all. Everything I thought I knew about myself seems to evaporate with every step up to the front door.

I ring the doorbell and move back a bit. My heart plunges into my stomach when the door swings open. A man I can only assume is Cassidy's dad stands on the other side. His light blond hair fades to white near the roots, and the wrinkles in his forehead deepen as he looks at me with curiosity.

His pale eyebrows dip between his eyes and he clears his throat. "Can I help you?"

"Oh, um, yeah. I'm here to see Jonah. I'm Colton, a friend of Vada and Cassidy."

"Right." He nods. "Cass told me you might be coming by." He jerks his head back toward the hallway, allowing me to step inside. He doesn't wait for me. Instead, he starts walking, leaving me to close the door. "Jonah," he yells. "Someone's here to see you."

The man continues down the hallway, making it apparent he doesn't care whether I follow him or not. There's a slight limp to his walk, and his shoulder dramatically dips with every step he takes. I make my way forward, following the same path he did. He sits down in the recliner set back in the corner of the living room, and I look up when I hear quick footsteps pounding against the ceiling. They make their way all the way down the stairs then Jonah swings around the corner. He grasps the railing, using it to propel himself toward the living room. His eyes light up the second he sees me.

Despite my happiness at seeing Jonah, my nerves still hum inside my veins. I look at Jonah more closely, hoping he can give me the answers I'm looking for, hoping he can tell me why he has this keychain.

"Colton!" he yells. He's excited, bouncing on the balls of his feet like he does every other time I've seen him. Clasping his hands in front of him, he holds them up to his chin. "Aunt Cass told me you went to the park to look for my keychain. Did you find it?"

I kneel in front of him, bringing myself down to his eye level. I look over my shoulder, checking to see if Cassidy's dad is watching. He's not. His eyes are glued to a documentary he has playing.

I pull the keychain out of my pocket, and Jonah's eyes widen as if I've just given him the number one gift on his Christmas wish list. I hold on to it, looking down at it in the center of my palm, the faded blue star somehow looking more faded than it did outside.

Tears line his eyes, and I watch as one drop spills over, sliding down his cheek.

"Thank you so much, Colton. Thank you for finding it." He smiles through the second tear spilling over. "I know what you're going to say."

"What do you think I'm going to say?" I ask him. There's no possible way he could guess the thoughts running through my mind about a simple keychain.

"That I should take better care of my things."

I let out a small laugh and run my hand across my mouth.

"You have a point there. You should take better care if it means that much to you."

"It does." He smiles, rubbing his thumb across the star. The longer he looks at it, the more I get this unsettling feeling that he didn't simply find it. It's an heirloom, or it holds some sort of significance for him.

"Jonah, can I ask you something?" I flick my gaze to the keychain then back to his light brown eyes. The dark brown hair on top of his head is messy, as if he's been rolling around or constantly running his fingers through it.

"Sure." He shrugs, swiping the tears away. They've already stopped.

I take a deep breath and blow it out. "Where did you find that keychain?"

"Oh." He frowns, looking down at it. When he looks back up at me, a ghost of a smile appears on his mouth, and his eyes light up. "I didn't find it. Cassidy gave this to me when I was a baby. She said my mom had it the night she found out she was pregnant with me. She said it was my dad's."

The blood drains from my face, and it takes every ounce of strength to keep myself from falling over.

Jonah's face transforms back to sadness, his smile fading. "It's the only thing I have from my dad because I never met him. That's why I can't ever lose it again."

I try to pull myself up to stand, ignoring the twisting, aching feeling in my chest. My stomach flops and I want to throw up, but I also don't want Jonah to worry about my reaction.

I place my hand on the back of my neck, squeezing it until I'm focusing on Jonah. Then it all starts to make sense to me.

The keychain.

The initials etched into it.

Why Cassidy looked so familiar to me, even though I've never met her.

And then when my eyes move past Jonah to the picture sitting on top of the end table situated against the wall, it feels like a barrel has been rammed into my chest.

It's a picture of Cassidy, and there's a girl standing next to her.

CHAPTER TWENTY-THREE

Vada

"I STILL DON'T UNDERSTAND WHY YOU TORTURE YOURSELF."
I'm sitting on the curb outside my brother's house, watching as
he finishes out his run. Sloan is a few feet behind him, her hands
planted firmly on her hips.

I can tell she's been making a habit of running with Dallas
every morning. Her stomach is a bit more toned, and the expression on her face tells me she isn't as exhausted as she used to be.

"I swear," she huffs, struggling to catch her breath. "This is
the last time I'm running with him."

"I already said you don't have to." Dallas smiles. He walks
over to Sloan as she hunches over. Her back is arched, and her
hands are on her knees. She stands when Dallas places his hand
on her back. He wraps both his hands around her cheeks,
pulling her in for a kiss.

It's sweet, but it's also strange watching my brother being
intimate with someone, especially when they're both drenched
in sweat.

"I'm trying to be a good wife." Sloan laughs with her statement, and I bite back a smile.

She's teasing Dallas.

"You already are one." He pulls away from Sloan and sits beside me on the sidewalk.

"Thanks." She grins, swiping the sweat from her forehead. "But seriously, I think I mean it this time. It's the last time."

I wrap my arms around my legs and look up at Sloan.

"I'm going to go take a shower." Sloan's eyes move between me and Dallas before she swings them back to me. "We're still on for tonight though, right?"

"Yep," I tell her. "I'm bringing the margaritas."

"I'll have the glasses."

Sloan and I planned a girls night a while back. Ever since she married Dallas and I started my relationship with Colton, we haven't necessarily seen each other as much as we like to, not to mention work has been killing me on top of all that.

I fight the exhaustion in my head as Sloan kisses Dallas one more time and heads inside the house. I'm staring at Sloan's house across the street when Dallas breaks the silence. She has yet to sell it even though she and Dallas use his house most of the time.

"How is everything? You know, with work and Colton."

I turn to face him, squinting against the morning sun rising behind his head.

"It's good." I'm lying, and the more I let the lie sink in, the more I realize it's my go-to answer when everything is anything but good.

I haven't heard from Colton since yesterday when I asked him if he would be able to swing by the park and search for Jonah's keychain. Since I was swamped at work, Colton was supposed to come over to my place after he closed up the restaurant last night, but he never did.

When I woke up early this morning, he wasn't lying beside me. Instead, all I got was a text letting me know he'd taken Jonah his keychain. That was it, a simple ten words.

Colton: I found Jonah's keychain and brought it back to him.

I don't quite understand why he's been nearly silent since our conversation on the phone. Maybe he thought I was too tired after I left work yesterday. Maybe he thought he was doing me a courtesy. Maybe he was tired himself. I can only guess, but I can't ignore the pit that's been sitting at the bottom of my stomach since I woke up to a half-empty bed today.

It's easy for me to slip into old habits. My mind automatically shifts back to how Colton used to be, before he told me I'm his.

I replay his words in my mind from the night he held me against my sliding glass door, the fire still burning outside. The rational part of my brain constantly pushes against the emotional side, convinced there's a simple explanation.

Other than work, Colton and I haven't exactly been on the same wavelength. It's as if every time we're together, it feels the opposite. One minute he's unable to keep his hands off of me, ensuring me he feels the same. The next there's a distant look in his eye, as if he's anywhere but with me.

I stare at my brother, wondering if he's spoken to Colton. I'm wondering if he can see through the lie I've just told him by saying everything is good.

Whether he notices my lie or not, he doesn't let on. He doesn't press me on it, and I'm thankful. Then again, Dallas has never been the one to be intrusive in my life. It's always been the other way around. I'm always the one wanting to know what's going on with him.

"Nice." Dallas nods. "I'm glad things are working out for you." He presses his lips together as he lets out a breath through his nose. His nostrils flare and he looks down at the ground, resting his elbows on his knees. "Dad texted me yesterday."

I roll my eyes, feeling the groan already building in my

throat. I let it out and lean back on my hands. My palms press against the rough sidewalk. "What did he have to say?"

"Well, I didn't really care to look. I left it sitting unread in my messages for a while, but before I left for work, I decided to check. He wants to come down here and visit."

I scoff, pushing aside the sting in my chest at the thought that my father only bothered to message Dallas instead of both of us. He truly and honestly could not care less. "Do you want him to visit?"

"Not really." He thinks on it, scratching at the stubble on his chin. "But at the same time, I don't think I care enough to stop him. I think I've stopped expecting anything out of him. Because we all know what expectations give us."

"Yeah." I nod, agreeing. "Can I ask you something?"

"You're going to anyway." He chuckles. "It's you, Vada."

"Right." I sit back up, giving him a soft smile. "Seriously though, I wanted to ask you...did you invite Dad to your wedding?"

Dallas sighs, wiping his hand across his mouth. My question has triggered him. His jaw twitches as he works over my question, and it's clear in his blue eyes that the answer he's about to give me isn't a simple one.

"No." His voice is even and direct. "I didn't."

I wince, not sure if I want to get into this conversation right now, but I feel like I need to know. I've been wondering ever since my mother brought it up at the reception. "Can I ask you why?"

He sighs, his entire body moving with it. "Because he didn't deserve to be there. We may have had more people there than we intended, but I really only cared about two people: you and Mom. That's it."

My chest warms with his admission. There's pain laced in his stare, but there's also a strong sense of love there. Dallas is loyal to a fault, and aside from Sloan, I know our mother and I are the most important people in his life.

"If it makes you feel any better, I would have done the same."

"Yeah?"

"Yeah." I nod, pulling my bottom lip under my teeth. Emotion builds behind my eyes, and I know if I don't rein it in soon, tears will start falling. "I think it's because Mom always taught me to never settle for second best. Why put in the effort when he can't bring himself to meet me halfway?"

"You know," Dallas says, looking over at Sloan's house. I stare at his profile, examining the dip of his nose to the lines that crease in the corners of his eyes as he narrows them. "Mom hasn't always been the best at giving advice, but I agree with her on that one. You deserve someone who can give you the whole fucking world, Vada. Shit, scratch that—you deserve someone who's worthy of being in yours. It's your world, and they just live in it."

"Oh my god." I lean into him with my shoulder, never having heard him be this emotional with me. My laugh triggers one from him, and we both sit on the edge of the curb together, staring at the house Sloan still owns but doesn't live in. "I don't think I've ever heard you give me advice like this."

"Yeah, well I guess you could say it's the brother in me coming out."

"Sure." I laugh again and sigh, pulling myself to a stand. I swipe my hands on my leggings.

Dallas stands as well, wiping the sweat collecting on his forehead. "Do you have work today?"

I shake my head. "No, but I'm going to swing by the restaurant to see Colton. I know he's there prepping."

"Cool." He nods. "I might see you there later then."

"Maybe." I pause, swallowing down the tightness in my chest. "Did you see him last night?"

"I did." He nods, planting his hands on his hips. "We were pretty slammed all the way up until closing. After Colton closed up the kitchen, he stuck around to help me out front. We stayed pretty late."

I raise my eyebrows. "And you still decided to run this early?"

Dallas shrugs, the corner of his mouth curling into a grin. "It's a habit. Besides, I know Sloan doesn't particularly enjoy running, but I love that she does it just to spend some time with me. Sometimes she'll wait at the entrance of the park while I make my loop through there." He laughs. "So don't exactly believe her when she groans about running with me all morning."

"Are you telling me she cheats?" I ask, finding myself laughing as well.

"A little." He winks as he steps backward up onto the side-walk. "I'll see you later, sis."

"See ya."

I wait until Dallas heads back into his house before trudging over to my car. It's still early enough in the morning that I know Colton is at the restaurant by himself, starting a new round of meats to smoke for the day before the dinner shift tonight.

I text him to let him know I'm on my way to stop by. My conversation with Dallas unraveled the knot that's been squeezing in my chest since I woke up. Colton stayed late to help Dallas up front. It's not that I don't trust Colton, but with our long history of pushing our feelings aside for the sake of everyone else, I can't help the doubts that seem to creep in. It's a new feeling I'm just now learning to deal with, but it's hard denying the idea that he's reminiscent of the same Colton as before, the one existing in a world where we kept a secret buried, pretending as if it didn't exist at all.

When I pull up in front of the restaurant, I walk around the building, knowing the front door will be locked and Colton will be out back anyway. I round the corner to find the back empty. Smoke billows out from the top of each smoker, and music is blaring from inside the restaurant. The back door is propped open as it usually is when the kitchen staff is out here working.

Colton walks out of the back door as soon as I step up to the rows of smokers, and the smile that appears on his face the second he sees me is enough to melt my insides. It nearly dissolves all the bullshit that's been running through my mind.

"Hi."

"Hi." He stands in front of the furthest smoker from where I am and opens it. He grabs a set of tongs sitting on the counter and flips over a few whole chickens that have been split open. "What are you doing here so early?"

"I went by and saw Dallas and Sloan this morning."

"Oh." He nods slowly, frowning in thought. "How was it seeing them?"

"It was nice. Feels like forever since I've seen them." I cross the patio, closing the space between us.

He doesn't turn in my direction, keeping his focus on the split chickens. He simply nods.

"I'm going over there tonight to spend some time with Sloan."

"That's good." He nods again. I notice he's barely blinked since I've been standing beside him. He's still taken to wearing his contacts, and they do a poor job of hiding his emotions. He may not be looking at me, but I can feel the distance seep its way into my bones. He's retreating, and I don't understand why.

I open my mouth, ready to ask him why he didn't come over last night, but he beats me to it.

He clears his throat, still focusing on the smoker. "Sorry about last night."

"Everything okay?" I decide to ask him straight, no dancing around the bullshit like we used to do.

I'm missing his arms around me. I'm missing his mouth pressed against mine.

"Yeah." He finally looks up at me. "Of course. I just stayed to help Dallas out a bit and was more tired than I thought I'd be when I got out."

"Okay." I nod, watching as he grabs the tongs. He flips over a few pieces of chicken and rearranges the racks before closing the lid. "I bet Jonah was happy when you brought him back his keychain." I smile, knowing how important it is to him. I remember the day at the trampoline park when he asked Cassidy to hold on to it for him and she told me the story behind it.

Colton pauses, allowing his tongs to hover over the tray of meat. He presses his lips together, and his eyebrows furrow in thought. "He was. I don't think I've ever seen him as happy as I did yesterday."

"Good." I smile, my chest warming at the thought. "It means so much to him. Cassidy told me he's had it forever, so I couldn't imagine what it would have been like if you hadn't found it."

"Yeah." His voice is quiet, and I can hear the exhaustion behind it. "Well, I'm glad I was able to find it for him."

I tilt my head and cross my arms over my chest. "Are you sure you're okay?"

He finally brings his gaze up to mine, and then as if a light has been switched on, his entire expression shifts. "I told you I was." He attempts to make me feel better by reaching out to me. He grabs one of my arms, forcing it to unravel.

I take one step forward.

"Come here." He wraps both hands around my cheeks,

pulling me to him. I stumble toward him, and the toes of my shoes scrape across the concrete. I fall against him as he tilts my face up to his. He keeps his eyes pinned on mine.

I'm unsure if it's exhaustion I see or if it's something else entirely, but the usual honey brown flecks of his eyes are now a few shades darker. His eyes have turned down, and it looks as if he's carrying the weight of the world behind them.

He examines my face as if he's trying to remember every single freckle dotted across my cheek and every line that forms along my skin. He inhales a deep breath, his body stiffening against mine. "I am now."

A ghost of a smile appears on his mouth, and I want nothing more than to crash my lips into his. The palms of his hands gently press deeper into my cheeks. His long fingers weave in between my curls. I return his smile just before he closes the remaining distance between us, slamming his lips to mine.

The sun is shining, and there's smoke from the burning pecan wood surrounding us. My nose fills with the scent of the smoker and Colton's freshly washed shirt. The fabric is crisp under my hands as I fist it, tugging him toward me.

I moan against his mouth as he walks me backward, pressing me against the brick wall. He isn't rushed or hurried. He's slow yet commanding. It's a comfort to be feeling him this way again. Every kiss and every touch from him is a reassurance that we're okay.

All the thoughts I've had since this morning were for nothing.

He pulls back far enough to look me in the eye, keeping me pressed against the wall. One hand is on my hip, the other still wrapped around my cheek. He massages my bottom lip with the pad of his thumb. "I really am sorry I didn't come over last night."

My eyes flutter as I shake my head slightly. "Really. It's okay."

"I plan on making it up to you," he says. "In more ways than one."

"Oh yeah?" The Colton I've come to fall for the past few weeks has now returned, his exhaustion floating away with every word he speaks.

"Yeah." He nods, sucking in his bottom lip under his teeth. I start to remember what it feels like to have his mouth between my legs. I'm suddenly aching for him, but I know we can't right now, not when I know he's exhausted from the past two days. "Starting with me coming over..."

"Tomorrow." I finish his sentence for him.

"Well..." He laughs. "I was going to say I can come over once Frankie comes in. He should be here in about an hour."

"Oh." I raise my eyebrows. "Only if you're up for it. I figured you'd want to take a nap or a shower maybe."

"I can do those things at your place, right?"

"Yeah, you can. But remember I'm meeting Sloan for dinner later." I bite down on my lip, grabbing the back of his neck and pulling him down to me. I bring my mouth to his, parting his lips with my tongue.

He tastes like mint, and I taste like the red licorice I nibbled on the way over here. We're a tangled, mingled mix of strawberry and mint, sweet and refreshing.

I pull away, keeping my hand wrapped around his neck. He presses his hips into me, and his hardened cock presses into the space between my thighs. I close my eyes and calm my breathing, not wanting to get too carried away.

"What's the other way you're going to make it up to me?"

"Oh, you're going to love this one." His chest vibrates against mine as a chuckle rises from his throat. "I still plan on taking you to my parents' charity dinner next weekend, if you're still up for it."

"Hmmm." I tap my finger on my chin. "Let me think about it."

"Okay." He pulls me closer, bringing his mouth close to mine again. "Don't think on it too long." He places his lips to mine once again. His hand slides down to my lower back, and he playfully smacks me then pulls back.

"I should get the rest of this meat going."

I laugh, following him back over to the smoker. My heart hammers in my chest and my stomach flips. "I'll be at home then."

"Okay." He grins, shoving one hand into his pocket.

"By the way, I thought about it—the dinner."

"You have?"

I nod. "I'll go with you, as long as you go as my date."

"I thought that was already implied."

"I'm just making sure you knew." I shrug, giving Colton one more kiss before leaving. "I'll see you in a bit."

I leave him standing by the smoker and head back toward the front of the restaurant to where my car is parked. This time when I'm walking back, my steps are a bit lighter, and my shoulders don't feel so heavy.

I think about the look in Colton's eyes when he pulled me to him, the reassurance he gave me, and that's enough for me to go home feeling a million times better.

CHAPTER TWENTY-FOUR

COLTON

THE RESTAURANT IS AN EASY DISTRACTION. SOMETIMES when my thoughts start to wander back to the day I found Jonah's keychain, I'm quick to wipe them away while I'm cutting into a slab of brisket. Even more is when I'm thinking about Vada and how I'm going to tell her Jonah and I are closer than just friends.

For the past few days, I've struggled to wrap my mind around a situation I never thought I'd be in. Pieces of our lives are intended to be left in the past. Apparently, mine aren't.

It wasn't until that day I stood in front of Jonah with him telling me his keychain once used to belong to his dad that I realized I haven't been living my life to please others and meet their expectations as I believed I have for so many years. I wasn't doing it for my father, and I wasn't doing it for my mother. I've been living my life the way I was in an attempt to put my old one behind me. I guess in my mind, when you grow up in a house like I did, it's easier to make a whole new life than to constantly look back on the old one.

I haven't wrapped my mind around what happened with Jonah enough to talk about it with anyone else. I wanted to tell

Vada. The words sat on the edge of my tongue, ready to pour out, but the wall built up in my chest stopped me.

It's not that I won't ever tell her about my connection to Jonah. I will. Deep down, however, I know I need to talk to Cassidy first. I need to know what her sister told her about Jonah's dad, if she knows more than he does.

I step through the doors leading to the dining room of the restaurant. Dallas is standing at the end of the bar, talking to a customer, and when I look over, I catch Vada standing at the other end.

My chest squeezes when I see who's she's talking to on the other side: Cassidy and Jonah. I clear my throat and head in their direction when Vada sees me. She waves me over then turns her attention back to Cassidy and Jonah.

"Hey." I breathe out, trying my best to stay calm.

The restaurant isn't exactly filled, but there's enough of a crowd that I find myself having to talk louder than if it were dead in here.

"Hey." Vada leans on the counter and tilts her head back, her eyes roaming over me. "I was just about to head back and find you. Cassidy and Jonah stopped by for lunch, and they were just about to leave."

"Yeah," Jonah says. His eyebrows arch and his cheeks redden with excitement. "I finished that comic book you bought me. Aunt Cass is taking me to the store so I can get another one."

"Oh my god, you won't believe." Cassidy playfully groans. "He hasn't stopped talking about them since you took him."

"Really? Did you end up liking *Spider-Man?*" I ask him, leaning on the counter and crossing my arms over the top.

Cassidy and Jonah are standing behind the barstools parked in front of the counter. Jonah's head barely reaches the top of the stool, and his eyes are shadowed by the Rangers baseball cap he's wearing. It's covering his brown hair, but the ends peek out underneath, hanging above his eyebrows.

"I loved it. I really want to get another one." He leans closer toward me, wraps his hands around the top of the stool, and stands on his toes as if he's stretching to tell me a secret. "But Colton..." He lowers his voice to a whisper. "I'm going to try to convince Aunt Cass to get me two comic books instead of one."

Cassidy grins, rolling her eyes toward the front of the restaurant. I can tell she's holding back a laugh, wondering why he bothered to whisper when all of us could hear him anyway.

The second he giggles, my heart twists with an even deeper ache than all the other times I've seen him. The way his nose scrunches and the way he lifts his hand to his mouth, stifling his own laugh...it's all too familiar.

It's as if the wind has been knocked out of me. I stand up from the counter, unraveling my arms and shoving my hands into my pockets. "Sounds like you might have some convincing to do then."

"Well..." He sighs. "I have been trying to help more around the house."

"That's true," Cassidy says, placing her hand on his head. "He has been helping more when it comes to taking out the trash and helping Pop-Pop when he needs anything."

"Yep." He nods. "I've even sat with him a few times while he watches his documentaries."

"Oh man," Vada says, turning to Cassidy. "This kid definitely deserves two comic books then."

"I'll think about it," she muses, wrapping her arm around Jonah's shoulders. She starts pulling him away from the chair, and I wonder when I'll see him next.

"Maybe we can go together again sometime," Jonah suggests. "You and Vada."

"Maybe." I look at Jonah then Cassidy. I want to talk to her, want to ask her the million questions running through my mind. I want to tell her about the keychain.

But I can't, not when we're standing in the middle of my restaurant surrounded by strangers. That's not exactly the kind of conversation you have when you're in a place like this.

It pulls at me, the need to tell someone—Cassidy, Vada...but I can't. I still haven't been able to process it myself.

Before I can think on it any further, Cassidy and Jonah are already saying bye and heading out the door. I watch them as they step out onto the sidewalk and head down the street toward the comic book store.

"I was thinking of offering to help tonight if you need it."

Vada steps toward me. She grabs my hand, holding it loosely between us. Her touch warms me, dissolving the heavy weight bearing down on my shoulders.

"Um..." I think back to the schedule and who is set to work. "I think we have it covered. Are you not working at the paper today?"

"I am." She shrugs. "But Nate said my final edits could be turned in tomorrow instead of today, so I figured I could help out around here."

"I appreciate it though."

I tighten my fingers around her hand. Her skin is smooth, but her eyes shift, the green color fading as she allows my words to sink in.

The same feeling comes over me that crept in the other day. I could tell her now. I could open my mouth and say the words I know to be true.

Then again, I wonder how that would change things between us. For so long, Vada held herself back, fearing I would put her in second place, and for a while, I never shied away from telling her the truth. I couldn't put her first. I was honest, and at the time, I wasn't able to give her all of me.

The past few weeks with her have changed everything, and now that I'm finally able to put her first, I'm about to tell her something that could change it all.

But my feelings on whether it would change the relationship we've built doesn't matter. I know better than to keep this a secret for the sake of saving her feelings. I should tell her. Deep down, I know I need to.

I inhale a deep breath and open my mouth, ready to ask her if we can talk somewhere else, but I'm stopped.

"Is that you, Vada? I thought Colton here fired you a long time ago."

I turn around to find one of our weekly regulars sliding into the barstool across from where we're standing.

"Hey, Paul." She beams, glancing over at me before taking the few steps to stand in front him on the opposite side of the counter. "Colton did *not* fire me." She pins me with a stare before rolling her eyes back to Paul. "How are you?"

"Oh, you know." He shakes his head and laughs. "Same old shit, different day."

"Well, it is when you come in here five days a week." Vada laughs, and I can't help but laugh with her.

"I can't be comin' in here every day now." Paul shakes his head. "If I did, then hell, that would be too much. I won't lie though, I considered it in hopes I'd come in on the off chance you'd be here, even though your brother told me you've been killing yourself at the newspaper."

"I have not," she says. "If I were killing myself there, I wouldn't be here now, would I? Don't believe everything my brother tells you."

"Guess you're right." Paul pouts.

Dallas comes over with an already full glass of beer, knowing what Paul orders. I do too.

"Are you guys talking about me?" Dallas asks.

"No." Paul shakes his head. "Of course not."

"Usual meal, Paul?" I ask him, wanting to wash away the feeling coming over me. One minute I'm ready to tell Vada about Jonah, the next we're standing here laughing with Paul.

"Yep. Country fried steak on Texas toast, extra mayo."

"You've got it. Coming right up." I thrum my fingers on the counter and spin to head back to the kitchen, but I stop outside the swinging door when a hand wraps around mine, pulling me to a stop.

"Hey." Vada's green eyes are spread wide, staring up at me. "I just want to double check that you don't need my help. I figured with Paul coming in..." She sticks out her thumb and hitches her hand over her shoulder, pointing to where Dallas and Paul are deep in conversation.

"Yeah." I nod, pushing away my thoughts of Jonah. "If you want to, you can stay. It's up to you. I just didn't want you to feel obligated."

"I don't feel obligated." Standing on her toes, she plants a quick kiss on my lips then walks back over to the end of the bar.

I watch her walk away, figuring I can tell her another time... a better time. I just need to figure out when that is.

CHAPTER TWENTY-FIVE

Vada

I WANT TO VOMIT.

It's dramatic but true.

My stomach flips upside down the second my heeled shoe hits the gravel driveway outside Colton's parents' house.

I drop the bottom of my dress, letting it fall around me. The dark green fabric gathers at my feet, covering my black strappy heels. This is the first time I'm wearing them since I bought them three days ago. I've left my hair down, allowing my curls to flow freely across my back. A diamond barrette rests on the side of my hair, pinning one side away from my face.

When I agreed to come with Colton to the dinner, I don't think I fully understood what it meant. While I assumed I would wear a cocktail dress, I realized I was in fact supposed to wear a ball gown. While I thought Colton was going to wear a nice, pressed, button-down shirt and tie, I was wrong again. He's wearing a perfectly tailored black suit, and his black tie rests flat against his white collared shirt underneath. He's in a full-blown suit.

It's something I've only ever seen on him once before: Dallas and Sloan's wedding.

The house is fully lit from the inside out. Faint chatter and laughter filter through the open front door. A man dressed in a vest and bowtie stands near the door, opening doors for the guests as they drive up.

Wow.

Colton's parents have even gone as far as to hire a valet service. Colton hands the valet his keys. He leaves us with a quiet nod and hops into the driver's seat. He pulls away, allowing the next guest of the Adler's to flow in behind us.

Colton's standing in front of me, holding his hand out for me to take. I grab it, taking the first step toward the large house situated in the middle of nowhere.

I haven't told him about Nate's recommendation yet. When he picked me up, I could tell he was nervous, his mind set on getting through this dinner. From the second he saw me standing outside my apartment, I could tell he'd been worrying about how tonight will go.

I considered telling him anyway. I wanted to boast about Nate's recommendation, and I knew if I decided to tell him, it would put a smile on his face, but the faraway look in his eyes told me it wasn't the time. This night is about Colton.

I need to be here for him. I want to be.

The ride over was silent. Mostly we sat, listening to the radio through the speakers. He popped open his console, pulled out a piece of gum, and hasn't stopped chewing it since we crossed the Austin city line.

We only make it up one of the steps leading to the front door before he pulls us to a stop. He tugs on my hand, his fingers tightening their grip.

"What's wrong?" I ask him. He pulls us off to the side of the entrance, out of the way of the continuous flow of guests driving up. We're standing in front of a large bush, and I look past Colton, truly getting a feel of where we are. The field surrounding us is pitch black. I can't see past twenty feet in front of me. Stars dot the blue-black sky, and the golden light coming from inside the Adler's house behind me casts shadows across Colton's face.

His eyebrows arch across his forehead as he rubs his fingers across his skin. He's freshly shaved, the skin there smooth and bare. He's wearing his contacts again, displaying his perfect caramel-colored eyes.

"I don't know. I think I just need a minute before going in there."

"Okay." I wrap my arms around his shoulders and pull him closer as he bends, placing his hands on the small of my back.

He rests his chin on my shoulder, breathing me in. His lips brush against the skin between my neck and shoulder. His hot breath dances down my spine, causing a shiver to wash over me. I tense my thighs, breathing in his minty scent. For once, he doesn't smell like burning pecan wood. A part of me misses it when I pull back.

He looks different, slightly younger...more anxious.

I place my hand on his cheek, and fire smolders in my chest the second he reacts to my touch, leaning into it.

He grabs the back of my hand and squeezes it. He breathes out then lifts a few of my fingers, turning his face to place his lips against them. He stares into my eyes, and I search them for answers, clues as to what he's holding inside. Why is he looking at me as if I'm both causing him pain but also have the medicine to take it away?

"Thank you," he whispers.

"I didn't say anything."

"You didn't need to." He kisses my hand one more time, pulling me closer. "I need to remember that whatever happens in there, it doesn't matter. I have you with me."

"What do you think will happen?" I'm genuinely curious.

"I don't know." He lifts his other hand and pinches the bridge of his nose. He squeezes his eyes shut then opens them on a sigh. "I'm not saying anything will. I just never know when it comes to my parents."

"I get it. Everything will be fine. I'm here. It's only a few hours, and then we're out of here."

I know Colton has a habit of burying family secrets. He was raised in the type of family that hid any sort of situation that could be considered a scandal, keeping it away from the public eye. Colton's family isn't famous and isn't necessarily considered well-known, but to those who do know them, they are considered Texas royalty.

I've never been so nervous to meet the parents of anyone I'm dating. Meeting family is nerve-racking in itself, but meeting the Adler's? Now, that's a whole different story on its own.

Colton inhales a shaky breath, despite his solid body pressing against me as his muscled arms hold me against him. He's warm and everything I need to get through this night.

I might just be as nervous as him despite my attempt to sound confident.

I've felt distant from Colton these past two weeks, even more so in the past few days. But right now, as his eyes flicker with the lights coming from the house behind us, I've never felt closer to him. There's sadness in his eyes as he looks at me. He's conflicted once again.

He wraps his hand around the side of my face, pressing his thumb beneath my bottom lip. It's a habit he's formed whenever he's holding me this way, one I've grown accustomed to. My stomach flutters as he softly moves the pad of his thumb back and forth across my lip.

"Vada." His whisper is barely heard over the chatter coming from inside. "I need to tell you something before we go in there."

I inhale a deep breath, and my heart nearly stops. It slows, echoing across my body before it beats again. "What is it?"

"Colton, dear, there you are."

A woman's voice coming from behind me pulls his attention away. His eyes dart over my shoulder, causing me to turn in that direction.

I turn around, grabbing the fabric of my dress, pulling it with me.

A woman with the same smile as Colton's walks past me, pulling him in for a hug. She wraps her arms around him, and when she does, I catch Colton staring at me over her shoulder. He's bent down to hug her, wrapping his arms around her small frame. She's quite a bit shorter than he is, even shorter than me.

When she pulls away from him, holding him at arm's length, I can tell she's quite beautiful. Her brown hair is swept back into a tight low bun. Not a hair is out of place. Her silver dress sparkles with her every move, the perfect complement to her smooth skin.

The corners of her eyes crease as she grins, taking in Colton's outfit. "You look sharp, son."

"Thanks, Mom." His eyes move from her toes to her feet. "You look beautiful."

"Thanks."

Her smile deepens, but it's almost as if I see what Colton has been saying all along. There's a sadness hidden behind her smile, covering the way she truly feels on the inside. Maybe I'm only seeing it because Colton's told me of the pain she constantly carries with her after losing Ryan. To everyone else, she's the studious wife of a big-time Texas business mogul. The ones who know her or even know the truth of the family can see the façade she uses to hide her grief.

"This must be Vada." She turns to me, widening her fake grin.

She smells like strawberries. It's the first smell that hits my nose as she places her hand on my arm.

"Yes, Mom," Colton says, giving me a smile. "I'd like to introduce you to my girlfriend, Vada. Vada, this is my mom, Faye." He stands beside me and places his hand on the small of my back. His warm fingertips touch my skin, kissed by the cool night air.

"It's nice to meet you," I tell her, hoping she sees me differently than the way I know her husband does—no better than the dirt we're standing on.

"Mmm." It's the only word she says before she looks up at Colton. Her expression changes. Her shoulders stiffen and she looks toward the entrance to the house where guests are still arriving. Car after car continues to drive up. The valet looks exhausted already.

I brush off Faye's sudden change of mood. Her reaction to seeing me leaves me confused. She's the one who invited me here after all. She's the one who made the suggestion to Colton. Her rigid response to my introduction is a quick pinch to the chest. One second it stings, the next it's faded.

"I actually came out here to see if you had arrived yet. Your father is concerned that you aren't inside with all these guests arriving."

Colton presses his lips together, blowing out a hot breath through his nose. His nostrils flare slightly and his jaw ticks. We're not even inside yet and Colton's already irritated.

"Vada and I were just on our way in."

"Great," she says. She hasn't once bothered to bring her eyes in my direction. "I'll tell your father you're right behind me then."

When she leaves to head back into the house, she still doesn't bother glancing in my direction. To be honest, it's almost as if I'm not even here.

I turn back to look at Colton. His mouth is still pressed into a flat line, and his jaw is still working, the muscles pulsating across his jawbone.

"Colton," I whisper, placing my hand on his cheek, urging him to look down at me.

When he does, his eyes have darkened. I hate how he hates being here.

"I'm fine."

I giggle and shake my head. "That's the word someone says when they are anything but fine."

That brings his attention back to mine. He stares into my eyes half a second longer before grabbing the back of my head and pulling me in for a kiss. He firmly plants his mouth on mine then pulls back.

"At this rate, I'm going to need to reapply my lipstick." I swipe my finger across my mouth, checking to feel if it's faded.

"You look gorgeous."

"Thank you." I grin and nod my head back toward the house, turning halfway. "We should head in there before your mom comes out here looking for us again."

"I'm sorry she didn't give you the warm welcome you were expecting."

"I wasn't expecting anything, Colton. Besides, if I can handle her, I'm sure I can handle your father."

Colton laughs then shakes his head.

"Well..." He grabs my hand, leading me toward the house. "That was just the opener. We haven't even made it to the main event yet."

CHAPTER TWENTY-SIX

Vada

I'VE NEVER SEEN A HOUSE AS LARGE AS SCOTT AND FAYE Adler's. When Colton told me they had money, I didn't realize he meant *this* much.

The floor in the entryway is laid with shiny, pristine white marble tiles. They meet near the middle of the house, transitioning to a rich, dark hardwood running throughout the rest of the space. Each wall is decorated in some version of Texas-themed art. On one wall hangs a picture of a steer, and on the next there are actual longhorns mounted above a large sheet of metal cut into the shape of Texas.

Everything about this house screams Texas—Texas and money.

Colton squeezes my hand and holds it tight as we make our way through the house. He avoids the grand staircase situated in the middle of the entryway, and at least three waiters pass by us as we continue walking through to the backyard. Several guests recognize Colton on the way. They shake his hand, exchanging basic polite greetings before he introduces me.

I watch in awe as Colton changes from the man I've come to know for the past few years to the man I'm watching in front of me. I'm used to seeing him in plain shirts and torn jeans, serving up barbecue sandwiches, all while country music blasts in the background.

This Colton is different, sharper and cleaner around the edges. He stiffens when a guest pulls us to a stop. His voice is smooth and slow as he speaks to them before politely excusing himself. It's all very robotic and unlike the Colton I've fallen in love with.

Watching Colton slip into this role the second he walked through the oversized wooden doors makes me realize just how different his life used to be. Cocktail parties and money, fake smiles and money—all of it for the sake of appearances, to keep up the Adler image.

All four large French doors are spread wide open, creating a seamless transition from the party inside to the guests outside. Large round tables draped with white tablecloths are scattered through the field. They stretch as far back as an entire ballroom length. It's as if we're back at Sloan's wedding, only now we're standing outside.

Colton hands me a glass of champagne from one of the waiters' trays before we start walking down the three steps to the yard. String lights hang from tall wooden posts sticking up out of the ground. Toward the back of the field, past the endless rows of tables, is a large open white tent. From what I can tell from where we're standing, that's where the auction is being held. It's filled with pieces of furniture and artwork enclosed in glass cases.

"Oh shit."

"What?" I turn to Colton, following his gaze as a tall, stocky man ambles toward us.

Where Colton shares his mother's smile, he shares his father's eyes. They aren't the same color, but with the way they widen at the sight of us, there's no mistaking the similarities.

Colton squeezes my hand once more before his dad reaches us, sending me a silent signal that this is why he muttered the words he did, causing me to look in this direction.

"It's about time, Colton," Scott says. "I was wondering if you'd forgotten about tonight altogether."

"Of course not, Dad."

"Well, you know, from what I remember, Ryan was never late to a dinner. Not once." His voice wanders as he flicks his eyebrows and lifts his glass to his mouth. A dark amber liquid freely sloshes around inside of it. He tips it back and swallows, curling his lips inward. He hisses between his teeth before his gaze finally lands on me. "You must be Vana."

"Vada," Colton says quickly.

I gently squeeze his hand, truly not caring if the man gets my name right or not. I just need to get Colton through this night.

"Right." He grins, nodding his head once and extending his hand. "My apologies. It's nice to meet you."

"You as well." I release Colton's hand and return his father's handshake. His grip is firm, his large hand tightening around my fingers.

"Colton tells me you work for a paper. Which one is it again?"

"*The Austin Chronicle.*" I grin. I shift my gaze up to Colton, knowing I have yet to tell him about my promotion. "I'm managing editor."

"Huh," Scott says, giving me a curt nod.

I release Scott's hand, and Colton is quick to move, reclaiming it.

"I'd offer you a few hors d'oeuvres, but it seems you're a little late for those." Scott narrows his gaze then looks around the party. "Dinner should be starting soon at least."

"Okay, Dad." Colton's voice is flat and emotionless.

Scott's focus turns back to his son. "After dinner, I'd like to introduce you to a few investors, Colt. They're very important businessmen in the state, and I think it would benefit you to meet them."

Colton pauses, considering his father's proposal. Lifting his champagne glass to his mouth, he takes a gulp and swallows before responding. "Sure."

Scott gives us both a silent nod before turning his attention back to his guests. He lifts his hand in the air and waves down another man in a tuxedo across the patio. When he leaves, I can feel Colton's body exhaling beside me. His whole body shifts, and it's as if he was holding his breath the entire time Scott was talking to us.

We stand in silence for a few more minutes before we make our way to our table. One of the announcers stands up to a microphone between the tent and the rows of tables. There's a small podium with a single microphone standing in the middle of it.

The announcer leans forward, asking if everyone can take a seat at their assigned tables. Colton leads us to one near the front. His mother is already sitting down when she sees us. Colton holds out my chair before he sits down in the seat between us. There's an empty seat next to Faye, a chair I can only assume is reserved for Scott.

One of the servers automatically brings us each a fresh glass of champagne. A full one appears in front of me like magic. I pinch my fingers around the stem and glance over at Colton. He's staring at me with a relieved expression.

He leans forward, bringing his mouth to my ear. "I swear to God, Vada, looking at you surrounded by all these people makes me realize how fucking lucky I am. You're the most beautiful woman here."

My eyes flutter closed, feeling his breath dance across my

skin. I squeeze the stem of the glass, my nails pressing into the flesh of my fingertips. "You, Colton Adler, are insatiable."

"That's what I'm counting on," he answers, pulling away from me and sitting back in his chair just as his dad ambles up to the podium. Bright yellow spotlights shine down on his stout frame, his eyes wincing against the light.

"Attention, distinguished guests and friends. I would like to thank you all for coming out tonight. We hope you enjoy delicious drinks and food, all while raising money for the incredible charities we've chosen this year." He clears his throat. "A special thank you to my wife, Faye. As always, you did an exceptional job putting this event together. Let's all give her a round of applause."

The crowd surrounding us erupts with clapping. Faye doesn't stand. Instead, she nods her head in several directions, pulling her smile together long enough to fool the crowd. But again, I can see straight through it.

It's the same expression that's on Colton's face. He isn't clapping, and his focus isn't on his mother. It's on his father, standing at the podium in front of one hundred people.

I look from Colton to Scott and find him staring back at him in the same way. It's as if their sights are fused to one another, battling one another in silence.

The mood surrounding us swiftly changes, and I can feel Colton's body start to harden again. He stiffens as the applause dies out and his mother's artificial smile fades. His jaw ticks as he works his mouth, pressing his lips into a thin line. My heart pounds in my chest, unsure of what's happening. They haven't spoken a word to each other, but I can see the war in their gaze.

"As many of you know..." Scott's eyes sadden as he surveys the crowd. He takes a moment and looks down at his feet then rubs his fingers across his mouth before he continues. "As many of you know, I lost my son, Ryan, last year to a drunk driver."

I take note of Scott's use of the word 'I' instead of 'we', not including Faye or Colton in the loss. It's a subtle word choice and most wouldn't notice, but I know Colton does. He lowers his hand below the table and rests it on my leg. He stretches his fingers out, flexing them against my flesh. The smooth fabric of my dress bunches under his grip. I place my hand on top of his, urging him to stay calm, though I don't know how effective I am.

"I won't lie...his loss has been a struggle. Most of you knew how dedicated of a man he was. Studious. Hardworking. Most of all, he was dedicated to this company. He spent many years attending the University of Texas, eventually earning his PhD. From a young age, Ryan was always eager to learn the family business. He was valedictorian of his graduating class, a Texas scholar, and even received multiple offers to Ivy League schools around the country. But of course, he stayed true to his Texas roots, never roaming far from home." His gaze moves to Colton's. Both Faye and I shift our attention to him, following where Scott's eyes are narrowing. Colton removes his hand from my leg and straightens his back when Scott continues. "He was everything I could ever ask for in a son, in a man to carry on the business. I was proud of him, and having a son like him made me the proudest I could ever be. No one could ever measure up to the kind of man he was, to the kind of son he was. And because of that, I will forever feel his death until I die."

I'm still staring at Colton as Scott's words ring in my ears. I can see it in Colton's eyes, the way they swell and turn glassy. The reflection of the lights flickers in his eyes. Fire and ice intertwine. The pain in Colton's face is undeniable as he stares up at his father in disbelief.

Those words cut like a knife. They were meant for Colton, slicing straight through him.

"But as for the true reason for tonight..." Scott's voice fades into the background. Colton and I are no longer listening when he leans toward me, whispering again.

"I have to get the fuck out of here."

Before I'm able to turn to Colton or convince him to stick it out, he's sliding his chair back, spinning around. He fastens the button of his suit as he stuffs one hand into his pocket and makes his way toward the outside of the tables. He's quick to head toward the house.

I turn back to Faye, holding my breath. There's sadness in her eyes, but she doesn't move. It's as if she's completely shut down, unable to speak up for herself or, more importantly, Colton.

I get up from my chair, not caring that Scott has finished with his speech. The crowd bursts into applause again. A few eyes follow me as I pass, but all I can focus on is finding Colton.

By the time I make it through the open French doors, Colton is passing through the living room on his way to the entrance. His feet move from the smooth, dark hardwood to the cold marble.

I've caught up to Colton when I hear Scott's voice booming behind me.

"How dare you get up and walk away in the middle of my speech."

Fuck.

I'm standing between Colton and Scott when he finally reaches Colton. His narrow face is pinched tight, his eyebrows knitting together in anger. His cheeks are flaming bright red, much like Colton's.

I move next to Colton, unsure of what Scott's intentions are.

"Talk to me like a fucking man, will you?" Scott has lowered his voice. It's deep and venomous.

Every guest is still seated outside, digging into dinner and sipping on the free endless cocktails.

"You want me to talk to you like a man?" Colton asks. His words come out in heated breaths of disbelief. "You clearly didn't sound like a man up there on your stage."

"How dare you talk to me like this in my house." Scott takes a step closer to Colton, glaring once again.

"I don't give a fuck how I'm talking to you now. I won't sit here and listen to you spout off your bullshit. I know what you meant up there. None of that was about your grief from losing Ryan. None of that was true. You were only saying those things to get back at me for not being the son you wanted me to be."

Scott's eyes narrow before he shifts them in my direction. He stares at me for a few seconds, and his hard, cold eyes are a punch to my gut. I want to vomit with the way his stare hits me. He shifts his focus back to Colton.

"No. You aren't the son I wanted you to be."

"What the fuck is wrong with you?" Colton asks, shaking his head. "I don't know why I bothered to come. I should have known you would treat me this way. You always have."

"I have not." Scott clenches his hands into fists. "The fact is, you never learned. You never took the initiative Ryan did. He was everything you should have been. He was everything you should be. I told you from the start you shouldn't have opened that restaurant of yours."

Colton laughs, but there's no humor behind it. The anger raging inside him has now radiated across his body. The muscles in his arms strain against the sleeves of his suit, and the vein in his temple is raised against his skin, pulsating as he clenches his jaw. "You know absolutely nothing about Ryan."

"Are you kidding?" Scott shouts, pointing a stern finger to the ground. "He was my son."

"And he was my brother," Colton yells back. Silence fills the air between the three of us. The two men stare at one another.

Colton's eyes line with unshed tears. He holds them back, not allowing them to fall in front of his father.

My chest aches as the silence continues, but it's quickly replaced by the sound of Faye's heels clicking across the marble.

She doesn't speak a word or try to intervene. A tear spills over, sliding down her cheek as she stands behind her husband. Although she's standing behind him, she keeps her distance, not letting herself get too close.

I grab Colton's hand, urging him to leave. I know we need to get out of here before Scott takes this argument a step further. Thankfully, the guests outside are still distracted, but I don't know how long that'll last when the entire hosting family isn't present.

"Colton," I say gently, "we should probably go." I shift my focus to Faye, giving her the softest smile I can manage. It's filled with both regret and sadness.

"That's right. You should probably listen to that girl of yours. Lord knows your brother wouldn't have left, much less let a woman tell him what he should do."

Scott's lip curls as Colton steps forward. He's within a foot of his father. They're nearly the same height, neither of them having to look up at the other with their heated stare.

"Like I said, you have no fucking clue who Ryan truly was." Colton takes a step back, his gaze floating back and forth between his mother and his father. His voice wobbles, emotion taking over the anger. "You want to know how fucking perfect Ryan was? You think you knew him so well? He has a son."

CHAPTER TWENTY-SEVEN

COLTON

"What?"

It's the first word I've heard my mother mutter since we saw her out front when we first arrived at the house.

My father's once narrowed eyes have now widened into shock with my sudden confession. I couldn't help it, couldn't hold it in any longer. The secret of knowing my brother had a son was eating me alive. In time, I guess I intended to tell them. It was a secret they deserved to know, but with the way my strained relationship with my father only seemed to worsen, I didn't know when the right time to tell him would be.

Listening to my father spouting off bullshit about how perfect my brother was, was the last straw. My heart pounded in my chest as it filled with hot anger. The words spilled out of me before I even had time to realize what I was saying.

My mother takes a step closer to us, her face paling.

"A son?" she whispers.

"Yep," I snap, voice clipped. I focus back on my dad, allowing my anger to pour out of me. I've broken a dam, and now the flood is rushing out. "His name is Jonah, and he's seven years old."

From the corner of my eye I can see Vada snap her head in my direction. She looks up at me, her jaw dropping in shock. Her hand falls away from mine and she steps back, placing it over her mouth.

"Jonah? What are you talking about?" The blood drains from her face as tears line her green eyes.

I tilt my head to the side, dipping my eyebrows as regret replaces the anger I had for my father. I should have told Vada. She didn't deserve to find out this way, and she doesn't deserve to know I've been keeping this a secret from her.

"I'm sorry," I start, pulling my hand out of my pocket and holding it out to her. "I meant to tell you when I found out, but—"

"Ryan had a son?" my mother asks again, interrupting me. This time her voice is above a whisper. It's the most direct I've heard her speak in a long time.

My father hasn't uttered a word since I brought up Jonah. Everyone is staring at me, waiting to hear my explanation, but all I can do is focus on Vada. Behind the shock in her eyes, there's pain—pain caused by me not telling her, me keeping another secret from her. The hurt is visible in her eyes. It stings, knowing I'm the one who put it there.

I try to explain. "I only found out a couple weeks ago, when I brought Jonah his keychain."

She quickly moves her hand to her stomach and looks down at the floor. Her dress is fanned out around her feet, lying against the cool, white marble.

I want to wrap my arms around her and hold her to me. I want to explain every bit of detail of why I know Jonah is Ryan's. Most importantly, I want to explain to her why I haven't been able to tell her since I found out. The more I look between my mother and Vada, the more I'm having a hard time deciding who to focus on more.

"You've known for two weeks?" Vada asks me, still keeping her hand placed against her stomach. I noticed she's slowly been backing away from me. "And you didn't tell me?"

Secrets...Vada and I have always kept secrets, but those have only been between us. This is the first time I've kept one from her, the first one like this. This is the only one where I've kept her in the dark.

"How—" My mother stutters, swallowing the emotion thick in her throat. "How do you know he has a son? That would mean he was..."

"Twenty." I finish the thought for her. "He was twenty when Jonah was born. Lyla was eighteen."

I hold my breath, remembering how keeping Ryan's relationship with Lyla a secret used to be a big deal to him. At one point, he made me swear not to tell anyone or else he'd make me eat a handful of hay from one of the horse's stables. I never told a soul after that conversation.

But now, eight years have passed, and it's been nearly a year since his death. Life is different, and judging by the look on my mother's face, it's time I lay it all out.

"Ryan met Lyla when he was a senior in high school. He went to an out-of-town football game. She was a cheerleader for the opposing team, and one of his friends introduced them." I flick my gaze toward Vada before swinging it to my parents. "He never told anyone about her...except me. I only met her a few times when he would drop her off at her house after school. He was with her for almost two years before she broke it off with him before she graduated high school."

"No." Vada shakes her head. "Cassidy told me her sister said Jonah was conceived from a one-night stand. You must have them mixed up."

"I don't," I say, shaking my head. "She must have lied to Cassidy. Maybe she kept Ryan a secret from her family too."

"Who is Cassidy?" my mother asks.

"She's my friend and a photographer for the newspaper," Vada answers, briefly glancing at my mother before bringing her gaze back to me. "She's Jonah's aunt."

"Ryan never kept secrets from me," my father says, still staring at me as if he's waiting to call me out on my lie.

"Oh, he did. And you know what? He was considering leaving your company. He didn't want to take it over anymore."

"You're a liar."

"No." I shake my head, clenching my teeth together. "He texted me the night he died. It was after he had dinner with you. He was begging me to reconsider not working for you because he didn't want to." My anger is still simmering under the surface, burning with every single word my father manages to utter. In a way, I guess I've always felt my father had a part in Ryan's death. Only because he was the last person to see him before his head-on collision with a drunk driver. I glance back over at Vada, thinking back to all the moments when my father has made backhanded comments regarding her. "And honestly, I can see why he didn't want to tell you the truth. I don't blame him."

"How do you know this boy is his?" my mother asks softly, pulling me away from both Vada and my father. I can tell she's eager to learn more about Jonah and how he's a piece of my brother, a piece of himself that he left behind. "How do you know he's Ryan's?"

"Because Jonah has a keychain he says belonged to his dad." I hold my breath, remembering seeing the faded blue star and initials etched onto the back. I remember the way it looked as it sat in my palm and feeling like I'd lost Ryan all over again. "He lost it at the park, and when I went looking for it, I found it buried under the mulch below the monkey bars. When I pulled it out, I remembered Ryan had the exact same one. At first, I wasn't sure it was his, but then I saw the initials carved into the back: ROA. I remembered he did that with a pocketknife after he bought it. He told me he did it in case he ever lost it one day. Then whoever found it would know who it belonged to."

"Enough." My father's deep booming voice echoes around the entryway. Several of the guests at the outside tables closest to the house turn their heads in our direction.

My heart stops, and I hold my breath. My father takes a step closer to me, bringing his face within inches of mine. I can smell the red wine and cigar scent on his breath.

"You're lying," he seethes, curling his lip in anger. His forehead creases and his skin flames red.

"I'm not lying." My vision turns red with his immediate dismissal, though I shouldn't be surprised.

"Get out of my house." He straightens his arms at his sides and curls his hands into fists.

I clench my teeth in disbelief as his refusal to hear the truth barrels into my chest like a speeding train.

"Get the fuck out of my house, right now!" he yells, pointing toward the door behind me.

"I'm telling you that you have a grandson and you're telling me to leave? Ryan had a son, Dad. You have a grandson out there in the world, and you don't give a shit. You know what?" I ask, my anger now starting to return. I backtrack my steps and close the distance between us, matching my stance with his. We're about the same height, so I tip my chin higher and narrow my eyes. "It isn't me who's a failure. It's you. You can't admit that you failed with me, and you can't admit that you failed with Ryan either. Because in your eyes, him having a child at twenty while unmarried is a failure. You may have convinced yourself he was the perfect son, but the fact is, this proves you didn't know him at all. Whether or not you believe me, you have a grandson out there, and you're denying him the right to a family. You're the one who is a fucking failure."

"Get out," my father says, this time keeping his voice low.

I give him a smirk in disbelief and back away. "Nothing I haven't heard before." I give him a nod and shift my focus to my mother. Tears are streaming down her face, and I can sense the hurt in them. I want to walk over to her and hold her, wrap my arms around her and tell her everything will be okay, but I'm not sure now is the time. She steps closer to my father but doesn't look in his direction. Her focus is on the floor. Her eyes are wide and vacant, the thoughts in them clear. She's mulling over everything I've told her, but still, she manages to stand beside my father, making her position known. I don't know if it's love or fear keeping her beside him. It could be both.

"I love you, Mom," I tell her, uttering the words around the lump in my throat. "You did a wonderful job putting on this dinner."

Despite the anger I have for my father, I'm still sad for my mother. I've always felt the pain of her grief, and tonight is no different. As much as I want to be there for her and pull her out of her sadness, I know she doesn't want it.

She doesn't say anything when I turn around and grab Vada's hand, leading us through the front door.

The second my lungs breathe in the cool night air, a feeling of weightlessness washes over me. Of course I feel terrible that my parents don't understand how Ryan could have had a son and can't wrap their heads around the idea that they have a grandson. Honestly, if they don't want to know more about Jonah and the amazing kid he is, that's on them. They're missing out on keeping a piece of Ryan with them.

Vada and I reach the bottom step as she releases my hand. The valet sees me and immediately leaves to grab my truck.

We're left standing at the edge of the driveway, and I turn to face her.

Like my mother, there are tears streaming down her face. She's staring up at me with glassy eyes and a trembling lip.

I see the hurt in her gaze. I've broken my promise to never allow secrets to come between us, and the expression on her face is enough to shatter me into a thousand pieces.

"Vada, I—"

SECRET #5

Love is one secret that can never be kept forever.

CHAPTER TWENTY-EIGHT

Vada

Secrets are often used as a way to bond people together, but they can also tear you apart.

That's what Colton's secret has done. I feel like I'm being torn from the inside out, every inch of my soul caving in on itself.

I'm staring at the gravel driveway, watching as each pebble sparkles in the moonlight mingling with the warm yellow lights coming from inside the house. The party is still in full swing, the echo of the band in the backyard surrounding the entire ranch. It can probably be heard from a mile away.

I wish I were a mile away. Hell, I wish I were hundreds of miles away.

I'm looking up at Colton, feeling his secret about Jonah tearing me in two. My chest burns, and the pressure behind my eyes builds to the point where there's a constant flow of tears streaming down my blushed cheeks.

"Vada." Colton says my name on a heavy breath, urging me to look him in the eye. His brown eyebrows knit in confusion. "I—"

"No." I lift my hands to stop him from reaching out. "I just...

I just need a second." I hold my breath and turn to look back out at the driveway. The gravel extends past the circle drive, spreading all the way out to the main road leading back to the city. We're surrounded by absolutely nothing, yet I feel as if I'm standing in the middle of downtown Austin, surrounded by hundreds of people. I'm struggling for a breath trying to wrap my head around the idea that Colton could keep a secret as big as this one from me. I try to grasp the fact that he broke our deal to never keep secrets from one another.

My chest squeezes as I think of every single thing that's happened to us since I first met him.

First, he was my brother's best friend.

Second, he was a friend.

Third, a one-time secret.

Fourth, a stranger.

And last, a man I've simply fallen in love with.

But as I think of each version of Colton I've had over the years, I realize they're nearly all the same. I think about all the circumstances surrounding each version, wondering if Colton could ever make me a priority, if Colton ever truly saw me as someone he loved like I do him.

I think about how Jonah clings to the only piece of his father he has. I think about how Ryan died less than a year ago, all the while having had a son he never knew about. And then I think about how Ryan's death nearly shattered Colton, how he kept me at a distance in the process.

Then, part of me wonders if Ryan knew about Jonah at all. Maybe he kept him a secret as well. If that were true, Cassidy's story would be false, and that would make Ryan no better than the man I call my father—abandoning, being unloving, making his child feel unwanted.

If that were the case, I'd understand Jonah more than I ever have.

I move my gaze around, swallowing back the tears. As much as I'm trying to comprehend Jonah being Colton's nephew, I'm finding Colton's secret to be more painful than that.

Finally bringing myself to ask, I turn to face him. My vision wobbles with tears, my eyes turning to pools of liquid. Colton's eyes get lost, and he becomes one blurry mess. I blink the tears away, bringing him back into focus.

"Why?" Emotion catches in my throat. I clear it, asking him again. "Why did you not tell me?"

His shoulders fall and he reaches for my hand, but I take a step back. I want to feel him near me, but I can't when I can't get over this secret he kept from me. My body aches for him, but I hold back, my need for answers outweighing my need for him.

He sighs and wraps his hand around the back of his neck. He tilts his head, looking up at the sky. "I wanted to." He looks back down, his eyebrows knitting with regret. "I tried several times, but it never seemed like the right time. I'm sorry, Vada. I never meant to keep it from you."

Quickly, my hurt is replaced with anger and disappointment. Disappointed at the fact that despite everything Colton and I have been through these past few years, growing from our own secrets, he couldn't tell me this. He couldn't tell me the one thing that bonds us together. And with that disappointment comes the realization of knowing things between Colton and me haven't changed.

"Never seemed like the right time?" I place my hand on my chest, feeling my heartbeat against my palm. My cheeks heat and my throat burns. "You've known for two weeks, Colton. There were plenty of chances for you to tell me, but you chose tonight to say it? In front of your parents?"

I didn't realize it until now, but I wish the Adler's had found out about Jonah in a different way. As much as I hate Colton's father, especially after the way he was treating both me and Colton tonight, he didn't deserve to find out this way.

The anger and disbelief from Scott cut Colton deep. I could see it in the way Scott was quick to discredit Colton, as he always does, but it was the immense sadness in Faye that had me feeling for her. Despite the way she introduced herself to me when we first arrived, I could still see the pain inside her. She wears it like a bright blinking sign. Apparently the only one too consumed with themselves to see it is her own husband, Scott.

"I know." He sighs. "I just couldn't take any more of my father's bullshit about Ryan being perfect. He didn't know Ryan as well as he thinks he did. In fact, I'm left wondering how well I knew him for him to have a child I didn't even know about."

"What—you think he knew about Jonah and didn't tell anyone?" The thought of Ryan abandoning Jonah the way my dad did me causes my stomach to flip. I feel sick.

Colton's eyes widen, and the muscles in his jaw tick as he thinks. "No. I don't think he knew about Jonah. He wasn't the kind of man who would've done that. He would have done everything in his power to be the best dad he could be. I'm just saying Ryan had his secrets too. He told me about Lyla, but I never truly knew what their relationship was like. I mean, Cassidy didn't even know her sister was with him. She told her Ryan was a one-night stand. No one truly knows anyone, Vada."

"Does Cassidy even know?"

I widen my eyes, not sure what will hurt worse—the fact that Cassidy still doesn't know or that Colton could have told Cassidy and asked her to keep it from me. If he did tell her, I have a strong feeling she would have at least said *something*.

"No." He shakes his head, frowning. "Like I said, I've still been trying to deal with the fact that Ryan has a child."

"I can't believe you." I shake my head, crossing my arms over my chest. My breasts push together, swelling over the deep V neckline of my dress. A shiver trickles across my arms, as if the temperature has gone down ten degrees. "You need to tell her."

"I know. I am going to. I planned on telling her after I told you. Why would I not? Do you honestly think that low of me, Vada? She's his aunt—of course she deserves to know who Jonah's father is."

"I don't think low of you, Colt." I press my hand against my chest, feeling my heart beat against it, twisting with an ache I can't describe. I look at Colton, not knowing what to do. "I just can't keep going back and forth with you. How will I ever know you truly want to be with me? How do I know you want a life with me? For as long as I can remember, my father used to do the same to me, and I can't be with someone who will put me second."

"I've never thought of you as second, Vada." His voice strains against his words. I've clearly wounded him where it hurts the most. "You're everything to me. Up until these past few months, I was honest when I said I couldn't give you every-thing you wanted, but I can do that now, and not because I feel obligated to."

I pause, pulling in my bottom lip. I bite down on it, letting Colton's words sink in. Maybe I don't know anyone like I think I do. Maybe I don't know my father and how he truly feels about me. Maybe I don't know all the struggles my mother went through as a teen mom. And maybe I don't know the depth of Colton's grief over losing Ryan or his love for me.

It's then, as I'm staring into his light brown eyes, that I realize my pain doesn't come from the secret Colton was hiding. It comes from knowing he kept one at all, one that clearly affects not only his life, but mine as well. The truth is, I've always been Colton's secret.

"Maybe we don't know the deepest darkest parts of anyone, Colt. What hurts is not that people keep their secrets. What hurts is knowing you knew about Jonah, but you didn't feel the need to tell me at all. That's what hurts the most. I get that you may have had your reasons but I don't want to keep doing this with you if you'll never see me as anything more than what we are."

It's true. My pain comes from the insecurity my father laid into me all my life. Up until I met Colton, I only relied on putting myself first. I allowed Colton access to my heart only for him to close the door on me.

"Vada, I didn't mean to hurt you." Colton saying my name again feels like a hot iron pressing against me. "I'm sorry. I meant to tell you right away. I think I just needed time to understand it. Between Ryan dying and finding out about Jonah, it was a lot for me to deal with. It's not often you find out your brother left behind a child you didn't even know existed and neither did he."

He's pleading with me to understand. I coil away from him as the valet brings his truck around the circle. The tires crunch against the gravel and the engine rumbles, drowning out the music playing behind the house. The more I look at him, the more I see the secrets piling on top of us.

"Right," I say, not moving toward the truck. "I understand the pain you felt when Ryan died. It broke my heart seeing how much you were hurting and knowing there was nothing I could do to help you. I wanted to be there for you in the same way we were there for each other when Hailey died." I let the tears fall, my heart sinking to the bottom of my stomach. "But even when you put all of that aside it doesn't change the fact that you broke our deal, Colt."

The valet steps out from the driver's side and hands Colton his keys, but like me, he doesn't move.

Another rush of tears slides down my cheeks. "You found out your brother has a child, and you couldn't bring yourself to tell me. Instead, you kept me at a distance. I felt you pushing me away like you did the first time we had a secret between us. I convinced myself I was imagining it. I convinced myself you weren't pushing me away like the last time because of what you said that night at my apartment, but I was only fooling myself, wasn't I? The first time we kept a secret, it was ours." Another sob escapes my chest. "But this time? This time I didn't even know. You kept me away from it. You don't have to tell me everything, but if you can't tell me things like this, what are we even doing?"

"What do you mean what are we doing? I'm with you, Vada. *You*. And I do tell you things. I talked to you about my parents. I talked to you about how I've felt about you since the moment Dallas introduced me to you." He's quick to close the distance between us. I try to step back, but he stops me, wrapping his hands around my cheeks. His fingers entangle with my hair, weaving in with my curls. A slight breeze dances across my skin.

Tears slide down my cheeks, and when he places his hands on them, they soak into his skin. I choke back another sob, thinking of my dad and how my chest twists, aching in the same way it did when he would push me aside. I know Colton is different than my dad. I know he isn't the same.

Where I know Colton cares for me, I can't say the same for my father. Nonetheless, the ache from it is all too familiar. The only way I can describe the way I'm feeling is that I'm heartbroken. Colton has left me heartbroken.

"I still don't understand why you couldn't tell me." I choke my words out. "You say it was because there was never a right time, but to me, there were plenty of chances. Maybe I don't mean as much to you as you say I do. Maybe a part of you deep down doesn't want me."

"What?" He breathes out, pulling me closer. Hurt and anger now replace the regret. "That's absolutely ridiculous. I thought I made myself fairly clear these past few months. I want you, Vada. I've always fucking wanted you, ever since Dallas introduced me to you. I've wanted you ever since you offered to help with the opening of the restaurant, when you were standing outside it chewing on that piece of fucking red licorice."

I sob again, pressing my hands against his chest. I don't know how to feel, and the longer I stand here with him, the more confused I feel. "I don't know if it's enough for you to want me, Colt. I don't know if it's enough." I swallow. "It feels as if you've kept me at a distance so far that I don't feel like I'm a part of your life. I don't even know what we are."

Colton's breaths have slowed, and the redness from his cheeks has paled. He pins his eyes on mine, and I can feel him slipping away with every second that passes.

The quiet rumble of his truck looms in the background. It's still running, the valet having left the passenger door open. I look behind Colton's shoulder. No one is standing out front. The party is still going, but there's no one out here with us. They must have walked away after hearing our conversation.

"I know I broke my deal with you on no more secrets." He takes a deep breath, his eyes lining with unshed tears. "But you need to understand where I'm coming from, Vada. You have to know that even though I wanted to tell you, I needed to reconcile it with myself, first. I truly wanted to tell you. You have to know you're everything to me."

I can't bring myself to look at his pleading face. I place my hand over his, prying his fingers away. Hurt washes over his expression as he allows his hands to fall at his sides. He doesn't fight me, knowing he can't change what's happened.

"I understand how finding out about Jonah being Ryan's son is a big deal, but there's so much more that I don't understand about you, Colton." The hurt and pain are overwhelming as my words spill out of me. "You say you're with me, but you shut me out. I feel like you want me one minute and then the next, you don't. You let me in just enough only to turn around and shut the door on me. There's only so much my heart can take. I told you from the start that I wanted you, but that I didn't want to be with someone who couldn't be in one hundred percent. I understood when we forged our deal that night in the restaurant. That was on both of us. I also understood when Ryan died. You needed time to heal, and I knew nothing I could say or do would help you in that moment. Nothing can ever bring Ryan back."

A tear slips from his eye and he presses his lips together, breathing through his nose. His heart is breaking too.

"But I can't help feeling this way every time you keep me away. I can't help feeling as though you will always have these secrets."

"Vada." My name falling from his mouth is bittersweet. "There's nothing I can say to you that will change what's happened, but I can tell you I meant every word I've ever said to you. We may keep our secrets, but I've always told you the truth."

I nod, tears still filling my vision. I can't help it. I take a deep breath, knowing I can't stay here any longer. I can't stare at the man I know I'm falling in love with, knowing it brings me nothing but heartbreak.

"That's the thing about secrets, Colt...they lead to nothing but heartbreak. I think this needs to end." I sniff, wiping my fingertips across my cheeks. I take a deep breath, wanting nothing more than to get away from the Adler's house. My feet ache in my heels and my eyes are tired from crying, but most of all, my heart breaks more with every second I stand here looking at the man I love.

"End?" Colton asks, and I know exactly what he's thinking.

He dips his eyebrows, confusion written all over him. "What do you mean end?"

I swallow, allowing the tears to fall. "I think we need to end this feeling of thinking we're in a place to give each other what we want when we can't."

I press my lips together and force myself to stand my ground. It's hard to not want to go to him when my heart is breaking.

"I know exactly what I want," Colton says. "I've wanted you from the beginning."

I shake my head, knowing I've heard him say this before, the night of the wedding. "Or maybe we need time. Time to figure this out. I don't know."

A part of me has always known I've been in love with Colton, which makes this all the more painful. I have yet to tell him, but the way my stomach does somersaults and the way my thighs tense every time I'm around him tell me I am in love with him. I have been since the day I offered to help him open the restaurant in the midst of Dallas' grief, but Colton's constant need to keep me at a distance concerns me.

"Time?" he asks.

"Yeah." I shrug, not completely confident in my decision but knowing I need to give him this in order to figure us out. "I think we both need time to let ourselves heal...without each other."

He holds his breath, his chest freezing under his shirt. His tie rests loosely around his neck, the top button undone. When we first stepped out here, Colton's face was filled with anger, but now, all I see is pain, pain from knowing everything between us is ripping at the seams.

I'm in love with Colton. That much I already know, but I need to hear him say it. In order for me to move forward with him, I need to know he wants me more than what he's been giving me, but I can't ask him to say it now, not when there are so many secrets between us.

Another tear spills down my cheek as I inhale a deep breath, knowing I've never loved anyone more than I have Colton.

"I need you to take me home," I tell him, lifting up the bottom of my dress. I climb into the passenger seat without another word, unwilling to look at Colton. I know I'm leaving him standing there broken. I'm left broken as well, but the thing is, it's not just my heart.

It's all of me.

CHAPTER TWENTY-NINE

COLTON

It wasn't until I saw the look in Vada's eyes that I realized every decision I've ever made in my life was never for myself. Every decision I have ever made was to please my father. Even before Ryan's death, I felt the need to always put on a face for the sake of the Adler name. Never step out of line. Never fail.

Every day I was constantly pretending to be someone I could never be, and surprisingly enough, the older I got, the more pressure I felt to please him.

I only wish I'd known then what I know now. Because now I know, no matter what choices I would have made, my father would have treated me the same.

Maybe there was truth to what Vada was telling me. Maybe I did keep her at a distance, but deep down, I know I wanted to tell her about Ryan and Jonah; I just couldn't bring myself to speak the truth out loud, because doing so would mean admitting it was real. It's not that I didn't want to admit Ryan being Jonah's dad was real. It's that I would have been admitting that even though I know who Jonah's dad is, he'll never be able to meet him. Jonah will never have the privilege of knowing his dad, and Ryan will never have the privilege of raising his son.

The truth of why I couldn't tell Vada is like a punch to the gut. If I had told Vada my secret, maybe she wouldn't have walked away from me last night, asking me to take her home. If I had told Vada I'm in love with her, maybe I wouldn't be standing here, alone.

Instead, she'd be standing next to me right now, outside Cassidy's house. I swallow down the memory of the tears streaming down Vada's face and the way she walked away after getting out of my truck last night without looking back. I lift my shaking hand and ring the doorbell, recognizing Cassidy's car in the driveway. I'm hoping she's home. I don't have her phone number and want to give Vada the space she's asking for, so I just came over on the off chance she'd be here.

I can't deny that Vada's silence has been torture. I felt like shit when I woke up, the pressure behind my eyes was proof of what little sleep I got last night. My chest feels hollow and heavy at the same time. I'm gutted by her absence. I check my phone once more, hoping to find her name next to a message or missed call. My stomach dips when I don't see anything.

I run my fingers through my hair, pulling on the ends before pushing them back. I brush my hair off my forehead and take a deep breath. Vada's right; Cassidy deserves to know. But most of all, Jonah needs to know who his dad is.

I don't have to wait long before Cassidy opens the door.

"Hey, Colton." Her eyebrows immediately dip in confusion. She pouts and looks behind me, even tipping her head to get a better view of the driveway. She must be looking for Vada, assuming the only reason I'd be here is if she were with me.

I try not to think about Vada because it only makes me feel worse.

"It's just me."

"Oh." Cassidy leans back, her eyebrows settling back in their natural place. "Well, come in. Is everything okay? Is Vada okay?"

"Um…" I wrap my hand around the back of my neck, watching my boots move across the floor. The last time I was in this house was when I brought Jonah's keychain back to him. "If you have the time, I need to talk to you." I avoid bringing up Vada, mostly because I don't know where we stand after last night, and I don't want to tell Cassidy anything unless Vada does. She's her friend, and it doesn't feel right for me to say.

If Cassidy's worried that I dodged her question, she doesn't say so. Instead, she looks at me with more curiosity and nods once. "Yeah, I have a little time before Jonah gets home from school."

"Great."

"We can talk out back if you want. My dad is in the living room taking a nap." She giggles. "He always falls asleep watching his shows."

"So I've heard." I give her a weak smile, looking at the pictures lining the hall as I follow Cassidy to the back.

Cassidy's father's snoring can be heard throughout the entire first floor of the house. We don't speak a word, making sure not to make too much noise.

I'm nearing the end of the hallway when I catch sight of the picture of Cassidy and Lyla. It's the same one I saw the day I came in here and gave Jonah his keychain.

My stomach flips, remembering the sound of Lyla's voice. I used to sit in the back seat of my brother's Jeep, watching as he'd reach out across the center console and place his hand on her leg. She'd place her hand over his and leave it there, not moving it until Ryan pulled up in front of her house…this house.

White, puffy clouds litter the otherwise clear, powder blue sky. The air is cool today, and I'm thankful Cassidy suggested sitting outside. After the night I've had, I could use the fresh air. Every breath I take in is a temporary fix, making me feel only slightly more whole, despite me being without Vada.

"So," Cassidy says, sitting down on the small brick wall lining her patio. "What's going on? You never did answer my question."

I sit on the wall opposite her and lean forward, resting my elbows on my knees. I look up, giving her a confused look.

"About Vada…is she okay? Last time I talked to her was yesterday before your dinner. How did it go?"

I bounce my leg up and down, nerves starting to bundle inside me. At this rate, I still won't have told her about Ryan by the time Jonah gets out of school.

"Nothing is wrong with Vada. But honestly?" I wince, shaking my head. "I've never been a fan of my parents' charity dinners to begin with. The odds were stacked against us from the moment we got there."

"Oh." She frowns. "I'm sorry. Vada didn't tell me much about it. I just knew this was the first time she was meeting your family, but something must have happened if you've come all the way out here to talk to me…without Vada."

"Yeah." I swallow. "I fucked up, and I honestly don't blame Vada. She has a right to be upset with me, and I'm hoping to make it right." I sit up, stretching my arms out while still keeping them on my knees. "That's actually why I'm here to talk to you." I take a deep breath and let it out, ready to tell Cassidy. "Vada told me Jonah never met his father, and neither did you."

Cassidy immediately sits up, her back sticking straight up. "No, my sister left without telling us. We never even knew his name. It's been rough for Jonah not ever knowing who his father was and my sister leaving so soon after he was born, but we've made it work. He has me and my dad."

I nod, giving her another weak smile. It's all I can manage. "I know Jonah has been blessed to have you and your dad, but Cassidy, I know who Jonah's father is."

Her cheeks flame red and her bottom lip pops away from her top. Her mouth opens, allowing her to breathe in what I'm telling her. She's caught off guard by what I'm saying, and within seconds, I can already see the tears lining her eyes.

"What?"

"The keychain Jonah has? My brother had one exactly like it. He bought it years ago at the state fair when our family took a trip out to Dallas. He carved his initials, ROA, into the back." The more I tell my story of how I know Ryan is Jonah's father, the more Cassidy's tears start to spill over. She's holding her breath, holding her hand over her mouth, but I continue anyway. "He lost it about eight years ago. I'd forgotten about the keychain until Vada asked if I could stop by the park and find it for Jonah. I didn't want to believe it at first, thinking maybe Jonah had found it somewhere. But then given the initials, I asked Jonah where he got it, and he told me he'd had it since he was a baby...and it was his father's. It wasn't until I looked over and saw that picture..." I lift my hand and point to inside. The end table with the picture of Cassidy and Lyla can be seen through the sliding glass door from where we're sitting. "That I knew why you seemed familiar to me. I knew where I'd seen your sister before. Lyla was my brother Ryan's girlfriend."

"Oh my god." Cassidy lowers her hand. She quickly swipes her tears and stands, wiping her hands on the front of her thighs. She paces back and forth, staring at the ground. "She never mentioned him before. I can't remember her ever talking about a boyfriend. I mean, she mentioned sleeping with him one night, but that was it. I guess I can't be too surprised. She left after Jonah was born, so I don't know why I'd believe anything she said."

"I think they kept their relationship a secret because of our parents."

"Really?"

I nod. "Yeah, they were always very hard on us, especially Ryan. He was the oldest and set to take over our dad's company. I remember he told me not to tell anyone he had a girlfriend, and I think that's why. I think he was trying to protect himself, and Lyla."

"I don't know what to say." She shakes her head. She still hasn't looked at me, keeping her focus on the backyard.

I stand, walking a bit closer to her. "I want to apologize to you, Cassidy."

"For what? You have nothing to apologize for."

"No." I knit my eyebrows. "I do, for many reasons. First, I want to say I'm sorry Jonah will never get to meet Ryan. I truly believe he didn't even know Jonah existed, or else he would have been in his life. He was one of the most genuine, loving people. He would have loved Jonah."

Cassidy simply nods, holding her hand to her chest. Her chin quivers.

"The second thing I need to apologize for is not telling you sooner. I knew the day I found Jonah's keychain. I should have said something to you. I should have told somebody, but I think I was too wrapped up in realizing Ryan had left a part of himself behind in the world, and I didn't even think to share it with the people it affected most."

Cassidy reaches out, placing her hand on my shoulder. She keeps me at arm's length, sadness filling her expression. She's still processing what I've told her, but now she's looking at me as if I've answered every question she's ever had surrounding Jonah and his family. In a way, I have.

"Is that why you dodged my question about Vada? You didn't tell her when you found out?"

"No." I thread my fingers through my hair again, tugging on the ends. I don't want to talk about Vada, at least not here with one of her closest friends and co-workers, but here I am. "I didn't."

"It's okay, Colton. I understand why you didn't tell me at first. Sort of." The corner of her mouth curls into a smile. "But I can't tell you how much I appreciate you telling me now. It's nice to know Jonah has more family than just me and my dad."

It makes me sad hearing Cassidy say Jonah has more family now that we know who his father is. The immediate dismissal from my father told me everything I needed to know about what kind of grandfather he'd be even if he was in Jonah's life, and if he treated Jonah the way he treated me or Ryan, I wouldn't want the fucker near him anyway.

"As far as Vada's concerned..." She sighs. "She'll come around."

"I'm not so sure." I shake my head, pushing back the pain growing in my chest. "I hurt her, and I'm not exactly sure how to fix it."

Cassidy seems confident Vada simply needs time, but I'm not so sure. The ache in my chest squeezes and twists even tighter.

I inhale a sharp breath. "I'm not so sure Vada will ever forgive me. I promised her I wouldn't keep any more secrets from her, and this was a big one. I already broke her heart once before, and now I'm not so sure she'll be willing to take me back."

"I know Vada has been through a lot when it comes to trust," Cassidy says. "I don't know much about her family, but from what I do know, she hasn't had it easy. And from what I know of yours, it sounds like you've had a similar experience. She understood the first time you didn't talk because your heart was broken as well."

I slide my hands into my pockets and nod, knowing she's talking about after Ryan's death. My head pounds, as it has since this morning. "I never thought about it that way, but I guess we have." Cassidy may be right. My father has never treated me with the same respect he ever gave Ryan, and the same is true of Vada's father. He always put Dallas above her, never giving her the love and attention she deserved.

"I may not be an expert on the matter, but I know Vada loves you."

I scoff, not believing her. It's not that I think Cassidy is lying to me, but I know I've screwed up my chances with Vada more times than I can count. She deserves better, someone who can give her one hundred percent, what she's always wanted.

"I don't know if she does anymore. How can she love someone who's broken her heart as many times as I have?"

"I don't know." Cassidy shrugs. "That's the thing about broken hearts—they can always be mended. Right?"

I give her a soft smile before I turn my head to the sliding glass door at the sound of it opening.

"Colton!" Jonah yells, running across the patio. "I've missed you."

It's the first time I'm seeing him since I returned his keychain to him. Knowing Ryan is his father makes me see him in a whole different light. It's as if I'm noticing his features more, picking out the ones that resemble Ryan's. The way his brown hair catches the sunlight, slivers of gold peeking through. The way one corner of his mouth curls higher than the other when he smiles.

My chest aches for Ryan, but part of me is so thankful to know Jonah. I'm so thankful a piece of Ryan lives through him.

"I've missed you too, buddy." I tousle his hair with my fingers when he runs up to me. His dinosaur backpack is still resting on his back. Holding on to the straps, he bounces on his heels and grins.

"Are we able to go to the comic book store again? Is Vada with you?" he asks, trading glances between me and Cassidy. I give him a soft smile, ignoring the way the usual sickness takes over when I think of last night, when I think of the look on Vada's face when she said she needs time, time away from me.

"Not today," I tell him. I'm hoping this sinking feeling goes away as time goes on. In all honesty, I'm hoping I haven't lost Vada altogether. Because the more I look at Jonah and see Ryan in him, the more I'm realizing just how short life is. We only have the one, and I know if Ryan had been given the chance to know about Jonah, he would have loved him with his whole heart.

I may not have children yet, but I already know I've loved someone with my whole heart. I've just been too scared to admit it to myself until now.

"Actually," Cassidy says, pulling his attention away from me. Her gaze moves to mine. I already know what she's thinking, and without a second thought, I give her a reassuring nod. "Colton came over to talk to you."

"To talk?" he asks. "With me?"

"Yeah." I grin, my chest swelling. "I came to tell you about your dad."

CHAPTER THIRTY

Vada

I never thought I would feel this way.

I'm sitting at my desk scrolling through an article submitted to me by one of our reporters, but I haven't been able to focus. It's the fifth time I've read through it. Even when I get to the end, I reread the same sentence a few times before starting over.

I check my phone knowing if I don't get this article done soon, I'll be here all night. It's late in the afternoon, and I've been working on the same piece all day. My mind is anywhere but on work today, and I hate it.

It's stuck on Colton, and on the fact that I haven't spoken to him since the night of the dinner, since I asked him to take me home and we agreed to give ourselves some time and space to figure out what's between us.

I'm still unsure if Colton will ever be able to put me first, but my mother's words ring in my ear like a mallet banging against a bong.

Never settle for second best.

I understand the reasoning behind Colton's need to keep Jonah's true relation to him a secret, but that still doesn't erase how it makes me feel. It's not that I'm completely cutting him out, but I need to make sure I know where we stand before I make a decision. I need him to figure out whether or not he truly wants to be with me. I need to know if he loves me, because I love him.

The otherwise loud newsroom is unusually quiet today. Most everyone is out attending one of the music festivals Nate wanted to cover. I peek my head around my computer, looking through the doorway of my office. Cassidy's desk is nearly straight across from mine, all the way at the other end, and even she's gone. The lamp above her photo editing table is turned off. I look over at Levi's cubicle. He must have left as well.

I click on my thread of messages with Colton, reading the last one he sent me. He sent it as soon as we sat down at the table at his parents' charity dinner, just before his father's speech.

Colton: I can't stop staring at you. Maybe if you'd decided to wear a burlap sack, I'd have an easier time concentrating on this stupid fucking dinner, but I'm only kidding myself—you'd make even a burlap sack look sexy.

I try to read through the text without watery eyes, but I can't help it. Everything in me feels heavy and tired, echoes of the pain of knowing Colton and I are over before we could barely begin. There are so many unknowns. I don't know if Colton and I will ever get back together, and if we don't, I'm not sure I'll ever fully get over him. *Shit.* I wasn't able to before, when we'd forged our secret.

I haven't seen him since the night of the dinner two weeks ago, and every day that passes is more difficult than the one before it. I've tried burying myself in work, but even then, it's difficult. It's hard to pour myself into something I love when I've lost another part of me that I love.

I decide to turn my phone off. I hold down the button on the side and wait for the screen to turn black before stuffing it into my purse. If I keep checking it at this rate, there's no possible way I'll get this article done.

I'm halfway through my last read-through on this piece when I hear three knocks against the door frame to my office. I bring my eyes up from the computer to find Nate standing in the doorway.

He looks tired. His greying hair is ruffled near the front, and his sleeves are rolled up to his elbows. His tie is loosened around his neck.

"Hey, Vada. Do you have a minute?"

I sigh and sit back in my chair as he steps into my office. He leans against the wall and crosses his arms over his chest.

"Sure," I tell him, resting my hands in my lap. "I'm just finishing up the edit for the story on the new electric car factory they built."

Every muscle in my back contracts then relaxes as I lean back in my chair. I didn't realize how tense I've been while sitting here.

"Great." His eyes narrow as they move past me, looking out the window behind me. He pauses then shifts his gaze back to me. "I've been offered a position as editor-in-chief for a news-paper out in Lubbock."

"Lubbock?" I can feel my eyebrows shooting up, arching across my forehead. My stomach sinks and worry starts to take over. Is this the same shit my last boss pulled? Am I somehow living some sort of déjà vu nightmare?

I tell myself it's different. At least Nate is coming to tell me himself, warning me. At least this time there's no promotion promised to me.

"Yeah." He nods. "I realize it isn't as great as Austin, but that's where I'm originally from. My family lives out there, so I couldn't exactly turn it down."

"I didn't know you were from Lubbock."

"My wife and daughter live there. Every other week I drive up to see them since she works at Texas Tech."

I giggle. "How am I just finding this out about you? You have a wife and daughter?"

"Yeah." He reaches behind his head, wrapping his hand around his neck, massaging it. "We got married right out of high school. Our daughter is in middle school, and when I was offered the position out here a few years ago, I didn't want to leave my family, but I also didn't want to turn it down. The money was too good, not to mention the credibility it would give me."

"You're right there."

"Anyway, I've been trying for a while to get a job back there so I can be with them, and a position opened up with a magazine."

"Wow, congratulations." I give him a smile, truly happy for him. Mostly, I'm happy that he'll be reunited with his family—a family I had no idea he even had.

"So, who's going to take your place?" I ask, leaning forward. I rest my elbow on my desk and my chin in my hand, staring up at him.

Nate still hasn't moved from the wall. His stance is casual as he keeps his arms crossed over his chest.

"Actually, I put in a recommendation for you as my replacement."

"What?" I gasp, the air leaving my chest in one breath. "You did what?" I can feel my skin paling as I stare at Nate, replaying the words in my head.

He laughs, pushing off the wall. "They asked me if I might know anyone who would make a great editor-in-chief, and I gave them your name."

"Me?" I point to my chest. "You mean, me as in Vada Beckett?"

"Yeah." His eyebrows dip in confusion. His expression matches how I feel on the inside. "I'm not aware of how many other Vada Becketts there are in the world, but I'm fairly certain they knew who I was talking about."

I straighten my back, stunned by what I'm hearing. I've been promised promotions before. I've been told I was moving up only to have it completely ripped out from under me. I'm cautious to believe what Nate is telling me.

"I'm sorry." I hunch my shoulders, still unconvinced. "I'm not sure I understand."

Nate crosses the space between the wall and my desk. He leans forward, pressing his palms against the top. My eyes fall to the wedding ring on his finger, one I hadn't noticed before. At least I know he's telling the truth about being married.

"Vada, you're an incredible managing editor. You're dedicated, and you know which stories should be published and which ones shouldn't. You've been able to sift through the bullshit since day one, and you've honestly made my job a thousand times easier since you walked through my door. You also brought an incredibly talented photographer with you. What other name should I have said when they asked me who would be best suited to replace me?"

I want to cry. I can feel the emotion clogging my throat, threatening to spring free, but I hold it back, not wanting Nate to see.

"I don't know what to say, other than thank you." I clear my throat and stand because it feels like something I should do. I cross my own arms over my chest.

"Great." He nods once and smiles, satisfied. "I'm glad what I'm telling you finally sank in." He laughs again, turning to head out of my office. He reaches the door and turns around. "I won't be leaving for another few weeks, and we're set to have a meeting with the owners before I go. Be prepared, Beckett. I don't need you making me look bad."

I'm still standing behind my desk with my arms crossed when Nate disappears down the hallway. When I look down at my computer, I check the time again.

I sit down in my chair, allowing the silence of the newsroom to swallow me up. I mull over the past ten minutes, replaying Nate's words.

Me—an actual promotion. Me—editor-in-chief. It isn't official yet, but I've never been this close. I've never been personally recommended for a position as high as this one.

I try to get back to work, reading through the last bit of the article I need to finish, but I can't seem to focus. I save the edits I'm working on and send it to myself in an email, just in case. Turning off my computer, I grab my purse and leave my office.

The entire ride down in the elevator is utter torture. I want to believe I can get this promotion, but I heard Nate—I need to prove it to the owners of the paper first. I inhale a deep breath, forcing myself to stay calm. There's nothing I can do about it now. I have a few weeks to prepare and that's it.

Honestly, the first thought that comes to mind is Colton. I want to tell him. I want to tell him I'm being considered for a promotion, again, and this time the rug isn't being pulled out from under me by my boss disappearing. The owners know about Nate's recommendation.

Then I start thinking about the space I told myself I'd give us. It's not that I'm wanting to end things with him. It's more that I don't know what's truly best for my heart, and his.

Would I be better off with him? Or without?

The thought of Colton slipping away from me again is enough to crack my heart in two.

"VADA, OPEN UP."

I jolt awake at the sound of my brother's voice coming from the hallway. I toss the blanket aside, roll out of bed, and head out to the living room.

I stop when I see Dallas standing at my dining room table with two large foil-wrapped burritos.

"What are you doing?" I narrow my eyes at him then look at the clock on the stove. It's nine o'clock at night. I forgot he has a key to my apartment, like I have a key to his house. We're supposed to keep them for emergencies. I guess Dallas considers late-night breakfast an emergency.

"I brought you dinner." He shrugs.

"If they're from the place I think they are, those are breakfast burritos." I point to the two burritos and sit down on the couch, tilting my head back. I close my eyes, ignoring Dallas as he unwraps the burrito. The scent of warm tortillas and sausage immediately fills my living room, traveling to my nose.

"They are." He laughs under his breath, and then there's silence. I crack one eye open and roll my head to the side. "Come sit with me and eat."

"I'm not hungry," I mutter. I open my eyes completely and watch as Dallas picks up his burrito.

He holds it in front of his mouth. "Do you want to know why I brought breakfast burritos over at nine o'clock at night?"

I chuckle, giving him a weak smile. "Not really, but I'm sure you're going to tell me anyway."

He huffs. "I remember a time when I felt the same way you do now. I felt like shit after losing Sloan, and you brought me a burrito."

"From what I remember, you didn't even eat it." I remember that day. I brought him a burrito after Sloan found out Dallas had lied about knowing her mother. He had his guitar case out, deciding whether or not he would start playing again.

"No, I didn't," he admits around a mouthful of food.

"There's a difference between us though, Dallas."

"What's that?"

"I'm the one who ended it with him, not the other way around. You should be bringing him burritos."

"For one, I don't care if you were the one to end it or not—you're my little sister. And two, I already took Colton a burrito earlier."

I grin, loving my brother more now than probably ever. "Of course you did." I press my lips together and blow out a heavy breath, keeping my focus away from Dallas. "So you know then? You know everything about Ryan and Jonah?"

"I do." He nods.

"He didn't tell me. He knew for two weeks and didn't say a word." My words are straightforward and flat. There's no emotion in them because it's not truly what pains me. It's the thought that Colton could possibly never have cared for me as much as I have for him.

My breath is shaky as I think about my life up until now, my father's constant disdain for me coursing through my blood—the same blood as his. I think about my mother and how she always seemed to expect more out of me than Dallas, making up for my father's inadequacies. I swallow down the life I was raised in, fighting the emotion clogging my throat.

"Ever since I was a little girl, Mom has always told me to never settle for second best. I think she did because of Dad and how he always treated me compared to you." I finally bring my attention to him. "Do you think there's any merit to it? To what she said?"

He lays his burrito on the foil and wipes his hands off with a napkin, mulling over my words. He rests one elbow on the table and drops his napkin. Resting his chin in his hand, he looks out toward the sliding glass door through the living room.

"I think Mom had her reasons." His voice is low and quiet. "I see where she's coming from. I've never agreed with Dad treating us differently simply because I'm the oldest. I think Mom was doing what she thought best under the circumstances she was given, but Vada, you've never been second to anyone who mattered. Not me, not Sloan, not Colton, not even Jonah."

Water fills my vision as tears quickly line my lashes. I blink, and they immediately spill over. One lands on my hand, soaking into my skin.

"I want to ask you something," Dallas continues.

"What is it?" I still haven't touched the burrito even though I have it completely unwrapped. I swipe at my cheeks, quietly sobbing.

"Normally, I don't involve myself in your personal life. I've never been the kind of brother who hated the idea of you dating one of my best friends. Colton is one of the best people I know. But I have to ask you." He clears his throat and sighs. "Do you love him?"

I don't hesitate , already knowing the answer deep in my gut. I've always known it. "Yeah. I do."

"Good." He nods, finishing off the last bit of his burrito.

"What?" I sniff. "That's it? No sage words of advice? Dallas Beckett has never been afraid to share his opinion. Don't tell me you're starting now."

Unscrewing the cap of his water bottle, he lifts it to his mouth, shrugging before he takes a sip. "You've always been the smart one out of the two of us. You don't need me to tell you what to do. I know you already do."

"Sometimes I'm not so sure."

"Okay, fine. Maybe I'll share a few words of wisdom, but that's all you get." He takes a deep breath and scratches at the stubble on his chin. His black wedding ring reflects the light from the fixture hanging above. "I'll tell you a problem I've come to learn exists between our heads and our hearts. We always think they're two different things, running independently on their own, but they aren't. One can't live without the other. It's up to you to decide." He takes a swig of water then points to the burrito still laying in front of me. "You should probably eat."

I pick up one half and hold it in front of me. The sausage and cheese inside it are still hot as steam pours out. Before I take my first bite, I look up at my brother, knowing exactly what I want in my life.

Aside from admitting I love Colton out loud, I'm ready to not keep any more secrets.

"My boss is leaving in a few weeks and recommended me to the board of owners to be his replacement. I have a meeting with them coming up."

When I take a giant bite of my burrito, my chest doesn't feel as heavy anymore knowing for the first time in what feels like forever, I've been able to speak the truth out loud.

I've always been in love with Colton Adler.

CHAPTER THIRTY-ONE

COLTON

It's been three weeks since I've seen Vada, and I feel no better than I did the day she walked away from me.

I've tried to distract myself with work as usual. The bar is closed for lunch today, and other than a few prep cooks in the back, I'm the only one who's bothered to come in this early.

I'm sitting on a stool at the bar, going through the menu to see if there's anything that needs to be changed or updated. With one arm bent and resting on the counter, I use my other hand to flip the menu over, but my attention shifts to someone standing in front of the window.

When I look up, I find my mother staring at the front door. She isn't standing close to it. In fact, she's standing back, nearly on the other side of the sidewalk, along the curb of the street. She stares up at the sign hanging above the front door, her body stiff. It's almost as if she's a statue. I watch as she stares for a few minutes before she finally looks back down. Her eyes catch mine as I slide off my chair and cross the dining room to let her in.

I unlock the door and hold it open for her. I glance around

and down both sides of the street, not seeing my father or anyone else with her. She's by herself.

She doesn't speak a word as she walks in, her eyes taking in my restaurant. She surveys it in silence. I lock the door behind her and stay near the front door. Her eyes roam around the space as she spins around, stopping to face me. I cross my arms over my chest and let out a heavy sigh.

Seeing my mom in my restaurant is something I've always wanted, but I never imagined it like this.

"This place is very nice." She wraps both her hands around the strap of her purse resting on her shoulder. Her fingers grip the leather as she continues to look around.

"Thanks." I unravel my arms and slide my hands into my pockets. Silence falls between us. It pulls at my chest, swelling like a balloon. I decide to pop it by getting straight to the point. "What are you doing here, Mom?"

Her eyes finally fall to mine, and they're immediately lined with tears. One slides down her cheek, and her chin quivers. "I, um..." She inhales a deep breath then blows it out. "I wanted to apologize."

Honestly, I'm shocked by how emotional she is. She just walked in here, and I've barely said a word to her.

"For what?"

"Where do I start?" She lets out a humorless laugh, lifting her hand to her mouth. She wipes it across her lips, inhaling a breath. "I never claimed to be perfect, and I never assumed when I became a mother that I would get everything right. I mean, no matter how prepared you think you might be, you truly don't know what you're getting yourself into when you have a child. Sometimes, you feel as if you have absolutely no clue what you're doing."

I stay where I am, my mother's words grounding my feet to where they are. This is a conversation probably best suited for sitting down, but I can't bring myself to move. This is the most I've heard her say in I don't know how long.

"But I failed you and Ryan the moment I decided to not speak up against your father." Her sobs grow louder, her chest shuddering. "I didn't protect you."

"Mom." I walk toward her and wrap my arms around her, holding her to my chest. My heart breaks for her. It compounds on top of the sadness I'm already feeling about Vada.

She wraps her arms around me, resting her head on my chest, her sobs growing louder and harder. I place one hand on the back of her head, feeling her smooth hair under my palm. It slides between my fingers. Despite the distance I've felt from her, she smells like home. This is the first time she's wrapped herself around me. She's the mother I remember. Even if it's only for this moment, it reassures me she's been here all along. She simply lost her way, like Vada said.

She pulls away from me, wiping away her tears. She runs the back of her shaking hand across her cheeks. "I'm sorry. I told myself to keep it together long enough to tell you "

"Don't be."

"There are so many things I want to say," she admits. "I guess the first would be that I don't share the same opinion as your father. I'm incredibly proud of you." Her gaze moves across the dining room again. "How could I not be?"

"You're proud of me?"

"Yes." She pins her stare on me. She's never been more direct. Her expression firms, telling me she's serious. "In fact, I'm proud of you for taking your own path instead of your father's. You made a life of your own, one that wasn't his. I didn't know it until you told us at the dinner, but I'm proud of Ryan too. He may have never been able to do it, but I'm proud of him for wanting to walk away."

"I don't understand." I shake my head, squeezing my eyes

shut. I pinch the bridge of my nose and open my eyes. "Why would you want Ryan and me to not follow in Dad's footsteps? That's all you ever driven into us since we were kids."

"Him, not me. He drove it into you. I merely sat aside and let him. That's a burden for me to bear."

I move my feet, working my mother's confession over and over in my head on repeat. I sit down in the same seat I was in before she came. I rest my arm on the back and watch as she walks over to me. She doesn't sit down, but she stays close.

"I understand how Dad is," I assure her. "I may not be in your shoes, but I can understand why."

"Your father is not an easy man to stand up to."

"Right." I nod. "Even Ryan had trouble with that."

She nods in understanding, pressing her pink lips together. "I wish I had known. I wish I were as brave as you and Ryan."

I wince, urging the tears not to come. I don't want to cry. It'll only make me feel worse. "I'm not as brave as you think I am."

"Somehow..." Her voice softens. "I don't believe that."

I swallow down the queasiness rising in me with my mother's confession. I haven't heard her speak like this before. There's a vulnerability to her, one that shoots straight to my chest.

"Mom?" I know in my gut there's more to why she's here. "I love that you're here in my restaurant, but I have to ask...is there another reason you're here?"

She sighs, her shoulders falling. Her tears have subsided. "Losing Ryan was incredibly painful. The loss of a child is something I never thought I would experience. I don't wish it on anyone." She swallows, a ghost of a smile spreading across her mouth. "But when you told me he has a son, Jonah...well, I can't tell you how it made me feel. It was like you'd given me the sun on a cold, cloudy day." She lets out a light laugh. "Dumb comparison, I know."

"It's not dumb. I get it, actually. The same thing happened to me when I saw Jonah with Ryan's keychain."

"Yeah." Her smile fades. "I understand if it would be too much trouble and I don't know if it's even a possibility, but I'm hoping I can meet him one day. I'm sure I would have to speak with Cassidy or um, I don't know..." She waves her hand. "I've never been in this situation, so I don't know the right way to go about it."

"I get it, Mom."

"I just..." She sighs, sniffing. "I don't know if he knows about us or our family. I would just love to meet my grandson if given the opportunity."

"He knows about Ryan." The emotion swells inside me again. "I told him."

"Really?" She looks relieved. "I'm glad he knows he has an uncle in this world at least."

I pause, taking a moment to think. I twist my mouth in thought, chewing on the inside of my cheek. As far as my father, I'm unsure how he feels about Jonah or where he stands on wanting to get to know Jonah. Does he feel the same way as my mother? Does he even know she's here?

Something tells me he doesn't, but something else tells me my mother doesn't care whether he does or not.

"You know," I say, "a couple weeks ago, Jonah was telling me about how he'd never ridden a horse before but always wanted to."

I give her a small smile, and for the first time in forever, I see her give me a genuine one back. Her cheeks flush with pink and her eyebrows arch, knowing exactly what I'm offering.

"Oh," she says. "That would be great."

"Good." I give her another nod and tuck the menu I was looking at back into the holder at the end of the bar.

"There's something else I wanted to mention."

I spin around in my seat and look back at my mother. She's moved closer to me now, resting her hand on the back of the chair next to me.

"I wanted to let you know I think Vada is great for you. She's beautiful, and from what I've been able to tell, she seems like a smart woman."

My stomach flips before it completely jumps up my throat. I start to feel sick. Everything I thought I knew about my mother is wrong, and everything she's saying about Vada is everything I already know to be true.

I've always known Vada is beautiful and intelligent, but my mother doesn't know about what happened after we left the dinner that night. She doesn't know the history we've shared, all the secrets and untold truths.

"She is beautiful and smart, Mom."

She pauses, tilting her head to the side. "But?"

I shake my head and rise from the chair. I need to move my feet. I need to keep moving, anything to not let me sit here and think about how I fucked up my chances with the most incredible woman I've ever known. "It's a long story, and it all ends up with me ruining the only good thing I've ever had."

"I don't understand what you mean. I know I wasn't exactly welcoming when I spoke with her—you can add that to the list of all the things I need to apologize for—but I saw the way she looked at you."

"In what way?" I ask her, walking around to the opening of the bar. I stand behind it and grip the edge, stretching my arms out. I'm standing across from my mother now, and I still can't get over her being here, in my restaurant, talking to me about Vada.

Honestly, it's a bit odd. I've never talked to my mother about relationships. Now it feels even more odd talking to her about this at the age of twenty-six.

"Colton." She sighs. Her tears have all but disappeared. Her cheeks are dry, and her face is bright. "I know the look on a woman's face when she's in love, and that's how she looked at you."

"I love her, Mom. I do."

"Have you told her that?"

I shake my head, my chest squeezing. "I just don't know if she'd ever give me another chance. I'm not entirely sure I deserve one. I screwed up too many times, and she deserves someone better—someone who can give her everything she wants, someone who can put her first."

My mother leans forward, resting her arms on the edge of the counter. She tilts her head to the side and studies me for a moment. Her expression shifts from confusion to happiness. It's hard for me to understand the thoughts running through her mind when her expressions are all over the place.

"I'm not exactly sure what the details are and I'm probably in no position to say this, but if there's anything to come from losing Ryan too soon, it's knowing life is too short to be caught up in all the what-ifs. It's too short to keep secrets from the ones we love. I've spent too many years shutting you out, never sticking up for you. I can't change how I kept my silence with Ryan. That's a choice I'll carry for the rest of my life. But you..." She reaches out and grabs my hand. "You have a choice now to not let fear and secrets keep you from the life you should be living. Trust me. It's not a life you deserve. You both deserve to be happy."

I give my mom a simple nod and press my lips together, releasing a breath through my nose. Every muscle in my body is wound tight. The pressure builds in my eyes and my chest, my entire body feeling the weight of Vada's absence. Even though it's been three weeks since I last saw her, it hurts worse than the four months of silence I gave her after Ryan's death. It's different this time because this time I know I'm in love with her.

I've always been in love with her; I was just too self-involved to admit it to myself.

"You're right." I return my mother's squeeze, tightening my fingers around her small hand.

My mother gives me a warm, comforting smile before she straightens her back and inhales a deep breath through her nose. She reaches for the menu I placed back in the holder at the end of the bar. She starts scanning it, flipping it from front to back. "I know you aren't technically open and this is far past due, but I was hoping I might be able to try some of this barbecue I've been hearing so much about."

"We're not open," I say, and her eyes shoot straight to mine. "But I might be able to make an exception for family."

♥

I AGREE to meet Cassidy and Jonah at the comic book store after my mother leaves. I have a bit of time before I need to be back at the restaurant to start prepping for this afternoon. The store isn't far from the restaurant, so I decide to take the time to walk. It'll give me a chance to think.

I've walked down this street plenty of times, but I've never felt as light as I do now. Seeing and talking to my mother has changed me more than I ever thought it could. I didn't realize how distant we'd grown until I felt my chest swell seeing her standing in the middle of my restaurant in awe of what I've created. There's nothing like the experience of seeing your parents proud of what you've accomplished in life, especially when it's something they haven't agreed with.

But despite my mother's visit to the restaurant, I still feel the empty hole inside me that Vada left behind. I know I want her back. I replay my mother's words in my head, knowing she's right. I may have fucked up more times than I can count with her, but I love Vada more than I've loved anyone. She's always seen me for who I am, even through my flaws. I'm perfectly imperfect when it comes to her.

I'm starting to figure out what to do when my attention is pulled away. Jonah runs toward me. His brown hair bounces as he runs, holding his arms out to me. "Uncle Colton."

It's not the first time I've heard him call me uncle since I told him who I am to him, who Ryan was to him.

His tears only lasted for a few minutes before the questions started pouring out of him. I told him all I could that day, every bit I could think of that Ryan would want me to tell him. I have yet to work out a schedule with Cassidy on how often I'll be seeing Jonah, but there's plenty of time for that.

Jonah wraps his arms around me, giving me a quick hug before he leads me back over to where Cassidy is waiting. She's standing by the door, holding it open for us.

"Thanks," I tell her. I can't help it—every time I see Cassidy, I think of Vada.

"How is everything?" she asks.

Jonah runs ahead of us, stopping to flip through a few different comics on the shelf.

I frown, scratching at the stubble on my chin. "Pretty good. My mother came by the restaurant." I turn to Cassidy. "She would like to see Jonah sometime and meet him. I told her I would talk to you first and let her know, of course."

Cassidy grins, her cheeks warming. "That's very sweet. I think it would be great for Jonah to meet his father's side of the family. I'm sure we can work something out."

"Thanks." I pause, watching as Jonah moves down another aisle. I swallow the lump forming in my throat.

"You can ask me, you know."

"Ask you what?" I pretend to not know.

"How Vada is doing." She giggles. "I can see it written all over your face. You can't hide your feelings for shit."

I shrug, laughing under my breath. "It's because I got rid of the glasses. You can see my expression better.

"No," she disagrees. "It's because you still love her."

"I do." I nod, pressing my mouth into a thin line. I blow a hot breath out of my nose, knowing there's no way I won't see Vada tonight. "Well..." I clear my throat. "How is she?"

"At least you're honest." She winks, grabbing a comic book from the shelf. She flips through it as if she's actually interested in it then puts it back on the shelf. "For the most part, she looks just as bad as you do."

The truth coming out of Cassidy is enough to make my stomach turn.

"Other than that, she's actually doing okay. She has a board meeting with the owners of the newspaper today."

"Why?"

"Our boss is leaving the paper and recommended her as his replacement."

"That's incredible." My breath is nearly knocked out of my chest. This is the promotion Vada was waiting for, the position she's dreamed of her whole life.

"It is. She was worried she wasn't going to get it, but I told her there's no way she wouldn't with her reputation."

A sickening feeling passes over me, knowing I wasn't there when she found out about the recommendation, and I'm not there for her today.

As I stare at Jonah, clutching a pile of comic books to his chest, I know my mother was right. Life is too short to not go after what you truly want, and there's nothing I've ever wanted in my life more than I do Vada.

CHAPTER THIRTY-TWO

Vada

Never settle for second best.

I've run my mother's words through my mind for three weeks, dissecting them and picking them apart. It seems the more I play them on repeat, the more I realize how they sound.

The deepest part of my soul honestly and truly believes my mother had good intentions when she was telling me these words. Growing up with a father like mine, the kind who valued one sibling over the other, can be damaging, and I can't imagine my mother using them for any other purpose. But I can't help thinking maybe she drilled them into me hard enough that I started to believe anything more than second best was impossible to achieve. I was forever stuck being second, whether I intended to be or not.

That is until today.

I still can't believe I've been promoted to editor-in-chief as I stand in the elevator, riding down to the main lobby. The marble tile beneath my heels glistens more than ever before—either that or I've just never noticed.

I stare at my reflection in the mirrored doors. My hair is still resting on my shoulders, the curls framing my face. Not a bit of my makeup is out of place, and I'm wearing my favorite black dress. I usually play it safe at work, trying to balance between comfortable and professional. Today I've picked my favorite dress, the one I feel most powerful in, and it worked.

It fucking worked.

I want to smile back at the woman in the mirror. I want to praise her for breaking her mother's mantra of never settling for second best. Because I fucking did it.

I'm now the new editor-in-chief of the *The Austin Chronicle*.

Well, at least I will be when Nate moves to Lubbock in the next two weeks.

Pride in myself swells in my chest like a hot air balloon. It rises and rises, filling every bit of my body. But then when the elevator doors open and I find myself walking out to my car to go home, the fire dies out, sinking the balloon to the bottom of my stomach.

Just when I feel like I've gotten everything I've ever wanted out of my career, I realize the first person I thought of when I walked out of that boardroom was Colton. The need to tell him swells inside me, but I know I can't, at least not right now. Maybe he'll find out through Dallas, or through me, later on.

I'm not naïve enough to believe I will never see him again. Colton is Dallas' business partner and best friend. He's Jonah's uncle. It would be impossible.

But I can't help wondering how long it'll be before the sting of our separation becomes nothing more than a dull, echoing ache.

The silence between us has been difficult. A large hole still exists in my chest where he once filled it. Every day I wake up, hoping the hollowness I feel will disappear, wondering if I'll ever have the privilege of his lips pressing against my skin or him burying himself inside me.

Thinking of Colton being inside me brings me back to our first time together, the night we grieved for Dallas' pain together and gave in to the thoughts we'd stifled for as long as we'd known each other. Between his kisses and sweltering touch, he ensured it'd be a moment I'd never forget.

I guess in that respect, Colton stayed true to his word. I haven't been able to forget—it's nearly impossible when you're in love. Colton has ruined me. He's left my heart a tangled mess.

After stepping out of the elevator, I head toward my car and text Dallas to let him know I got the promotion. I know he's finishing up his shift at the restaurant, most likely with Colton. Sometimes both of them work the same shift, giving themselves a few nights a week to see each other outside of work. Ever since they hired a few assistant managers to fill in on the nights they aren't there, it's given them a bit of a reprieve from having to close every single night, at least on the slower nights.

When I get to my car, I don't immediately go home. I run to the grocery store so I can make dinner for myself, and I consider inviting Sloan and Cassidy over to celebrate. While I'm at it, I swing by the liquor store and grab some tequila. Working at the restaurant for over a year taught me how to make a killer margarita.

Under normal circumstances, I'd want to go out to my favorite bars or clubs. I'd invite Sloan and Cassidy, insisting it would be the proper way to celebrate.

But my fractured heart retreats at the idea. Forcing myself to go to a place filled with hundreds of people, knowing not a single one would be Colton sounds like the worst idea. Instead, I'd rather celebrate in the comfort of my home. Maybe in time I'll want to venture out, but this bottle of tequila will do for now.

To make up for the fact that I'm not wanting to go out, I message Sloan and Cassidy. They'll be sure to bring up my mood and pull me out of this rut I'm in. I should be happy. I should be thrilled to have broken through the glass ceiling I've had placed over me by my father and anyone who ever believed I wouldn't make it, but the constant pricking in my chest keeps me from completely letting it sink in.

When I get home, I park my car in the lot and push through the wrought iron gate. The complex is quiet aside from the water pouring from the top of the fountain situated in the center of the courtyard. I round the corner leading to my front door but abruptly stop when I see the person standing in front of it.

Colton's eyes shoot from the ground when he sees me standing in front of him. They flash under the golden lights of the courtyard and roam over me, examining me from my feet to the bag in my hand before they stop on my face.

My heart thrashes inside my chest. The more it beats around, bouncing from one side of my body to the next, the more unsure I feel about how long it'll be before it breaks free. My palms sweat as I tighten my hold on the grocery bag I still have in my hand, willing myself to stay calm.

His black t-shirt clings to his muscles, highlighting the plains and valleys of his arms and chest. His subtle tan skin contrasts with the faded color of his shirt. One hand is wrapped around the neck of a bottle of champagne. In the other, he's holding the largest bag of red licorice I've ever laid my eyes on.

"Hi," he whispers. The deep, velvety tone of his voice travels through my ears and straight to my heart, forcing it to stay in place.

I draw my gaze to his, the emotions from seeing him already hitting me.

"Hi," I whisper back.

"Um..." He clears his throat and steps forward, his voice now back to normal. "I wanted to say congratulations."

I give him a confused expression, wondering how in the hell

he even knows I was promoted. It's barely been two hours since I left the meeting with Nate and the owners.

"How did you know?"

He smiles, the corner of his mouth curling. It's enough to spark the familiar fire in my stomach. "Dallas told me. We were at the restaurant together when you messaged him."

Well, that solves my problem of wondering when Colton will find out about my promotion.

"Oh." I nod, tucking my bottom lip under my teeth. I bite down on my soft flesh, wondering if he's only come over here to wish me congratulations or if there's more. I hold my breath. Hope is a foolish notion, one that should be handled lightly. It's easy to fall into a pattern of hope with Colton. It's happened in this very place before.

I ignore the way my palms sweat and my throat burns with the ache to kiss him.

"I told Cassidy about Ryan and Jonah." The words fall quickly from his mouth as if he's been holding them in like a deep, weighted breath.

"I know." I nod. "Cassidy told me after you went to see her. I'm glad you did, and I'm glad Jonah knows who his father is."

Silence. It hangs between us, causing me to become painfully aware of just how hard my heart is beating.

"Are you here simply to tell me you told Cassidy and Jonah about Ryan?" I tip my head toward the candy clenched in his large hand. "And to wish me congratulations by bringing me a ginormous pack of licorice?

He doesn't break his concentration as he tentatively steps forward, closing the distance between us. When he stops directly in front of me, he places the bottle of champagne and candy at his feet.

His eyes are fastened on mine as he reaches out, wrapping his hands around mine. He pries the tequila and bag from my hand, slowly taking them and placing them next to the candy and champagne.

"No," he whispers. "That's not the only reason I'm here."

That fucking hope again...it jumps and rattles inside me, springing my heart to life. My whole body perks with Colton's admission.

I want to be cautious. My defenses are fragile when it comes to Colton.

Deep in my soul, I know I love him. I've always loved him.

"Then why?" I ask him.

"I think it's about time we were honest with one another, from here on out." He swallows, his eyes turning glassy under the golden lights of the complex. "I came to tell you I've only kept one other secret from you."

"Oh." I frown, looking down at the points of my bright red stiletto heels against the concrete. It's not what I was expecting him to say. The thought of Colton keeping another secret from me causes my stomach to turn sour. I hold back the urge to wrap my arm around my waist to keep myself from falling apart in front of him.

"See, the thing about secrets is they can either break your heart into a million pieces, or they can mend it with one simple confession." His voice drifts over the trickling water of the fountain behind us. "I love you, Vada. I always have. I just think this is one secret that has been buried in me since the day I met you."

"What?" My heart stops. This is the first time Colton's ever told me he loves me. This is the first time I've heard the word pass his lips.

"I..." He pauses, his eyes searching my face before they meet mine again. "I love you. I can't say it more simply than that."

He lifts his hand and places it against my cheek. His palm is warm, the sensation shooting straight down to my chest. His fingers weave through my curls, gripping the side of my hair. I lean into him on instinct. The familiar scent of smoked pecan wood and mint fills my nose. I clench my thighs and swipe my tongue across my mouth, breathing him in.

Tears spring up behind my eyes, welling and causing pressure to build. I bite them back, not wanting to let my tears blur my vision of Colton standing in front of me. His eyes spark, his own admission of loving me lighting him up from the inside.

"I do. I love you, Vada."

"But..." I swallow. A tear spills over when I blink. "You—"

"I know. I know you think I can't put you first, and I know I don't have a very good track record when it comes to it. But everything I've ever done has come to this, to loving you. Even though you may think you've come second in my life, you never have." He removes his hand from my cheek and grabs mine. He wraps both of his hands around mine, pressing it to his chest. "I've loved you since the moment we met. You've healed me, you've wounded me...you've marked me, you've ruined me. It never mattered if I had my parents' approval or if I was too busy to see past my business and school. I think I grew into this habit of pouring all my focus into the parts of my life that don't truly matter. I tried too hard to satisfy everyone else—my father, my mother. In a way, after Ryan died, I think I felt guilty for allowing myself to indulge in a life that involved anything around happiness. I felt guilty for living a life he never got to have. Most importantly, I allowed secrets to stand between me and the ones I love. I let my fear of disappointment overrule the decisions I should have been making for myself."

"What decisions are those?"

"I shouldn't have pushed you away when Ryan died. I let my grief push away the only person I knew could pull me out of it. And I should have told you about Ryan and Jonah. I think I pushed everyone away for so long it was hard for me to believe I was worthy of anyone's love."

I hold my breath and close my eyes, wondering if this time is different. Colton and I have come a long way from those two shattered people forging a secret under the dim neon lights of his bar. Colton has loved and lost. I've lost out on my career, only to build my way back up.

When Colton points out how he had trouble believing he was worthy of anyone's love, I don't think I've ever understood him more than I do in this moment.

I give him a light smile of understanding, even through the tears. "I know what you mean." I inhale a sharp breath, uttering the words I've held in for so long. "I've spent my life under the constant affirmation from my mother that I should never settle for being someone's second. My father consistently put her on the back burner, and when I was born, he did the same to me. But I think somewhere along the way, in the past twenty-plus years, I got it into my head that I wasn't worthy of being any more than second." I pause, catching my breath long enough to get the next words out. I need Colton to hear them as much as I needed to hear his. "You've ruined me. You've ruined me in the best way possible, and I'm fucking hopelessly in love with you."

Colton moves his hands from around mine, gripping both sides of my face with them. I study every strand of his brown hair, the sharp angle of his brooding eyebrows down to the equally sharp angle of his nose. It's a feeling I can't explain, but I've always known it was there. The sensation I get when I look into Colton's eyes...it's as if he's able to see straight into my soul.

With both fingers buried deep into my curls, his eyes swirl with the pain of knowing I thought of myself as anything less. "You have always been worthy, Vada. Always."

"I once told you your mother lost her way after losing Ryan, but I think everyone does at some point in their lives. We both lost our way, believing we were less deserving of love. Despite getting lost, I know it's always been you. I found my way to you."

He breathes a sigh of relief, his shoulders falling. He doesn't release his grip around my face, gently pressing his fingers deeper as he pulls me toward him. His shoulders tighten and his arms flex as he pulls me close, slamming my body to his. I stand on my toes as he lifts my head upward to meet his mouth.

He presses his mouth to mine, claiming it with his soft lips. His hot breath dances across my skin, and I can't stop the flutter inside my chest as he removes one of his hands, placing it at the small of my back. He keeps me pressed against him as I walk him backward, toward my front door. We leave the food and liquor on the ground, not caring to stop to retrieve it.

His back presses against the brick wall of the alcove around my front door. "I love you, Vada. You've always been first." He breaks his mouth away from mine to tell me before he returns. Then he pulls away again. "I will spend the rest of my life making sure you never doubt it ever again."

When he brings his mouth back to mine, his lips land on my smile. Tears are still streaming down my face, a few drops sliding between our joined mouths. The salty taste of my tears mixed with the mint in Colton's mouth causes my throat to warm.

I break my mouth away from his, allowing my lips to ghost along his as I speak. "I love you, Colt."

"Fuck," he says, his eyes moving back and forth between mine. "I love you."

Gripping my waist, he spins us around to where my back is now pinned to the wall. He pushes his hips into me as he slides one of his hands down the curve of my waist and the side of my thigh. My skin heats with his touch. It's searing and soothing all at the same time.

I tilt my head back as he moves his mouth down my neck. He breathes in, and the tingling sensation it gives me shoots straight down to my center. His breaths are deep and rushed as he slides his mouth along my skin, tasting me along the way.

"God," he says against my collarbone. "I've missed you."

I smile, not wanting to bring this up now, but considering where we're standing, I'd hate if Sloan or Cassidy were to walk up on us like this. My front door is set back slightly with a few feet of brick standing between the door and the courtyard. We're shielded by most of the complex unless someone were to walk up on us.

"I invited Sloan and Cassidy over to celebrate my promotion. They're supposed to be here any minute."

"No," he says, still kissing my skin. He refuses to pull away. "They know I'm here. I told them we'd celebrate later."

I laugh, not in the least bit surprised. It sounds like something Colton would do. My laughter subsides when his fingers start sliding under the bottom hem of my dress, finding my inner thigh.

"Fine." With every nerve in my body sparking with electricity, I lift my hand and hook two fingers under his chin. I force his gaze up to mine. "Show me exactly how much you've missed me then."

As if my words flipped a switch, Colton's hands wrap around my thighs, lifting me up. He slams his mouth to mine again, kissing me with more force than before. He's all heat and touches, holding nothing back.

"Wait," I tell him, really not wanting to stop him, but I have to. "My key."

"What?" He pulls back.

I bite down on my lip, my cheeks flaming red from having him all over me. "The key to my apartment is in the bag over there."

I nod my head to the side, to where he dropped my stuff on the ground. He lowers me and quickly walks over to it. He scoops everything into his arms, but he doesn't carry it far. He drops it all near the entrance of the alcove, fishing for the keys in my bag. When he grabs them, he quickly unlocks the door then makes his way back over to me.

Wrapping his arms around my legs, he lifts me up again, and my warm center presses against his waist as he carries me in. I don't wrap my arms around his neck. Instead, I wrap one hand around the back of his head, grabbing his hair and dragging my nails across his scalp.

With my other hand, I try to lift his shirt from his waist. He doesn't carry us far, stopping at my dining room table. He sets me down on the edge, and I'm finally able to lift his shirt over his head. I'm quick to unbuckle his jeans. I grip his boxer briefs and his jeans, sliding them down together. He steps out of them and reaches behind me, drawing the zipper on the back of my dress far enough down to allow the top to reveal my shoulders. My breasts pop free, my nipples already teased into two hard pebbles. Colton's eyes roam over my body as his jaw ticks. His cock is hard as stone, pointing straight at me. He slides his hand up and down his length as he watches me. I lift one hand and cup my breast in my palm, twisting my fingertips around my nipple.

He stops stroking himself, moving his fingers between my legs. He parts them further, ghosting his fingers along my thighs until he slides them between my folds.

"Fuck, Vada. You're so fucking wet for me already."

I let out a sharp hiss through my teeth, thankful I decided not to wear underwear today.

"Now," I moan on a breath, tilting my head back. "Now you know how much I've missed you...how much I've missed your touch."

"I have missed this." He presses his other hand flat on my sternum, between the swells of my breasts. "Lay your head back."

I do as he says, lowering myself back until my head lands on the dark wood table. I stare up at him, feeling my stomach light with fire as he works circles over my clit. Our breaths are heavy, filtering through the stifling air of my apartment. I don't know if I accidentally left the heat on or if it's from Colton's touch, but my skin is already damp.

He keeps his hand pressed to my chest as he centers himself in front of me. I wrap my legs around his waist, lifting myself higher to be more in line with him. The faster he works me, dragging his finger over my clit, down my center before sliding it inside me, the more I feel myself reaching the edge. I'm going to cum on his hand before he's even had the chance to be inside me.

"I need you." I breathe out, staring up at him with hooded eyes. "This time I don't want you to fuck me, Colt."

"What do you want then?" he asks, pulling his hand away from me, grabbing his hardened cock and pressing it between my wet folds, right at my entrance. "Tell me."

"I don't want you to fuck me." I stare up at him with hooded eyes, and my chest nearly explodes when I tell him exactly what I want. "I want you to make love to me."

With those words, he pushes himself inside me. I tilt my head back on the table, closing my eyes. The darkness of my apartment deepens with my eyes closed, but when I feel Colton's hand grab my chin, pulling my attention back to his, I open them.

I open my eyes to find Colton moving above me. He slides himself in and out. He's not rushed or hurried as he's been in the past. This time he's slow, making sure he's filled me completely before pulling back far enough to slide back in.

He leans forward and kisses me before he straightens his back far enough to keep moving inside me but close enough to reach out and press his thumb to the center of my bottom lip, as he's always done before.

The sensation of his touch and the way his hips slam into me over and over again, slowly quickening our pace, is enough for the fire simmering in my belly to expand across my skin. My legs tingle and quiver, tightening around him as I feel my orgasm coming.

"Oh my god, Colton." His name falls on a breath.

"I love you, Vada. First and forever."

I look into Colton's eyes as I fall apart around him, my chest expanding as I scream his name. My back arches and my toes curl inside my stilettos. I wrap my hands around his arms on either side of me, pressing my fingertips into his taut muscles.

When I reach the end of my orgasm, I catch my breath and look down at Colton as he continues to move inside me. I lift myself up but lean my hands back on the table, slamming my hips into his. He pushes into me several more times before he stops, his body quivering with his orgasm. He spills himself into me as his cock throbs. That sensation alone is enough to make me orgasm a second time. I wrap my hand around his face, feeling his stubble prickle the sensitive skin of my cheek as I pull his focus up to mine. His chest moves up and down in quick succession, and that's when I see it.

There's a fire in his eyes, similar to the one I've seen in them every other time we've been together in this way.

And this is the moment I realize Colton has always loved me.

The truth of it is I was never settling for second best when it comes to Colton. I've always been first. First and forever.

Vada

"Vada, Uncle Colton, watch this." Jonah clicks his feet on either side of his horse. The horse obeys, taking several steps forward around the outer edges of the pen, along the inside of the fence. Holding on to the reins, Jonah takes the horse in a slow circle, slow and steady.

"You're doing great, Jonah. Pretty soon you'll be a pro." I cross my arms over the top of the wooden fence and smile, watching as one of the handlers leads Jonah. He's been practicing the past few months, coming to the Adler's ranch every weekend, learning how to ride a horse. In a way, it's been great for Colton's mother. She's slowly built her relationship with her grandson, starting with offering Ryan's horse to Jonah for him to learn to ride on.

The gesture of Faye's offering to her grandson made my heart swell. It's been a beautiful sight to watch her find her way back to enjoying life. For her, she was able to grab a small piece of Ryan back, all the while getting to know an amazing fucking kid.

As far as Colton's father is concerned, he has yet to come around to the idea of having a grandson, or so Colton says. He claims to miss Jonah's visits due to his weekly golf sessions with business contacts. It's all bullshit, and we all know it. Even Faye knows he avoids him on purpose, but none of us care enough to fight it as long as Jonah is happy.

"So, what'll it take for you to finally agree to ride?"

Colton's hands slide along my waist from behind. His chest presses against my back, warming me as his tall frame surrounds me. I laugh, resting my head back on his hardened chest. He lifts his hand and delicately trails his fingers across my neck. I break out into shivers, goosebumps dotting across my arms.

"Um, I don't think there's anything you can say that will get me to ride one of those."

"Oh, come on." He dips his head low enough to place a kiss on my neck. "Horses aren't that scary. They're gentle animals."

Fuck, his minty breath and warm mouth press into my skin, and I want to both push him away but have him keep going. It's a conundrum as we stand out here, watching Jonah ride in circles.

"That's what you think, but they scare the shit out of me, Colt. They're twice as tall as me, and they're completely unpredictable." I scoff, resting my head harder against his chest as he watches Jonah over my shoulder with hooded eyes.

"If Jonah can ride one, surely you can," he teases. "At this rate, he'll be teaching you how to ride by the time you finally agree."

Colton has been trying to convince me to ride one of the horses ever since we started bringing Jonah here on the weekends, but I didn't realize just how terrified I am of horses until I was standing next to one. Hopping on one to ride it? Forget about it.

I don't mind standing on the outside, watching Jonah's face light up every time he rides Ryan's horse.

"I have a question for you," Colton says. His voice breezes

across the hollow of my ear, and I feel it shoot straight for my chest, causing my heart to skip a beat.

Ever since Colton showed up on my doorstep three months ago, telling me he's been in love with me from the start, we've been nearly inseparable. Falling in love with Colton was as easy as breathing for me, and I didn't realize until he was gone just how starved for oxygen I had been.

Now editor-in-chief of the newspaper, my schedule has been pretty packed, but not a day has gone by where Colton hasn't found a way to see me or talk to me. For the first time in forever, we have no secrets. Everything is laid out on the line, no matter how ugly it might be.

"Ask away." I fight the urge to lean my head against him, breathing him in, knowing I won't be able to stop from taking it too far.

"If you had a choice, would you want to stay in the city or live out in the country?"

"What? You mean on a ranch like this?"

He shrugs. "Could be."

"Hmm." I think about my answer before giving it to him. "Would we have to keep horses?"

Colton's chest shudders with laughter against my back as he wraps his arms tighter around my waist. "We can keep whatever animals you want, or none. That's up to you."

I twist my mouth, biting down on my bottom lip. "I don't know. I've never really thought about it. I've always thought I liked the city, but this is nice too. I like how quiet it is out here."

"So, what you're saying is you're undecided."

"Maybe." I smile. "I'll get back to you with an answer later."

"Okay." He nods.

He pauses long enough to watch Jonah take another lap. He waits until he passes us for the third time before bringing his mouth close to my ear again, whispering against my skin.

"I have another question for you, but this time, I'm hoping your answer won't be as undecided as the last one."

He unravels one of his arms from around my waist, moving it behind me. I hold my breath when his hand reappears in front of me, this time holding a ring.

It's a simple silver band with a black diamond in the center, surrounded by a row of tiny blue sapphires. The sunlight reflects off the stones, glinting between Colton's pinched fingers.

Tears immediately spring from my eyes, and I bring my hand to my mouth, covering it as I spin around. I lower it and stare into Colton's eyes. Tears are lining his as well, and I don't think I've ever been as in love with him as I am in this moment. He grabs my left hand and holds it while he keeps the ring pinched between the fingers of his other hand.

"What are you doing?" I ask him, my voice already wobbling from my throat swelling.

"Vada Beckett, I've spent most of my life aiming to please others, afraid of disappointment—that is until I met you. You started out as my best friend's sister. Then you became my friend. Then you became my one-time secret." He pauses long enough to clear his throat. "Then you finally just became all of those wrapped into one, but you became even more than that. You became my first and forever."

I let the tears slip from my eyes as Colton slides the ring over my fourth finger.

I laugh through my tears, watching as he slides it down, stopping when it gets past my second knuckle. "You haven't even asked me yet."

His brown eyes spark, and he places one hand on his chest, catching his breath. "Well, shit. I should probably ask my question then, huh?" He moves his hand to cup my cheek, pinning my gaze to his. "Vada Beckett, will you marry me?"

My heart pounds in my chest as I stand on my toes, leaning up to kiss him.

I press my lips to Colton's, and against his mouth, I finally utter the words, never having been so certain of anything in my life. "Yes, Colt. I'll marry you."

Sneak Peek
Cassidy
Five years earlier...

HATE IS A PRETTY strong fucking word. Reserved only for the most extreme cases.

Although I've never outright stated I've hated someone, there's only one person who's ever come close.

Levi Hawkins.

Quarterback of our school football team and the bane of my existence.

Not that I've ever actually held a decent conversation with the guy. He's only ever muttered all of a few sentences to me over our nearly four years of high school together. I'm basically invisible to the same man who is everything but to the rest of the world.

Still, I know how Levi Hawkins truly feels about me. Between the constant glares and back handed comments to his other teammates, it hasn't been hard to miss.

Even still, I don't know where his contempt for me comes from. How can you possibly hate someone when you've never actually spoken to one another?

Being the photographer for the school yearbook requires me

to have a certain level of interaction with our varsity football team. Especially in a state like Texas. Where football is as sacred as the iced tea in their glasses and the barbecue on their plates.

On the days where I've been forced to stare at Levi for the sake of my yearbook duty, I've considered all possibilities of why he seems to curl his full lips and narrow his piercing blue eyes in my direction every chance he gets.

Maybe he considers me an inconvenience to the team, always sticking a camera in their faces. Football games and team photos. I've been there, camera in hand, snapping shot after shot.

Or maybe it's because for guys like Levi, it's impossible for them to bother to associate with anyone who isn't on the team or shaking those obnoxious black and gold pom poms.

Those are only a couple of the reasons I've thought of as to why he can't stand to be more than within six feet of me.

Despite all the viable reasons why Levi Hawkins can't stand my presence, the same could be said for me. Staring at Levi through my lens has only made my chest burn and my legs tighten even more.

He's impossibly gorgeous and I fucking hate it.

I loathe the times where my eyes are forced to look in his direction. Only because of what it does to me.

There have been too many times where I've imagined what it might feel like to have his mouth press on mine or how it would feel to see his eyes looking up at me as he buries his face between my legs.

In all honesty, I can't stand the power he has over me. It's incredibly frustrating to want the guy who gives you absolutely no indication he has any interest in you at all.

My only saving grace is graduation in eight months. In eight months I'll be off to college and far away from here.

Eight months and I'll never have to see him ever again.

But I know even then, I'll remember how Levi Hawkins has always been trouble.

Want to read Cassidy and Levi's story?
Read their story in *The Troubles with Heartbreak*.
CLICK HERE

Want to read the beginning of Colton and Vada's story in One-Time Secret?
Grab the FREE short story HERE

Thank you for reading Colton and Vada's story! There's more to come in The Heartbreak Series. If you enjoyed the book, I would absolutely love if you left a review. Reviews mean the world to us indie authors and it would mean so much to me.

XOXO

Want to sign up for my newsletter and be notified of my upcoming releases?

You can also join my reader group, Brittany's Book Lovers

ALSO BY BRITTANY

Standalone

What are the Chances

See Through

Paper Hearts

The Wrong Pitch

Without You Duet

Without You

Without Me

The Back to Me Series

Dissipate

Mine

Back to Me

The Heartbreak Series

The Rules of Heartbreak

The Secrets to Heartbreak

The Troubles with Heartbreak

Harding Brothers Series

Gorgeous Lies

Sweet Nothings

Pretty Heartache

ACKNOWLEDGMENTS

Honestly, when I was writing The Rules of Heartbreak, I was under the impression Colton and Vada's story would be easy to write. Between their quirky yet witty banter back and forth in *The Rules of Heartbreak,* I had a plan on where I wanted their story to go. I always knew they would get their HEA and how they would get there was clear.

In the beginning, at least.

Just like Colton's stubborn streak, so were these characters. I loved them dearly, but they were insistent on how they wanted their story told. They had me rearranging and cutting out whole chapters only to start over. It was all-consuming but at the same time, I wouldn't expect any less from Colton and Vada.

I'm so glad they finally got their HEA and I'm so happy I was able to share it with you.

As always, I would like to thank my husband and my two boys. Every single time I'm put on a deadline you're there for me. I seriously don't know how I would do this without you. You're my biggest cheerleaders. I love the three of you the most in this world.

To my family for always having my back. Not going to lie, imposter syndrome hit real hard this time, but you never wavered in reminding me how worthy I am and how there is space for me in this big vast book world.

My betas. Amy, Ashley, Amanda, and Dani. Thank you so much for your honest feedback. I don't know how I can ever properly thank you for keeping my vibe in check and for helping me keep this story on track. Love you guys.

To my designer, Amanda. Girl. Like this story, this cover took a few drafts before landing on the right one. Your patience will never be under-appreciated. I love you so freaking much for always killing it with your covers.

To my editor Caitlin. I don't ever want to lose you. Seriously. You're magic.

My assistant, Tiffany. You're the glue that holds me together. In all ways. It's indescribable how much I appreciate you.

To Shauna and Wildfire Marketing. Thank you for working with me on this series. Can't wait for The Troubles with Heartbreak!

Last but not least, BookTok. Book. Tok. What can I say about all of you other than THANK YOU? You have seriously changed me as an author and propelled my career to places I never thought I could go or that would take me forever to get to. Your support and love has been incredible, and I don't think a day will pass where I don't think about how your passion for reading drives my passion for writing. Thank you for reading my stories. From the bottom of my heart, thank you so freaking much.

XOXO

Brittany

ABOUT BRITTANY

Brittany Taylor grew up all over the world including places such as California, England, and Texas. Her love of reading started at a young age. Finally deciding to fulfill her lifelong dream, she took the plunge into the writing world and published her first book when she was twenty-eight. Today she resides in Connecticut with her husband, two sons, two cats and one dog.